By Adam Hamdy

Out of Reach
Battalion
Pendulum

PENDULUM

ADAM HAMDY

New York • London

Quercus

New York • London

© 2017 by Adam Hamdy
First published in the United States by Quercus in 2017

Any member of educational institutions wishing to photocopy
part or all of the work for classroom use or anthology
should send inquiries to permissions@quercus.com.

ISBN 978-168144-135-1

Library of Congress Cataloging-in-Publication Data

Names: Hamdy, Adam, 1974- author.
Title: Pendulum / Adam Hamdy.
Description: First edition. | New York : Quercus, 2017.
Identifiers: LCCN 2016041032 (print) | LCCN 2016050161 (ebook) | ISBN
    9781681441351 (hardback) | ISBN 9781681441344 (paperback) | ISBN
    9781681441337 (ebook) | ISBN 9781681441320 (library ebook)
Subjects: LCSH: Serial murderers—Fiction. | BISAC: FICTION / Suspense. |
    FICTION / Technological. | GSAFD: Suspense fiction.
Classification: LCC PR6108.A5 P46 2017 (print) | LCC PR6108.A5 (ebook) | DDC
    823/.92—dc23
LC record available at https://lccn.loc.gov/2016041032

Distributed in the United States and Canada by
Hachette Book Group
1290 Avenue of the Americas
New York, NY 10104

Manufactured in the United States

10 9 8 7 6 5 4 3 2 1

www.quercus.com

For Amy

PART ONE
London

1

Burning sour acid caught in the back of John Wallace's throat, and he knew instantly that he had been sick. He opened his eyes, but the world remained dark. Wallace felt his eyelids twist and his lashes turn inward as they moved against the blindfold. His heart raced, pounding in his chest with the jackhammer pace of a full-blown panic. He was familiar with the vicissitudes of an anxiety attack, but this was different, no trick of the introspective mind; this was all too real. Trying his arms, Wallace felt the strong grasp of surprisingly soft bonds around his wrists; it felt like silk. His ankles were similarly bound. Wallace could no longer feel his clothes, just his underpants; someone had all but stripped him. He heard movement nearby; soft footsteps against his thick rug. *Stay still. Stay silent.*

Wallace listened to the movement around him and tried not to give the slightest indication that he was awake. A sudden rush of air and a blow to his stomach made him cry out in pain.

"Please don't," Wallace tried, hearing the crackling weakness of fear in his own voice.

Movement across the room, and then noise—the familiar sound of "The Pretender" by the Foo Fighters. Powerful speakers blasted the heavy guitar at full volume, and Wallace doubly regretted his inability to conceal his consciousness, knowing that the loud music would drown out any cries for help. And help was what he desperately needed. He imagined Leona, the sultry fire breather who lived above him. He fantasized about her knocking on his door to ask him to turn the music down, realizing something was awry and urgently calling the police. The fantasy instantly died away; Leona had never once complained about noise. Neither had the Levines, who lived below. The solid brickwork of the converted church provided effective soundproofing, which, when combined with the residents' laissez-faire approach to life, meant complaints were rare.

Wallace didn't know how long he'd been unconscious, but, until the knock at the door that started this nightmare, he'd been confident that his solitary existence was the safest way to go through life. Real connections brought nothing but suffering, so Wallace limited his relationships to the smilingly superficial. Until Wallace had risen from his desk and walked away from his computer, he'd been certain that very little good could ever come from other people. All they offered was disappointment, betrayal, and pain. Now, lying vulnerable and afraid, Wallace realized that one person, *just one person*, might bring salvation.

Noise. Activity somewhere above him. Something hit one of the wooden beams that the slick real estate agent had pointed out when showing this feature-rich desacralized church. Second-floor views of one of London's most expensive streets through original arched stone windows. A landscaped communal garden. A walk-in shower. A dressing room. A bright studio space. A large kitchen/dining area. A list of things that had seemed so essential, so important at the time, but that now wouldn't even figure as footnotes in his life. *What really mattered was freedom. Escape.*

Movement. Near his head. Wallace's heart raced faster and his breath grew shorter as panic gripped him. Someone—the person he had opened his door to—moved his head. Something. *No! No! No! This can't be happening.* Something was slipped over his head. If he didn't admit what it was, it wasn't real. *It's not real. This is a trip. A dream. This isn't life. No!*

The noose tightened and Wallace couldn't pretend anymore.

"It's easier if you stand," came the voice. It was somewhere above and behind him. Deep, serious, unfamiliar, and delivered with a bland Transatlantic accent. Wallace clung to the faint hope that this was a practical joke taken too far. A colleague. A friend. A neighbor.

Someone he knew seeking to repay some act of unkindness. But he didn't recognize the voice. If this was a joke, someone had paid money for an actor. *Please let it be an actor.*

"Please," he said hoarsely. "Please don't do this."

Wallace remembered Kabul. He remembered the condemned men shuffling slowly to the gallows. He remembered wondering why none of them tried to run. He remembered pressing his cheek against his camera and peering into the viewfinder, searching for the answer in their eyes. The men, foot soldiers in a militant group determined to overthrow the Afghan government, had cast their faces at the ground, and it was not until they reached the foot of the small run of steps that Wallace saw the first man's eyes. He had seen the man look up at his destiny, and, as the shutter chattered away to capture a stuttering record of the moment, Wallace saw the hollowness of defeat in the man's eyes; such fire that animates the human soul had already been extinguished. *You're not one of them!* Wallace told himself, as he felt the fire of life burning fiercely within.

If I stand, Wallace thought now, as the noose choked tighter, *I might be able to lash out and catch this guy off guard. Risky, but if I do nothing, I'm dead anyway.* He fumbled to his feet, his upward progress aided by the taut rope around his neck. Once on his feet, Wallace strained his ears, listening for movement. The rope tugged at his neck, squeezing his windpipe, but it wasn't getting any tighter. Wallace tensed his muscles. For almost two decades he had trained for just such a moment. He remembered his first aikido instructor, Shiodin Bal, telling him that true warriors had to be willing to greet death as a friend. As glorious as that sounded to a fourteen-year-old from West Hampstead, the combat techniques Wallace had learned in the intervening years all relied on him having free movement of his hands and feet. There was no glorious grace in fighting from the end of a noose, just simple, ugly survival.

A creak and movement in the air ahead of him. Wallace jumped up and kicked out with both feet, holding nothing back and committing himself to the maneuver entirely. All in, high stakes, no holds barred. He visualized his feet connecting with his attacker's head, the man going sprawling; freeing himself and living to tell his triumphant tale to the amazed police officers who arrived to arrest the villain. Reality had other plans. Wallace's legs barely climbed above knee height, such was the difficulty of jumping while bound. His limbs connected with nothing but air, and he fell flat on his back, his neck catching the rope at a perilous angle. If his attacker hadn't fed him some slack, Wallace's neck would have snapped under his own weight. He felt the terrible blow of failure, and he realized that his effort would have looked less like an escape and more like an attempted suicide.

"It's easier if you stand," came the deep voice. No anger, no disappointment, just factual, like a doctor delivering a diagnosis. Or a vet talking to an animal.

Wallace found himself trembling as he got to his feet. The music had changed: "Polarized" by Seven Lions. Haunting, moody, atmospheric, Wallace felt he finally understood the significance of the track. It was about second chances, a celebration of life. *I don't deserve to die here.* Even as the words formed in his mind, Wallace knew that they represented the desperate plea of a fool, not a man who had seen enough of the world to know that tens of thousands of undeserving people die every single day.

"Please. I'll give you anything you want." Tears soaked his blindfold, and his tremulous voice said it all; he was broken. There was no practical joke, no action movie escape. Just him in a room with a stranger who controlled the noose around his neck.

Movement. Something touched his skin. Wallace recoiled, but then realized it was a hand. A gloved hand. Leather or rubber. Cold but malleable.

"Please don't," he blubbered.

The gloved hand grabbed his arm and held it firm. He felt movement in between his wrists, and his arms were suddenly free—his bonds had been cut. Relief beyond any he had ever experienced rushed through him, as the man cut the ties that bound his legs.

"Thank you, thank you," Wallace croaked.

He didn't care who the man was, or why he had felt the need to punish him, Wallace would forgive him. He had come face-to-face with his own mortality and it had taught him many valuable lessons. *Get a chain for your door*, Wallace thought to himself as he giggled inwardly, drunk with hysterical euphoria. *Don't trust strangers. Buy a dog. A big dog.*

He sensed movement around his head and the blindfold fell away. Every valuable object in his luxurious flat was undisturbed; this was definitely not a robbery, but there was no sign of the practical joker.

"You can lose the noose," Wallace suggested, his confidence returning. He tried to turn his head, but the noose was pulled tight. "All right!" he cried out hoarsely.

He heard the shard of doubt in his voice and his confidence faltered. It crumbled completely when he saw something being pulled toward him. Out of the corner of his eye he saw a black-gloved hand holding one of his kitchen chairs, the ends of the chipped wooden legs brushing the long hairs of the woven rug as they traveled the short distance to his side.

"Up," his assailant instructed, with a firm tug of the rope. The noose tightened and pressed his Adam's apple into his throat with such force that he wasn't able to talk. Every breath became a strain as he gasped for precious air. He hated his legs; he knew they were deceiving themselves because they believed there was blessed relief on the chair. Legs that could carry him fifteen miles at a run were weak enough to fall for a lie. He cursed his treacherous body as it mounted the chair, the crushing noose pulling him ever higher. He looked at the weathered, pockmarked beam and regretted his decision to have it treated for woodworm even after the structural survey had found none. Wallace wished that for once he had not chased perfection. If he'd been the kind of person who'd let things slide there was a chance that the beam would have been weakened by woodworm and that the weight of the heavy rope and his even heavier body would have brought it crashing down.

With the blindfold gone, Wallace could feel tears cutting gullies down his chiseled cheeks. He was too wrapped up in the prospect of his own death to maintain the pretense that he was anything other than an abysmal failure. He'd made a living chronicling other lives, but he had done nothing with his own. He would leave the world without having made the slightest difference; his only legacy was a few photographs that would soon be lost and forgotten. *We're all weak. We all fail. And then we die.* Staring up at the beam, Wallace realized that something inside him had died: hope. Like the men he had photographed in Kabul, he felt nothing but the hollow emptiness of defeat.

Movement at the edge of his vision. Wallace cast his eyes down, and what he saw filled him with dread. A man dressed in heavy black boots, black leather trousers, and some kind of black body armor over his torso. A black combat mask with a mouth hole covered with a wire mesh, and round, opaque black goggles. Wallace could see his reflection in the lenses—a sickening echo of the ghost he was about to become. A full-length black leather coat with a beautifully rich purple lining completed his attacker's attire. *A superhero,* Wallace thought darkly. Only there was nothing heroic about the figure before him. Even through the mask Wallace could sense brooding hatred.

Who was he? *Serial killer. No. There's no hope with a serial killer. Don't go there.* Wallace ignored his fears and continued reaching for a memory; searching his past for someone he had wronged. His relatively blameless life frustrated him and he could think of nothing that merited murder. This lunatic had the wrong guy.

"You've got . . ." Wallace tried, but the words were trapped in his throat, his voice box crushed by the noose. Anger overtook fear and the tingling fire of indignation coursed through his body. He was going to die for no reason, because a monster had got the wrong address.

He tried to shout, but his throat wouldn't open enough to get the words out, and he watched in horror as the masked man kicked the chair away.

Time slowed.

Wallace felt himself suspended in midair, free of any support, outside the laws of gravity; he was weightless, flying, he would live forever. He'd make some changes. Start fresh. Find purpose in life.

Maybe find someone to share it with. Connie . . . Why was he falling? *That's not right. I can't die.*

Time kicked in and Wallace fell, his full weight pulling against the noose, which tightened around his neck like a hand squeezing a tube of toothpaste. He was surprised by the lack of resistance his neck offered—it collapsed under the rope without any argument. Unlike the condemned warriors in Kabul, he hadn't fallen far enough to break his neck, so Wallace knew he would choke to death. Slowly. His hands clawed at the noose, but it was so very tight, the fibers cutting into his neck, fusing with his flesh. Wallace's fingers went farther up, to the rope that rose behind his head. He pulled at it, lifting his own weight, and the noose stopped tightening, but it did not get any looser. Wallace was shocked at how heavy he felt, and how quickly his arms began to burn with the strain. All those hours spent in the gym, obsessively training his body to ensure it could meet the physical demands of his work. That obsession would finally pay off. He'd pull himself up to freedom and somehow overpower his misguided attacker.

He trembled with the effort of keeping himself aloft. He was strong, fit, and determined. He would never give up. Letting go of the rope, letting the noose take his weight, he'd be almost as culpable in his own death as the masked man who put him there. He would endure whatever pain it took to pull himself up the rope, to the beam, out of the reach of his would-be murderer. Aikido had taught him that he was master of his mind and body. John Wallace was not about to give up.

Like his treacherous legs before them, his arms betrayed his mind. They were weak when he most needed strength. Despite his desperate commands for them to ignore the pain, they dropped to his side. His legs kicked the air as his neck took his full weight. Wallace finally realized that there would be no escape. *I'm dying.*

The old cliché wasn't true; his life didn't flash before his eyes. Instead Wallace found himself reliving only the most painful moments. The death of his parents. The mutilated bodies of the Afghan children that had finally sent him home. And Connie. Warm, sweet, tender Connie, her sad, tear-drenched face looking up at him, full of love. She had been right, and now, more than ever, he regretted letting her go.

Through the free-flowing tears, Wallace looked down at the masked man, who watched impassively as his life was choked away. Wallace's lungs, full of stale, fetid air, burned with the desire to expel their contents. His eyes pushed farther and farther forward, edging their way out of their sockets. *I'm sorry. I'm sorry. I should have done better.*

Remorse was the very last feeling Wallace experienced before he blacked out. Inertia kept his body swinging after his legs had stopped kicking. A pendulum marking the final moments of existence.

The masked man watched Wallace's body until it fell still. Satisfied, the killer began the next phase of his work.

2

Primal pain stabbed searing barbs that jolted Wallace back to consciousness. The sensation was unlike anything he had ever experienced in its sheer brutal ferocity. It overshadowed being shot on the road out of Kandahar and made the resultant fleshy shoulder wound seem like an alluringly benign experience. Wallace forced his senses through the pain and realized he was lying on his back covered in heavy timber, plaster, and rubble. The beam had collapsed. *The beam had collapsed!* Euphoria trumped agony, and the pure joy of being alive surged through his body.

The impact of the beam landing on him had rapidly compressed Wallace's lungs, expelling the toxic air, and shocking him awake. He instinctively tugged at the noose, loosening it enough to take a breath. The relief he felt was instant, and a warm, divine feeling flooded his body. It was the most intoxicating moment of his life. His heart pounded, pumping euphoric adrenaline everywhere, and this time his limbs didn't betray him; he got to his feet as he removed the noose. The room was empty; no sign of his attacker. *Phone. Police.* Wallace's brain kicked into gear.

He started for the door only to be greeted by the sight of his masked killer running into the room from the inner recesses of his flat. Drawn by the noise, the killer seemed momentarily shocked to find Wallace alive. The moment didn't last, and the killer took action, producing something—a Taser?—from beneath his long coat. Wallace didn't wait for his attacker to use the device. *Get away!* Distance was life. Proximity was death. The logic was simple, but the execution was not. The killer stood in the only exit, a doorway that led to the entrance hall that led to the front door that led to the sweeping staircase that wound down two flights of converted church to the main entrance. Wallace's only way out was past the killer. The killer with a weapon. *Not the only way.* Wallace's legs were moving before he'd even fully registered the thought. He would risk the chance of dying over the certainty of it.

He crashed through his large living room window and heard himself scream as he tumbled two floors and hit the well-groomed lawn of the front garden, landing on his back. Even in London, where citizens were adept at ignoring the most terrible sounds, the noise of his fall would draw attention. But Wallace didn't want to be found, not here, not in sight of the man who had tried to kill him. He fought back the dark mass crushing his consciousness and looked up at his window. The killer thrust his head through the jagged hole in the glass and looked down at Wallace before withdrawing. *He's coming.*

Wallace felt the dark mass grow heavier as oblivion beckoned, but knew that he had to stay awake. He reached for his chest, the part of his body that was causing him the most pain, and felt something bony and wet—an exposed rib. He pushed it, hard. The ensuing agony was so severe that it cut through his drowsy mind like a searing laser and startled him to life. Wallace staggered to his feet, ignored the screaming pain that came from almost every inch of his body, and stumbled down through the front garden to the street.

Death is hunting you. Think. Think. Think. Wallace's creativity made him a living, but this wasn't a matter of lighting and composition, this was real. He was badly injured, wavering on the edge of consciousness. He had no clothes, no money and no weapon. He considered appealing to his neighbors for help as he stumbled down Hamilton Terrace, but this was one of London's most exclusive addresses and nobody in their right mind would open the door to a battered lunatic on a dark September night.

He tumbled down Abercorn Place, the gentle slope drawing him toward the throng of Maida Vale. The yellow streetlights hanging high above the busy road looked like the glowing hearts of angels.

Salvation, Wallace thought. If it wasn't a mistake, if the killer had come for him, Wallace knew his safest bet was anonymity—losing himself in the teeming city would rob the murderer of a second chance. Rush hour had long passed and traffic was moving freely on Maida Vale. He looked up Abercorn Place and saw no sign of his assailant. Then something in one of the gardens, a figure pulling himself over a wall—he was being followed.

Fear injected him with energy and Wallace staggered toward a bus stop where one of London's double-deckers was discharging its contents. He leaned against the bus while commuters stepped off, and then slipped through the doors as they closed. If the driver had spotted him, he didn't say anything. He'd probably been on the job long enough to know that it wasn't worth confronting nutters over their bus fare. With his last reserves of strength, Wallace hauled himself upstairs. He barely registered the looks of disgust as he made his way along the upper deck. As one of London's rare considerate drivers finally gave way, and the bus pulled out, he collapsed on a seat near the back of the bus. His nearest neighbors gave him concerned glances and moved toward the front, but Wallace didn't care. He leaned against the cold glass and looked out of the window, scouring the gardens of Abercorn Place for signs of his killer. When he saw none, he finally relaxed. The bus rolled along Maida Vale, and he felt the gentle warmth of adrenaline subsiding before comforting darkness closed in.

3

One word stuck in Wallace's mind as he came round: *suicide*. He'd heard it a great deal over the past few kaleidoscopic days. *Suicide. Suicide attempt. Suicide watch.* He'd tried to explain, but he hadn't been making much sense, and the world flickered by like a zoetrope. Wallace caught spinning moments that gave the illusion of being connected, but in reality he had no idea what games time was playing. His only certainty was that everything around him seemed to be urgent and important; things happened quickly and seriously. Wallace didn't mind; during his conscious moments he felt like he was swaddled by a white world of soft clouds, and when he was asleep he dreamed the most colorful nightmares. Horrors so terrifying they made everything else seem utterly blissful. Wallace drifted and drooled as he was eased in and out of life, the zoetrope whirling on. While doctors operated and nurses drained, orderlies pushed, anesthetists had him count in reverse, lights shone brightly, steel gleamed, blood flowed, and life continued. And that's what made it all so pleasurable: *life*. Wallace recalled the crushing, unconquerable grip of death and it made everything that came after it a joy. Each breath, each blink, each simple movement was a prize that he had stolen from the man who'd tried to kill him. He drifted in and out, half-registering the world around him, existing in a place without time or meaning.

Then he woke up. *This is different*, Wallace thought as he looked around the hospital room. He felt the self-awareness and mental acuity that came with sobriety. He guessed they must have dropped the dosage of whatever was keeping the pain at bay. Three months on a photo assignment in Nepal had given him a passing familiarity with opiates and he recognized the muted feeling of withdrawal rooted somewhere deep in his gut.

Laminated vertical blinds cut the sunlight that shone through the frosted window and illuminated Wallace's private room. There was nothing unusual about it: an electric bed, a tray table pushed to one corner, a stand supporting a bag of clear liquid that ran through a tube into the needle embedded in his arm, a heart rate monitor, a television attached to the wall, and an old lady. The old lady smiled as Wallace did a double take. She sat in a low chair positioned against the wall opposite his bed. She wore a floral sweater and a long black skirt and held a book: Gibbon's *History of the Decline and Fall of the Roman Empire*. Her smile was joined by wide eyes that conveyed a perfect mix of sympathy and pity. *Should I know you?* Wallace tried to place the face, but he didn't recognize her.

"How are you feeling?" the old lady asked.

"Okay," Wallace croaked, his throat raw.

The old lady stood and went to the tray table to pour a glass of water from a plastic jug.

"They said you would find it difficult to talk," she said as she brought it over. "This might help."

Wallace nodded his thanks and took a sip, which immediately caused his throat to clam up with what felt like the worst case of tonsillitis he'd ever experienced. He mouthed an oath and grimaced as he held the glass out for the old lady.

"It may take a while," she observed as she replaced the glass on the tray.

"Police," Wallace rasped, the searing sensation now registering through the diminished painkillers.

"No, I'm just a volunteer. We sit with some of the more . . ." the old lady hesitated, searching for the right word, ". . . vulnerable patients."

Suicide watch. Great. Wallace shook his head at the old dear.

"Police," he said again, willing her to get it this time. He wasn't sure his throat could take much more.

"Oh!" she exclaimed with sudden realization. "You want me to fetch the police. Of course. I'll ask one of the nurses to call someone."

Wallace was surprised at how tired he'd become; that simple attempt at communication had exhausted him. He passed out shortly after the old lady had left the room and came round to find someone gently touching his shoulder. A moment to focus; then recognition, one of the faces from the zoetrope; a doctor.

"Mary said you were awake," the doctor began. "We were wondering if you could tell us your name."

The doctor wasn't wearing a badge. Wallace put him in his mid-forties. He had a harsh Afrikaans accent and a severe, unfriendly face, which reinforced Wallace's paranoia.

Wallace touched his skull and shook his head to indicate that he didn't remember.

"Don't you remember?"

Wallace nodded.

"Odd. You don't show any signs of neurological damage," the white South African continued. "It's one of the few parts of your body that was okay. You suffered serious bruising to your legs and back, three broken ribs, one compound, a fractured collar bone, broken wrist, lacerations of the neck and a collapsed windpipe."

Wallace's eyes widened.

"You're lucky to be alive," the doctor said as he studied Wallace in puzzlement. "I'm going to order another MRI. Make sure we didn't miss anything."

Wallace smiled and nodded.

"There's a police officer outside. Are you up to seeing him?"

Wallace nodded as emphatically as his damaged neck would allow.

"If you need help with anything, just press this button," the doctor gestured toward a green button that hung from a cord beside Wallace's bed.

Wallace smiled and waved his thanks as the doctor withdrew. Moments later the door opened and a young black man in a shabby, crumpled suit entered.

"Hi, I'm Detective Sergeant Bailey. The doc tells me you can't remember your name. Is there something you'd like me to call you?" Bailey was tall and slim but had round cheeks that gave his face a babyish look, making him seem kinder and more approachable than he probably was. His closely shaved hair was almost certainly an attempt to give himself a menacing edge.

"John," Wallace croaked.

"John. Okay, John, how can I help you?"

Wallace beckoned the police officer closer. The pain each word caused him meant he didn't want to repeat anything. Bailey drew near. Wallace could see that his eyes shone with intelligence.

"Someone tried to kill me," Wallace rasped.

"Okay. Someone tried to kill you," Bailey said with more than a hint of skepticism.

Wallace glared at him. "Man in body armor," he said through the pain.

"I don't mean any offense," Bailey replied. Wallace guessed he was somewhere in his midtwenties, young enough to be eager, old enough to know that things aren't always exactly how they seem. "It's just that, well, patients' records are confidential, but I've been waiting out there awhile and I've always found that if you chat to the nurses, maybe buy them a tea, you can learn way more than you'd ever learn from a file. They say your injuries are consistent with a suicide attempt and that maybe you panicked when it went wrong. You were found passed out on a bus in Victoria Station."

Wallace had wanted to get lost, but couldn't believe he'd made it all the way to the depot without any of the other passengers alerting the authorities. He shrugged inwardly: *London, the place where nobody wants to get involved*.

"Man tried to kill me," he protested, his hoarse voice making him sound menacing and inhuman.

"I haven't dealt with many situations like this," Bailey responded, "But I do know that a lot of people feel embarrassed. Rather than admit what happened, they're all like, 'I don't know how I finished up in front of the train, I slipped,' or, 'I miscounted the pills, I meant to take two, but I took sixty.'"

He smiled down at Wallace, who hadn't considered the possibility that he'd have to convince the police someone had attacked him.

"Not suicide. Murder," Wallace rasped. "Was working. Knock at door . . ."

He felt the world fade. His chest tightened and his mind became light and fuzzy. He could feel his heart pound and his palms grow moist. The memory of what happened was triggering a frightful reaction in him. Wallace felt the familiar haze of a panic attack, and his head grew light as reality drifted into a distant bubble.

Bailey drew close. "Are you okay?"

Wallace nodded and then shook his head. *Don't try to fight it. Breathe. He* focused on his breathing—slow and full. *Slow and full.* The tightness in his chest subsided.

"I died," he whispered. "Shouldn't be here."

"Let's start from the beginning," Bailey suggested, his demeanor changing from light skepticism to serious professionalism. "Have you really forgotten your name?"

Wallace hesitated. Someone had tried to kill him, and he'd watched *The Godfather* enough times to know that hospital was a prime place for a second attempt. Bailey produced a pad and pencil and looked at him expectantly.

"Promise me. Not tell anyone," Wallace said quietly.

"Any notes are confidential. They only get put on file if there's an arrest, in which case you'd have nothing to worry about. You're safe, I promise," Bailey replied reassuringly.

"John Wallace."

"Address?" Bailey asked.

"Flat four, sixty-one Hamilton Terrace, St. John's Wood," Wallace replied.

Bailey breathed a silent whistle. "Nice part of town. Where do you work?"

"All over. Photographer."

"You enjoy your job?"

Wallace's eyes narrowed. "Didn't try to kill self," he rasped.

"Do you live alone?" Bailey continued.

Wallace nodded.

"Why don't you tell me what happened?" Bailey asked gently.

Wallace hesitated. He could feel panic rising as he cast his mind back to that night. Bailey put a reassuring hand on his shoulder. "It's okay. You're safe."

"Ten o'clock," Wallace began. "Working. Uploading pictures. Knock at door."

"Does your building have a buzzer?" Bailey interrupted.

Wallace nodded.

"And you didn't let this guy in?"

Wallace nodded again.

"So either one of your neighbors let him in, or he broke in," Bailey observed before falling silent.

Wallace continued, "Opened door. Nobody there. Something sprayed in face. Passed out. Came round. Blindfold. Hands and feet tied. Put noose . . ." He trailed off, his hoarse voice cracking to nothing.

"It's okay," Bailey encouraged him gently. "I need to know what happened."

Wallace wiped his welling eyes and composed himself. "Noose on neck," he whispered. "Forced to stand. Blindfold off."

"Did you see him?" Bailey asked.

Wallace shook his head. "Not then. Cut bonds. Made get on chair. Then saw him. Black mask, black suit. Black goggles. Round, covered eyes. Long coat. Like superhero," he said as he remembered his dark observation.

"So you didn't get a look at his face?"

Wallace shook his head.

"What about height? Build?" Bailey continued.

"Six feet. Maybe taller. Strong."

"Did he say anything?" Bailey asked. "Tell you why?"

Wallace shook his head again. "He just . . ." He struggled with the memory, and his chest pounded with the unbearable pressure of fear. His throat tightened, making every breath an effort.

"It's okay, it's okay," Bailey said, his hand pressing gently on Wallace's shoulder. "You're okay. You're safe."

Wallace tried to suppress the panic, but it was an illogical force. He knew there was nothing to be afraid of, but try as he might to convince himself, there was something deeper and more powerful at play. Millions of years of instinct bred into mammals to ensure their survival, panic at the first sign of danger provoking a bestial fight or flight response that could not be satisfied by a wounded man in a hospital bed. No amount of reason or rationality could overcome this ancient, primal feeling.

"Sorry," he croaked.

"It's okay," Bailey said with genuine sympathy. "Take as long as you need."

Wallace lost track of how long he lay there without saying anything, fighting to tame his fear of the moment he almost died.

"He kicked chair away," he said, finally pulling himself together. "Hung there. Tried to pull myself . . ."

Another moment of panic, followed by more patience and sympathy from Bailey.

"Tried to pull self up," Wallace eventually continued. "Couldn't hold weight. Let go."

He broke down utterly as he recalled his abject failure. His life had literally been in his own hands and he'd dropped it. Fear, shame, anger and regret all swept over him as he sobbed in his hospital bed. His eyes were red and sore and his throat burned. *This is important,* he told himself. *This policeman needs to believe you. He needs to get out there and find the man who did this to you.* Anger took over and gave him the strength to continue.

"Blacked out. Came to. Beam had snapped. Stood up. Pulled noose off. Killer came back."

"He was still in your flat?" Bailey asked.

Wallace nodded.

"Why? He must have thought he'd killed you," Bailey observed, puzzled.

"Blocking door. Pulled something—Taser? Couldn't fight— jumped out window."

"You jumped out of the window?"

"Two floors. Killer followed. Got to bus. Safe. Now here."

Bailey digested Wallace's story for a moment, and then asked, "Can you think of any reason someone might want to kill you?"

Wallace shook his head.

"Ex-lover? A business deal gone wrong? You ever associate with any dangerous people? Criminals?"

Wallace shook his head again. "Not many lovers. Live alone. Work alone. Films, mostly. No danger."

"Anyone get angry with you recently?" Bailey pressed.

"No," Wallace croaked hesitantly. "Was part of Masterson Inquiry," he conceded eventually.

"I knew I recognized your name," Bailey remarked. "You think it might have had something to do with that?"

"Long time ago," Wallace replied. "Was discredited. No threat to those soldiers. No threat to anyone."

"Okay," Bailey conceded. "I'm going to check this out, talk to your neighbors and find out if anyone saw or heard anything. Is there anyone you'd like me to call for you?"

Wallace shook his head. Until he was in a firmer frame of mind and knew who'd tried to kill him, he wasn't inclined to see or trust anyone.

"Do you want me to let the hospital know?" Bailey asked.

"No."

"I only ask because you've been sectioned under the Mental Health Act. The doctors believe you pose a risk to yourself. If they knew all this, it might make a difference to how they assess you."

Wallace smiled darkly. "Don't believe me?"

"You've obviously been through a terrible ordeal, but my job is to find out exactly what happened," Bailey replied. "I'm taking what you've told me very seriously."

Wallace gave a small shrug; it was the best he could hope for in the circumstances.

"So do you want me to tell them?"

"No. No one. Safer."

"I'll be in touch," Bailey said as he walked toward the door. "Feel better."

As Wallace watched the young policeman exit he realized that he'd put all his trust, and his life, in the hands of a stranger. He prayed that it would pay off before pressing the call button. He needed the nurse. He longed for sleep. Whatever they had him on, he wanted more. He didn't want to lie in his bleak hospital room haunted by the harrowing memories of his murder.

4

The girl's toes reminded Wallace of the fallen columns he'd photographed at Karnak. Each digit comprised of three prominent phalanx bones lying haphazardly in line, joined by the past, being slowly eroded by the future. Wallace studied her face. Angular, almost jagged cheeks thrust out from pale, pockmarked skin. Sunken eyes, ringed by dark shadows. Lank blonde hair falling in matted tresses that hid much of her face. Sharp angles all the way down, from her collarbones, their skeletal outline punctuating her narrow neck, to her bulbous ankles. Her name was Heather, and she was talking, but Wallace was barely listening. He had heard her story many times before and knew that her words held no secrets. Instead, he was trying to find meaning in her fragile, distorted beauty; her ribs, which cascaded down her torso like the arched keys of a macabre glockenspiel, their painful outlines visible underneath her thin white blouse, elbows and knees all raw, the skin stretched tight around the joints beneath, twin bones running along the forearm, broken only by the sweatbands on her wrists. Occasionally Heather would nervously play with one of the sweatbands and Wallace would catch a glimpse of the white scars hidden beneath.

Heather, the saddest girl in the world, too fragile for happiness, too resilient to escape. Had she been born unhappy? Or had the storm of life weathered her soul, grinding it down until only misery remained? Wallace watched her thin lips as they moved slowly, signposting her thoughts, but never revealing the truth. He looked up at Heather's eyes. There, past the shadows, beyond the red rims, was the truth: *pain*. Life brought Heather nothing but pain. It trapped her in suffering, but her lips, the purveyors of comforting lies, would never share the truth with the group. Maybe she harbored the hope that she'd get better. More likely she didn't want to reveal the darkness within to Doctor Taylor, who might never clear her for release and forever deprive her of the ability to make one more attempt to escape the pain.

The group meant that it was either Tuesday or Thursday. Wallace was having trouble with the days. The group. Five broken individuals. Six including Wallace. Seven including the doctor. Wallace would watch Taylor, his shining, full-bodied wavy hair, his pressed shirts and polished shoes, his Mont Blanc pen and Gucci glasses, all signets of his sanity. Great seals of civilization that notarized the fact that Taylor was a functioning member of society. Only Wallace knew the truth. As the one vaguely sane person in the group, he could see the signs: the doctor's hesitant questions, the doubt in his eyes, the fear in his voice. Taylor's lips lied better than Heather's, but Wallace knew the doctor was just as broken as his patients. He had to be. No sane person would choose to be surrounded by such sorrow. He'd have to be mad to believe these people could be saved. This was Wallace's fifth, no, sixth—*got to keep on top of time*—session with the group and already he knew that Heather and her cadre of survivors were beyond help. The best any of them could hope for was to be patched up for a few more years of maladjusted misery. The bleak burden of what those people shared in that room weighed heavy on Wallace's heart. Taylor could not be sane and remain unaffected by it. The doctor's leery, bright-toothed smile and mind full of learning couldn't do anything for them; to think otherwise was lunacy.

Taylor had chastised Wallace in an earlier session—*third, definitely the third. Stay on top of time, John.* The doctor had felt compelled to highlight Wallace's lack of engagement. He spoke about the danger of distance and had begun to explore the perils of evasiveness before Wallace had been able to send his mind somewhere else. *Distance. Disengagement.* These were words he'd heard before, spoken by softer lips. Connie had initially accepted the distance. Learned to live with the long periods when he'd retreat into his mind and utterly ignore the world around him. But the more she'd accepted him and the closer she'd become, the further Wallace had withdrawn. Connections brought nothing but pain, and the people in this room were the starkest evidence of that truth.

He was finding it increasingly hard to keep track of abstract concepts like truth and identity. Robbed of the context of life, he was adrift. The very environment that was meant to cure these people made it all the more difficult to anchor the mind on something solid. Wallace had been medicated with a powerful cocktail of pills since admission. A miniature Tetris tray of oddly shaped pills that would all fit together in his gut to make him a whole, happy person. Taylor had explained what each would do to his body and mind, but the conversation now seemed too distant to recall in any detail. In the cinema of his mind, the screen was cracked and faded, and the audio a low monotone of indecipherable phrases. Maybe the pills were making him drift? Maybe they broke his mind down to a malleable mass that could be reshaped into a sane whole by the dedicated Doctor Taylor?

That's how it gets you, Wallace told himself. *Dark, insipid thoughts. The product of a drugged mind that has nowhere else to go. You're the same man you were four weeks ago.* Except Wallace knew that he wasn't. Someone had tried to kill him. He wasn't able to close his eyes without seeing the mask. He wasn't able to sleep without reliving the moment. The only difference between the dream and the reality was that in his dreams he died. But instead of painless oblivion, his death sent him hurtling through the most miserable moments of his life. Every single regret replayed and magnified by his nightly nightmare. When he was taken for his morning wash, the face that looked back at him from the mirror wasn't his. He'd declined the services of the hospital barber and the ragged hair and scraggly beard that had materialized in the intervening weeks—*three? four? definitely four*—made him seem wild. When Wallace looked in the mirror he hoped he would have his eyes back. More than the sunken cheeks, the haunted expression, or the pale skin, Wallace wanted rid of these eyes. Like Heather's, they spoke of his pain. The tips of black icebergs, Wallace's pupils were the start of a heavy darkness that plumbed the depths of his very existence. Everything about who he was, what he did, what he believed, the world around him—everything was a sham. His death. The noose. His final breath. That was reality.

"Are you okay?" Wallace became aware of a voice that wasn't his own. It was Taylor, leaning forward, his face a picture of concern. Perhaps that was why Taylor chose this life; being surrounded by the most fractured specimens was the only way he could feel good about himself. "John?"

Wallace saw Heather look at him, her eyes brimming with pity. He touched a hand to his cheek and felt wet tears.

"Did Heather's story resonate with you?" Taylor asked in a syrupy voice that oozed with concern.

Wallace looked round the room. There was Rodney, who had tried to gas himself in his garage. Tina and Ken, who had both tried to overdose, and wheelchair-bound Martin, who had jumped off a bridge. These sad, broken spirits looked at him with overplayed pity. He had taken the heat of Taylor's attention away from any of them and Wallace knew that they would applaud and encourage any attempt to keep it firmly fixed on him.

"I'm okay," he replied. He wasn't about to open up. Not now. He wasn't about to tell Taylor that the source of his tears was his recently discovered never-ending river of self-pity. Guilt. Regret. Existential crisis. All markers of a breakdown, but he was not about to discuss them here. He looked at the attempted suicides and found new resolve. He was not one of them. Someone had tried to kill him. A random event that had wounded him, physically and mentally. He might even be experiencing a breakdown, but unlike the people around him, he was not yet broken. Time, not some smiling doctor, would heal him.

"Are you sure?" Taylor countered. "It's been five weeks . . ."

Five! No. It's been four, Wallace thought as he suddenly wondered whether Taylor was playing games with him.

". . . and you still haven't shared anything with the group," Taylor continued. "I normally give people a maximum of eight sessions before insisting they tell their story. This is your tenth, John, and we still don't even know your full name."

"I'm just John," Wallace replied. Someone had tried to kill him, and until he knew who that was, no one would know his identity. "You know I can't tell you my name."

Taylor looked as though he wanted to roll his eyes, but his training prevented him from doing anything so unprofessional. "I know why you think you can't tell us. But once the police investigation is complete, we're going to need to know. If necessary we'll start canvassing for your name. Identity gives us context in life. It will enable us to help you get better."

Wallace smiled. "I don't need help. I really don't belong here."

"You keep saying that, John," Taylor countered. "But how can you expect any of us to agree with you if you don't tell us more about yourself?"

Wallace looked around the room. Why would he want to share anything with these strangers? Rodney's eyes were vacant, the result of spending too long in his monoxide-filled garage. His movements were like a distant swell, slow and languid, his arms and legs carelessly rolling, as though his brain was struggling to retain control of them. What could Wallace hope to gain by sharing anything with this damaged man? Wallace was not a suicide. He had nothing in common with these people.

"I've got nothing to say," Wallace responded.

Disappointment flashed across Taylor's face. A lesser mind would have felt the pressure of guilt and sought to please Taylor by spilling its contents, but Wallace was wise to the doctor's manipulation and simply stared at him defiantly.

"Perhaps next time," Taylor conceded. "Heather, why don't you carry on?"

Disappointment also clouded Heather's face, but she lacked Wallace's resolve in dealing with the doctor, and her lying lips continued their slow work. Wallace turned his thoughts to the future and wondered how he would secure his release without divulging his identity. Even if he told them who he was, they would never believe him without any evidence. He tried to recall the police officer who had visited him in hospital, but the man's name remained beyond the haze of drugs. If Taylor was right and he'd been institutionalized for five weeks he might as well give up hope of the police coming to his rescue. Like everyone else, the detective had probably dismissed Wallace as a failed suicide. He wouldn't have even bothered to follow up Wallace's story. Whatever the future held, Wallace almost certainly faced it alone.

Ellie had chewed him out, but Bailey didn't really give a shit. For all the advances in technology, forensics were there to support real detective work, which meant they did what they were told. And if he told them to sweep the home of an obvious suicide, that's what they had to do. But they'd come up empty and Ellie had come down on him for wasting her team's time. Fuck her. *Never*, Bailey thought. Too geeky, with a pastiness that comes from spending too much time indoors. Bailey preferred his women fiery and tanned. His relationships didn't last long, but they kept life interesting.

He parked in a resident's bay on Hamilton Terrace. When he climbed out of his Vauxhall, he realized how out of place it looked, flanked by a Range Rover and a Bentley. Growing up in Streatham, Bailey had dreamed of being rich. *But I'll never be rich*, Bailey thought as he crossed the pavement and started up the black-and-white tiled pathway that led to number 61 Hamilton Terrace. The converted redbrick church was one of the more modest buildings on the broad, tree-lined street. Next to it, concealed behind high walls and solid black gates, was a giant white mansion with opaque sky-blue windows. Here, in this fine neighborhood, that pile would set a person back at least twenty-five million. Bailey felt a pang of jealousy, but consoled himself with the thought that he never had to worry about anyone breaking into his one-bedroom flat in Hackney. No threat of home invasion. No concerns about being held at knifepoint while the house was ransacked. Still, it would be nice to have the choice, the freedom to drop twenty-five mill on a pad. The guy who owned the white palace probably wouldn't even notice the dent the purchase price made in his wallet. There were some people out there with way too much cash. *Whiners ain't winners.* Bailey recalled his grandmother's advice, which was doled out to him and any of his siblings whenever they complained they were getting a raw deal.

He focused on the job at hand: one more witness to interview. He'd made three visits to Hamilton Terrace over the past month. The first was to canvas the neighbors and find out if anyone had seen or heard anything. He'd interviewed Steve Kent, the banker who lived in the basement, the Wilsons, a young family who rented the ground-floor flat and the Levines, a retired couple who had the flat on the first floor. But he hadn't been able to reach Leona Stiles, the woman who lived directly above Wallace. Mrs. Levine had told him that she was some sort of showgirl, who had left a few days after the incident to spend a few weeks working in Dubai. She wasn't due back until the end of October. Beyond the immediate neighbors, Bailey had canvassed three homes either side of number 61. He'd only been able to talk to the staff in each of the adjacent properties and was told that the owners were away. No one with money spent autumn in London. Like the first ancients, these absentee landlords were sun worshippers. The only difference was that they had the resources to chase it around the globe.

None of the residents or staff had seen anything, suggesting that Wallace's story was a work of fiction. Bailey's second visit had been with Ellie and the forensics team, and, as he'd watched their meticulous work, he'd studied the collapsed beam and questioned whether a failed suicide really would follow an unsuccessful attempt with another immediate bid. It would take a particularly unhinged mind to leap out of the window after an abortive hanging, and, while Wallace had seemed distressed, he did not come across as unstable.

Even though the forensics team didn't find anything to suggest attempted murder, Bailey couldn't shake the nagging feeling that Wallace had been telling the truth. The man had been deeply shaken and seemed genuinely convinced that someone had tried to kill him. So Bailey made a third visit just over a week ago to walk the course. He had checked the walls, gardens and outbuildings around number 61, invoking the ire of more than one security-conscious neighbor and the attention of the local uniforms. He had found nothing. No trace of a supposed intruder either inside or outside the property. With a certain amount of satisfaction, Ellie had told him that her team had concluded that John Wallace had attempted suicide, first by hanging, and then, when the decorative beam had collapsed, by jumping through his second-floor window. Nonetheless, Bailey's instincts told him that the man had been telling the truth, so he had waited patiently for the return of the only remaining witness who could corroborate Wallace's story.

He climbed the single step and pressed the buzzer for flat number five. He stared at the camera and smiled when a voice answered, "Hello?"

Bailey held his ID up to the camera and replied, "Miss Stiles, it's Detective Sergeant Bailey. We spoke on the phone."

The catch on the door buzzed and Bailey pushed it open. He crossed the wood-paneled hall and checked himself in the large, gilt-framed mirrors that flanked him on either side. Hundreds of reflected images stared back at him: a strong, confident, young black man with looks that merited his ego. Bailey was pleased by what he saw. He passed the door to the Wilsons' flat and hurried up the carpeted stairs, taking them two at a time. The thick green pile muffled the sound of his steps. If someone was able to break into the building, it wouldn't be difficult to move around without being heard. As he walked along the first-floor landing, he saw the light change in the Levines' peephole. The door opened a moment later, and Mrs. Levine, a sweet, crinkled old white lady with a loose perm, smiled at him.

"Hello, Detective Bailey," she said. "Any news on John? We're worried about him."

"The doctors think he'll be okay," Bailey replied. "Just needs a little more time. If you'll excuse me."

"You'll let us know if there's news, won't you?" Mrs. Levine called after Bailey, who had already moved on.

As he rounded the next flight of stairs, Bailey looked back to see the old lady shut the door and heard her double-lock it. She claimed to have always been security conscious, even before the incident. She had plenty of time to read the newspaper and knew what happened to people who didn't look out for themselves. Mrs. Levine had been home the night of the suicide—murder—attempted killing, was the phrase Bailey had finally settled on. Mrs. Levine said she'd heard loud music and some banging about, but nothing unusual until the beam collapsed. The awful racket had convinced her that the building was coming down. After the sound of shattering glass, Mrs. Levine had looked out of the window to see John Wallace, half-naked, scuttling down Abercorn Place. She'd not been aware of any visitors, nor heard anything that would have led her to believe John Wallace wasn't alone.

As Bailey continued up the stairs, Wallace's front door came into view. It was secured by a temporary padlock and a caution notice warned any unauthorized visitors. Bailey had called Maybury Hospital to check on Wallace. The doctor he spoke to, Taylor, refused to divulge any information on Wallace's condition but said that Bailey was welcome to visit. Bailey couldn't bring himself to talk to the guy just yet. Not until he'd figured out for certain whether he was a genuine victim or a deluded liar. He continued up the stairs until he reached the top floor of the converted church where the roof began to gently slope toward its high apex.

He crossed the third-floor landing and found Leona Stiles's front door ajar. The smell of sweet incense drifted through the gap. Bailey knocked. "Hello?"

"Come in," came a soft voice.

He opened the door and stepped into a bright hallway. Light came through a couple of open doorways. The one on his right led into a kitchen with a wooden floor and low units. The other door was directly ahead of him. Another wooden floor, but this one covered by a rug. The layout seemed to be a duplicate of Wallace's, but the decor couldn't have been more different. A photograph of two nude women locked in an intimate embrace dominated the hallway.

Bailey wasn't sure how to describe the style, but the black-and-white image was overexposed so that one only caught the most pronounced features, an effect that accentuated the mystery of the subjects' embrace. A dozen smaller, framed black-and-white photographs of a woman in a variety of outlandish outfits filled what space remained on the bright red walls. The woman's face was covered with rich makeup that masked her true identity. Bailey couldn't help but marvel at the intricacy of the costumes and face paint. A burlesque peacock in one, a seductive deviless in another, the images could never be described as erotic, but Bailey found them strangely alluring.

"In here." The voice came from the living room.

Bailey entered to find the large space dominated by a tailor's mannequin adorned in what looked like a bridal gown. A long white train flowed from the dress and wound around much of the room until it finished bunched in the hands of a strange young woman. Strange because one side of her head was shaved and tattooed, while the other sported lustrous wavy auburn hair. Leona Stiles was probably a natural beauty, but her dichotomous appearance rendered traditional concepts of beauty useless. Bailey settled for fascinating. Leona stood and carefully deposited the end of the bridal train on the old leather chair that she'd been sitting on. She wore a floral tea dress that was split at her midriff, revealing part of her torso. Bailey tried not to look too closely but couldn't help seeing that a garland of roses tattooed the space between Leona's breasts. She crossed one of the largest Persian rugs Bailey had ever seen and offered her hand.

"Pleased to meet you, Detective," she said. "I'm Leona Stiles."

"Nice to meet you." Bailey floundered for his cool as he shook Leona's hand. Her grip was delicate but gave a hint of the strength that lay beyond it.

"Sorry it's such a mess in here. I'd offer you a seat, but I had to take them all out to work."

Bailey looked at the gown. "Someone's big day," he observed.

Leona looked puzzled for a moment before realization dawned. "Not quite," she responded with a smile. "I'm making it for a performance. I do all my own costumes."

"Mrs. Levine said you're a trapeze artist," Bailey remarked.

"Trapeze, high wire, fire breathing, anything that might kill me," Leona replied dryly. "This one's for a music video. They're going for a Miss Haversham vibe. The entire dress catches fire, liberating me to be an independent woman. Or liberating me of my clothes; I can never keep track of all the creative reasons why I find myself in my underwear so often."

Bailey was smitten. Dangerous, funny, and smart. The living room walls were pure white but were covered in brightly framed photographs and paintings of circus folk through the ages. As wild as it was, it was clear to Bailey that Leona revered her work.

"How's John?" Leona broke the extended silence.

"John?" Bailey snapped out of a romantic daydream in which he and Leona had married and sired a handful of circus-performing kids.

"My neighbor? I assume that's what you're here to talk about?"

"Yeah. Sorry. John Wallace, that's right," Bailey replied. Got to be smoother than that, he told himself. "Were you home the night of the incident?"

Leona nodded. "It was a couple of days before I flew out to Dubai. I was working on my costume."

"Underwear?" Bailey joked.

Leona smiled and shook her head. "Not in Dubai. Modesty is the watchword."

No more attempted jokes, Bailey chastised himself. This girl is as cool as anyone you've ever met. "How well did you know Mr. Wallace?"

"Quite well. We've been out for drinks. I've posed for him a couple of times."

"He seems to have a bit of a name," Bailey observed.

"He does. He photographed war until it got to him. Now he mainly does unit photography. Films. Big TV shows."

"You think it was suicide?" Bailey asked bluntly.

"No," Leona countered swiftly.

"Maybe the war—" Bailey began.

"What he saw in Afghanistan troubled him," Leona interrupted. "The Inquiry really got to him, but he'd moved on."

"Did you see or hear anything unusual that night?"

Leona shook her head. The tattoo on the right side of her scalp depicted an eagle carrying a rose in its talons. "There was loud music a few minutes before it happened, but I didn't think anything of it."

"Was he normally noisy?" Bailey asked.

"Hardly. John keeps to himself mostly," Leona smiled. "But every now and again he blasts a track to get him in the mood."

Bailey waited to be illuminated.

"In the mood for a project," Leona explained. "I assumed he was preparing for his next gig. He says the right music helps inspire him."

"You didn't see anyone?"

"Only John. After I heard the crash, I went to the window and saw him running toward the main road. I think he was naked."

"How long have you lived here?" Bailey asked.

"Four years. My father bought the flat for my twenty-first birthday."

Although physiologically impossible, Bailey now wanted to have her babies. Fascinating and rich—*jackpot*.

As he stood there studying her, Bailey was aware of a subtle change in her expression. He could only describe it as familiarity. Here was a woman who was used to being watched. More likely than not she was aware of how she captivated men. She had recognized the signs in Bailey, and while there was no obvious, outward reaction, the balance of power had shifted in her favor. *Way to play it cool, idiot*, he yelled inwardly.

"Sorry I can't be of more help," she said as she moved slowly toward the door.

"No need to apologize. You've cleared a lot of things up for me," Bailey responded, following her. He cast around, searching for an excuse to ask her out, or at the very least return for a follow-up visit. He dried up, and his arid, rough tongue stuck to the roof of his mouth. Damn! This girl was the real deal.

Bailey swallowed.

"Listen," he tried.

"I love this photo," Leona cut him off as she gently caressed the frame of the giant picture in the hallway. "John took it. It really captures who I am."

Bailey looked at it again. This time, through the burning, over-exposed light, he saw that one of the women seemed to have something on the side of her head. A bird, perhaps? An eagle clasping a rose, he realized with the encroaching numbness of defeat. The photograph captured a powerfully intimate moment of true tenderness between two lovers.

"It's really something," he observed. He never stood a chance. "Thanks for your help, Miss Stiles."

"If there's anything else I can do," Leona left the offer hanging.

"I think I've got everything I need," Bailey said as he opened the front door. "Thanks again."

He stepped into the carpeted corridor and didn't look back until he heard the door shut behind him. He gave a wry smile as he considered how close he'd come to making a total fool of himself and consoled himself with the thought that it was good to know there were still women out there who could have that kind of effect on him. With that minor consideration working to slowly extinguish the flames of embarrassment, Bailey started down the stairs.

5

The day began with a familiar burning behind the eyes. Wallace's head felt tight, as though someone was shrink-wrapping his brain. The meds pounded him with the murky pain of a punishing hangover. He rubbed his eyes. Five weeks. He couldn't believe it had been that long—he thought he'd kept better track of the days. Maybe it was Taylor's way of testing him, challenging him to prove his sanity by correcting the temporal deceit. No, the doctor's thinking was too prosaic for such subtle tests. Wallace had to face the fact that he might be losing his mind.

He rolled into a seated position and sat on the edge of his bunk. Everything around him was designed to be as safe as possible. From his benign sky-blue pajamas to his urine-proof laminated mattress, the Maybury Hospital offered the safest, blandest of all possible existences so as not to provoke the discordant mind, but, without life's sharper edges, there was nothing to give the inmates purchase. The languid haze of medication made it all too easy to drift through time. He rose from the fiberglass plinth that supported his bunk—no planks or nails to fashion a weapon that could be used for a violent exit during the night. He pressed his palms flat against the wall and looked out of the window as he tried to stretch his shoulders. The blinds rolled open at seven thirty. They were built into the window, resting between two thick panes of glass that distorted the view of the gardens beyond. The glass made the bare tree branches seem even more crooked, and people walking through the gardens wobbled and warped like reflections in a carnival mirror.

Wallace caught sight of his echo in the window. It wasn't a proper reflection, more like the shadow of one. He could make out his scraggly beard and unkempt dark hair. His piercing blue eyes only registered as black hollows on the thick glass, but his prominent cheekbones seemed even more pronounced than usual. He stood upright and ran his hands over his torso. His ribs danced under his fingertips, and Wallace realized that he'd lost quite a bit of weight. Normally lean and muscular, standing at just over six feet, in his current condition Wallace was in danger of being considered gangly. He looked down at his toes and realized they were starting to look like Heather's, the skin pulled in tight relief against the narrow bones. Perhaps this was what the Maybury did: deconstruct a person until only a skeletal outline remained, one that could be refilled and recolored in Doctor Taylor's image. Wallace made a mental note to eat more. He did not need to be reconstructed. He needed to get out. He needed to find the man who tried to kill him.

He relieved himself in the fiberglass toilet and then washed his hands and face in the adjacent basin. He sat on his bunk and waited for the daily routine to begin. At seven forty-five an orderly would open the door and escort inmates to the showers, where strong iodine-colored soap ensured cleanliness. Day clothes were provided in the changing area. Clothes were usually the inmate's own, but in Wallace's case a pair of jogging bottoms, T-shirt and Crocs had to suffice in light of his refusal to share his true identity. Breakfast in the canteen and morning medication. All done and ready for nine. Nine until one was activity time. Inmates were encouraged to participate in something that developed and reinforced constructive behavior. There were walks around the garden, reading groups, card games, jigsaw puzzles, table tennis, backgammon, chess, talks, discussions, and counseling sessions. Wallace tended to stay in the television room and watch daytime programming. Safe, bland, tedious shows that kept him comfortably distracted until lunch, when he would eat another outsourced, reheated meal in the canteen. Two until five was therapy time. Either as a group, which happened twice a week, or individually as required. Five until seven was free time, when Wallace went back to the television room and watched equally dull early evening programming. They weren't allowed the news lest the horrors of the world trigger adverse reactions in some of the more fragile inmates. At seven they had their evening meal, followed by evening meds: little pills to keep the big nightmares at bay. From eight until ten was movie time—usually family fare with nothing overtly violent or stimulating. Half an hour back in their rooms to decompress from the mayhem of the day by reading or masturbating. Lights out at ten thirty to give them plenty of time with their nightmares. This was the program the bright stars of mental health hoped would prepare the inmates for the rest of their lives.

Wallace heard the familiar sound of the buzzer, and moments later, Keith, his section orderly, poked his head round the door.

"Morning, John. How are you feeling?" Keith asked, his paunchy moon face curling up in a jovial smile.

"Like I don't belong here," Wallace replied honestly.

"I think we'd all rather be somewhere else," Keith chuckled. "Come on. Up and at 'em. It's wash time."

Wallace shuffled to the showers. He lathered up with the blood-red, hospital-strength shower gel before rinsing himself and then shuffling to the changing room to put on his layabout's uniform. He shuffled to breakfast and opted for the congealed Full English. Pills popped, he shuffled into the television room and settled into the armchair closest to the TV. Most of the other inmates were eager to be cured, so apart from a couple of lost causes Wallace knew only as Fat Bob and Button, he was the only one to waste his morning in front of the television when there were delicious, sanity-restoring activities taking place in other parts of the hospital. Fat Bob and Button sat on opposite sides of the large room. Fat Bob had the remote. Fat Bob always had the remote. Button watched the screen, but Wallace doubted anything ever registered because all he did was endlessly repeat the words "Push the button." Sometimes he said them under his breath like a quiet prayer. At other times they were sung like a Gregorian chant. Occasionally the words would be spat out at full volume, full of vitriol. As far as Wallace knew, Button had never said anything else.

"Fat Bob. Button," Wallace greeted the men. "What you watching?"

"Push the button!" Button yelled.

"Stuff. Buying stuff. Selling stuff," Fat Bob babbled enthusiastically. "They have this thing. Plays music in the shower. Why can't we have music in the shower, huh? They never let us have anything. We need more stuff!"

If Fat Bob was talking about stuff, that meant they were watching the shopping channel, and, sure enough, there on the screen was a bright-toothed, perma-tanned presenter selling a waterproof radio.

"Push the button," Button said quietly, as Wallace slid into a seat in the middle of the room.

A few moments later, just as he had done every single day since Wallace's arrival, Fat Bob came and sat next to him. Wallace got the feeling that Fat Bob liked him, but outside of an initial daily greeting, the two men never spoke. They just sat and watched whatever Fat Bob decided the screen should throw at them. Wallace was just getting into the hypnotic rhythm of the presenter's patter when he noticed Keith enter.

"John, you've got a visitor."

Visiting hours were between nine and nine. Wallace couldn't help but feel upbeat as he followed Keith to the meeting room, where visitors were made to feel comfortable around madness. He'd occasionally pass it in the hurly-burly of his daily routine and had come to recognize the embarrassed look worn by most visitors: *please forgive me for not knowing how to handle your grotesque insanity.*

Apart from the policeman, nobody knew Wallace was here, and when he entered the breakout room, Wallace was gratified to see the vaguely familiar face of a slim black man in a crumpled suit. Across the room, Rodney sat with his pretty wife, but they didn't speak. Instead, she wept quietly while Rodney held her hands. Tough to move on from the fact that your partner was unhappy enough to attempt suicide. Where do you go from there? Apart from Rodney and his tormented wife, and Keith, who took up a discreet position near the door, Wallace and the police officer were alone.

"Seems like a nice place," the police officer said, signaling their surroundings. Wallace quickly glanced around and took in the framed posters of hilltops, mountains, and other inspirational landscapes. A small bookshelf was lined with bound editions of the classics, no doubt a gift from a worthy benefactor.

"Don't be fooled. They put us in chains when visiting hours are over," Wallace said with a smile as he sat on the molded plastic chair opposite the officer. "You'll have to excuse me, I don't recall your name."

"Detective Sergeant Patrick Bailey."

"Nice to meet you, Detective Sergeant Bailey." Wallace extended his hand. "I don't remember much about our last encounter."

Bailey shook his hand. "That's okay. You were pretty messed up. How are you feeling?"

"Physically, I'm okay. The bones have almost healed. Collarbone will take a little longer. Just means I can't train," Wallace replied.

"No aikido for a while," Bailey observed.

"No," Wallace responded hesitantly, surprised that the policeman had gone through his life in such detail.

"I'm very thorough," Bailey explained. "I've seen some of your photographs. You've got a good eye."

Something about the man's demeanor set Wallace on edge. He was skirting the issue. Not a good sign.

"You didn't come here to commission me, Detective Bailey. You didn't find anything, did you?"

Bailey shook his head slowly.

"So you think I'm crazy?" Wallace challenged him.

"You've been through a difficult experience," Bailey responded.

"Difficult experience! A guy broke into my place and tried to kill me!" Wallace replied testily. He realized his voice had dropped in tone and risen sufficiently in volume to catch Keith's attention. The rotund orderly looked over with an admonishment of caution.

"We had a forensics team sweep the place. I spoke to all your neighbors. I checked the area. I even spoke to your old agent," Bailey reassured Wallace. "Nothing."

Wallace slumped, literally feeling the weight of the "truth" the rest of the world now accepted: he was a suicide gone wrong. Without evidence, Wallace couldn't convince Taylor he didn't belong here. Without evidence, he couldn't be sure why someone tried to kill him. Without evidence, he couldn't return to his life. He flailed for inspiration.

"What about cameras?" he asked hopefully. "CCTV. They're on every corner. One of them must have caught something."

"First thing I checked. A power surge fried all the cameras in St. John's Wood. They were out for about two weeks," Bailey replied. "Nothing in a six-block area."

"There was a man inside my flat. He tried to kill me," Wallace reiterated. "I'm not lying. And I'm not crazy."

"You ever seen a film called *Contact*?" Bailey asked. "Jodie Foster. Matthew McConaughey before he became all cool. She talks about some kind of razor being the simplest explanation for things."

"Ockham's razor," Wallace observed. "The simplest answer is the most likely."

"Exactly," Bailey's smile withered away. "One of your neighbors told me you used to be a war photographer. Your agent said you had a hard time in Afghanistan. You quit. Started working in film."

"What's that got to do with anything?" Wallace glared at Bailey. He could feel his anger rising.

"Sometimes when people live through a terrible event, it can cause long-term damage," Bailey explained. "Maybe this was a delayed reaction."

"So you think I tried to kill myself?" Wallace growled, struggling to control his temper.

"I'm going on the evidence, John." Bailey's response was infuriating.

"A man tried to kill me," Wallace protested loudly. He hit the table between them, drawing a harsh look from Keith.

"What do the docs say?" Bailey asked in a clear attempt at deflection.

"They think I'm nuts," Wallace replied. "And without any evidence, there's no way to convince them otherwise."

"I'm sorry, Mr. Wallace, there isn't anything I can do," Bailey said as he stood.

"That's it?" Wallace's anger bubbled into incomprehension. "I'm stuck here?"

"Until they believe you no longer pose a danger to yourself," Bailey offered. He held out his hand. "If you can think of anything else that might help me, I'm based at Paddington Green."

Wallace refused Bailey's empty hand and stared at the man. How did he know this smiling fool had actually done his job? Forensics? Interviews with neighbors? Talking to his agent? This guy was full of shit. How dare he bring up Afghanistan?

"I'd like to see your notes," Wallace said coldly.

"What?" Bailey's hand dropped to his side.

"I'd like to see your notes."

The policeman bristled, and Wallace knew he was onto something.

"Not going to happen, Mr. Wallace," Bailey replied flatly.

"How do I know you've done your job?" Wallace challenged.

Bailey shook his head as a tight smile stretched across his lips. He leaned down, drawing his face close to Wallace. "Because I told you so," he said harshly. "Move on with your life, Mr. Wallace. Nobody's buying your story."

Wallace brimmed with rage as the turbulent kaleidoscope of emotions he'd suppressed over the past few weeks spiraled through his body. He felt the humiliation of defeat, shame at having let go of the rope, frustration at not being believed, anger at the unfairness, but, most of all, the rage of impotence.

Wallace reacted instinctively, cocking his head like a pistol hammer before firing it forward. Bailey's nose broke with a noise that sounded like a gunshot, and the policeman went down, dazed. Out of control, Wallace jumped on the prone man and started pounding him with his heavy fists. Bailey put up scant resistance as Wallace gave vent to his anger. A Klaxon sounded, but Wallace hardly heard it. Moments later, Wallace registered a heavy blow to the back of his neck, but such was his fury, it did nothing to slow down his frenzied assault. Another blow, this one harder, and everything went black.

Fuck! Fuck! Fuck! Bailey cursed his stupidity. The guy could have killed him. The orderly had smacked him over the head with a cosh and now the prone, unconscious form of John Wallace pressed down on his chest. With the orderly's assistance, Bailey rolled out from underneath his attacker. Other orderlies soon arrived, along with a couple of nurses and a doctor.

"What happened?" the doctor asked.

"The patient attacked the detective," the orderly who rescued Bailey answered. "I was forced to subdue him."

The doctor turned to his team. "Get him to isolation."

The orderlies grabbed Wallace and dragged him from the room.

"I'm so sorry," the doctor said as he approached Bailey. "I never expected him to be violent. You need treatment."

Bailey tried to find something to take his mind off his humiliation, but none of the books or abstract prints of gentle shapes engaged him. He gingerly touched his newly set nose. A short Band-Aid concealed the wound, which unleashed nausea-inducing waves of pain as soon as he put his finger to it. The rest of his injuries were superficial, the most serious being to his pride. He was a professional with years of experience and should never have put himself in danger like that. A lucky strike was all it had taken to put him down, and if it hadn't been for the orderly, things could have been a lot worse. Bailey had received treatment at the Maybury's sister hospital, Southold General, and, after a barrage of tests that had given him the all clear, was returned to the Maybury to complete incident reports and give a witness statement to the local police. After almost an entire day, he was finally ready to go home. The doctor, who Bailey now knew was called Taylor, had informed Superintendent Cross of the incident. Bailey was certain he'd get his knuckles rapped for not exercising better judgment, and so carelessly exposing himself to danger.

The door opened and Taylor entered.

"We're all done here, Detective," Taylor said, beaming. "I hear your x-rays and MRI came back clear. No lasting damage. Other than the nose, of course."

"How's the patient?" Bailey asked.

"Remorseful. When he came round, the first thing he wanted to know was whether you were okay," Taylor responded. "I'm going to have to take a very different approach with him."

"His name's John Wallace," Bailey said. *Crazy fuck broke our confidentiality agreement when he cracked my nose*, he thought. "I wanted to make sure you got his name. Flat four, sixty-one Hamilton Terrace, St. John's Wood. I've written it down for you."

He produced a scrap of paper from his pocket and handed it to Taylor.

"Thanks," the doctor replied. "I'm very sorry about what happened."

"Don't sweat it," Bailey replied on his way to the door. "Just make sure you fix him."

6

Regret had dredged his mind for the past week, tormenting him relentlessly, dragging him further and further down. As he lay in his cell, Wallace felt the now familiar dank hollowness of depression. Regret gripped him the moment he regained consciousness. Regret held him as Doctor Taylor outlined his new treatment regimen. Regret consumed him the instant Taylor used his full name. The detective had told them. Wallace had attacked his only ally and had paid the price of his fury.

Alongside regret was a new feeling: doubt. Taylor had taken a very active interest in Wallace's treatment ever since his violent outburst, and Wallace now had daily one-to-one sessions as well as group therapy. He was also forced to participate in the mind-improving morning activities. In this hive of instability, he was deemed too unstable to be left to his own devices. In their private sessions, Taylor had been chipping away at him, forcing Wallace to open up about his childhood, about his life. Wallace knew what the doctor was doing; picking at the past until he created a wound that needed healing, but Wallace felt powerless to resist. Shame and regret created a debt that could only be repaid by satisfying Taylor's desire to fix him. Earlier that day, Taylor had finally struck home.

"What if you created the memory of this attacker to mask the fact you had attempted something you were profoundly ashamed of?" Taylor suggested from the comfort of his armchair.

"He was as real as you," Wallace protested, but, as he looked away from Taylor and gazed around the doctor's IKEA-inspired private therapy room, the seed of that evil thought took root.

Now, in the early hours of the morning, when the effects of the evening's sedation had worn off, the seed had flourished into a terrible, hideous tree of doubt with branches that shaded every aspect of his life. What if Bailey and Taylor were right? What if he'd had a delayed reaction to what had happened in Kandahar? What the soldiers did to those children—he'd raged against it. Righteous fury had consumed him, but he hadn't been able to do anything to stop the violence, and then, when he had found out that the Masterson Inquiry had ruled his testimony insufficient to bring the killers to justice, well, that was the day Connie left. She'd had enough of the desperate misery that fueled his incessant anger. Wallace knew the children's deaths had disturbed him, but perhaps he hadn't realized just how much. Was it possible he'd conjured his masked assailant to rationalize a suicide attempt? In some ways the growing tree of doubt was attractive. If Wallace admitted the truth of Taylor's theory, he could give himself over to the good doctor and embark on a course of treatment that would ultimately cure him. But accepting the fact that his assailant had been a phantom filled him with fear. If something that seemed so real, something that assaulted his every sense, something that had filled him with such terror, could be a figment of his damaged mind, how could he trust anything? Certainty involved destroying doubt. But if he clung to the certainty that the man who tried to murder him was real, Wallace could not see a way out of the Maybury. If he accepted doubt, he had a path to freedom, but would be forced to recognize that his mind could not be trusted. He felt a familiar tightness in his chest and recognized the shallow breathing of a panic attack. The stress of his situation was becoming too intense. Wallace had to concede that he wasn't well. He had to reach out for help. He had to . . .

The sound of the door buzzer cut through the still night. Wallace looked up uncertainly. There was no light between the tiny gaps in the closed blinds, so it was still dark outside. And yet the door was open. The emergency exit sign in the corridor beyond cast just enough green light to circumscribe the frame. Wallace lay still for a moment. Was this a test? Was he imagining this? Was his mind trying to trick him into trusting it? He waited, straining his ears, searching for a clue. Could this be real? The only answer was silence. There was safety in routine, and this was most definitely not routine. A dark thought swelled in the paranoid recesses of Wallace's mind. With his cloak of anonymity lifted, the killer had located him. He felt an urgent need to find someone. He rolled upright and got to his feet. His collarbone, which had fractured anew during his outburst, ached with reassuringly real pain. This didn't feel like a dream. He tentatively approached the door and put his fingertips around the outside edge, into the gap. He pulled slowly, and the door opened. Beyond it was the corridor, dimly lit by the green glow that came from the illuminated image of a man escaping through a door. *Escape.* Wallace remembered when the idea had dominated his thoughts.

He approached the door beneath the green sign. Large letters informed him that it was alarmed. Cause and effect; push the door and orderlies would come. Taylor would add an escape attempt to Wallace's ledger and extract an even higher price from his wayward patient. Such limited privileges as he had would be withdrawn. *There's a killer on the loose.* The words rose unbidden, but Wallace fought back the panic that accompanied them and resisted the temptation of the fire exit. He drifted away from the door and moved toward a small pool of light that emanated from the nurses' station. He would earn credit with the doctor by informing the duty nurse of the malfunction with his door. His feet slapped against the cold floor, and he made no attempt to conceal his presence. He didn't want the nurse accusing him of scaring her.

"Excuse me," he said as he came into sight of the hatch that opened onto the corridor. "I think there's . . ."

Wallace fell silent when he saw that the nurses' station was deserted. When unmanned, the station was normally sealed off by a window that covered the hatch. The window was open. Beyond it, Wallace could see files, folders, a prescription pad and a set of keys. He recognized them. The orderlies all carried them. They were access keys that opened the secure doors throughout the entire wing. Eight of them, and a key card that granted entry to some as yet unvisited section of the hospital. He looked around the deserted ward. He glanced up at one of the hospital's many security cameras, which was pointed directly at him, and saw that the red operating light was dead. The dark corridor was deserted in both directions and all the other cell doors were locked. The place felt wrong: empty and eerie. He fought back dark thoughts of imminent danger and reverted to the keys. Eight steps to freedom on a small metal ring. *No. I'll find the nurse and return them,* Wallace told himself, even though he was starting to think it was a lie. Keys in hand, he moved down the corridor toward the first security door. This time he crept silently across the thick rubber floor. *You're not trying to hide,* he told himself. *You're just being careful.*

The hospital was deathly quiet. No troubled patients screaming in the night. No pounding on cell doors. No orderlies running their truncheons along radiators. Instead, through the thin strips of reinforced glass that were cut into each and every one of the cell doors, Wallace could see the slumbering shapes of his fellow inmates in sedative-induced sleep. He padded quickly and quietly until he was at the first security door. He tried the keys, carefully inserting each one into the recessed lock, until number five opened the door. He pulled it slowly, thankful that it did not squeal. He stepped through and carefully shut the door behind him. The click the latch made as it tumbled into place seemed to echo along the corridor, and Wallace tensed, waiting for a reaction, but none came, and so he moved on.

He was in another ward, similar to his own. His pace quickened, aware that each step farther was another to justify to his captors. Best to avoid the whole mess of explanation by not getting caught. That would be neater, he thought, dispensing with the subterfuge that he was on a mission to find the duty nurse. He swiftly covered the ground to the next security door. Freed of self-deception and alive with hope, Wallace's mind raced. He'd need shoes, clothes, money, and a plan. He'd been committed, which meant they thought he posed a danger to himself or others. After the attack on the policeman, they'd almost certainly regard him as a threat in both categories, so police and public health agencies would be instructed to find him. He'd have to avoid capture and figure out a way to reclaim his life. *Small steps,* Wallace told himself. *Get out first.*

He cycled through the keys until he found the one that fitted the second heavy, reinforced door. He opened it and quickly stepped through to find himself in the day section. His beloved television room lay to his right, the showers were directly ahead, and the canteen was to his left. Beyond that was the administration block with the therapy rooms and offices. Wallace could not recall how he'd been brought into the building, but he thought the administration block represented his best chance for escape, so he moved to his left, quietly heading along the corridor that led to the canteen. Intermittent lamps broke the darkness, casting just enough light to make the hospital seem eerie rather than menacing. Wallace tried to ignore the growing sensation that he was being watched and that, at Doctor Taylor's command, a heavy orderly would suddenly spring out and drag him back to his cell. There was also the creeping fear that there was someone far more dangerous in the building, and his overactive mind started to see figures lurking in every shadow. He felt his heart rise into his throat, and his pace quickened.

Another key. Another door. This one granted him access to the canteen. Row upon row of stools attached to Formica tables, like miniature warriors standing to attention. The large, empty room was far too mundane for anything more terrifying than an undercooked chicken. Wallace felt his fear ebb away. It was replaced by a mixture of relief and mild embarrassment. His spirits were lifted by the dawning realization that his newfound, drug-fueled paranoia had fired his imagination to the feverish pitch of a five-year-old child. There were no figures lurking in the shadows. No monsters in the darkness.

With his thoughts turning firmly to the prospect of escape, Wallace picked his way through the canteen to the security door at the far end. He'd have to be careful as he moved into the administration block, where central security was located. He imagined a couple of security guards standing around while a technician worked to fix their camera system. Maybe they'd even revert to foot patrols. He hesitated at the door. He could still go back. He could return the keys and retreat to his cell. Nobody would ever know. As Wallace wavered, he realized that if he did go back, he'd be committing himself to Doctor Taylor. He'd be forced to accept that he had imagined his attempted murder and would undergo weeks, if not months, of treatment to earn his release. Wallace was suddenly gripped by resolve; he had been attacked, he was not insane, and he would escape from this place and prove it. He found the correct key and opened the security door.

The first difference was carpet underfoot. Even though it was thin, industrial pile, it acted as an acoustic dampener, making the administration block seem even quieter than the rest of the building. Wallace shut the door behind him and moved along the corridor, alert for any sign of activity. He passed the group therapy rooms and stepped through a dividing door into another section of the corridor, which was flanked by smaller therapy rooms and doctors' offices. It was in one of these rooms that he had opened up to Doctor Taylor. Wallace moved on, until he came to another security door, this one flanked by a card reader. He swiped the key card and was startled by a harsh buzzing as the reader informed him the card was invalid. He looked around, convinced the noise would attract someone, but he was alone. He rubbed the card against his pajama trousers and tried it again, offering a silent prayer of thanks as the light turned green, and the door buzzed open. He pulled it wide and stepped into another corridor lined with an equipment store, a linen room, and, halfway down, a dispensary, which was marked with large menacing letters that warned there was no unauthorized access. Immediately beyond the dispensary the corridor branched to the right and Wallace saw a sign that filled him with hope. Beneath directions to the security room, the staff canteen and the lobby was a final plaque that read "Exit."

He hugged the wall and then glanced around the corner to see that the corridor was deserted. At the end was a security door, and beyond it was a large open space and a desk marked "Reception." This was it; one more door and then only the main entrance stood between him and freedom.

Wallace was about to move when he heard a noise behind him and turned to see a figure that chilled him to his core. Stepping out of the dispensary was the man who had tried to kill him.

7

Wallace tried to flee, but his legs weren't quick enough. Before he could react, his assailant lunged for him and grappled him into a choke hold. Wallace tried to scream, but his throat was crushed into silence. The feeling was all too familiar and instantly filled him with panic. *Please let this be a delusion.*

Wallace knew that it wasn't. A black, armored forearm throttled his windpipe while a gloved, fiercely strong hand pulled at his hair and forced him back into the dispensary. Wallace kicked out, catching one of the shelves and sending medical supplies tumbling to the ground. As vials and bottles smashed, the spring-loaded door slammed shut. Steel bars cut the moonlight that shone through a high window. He tried to grasp at his assailant's arm to relieve the pressure on his throat, but the man was clad in Kevlar, which prevented his fingers gaining any purchase. Wallace kicked and thrashed wildly, turning all his strength to escape. Out of the corner of his eye, he saw a pharmacist's table, and there on the laminated top was a large syringe filled with a clear liquid. Wallace did not need to be told what was in it; an adjacent empty vial of morphine said it all. He was to have an overdose. He knew that he'd have one chance, one opportunity to save his life.

He continued struggling, but his efforts lacked their previous intensity. He wanted his assailant to think that he was giving up. Deprived of oxygen, his limbs grew heavy and tired, his vision started to blur, and he wondered how much was pretense and how much was real. Exhausted and asphyxiated, Wallace went limp. His assailant maintained pressure for a few moments longer to ensure unconsciousness, and then relaxed his grip to reach for the syringe. As his arm swung out, Wallace gulped a breath of air, leaned forward and for the second time in the space of a week used his head as an effective weapon. The back of his skull smashed into his attacker's mask and Wallace felt the satisfying crunch of a damaging impact. He didn't wait for a reaction. He pushed away from the masked figure, and lost a crop of hair to his assailant's tenacious grip. As his attacker floundered, Wallace remembered his years of aikido and unleashed a simple side kick at the man's midriff. It wasn't enough to injure him through his body armor, but it was sufficient to knock him off balance and give Wallace a moment's head start to reach the door. As he fled, Wallace pulled down the nearest shelf, bringing it crashing to the floor behind him. He didn't waste time turning to see what had happened, but as he yanked the door open, he felt hard fingers score his spine. He ignored the painful contact and pressed on through the gap, into the corridor.

Wallace banked right, and raised the key ring. He prayed for another card reader, but was disappointed to see a recessed keyhole. He could hear heavy footsteps behind him. Five keys to choose from. No time. Wallace slammed into the door and jammed the first key in. It would only go halfway, so he pulled it out and tried another. The footsteps were close. The second key wouldn't fit, nor the third. Wallace had just pushed the fourth key in, when gloved hands pulled him away from the door, spinning him round and slamming him into the adjacent wall. His head whiplashed back, crashing against the plasterwork, and the world started swimming as his masked assailant came into view. Wallace was disappointed to see that the face mask had only sustained a few superficial cracks as a result of his reverse head butt. Unarmed and exposed, Wallace didn't have a chance against this guy. Then he saw hope: pressed to its hilt, the fourth key hung in the lock.

He ducked a punch and charged his attacker, throwing all his weight into his shoulder. The pain the collision unleashed was agonizing, but Wallace ignored his broken collarbone and pressed on until he felt the impact of body armor against the far wall. It wasn't graceful, but it was effective and it gave him the split second he needed to make for the door. A hand grabbed his calf, but Wallace twisted and lashed out with his other foot. He connected with something and the pressure on his leg ceased. Wallace turned the key, pushed the door open and stepped through. He snapped the key in the lock and slammed the door on his attacker's arm, pushing against it as his assailant fought to get through. Wallace scanned his surroundings for relief and found something that just might work, but he'd have to move quickly. He leaped away from the door and, in one fluid motion, grabbed a large red fire extinguisher. As the door opened and his assailant lunged for him, Wallace swung the heavy metal tube into the man's face and sent him hurtling back the way he'd come. His attacker landed flat on his back. Wallace dropped the extinguisher and slammed the security door firmly shut.

"Hey!"

The shout came from above, and Wallace glanced up to see two security guards running along the mezzanine balcony, which led to a flight of stairs that landed near the main entrance. He set off at a sprint, hurtling through the lobby as fast as his bare feet would carry him. So much for shoes, clothes, and a plan. He vaulted a leather sofa and skidded to a halt by the automatic doors, which didn't seem to have a lock. He could hear the security guards closing and looked up to see them starting down the stairs. Both men loomed large as they produced retractable metal batons and flicked them to full extension. Wallace cast about desperately and saw a card reader on the other side of the doors, near the stairs.

This is going to be tight, he thought as he ran to the reader and swiped the card. A red light and "access denied" flashed, as the first baton came swinging toward Wallace's head. He caught sight of the bulbous metal tip reflected in the window ahead of him and ducked, with fractions of an inch to spare. The baton went whizzing overhead, and Wallace, fueled by adrenaline, resolved not to give his new attackers another chance. He barreled backward, hurling himself into the first security guard's midriff. Before the shocked man could react, Wallace stood up violently and brought the top of his head into crashing contact with the guard's chin. There was a hard crack and a yowl of pain. Wallace turned on the man and pressed the advantage by striking the security guard's ears between his two hands in a double yokomen'uchi: a devastating punch. Dazed, the security guard went down. Wallace grabbed the baton and brought it up just in time to parry a blow from the second guard. Somewhere inside this building was a maniac determined to murder him and make it look like suicide, and nothing would prevent Wallace from escaping. He turned inside the second security guard's reach and swept round, bringing his baton full circle in a devastating blow that shattered the guard's cheek. The man went down instantly.

Wallace looked at the two guards, and, while keeping a keen eye on the inner access points, stripped the nearest one of his shoes. A Klaxon sounded. Through the large lobby windows, he could see lights coming on in other parts of the building. Someone had raised the alarm. Someone determined to stop him escaping.

He tried the key card again, but it failed to work. Standing as far back as physically possible, he swung at the nearest window with the baton. The double glazing shattered but held firm. Wallace struck again and again. The first security guard stirred and Wallace redoubled his efforts, striking the window with such desperate force that the pane fell forward. He clambered through the jagged gap, stolen shoes in hand.

Once outside, he glanced back and saw silhouetted figures running along corridors. Then he looked around and saw something else. The shape of a man. A shadow. It was skirting the building line, heading directly for him. Wallace knew who it was, and renewed fear spurred him to action. He ran through the garden, heading for the twelve-foot-high brick wall that surrounded the hospital. He sprinted for an old oak, a remnant of whatever property the new hospital had replaced. He didn't even consciously scout for holds, but simply found himself bounding up the trunk and clambering along a thick branch that extended at an angle toward the wall. It was a perilous jump, but Wallace had no choice other than to attempt it. He took a step, and then leaped from the branch, aiming for the beveled top of the wall. He landed off balance, teetering on the rear edge, but rather than allow himself to topple backward, Wallace threw himself forward and plunged head first over the other side of the wall.

Tears welled in his eyes as nerves cried out all over his body. He had instinctively used his arms to break his fall, but had crumpled onto his shoulder and flipped over onto his back. His collarbone screamed. His only consolation was that he'd landed on a strip of grass rather than the concrete pavement a few inches away. Beyond the sidewalk was a main road. Pools of yellow phosphorescence illuminated a steady stream of fast-moving nocturnal traffic. Wallace fought through the agony. He wasn't safe. He rolled onto his right side and pushed himself to his feet. His left arm hung limp and the pain of his left collarbone dragged his body over. He looked down at the shoes and the baton that had fallen nearby, and stooped to pick up the weapon before scuttling into the road, hunched and shoeless, and throwing himself in front of a set of blinding headlights. He braced for impact, but instead heard the squeal of rubber as the car suddenly stopped. Caught in the lights, Wallace couldn't see the driver—it could just as easily be a South London drug dealer as a late-night shift worker, so he couldn't take any chances. He ran to the left and smashed the driver's window.

"Get out!" he commanded, his voice distorted by searing pain.

A terrified middle-aged white woman covered in broken glass stared up at Wallace in shock. Her eyes were focused on the baton.

"Move!" Wallace yelled, and the woman sprang into action. A couple of cars had gathered behind, and vehicles on the other side of the road slowed to a crawl as they passed. But they didn't stop, and nobody dragged him away from his hijack victim. Big cities bred witnesses, not heroes. Shaking, the woman exited the car, and Wallace pushed her out of the way before jumping in. The wind was knocked out of him as his shoulder hit the seat, but he ignored the pain and used his right hand to turn the ignition and start the stalled engine. He threw the gear stick forward and the car lurched ahead, roaring down the street in first gear. Reflected in the rearview mirror,

Wallace saw drivers finally emerge from their vehicles to commiserate with the hijack victim. They'd all be able to pretend they had been about to intervene, and she'd have an exciting story to tell everyone at work.

Wallace caught sight of himself in the mirror. In addition to looking a physical mess, he appeared frantic, so he took a breath as he checked the road behind him. No sign of anyone following. He rested his left hand on the wheel and, in a clumsy but effective maneuver, shifted into second with his right. The roar of the engine subsided, and the little car—the logo on the steering wheel signaled it was some kind of Ford—picked up speed as it rolled through South London. As the adrenaline ebbed and the driving panic died away, Wallace was left to consider his next move.

8

Bailey stood in the hospital lobby trying to figure out exactly what had happened. He was in the unusual position of being a guest on the scene. Croydon was running the case, but Doctor Taylor had phoned him out of courtesy, and Bailey had been able to wangle his commanding officer's permission to attend. Superintendent Cross usually let Bailey follow his hunches, and the humiliating experience of Wallace's attack hadn't done anything to change that. Local Croydon uniforms were combing the hospital and taking statements from the night staff, while employees arriving for their day shifts were being directed to an alternate entrance. The detective in charge was a woman called Scott, businesslike and brusque; she wouldn't have been out of place on *The Apprentice*. But she had brought Bailey up to speed and offered him total access to whatever they found. Not having to worry about the practical issues involved in dealing with a crime scene, Bailey was free to think.

The duty nurse had been found unconscious, passed out on the floor of her station. She'd been discovered after Wallace's escape and failed to respond to attempts to wake her until paramedics arrived with smelling salts. Residual nausea and dizziness suggested she may have been drugged. She claimed to have only had one cup of coffee all night, and the dregs had been taken away for analysis. The hospital's surveillance system had malfunctioned at precisely 02:43. Security had placed a call to the maintenance company, and an engineer had been en route at the time of the escape. There was no video of Wallace until he reached the street, where a distant bus lane camera had captured low-resolution footage of the carjacking. The two security guards who had tried to prevent the escape were in the hospital with their injuries. The pharmacy had been vandalized but it appeared that no drugs were missing.

Scott's working theory was that Wallace had somehow managed to dose the duty nurse's coffee earlier in the evening. He'd figured out a way to prevent his cell door from locking and, when he was sure the nurse was out cold, had left his cell and stolen her keys. On his way to the exit, he'd raided the pharmacy with the intent of stocking up on salable narcotics, but, fearing capture, had smashed the place up instead, before fleeing into the night. What the working theory failed to take account of was the malfunctioning camera system. Scott put it down to coincidence, but Bailey didn't believe Wallace was that lucky; someone had disabled the cameras. Someone who was either working with Wallace or trying to get to him. As he stood thinking about the evidence, Bailey was troubled by the nagging hunch that Wallace might have been telling the truth all along.

"So we're moving everything to a cloud-based platform," Ron Bickmore announced proudly. It was the culmination of a forty-five-minute speech that had given Constance Jones plenty of time to daydream. Cloud-based computing. Wow. Mainframe systems repackaged as clouds connected to thin client machines by hyperfast data links. In another ten years the fashion would be for superpowerful tablets that could store and share data individually. Connie had only been in the business for eight years, but she'd learned enough computing history to know that every few years IT directors were gripped by the latest fad that either centralized or decentralized data processing. None of it mattered; it was only done so they could shave 5 percent off their systems infrastructure costs, but most of that would be lost to the consultants implementing the change. The rest would be swallowed up by executive bonuses. It was change for the sake of change so that Bickmore could look like he was earning his vastly inflated salary. Connie looked round the conference room at the dozen people who would be tasked with leading the radical new program, which had been given the imaginative name "Project Cloud." None of them looked as bored as she felt. Some of her colleagues seemed positively excited by the new strategy. The four external consultants smiled like lions herding lambs.

"So we'll be making a briefing pack available on the project file server, and there will be a kickoff meeting next week," Bickmore concluded. "Exciting times, people."

A couple of Climbers broke into seemingly spontaneous applause. The Climbers were a particular genus of Good Capitalist: people who were willing to kiss as much arse, stab as much back, and climb as much greasy pole as was needed to Succeed. Only, you never did Succeed, you were always shown another branch higher up the tree, and so the Climbers kept climbing, always reaching for something tantalizingly beyond their grasp. Bickmore ignored the embarrassing attempt to curry favor and made a swift exit. Connie didn't hang around either; she slipped out of the twenty-fifth-floor conference room and made her way toward the elevators. She nodded at a couple of people she recognized and waited for one of the eight sets of doors to open. Even though she'd spent almost six years working at Suncert's headquarters, she never ceased to be amazed by the splendor of the building. A curvaceous crescent of glass and metal that cut forty-five floors into the London sky, it was a towering monument to the ingenuity of mankind.

A set of doors pinged open to reveal a familiar face; Karen, her earnest young assistant.

"Connie, I'm so glad you're out," Karen said. "There's a guy looking for you. He says it's urgent."

"Who is it?" Connie asked.

"He wouldn't give his name," Karen replied. "But he said you love Justin Timberlake."

Connie felt a sudden pang of panicked realization. The man was John Wallace. But why was he here? And why wasn't he using his real name?

"He's with security," Karen advised. "They say he's a mess."

Butterflies started swirling around Connie's stomach, as she went to find the man she once loved.

Wallace studied the security guard opposite him. They were seated across a table in a small basement meeting room that adjoined the building's security center. The guard's colleagues had called him Dwayne, and, as the team junior, he'd been given the dull task of babysitting Wallace. The stark contrast between Dwayne's sharply pressed uniform and Wallace's filthy blue pajamas reinforced the impression that they were from different worlds. Wallace was relieved that his wild dishevelment had led the guards to categorize him as "harmless crazy" rather than "dangerous crazy," which meant they would give him the opportunity to prove his story. He had already been warned that the police would be called if his claimed association with Constance Jones turned out to be a lie. As a "harmless crazy" Wallace didn't merit Dwayne's full attention, and the young security guard's head hung down over his mobile phone as his fingers danced furiously across the screen. He was lost in some sort of game. Wallace watched the fingers flicker, desperate for anything that would distract his mind from the gnawing pain.

After twenty minutes of sitting in silence, the door opened and Wallace saw the beautiful face that haunted his memories. Connie still looked great and was wearing a retro emerald-green lace dress. Her long, pale legs ended with a pair of green heels. Wallace was surprised by her hair. Instead of the cropped bob, Connie had let her deep-red hair grow out, and it cascaded around her shoulders.

"John?" Connie's tone betrayed her dismay. "What the . . ."

"Do you know him?" Dwayne asked as he swiftly pocketed his phone.

"Yes," Connie replied. "Give us a minute, please."

Wallace longed to embrace Connie, to fold his arms around her and feel her soft alabaster skin against his, but her expression broadcast her puzzled hostility, so he simply sat and watched her as the security guard left the room.

"I haven't confessed my Timberlake love to many people," she observed when they were alone.

"I couldn't risk using my name," he said with an edge of paranoia.

"Why? What's happened to you?" Connie asked.

Wallace had already decided that simple honesty was the best policy. "Someone tried to kill me," he said.

Connie smiled. "What?"

"I'm serious," Wallace declared. He noted Connie's expression shift as she picked up on his sincerity.

"A few weeks ago, someone broke into my flat and tried to hang me," he continued, his voice cracking slightly as he gave voice to the horror. "The beam—you know, the big one in the living room—it collapsed. I jumped out of the window."

He was gratified to see Connie's eyes widen. "You jumped out of the window?"

Wallace nodded. "The doctors thought I'd tried to kill myself."

"What about the police?" Connie interrupted.

"Same. They couldn't find any evidence of an intruder. I was committed to the Maybury Hospital for psychiatric treatment, which is where I was until I escaped last night."

"Escaped?"

"The officer leading the investigation told the hospital who I was. I don't know how the killer found me, but he tried to finish the job. I fought him off and stole a car. Now I'm here."

"You escaped?" she repeated.

Wallace nodded. "I need a place to stay. Somewhere safe," he said earnestly. "I need help."

Conflicting emotions swept across Connie's face. "John, I don't know—" she began.

"I came here because I trust you," Wallace interrupted.

"Don't you have friends? Someone you work with?" Connie asked.

"I can't trust anyone else."

"I've put the past behind me. I don't know if I could handle going back," she told him.

"It's not going back," Wallace protested. "I just need somewhere to stay. For a few days."

Connie wavered and Wallace could sense her inner turmoil as the latent feelings she had for him fought with the instinctive desire to protect herself.

"I can't trust anyone else," he repeated emphatically.

"I'll help you get on your feet," Connie said finally. "That's it. I can't go back, John. I can't go there again."

He nodded gratefully.

"I'm still in the same place. My keys are upstairs. I'll get them. And you'll need money for a cab," she said.

Wallace nodded again, trying to stem the swell of relief that threatened to overwhelm him.

"And clothes. I'll grab some when I finish work. Get yourself cleaned up," Connie advised. "I'll be home around seven." She opened the door and found Dwayne leaning against the opposite wall, phone in hand. "Could you escort this gentleman to the service entrance?" Connie asked him. "I'll meet you there in five minutes."

"Thank you, Connie," Wallace said quietly.

Connie gave her troubled, filthy, wounded ex-boyfriend an uncomfortable glance. "It's nothing," she answered. "You'd do the same for me."

And with that, she was gone, her heels tapping as they kissed the hard floor of the corridor beyond.

"Come on, mate," Dwayne said in a vaguely patronizing tone that he probably reserved for drunks.

Wallace hauled himself to his feet and slowly followed Dwayne out.

9

Dwayne led Wallace to the service entrance, which opened onto a narrow alleyway that ran between a cluster of high glass buildings. The alley was a popular route to and from Leadenhall Market, so if Connie had been hoping to spare Wallace embarrassment, she'd failed. Dwayne took the opportunity to snatch a quick smoke and leaned against the looming Suncert Building while he dragged on his cigarette. Barefoot, bearded, and bloody, Wallace was aware he cut a grim figure, but he was in too much pain to care about the bemused looks he was getting from passersby.

"D'you say something, mate?" Dwayne asked, and Wallace suddenly became aware that he was groaning. The pain emanating from his collarbone was relentless.

"Nothing," Wallace grimaced.

A couple of minutes later, Connie found them.

"I'll take it from here," she told Dwayne firmly. He pressed the stubby remains of his cigarette against the ash container and went inside.

Connie handed Wallace a set of keys and a thin sheaf of money.

"It's all I've got," she said as their hands touched.

"It's enough," he replied. "Thanks." He longed to pull Connie close to him, but she stepped away.

"I have to get back," she said, nodding in the direction of the building.

"I know," Wallace said. "Thanks."

Connie smiled uncomfortably as she walked away and Wallace watched her pull the service door shut before he started down the alley. *Pain*, he thought, *got to do something about the pain*.

Wallace hailed a black cab on Leadenhall Street and was surprised when it stopped. Uber must really be hitting their business, he thought as he climbed into the backseat.

"What is it? Stag night?" the driver asked jovially.

"Something like that," Wallace replied. "Stoke Newington, please. And I need to make a stop on the way."

"No problem," the driver replied, as the taxi pulled into the steady stream of traffic.

Wallace had the man stop halfway up the Kingsland Road and offered him ten pounds to run into a small family pharmacy and pick up some strong painkillers. After a few minutes the driver returned with two boxes of codeine compounds: Paramol and Co-codamol. As he handed over the boxes, he registered the full extent of Wallace's dishevelment for the first time.

"You're not a fucking junkie, are you?" he asked, as Wallace tore into the Paramol.

"No," Wallace replied in strained tones. "Terrible hangover. Stag night, remember?"

The driver responded with a look of profound skepticism, but said nothing more as he hurried round the cab and planted himself in the front seat. Moments later they were on the move again, and, as they slowly drove north, Wallace surreptitiously tossed down two Co-codamol.

By the time they reached Stoke Newington, he could feel the deliciously pleasant haze of the drugs beginning to blunt the sharp pain. He asked the driver to stop at the western end of Cazenove Road. Paranoia trumped exhaustion and pain; he didn't want the man knowing Connie's address. The taxi pulled to a halt opposite the Turkish supermarket that stood near the intersection with Kingsland Road and Wallace climbed out and paid the driver his fare and a decent tip.

"Thanks, mate," the driver said before swinging the cab round in a tight U-turn and heading back toward the city.

Wallace started walking east, his bare feet moving carefully to avoid treading on anything sharp. Nothing about Stoke Newington had changed in the two years since his last visit. The litter-strewn pavements, graffiti-scrawled walls, hustlers, loafers, and crazies manning the streets were all still there. It was one of the few places in London where a bloodied, barefoot man in pajamas could pass without comment. The painkillers were really kicking in, perhaps enhanced by a combination of fresh air, exertion, and fatigue. Wallace felt immune to the cares of the world, as though he was cossetted by the purest warm happiness. The colors on a painted graffiti mural truly popped, the images so alive that they were almost shimmering. Patterned light danced, its motion dictated by the leaves on the high sycamore trees that loomed over him like giant puppet masters. The light took on a magical quality, almost sparkling as it cavorted through the trees. Wallace longed for his camera. Light like this was too beautiful to go unrecorded. He made his way along Cazenove Road, past the mosque and the synagogue, and finally reached number 91, a once-grand corner house that had been carved up and converted into half a dozen tiny flats. He walked up the cracked path through the overgrown garden and used Connie's keys to let himself in the front door. Past the hallway with its yellowing, woodchip wallpaper and stained, thin brown carpet, he hurried up two flights of stairs and opened the door to Connie's top-floor flat.

The first thing he did was pour himself a large glass of orange juice, following it with a glass of water in an effort to quench his thirst. Then he made use of the toilet in the tiny bathroom. As he washed his hands, reflected in the bathroom mirror, he finally saw the mess that had greeted Connie. His hair was terribly matted, his scraggly beard caked with blood. His eyes were so sunken that they looked like they had been ratcheted to the back of his skull. He had lost a lot of weight, and his cheekbones, which had once been strong and defined, now protruded painfully. He needed to clean himself up. He stripped off the filthy blue pajamas and examined himself. His left collarbone was covered by a kaleidoscopic inkblot of green, blue, and purple hemor-rhaging flesh. Wallace harbored the vain hope that the garish intensity of the colors was a trippy side effect of the painkillers. The rainbow over his collar made the dull brown of his old bullet wound look positively monochrome. The rest of his body was marred by fresh bruises, cuts, and grazes. Halfway up his pronounced rib cage was a tight, raw scar, which, to Wallace's relief, had not reopened. Apart from his collarbone, all the other injuries sustained in his escape seemed superficial.

Wallace washed twice under the shower, shocked by the foul color of the effluence the first time round. Then he stood there for ten minutes, enjoying the gentle patter of warm water against his skin. After his shower, he found a pair of scissors and trimmed his beard before using one of Connie's razors to shave. Designed for delicate legs, the ladies' razor struggled through rough stubble and scored a handful of nicks, which didn't bother Wallace. He was simply pleased to see a far more familiar reflection looking back at him. He found his old, oversized bathrobe in the linen closet and put it on as he exited the bathroom.

He wandered into the living room and found that nothing much had changed. Everything in the flat was pretty but well worn; Connie had a preference for vintage. Old things were properly made, Wallace remembered her saying, it added to their beauty. Her fondness for vintage was probably a consequence of her childhood. Wallace had only met her parents, Peter and Sandra, once, but that was enough to know that they were anachronisms. He paused by a photograph of them that stood halfway up a set of shelves. Now in their seventies, Peter and Sandra smiled up at the camera as they sat by their swimming pool in Perth. They'd had Connie in their early forties, when many other parents were on the verge of becoming grandparents, and, as a result, Connie had been brought up in an old-fashioned world of cookstoves, classical music, and floral patterns.

On the next shelf, he found a photograph of himself and Connie. It had been taken the night they'd first met, three and a half years ago. Sue Furnival, a makeup artist he'd bumped into on set a few times, had cajoled him into coming to a barbecue. At first Wallace had thought Sue had romantic intentions of her own, but when she introduced him to her darling old school friend Connie, he realized that she wanted to play matchmaker. Now he studied Connie's face in the photo and recalled the honest vulnerability that he found so attractive. As she smiled at the camera, her eyes made a poor attempt to conceal her genuine joy at having met someone so perfect for her. Wallace's own expression was that of a man menaced by demons.

He wondered why Connie would choose to fill the room with memories and torment herself with the past. He knew better than most where such torment led. He walked over to the battered brown Chesterfield sofa and sat down. Everything was worn, nothing matched, but somehow Connie made it all work and had turned her flat into a warm, inviting home. The living room had four large sash windows that overlooked Cazenove Road. The mature trees cut out the worst of the surroundings, and when Wallace lay down, resting his head on the cracked arm of the sofa, all he could see were the tops of the trees and the crisp blue autumn sky. He could have been anywhere in the world. Whatever came next, he was simply glad to be alive. He lay watching the tops of the trees brush the sky until warm waves of relaxation swept him off to sleep.

For the first time in weeks, Wallace slept without dreaming. He experienced a moment of panic when he felt someone shake him and sat up suddenly, adrenaline coursing through his veins.

"Sorry," Connie said, looking down at him. "I didn't mean to startle you."

As he rubbed his eyes, Connie crossed the room, switched on a small china lamp, and pulled the curtains to shut out the graying sky.

"How are you feeling?" she asked.

"Okay," Wallace lied. His shoulder was screaming for more pills.

"I got you some clothes." She gestured to a collection of branded bags on the other side of the room. "I bought your old sizes, but you look like you've lost weight."

"Thanks."

The ensuing uncomfortable silence seemed endless, but Wallace was being assailed by an intense pain that crowded out rational thought, and he didn't want to open his mouth for fear he would cry out.

"Listen, make yourself at home," Connie said at last. "I'm going to get changed."

She turned and left the room, and Wallace waited a moment before following her out. He found the boxes of painkillers in the tiny kitchen and tossed down two Co-codamols and a Paramol. The stabbing pain screamed for more, but he knew it was dangerous enough to mix medication; he couldn't risk an overdose. He replaced the boxes on the counter beside the fridge and returned to the living room. Desperate for something to take his mind off the pain until the pills kicked in, he riffled through the shopping bags. Three pairs of jeans, four T-shirts, a sweatshirt, two pullovers, a pair of Adidas, and a couple of packs of socks and underwear. Wallace grimaced as he got dressed; pants, jeans, and a T-shirt—he could not face the pain involved in pulling on a pair of socks.

"That's better," Connie said as she entered. She was wearing a pair of dark-blue jeans and a gray tank top and had tied back her hair in a loose ponytail. Even through the pain Wallace could see that she looked fantastic.

"You want a drink?" she asked in a strained tone that suggested she was trying to make everything seem as normal as possible.

"Better not. Broke my collarbone and I'm on pretty nasty pills," Wallace replied, pulling down the collar of his T-shirt to reveal the angry flesh beneath.

"Ouch," Connie exclaimed, recoiling. "How did you do that?"

"When I jumped out of the window. Fractured a few ribs, too," Wallace answered.

"You don't mind if I have one, do you?" Connie asked the question on her way to the kitchen. Wallace followed.

"Not at all," he said, aware that she wasn't really waiting for an answer. He watched her pour a large glass of Chablis. "You know what, a small one won't kill me."

Connie produced another wineglass—different size and style, unsurprisingly. She poured generously and handed it to Wallace.

"Thanks," he said.

Connie didn't reply but instead knocked back about half her glass. She noted Wallace looking at her, and his expression must have betrayed his surprise.

"Well, it's not been a normal day," she said by way of explanation.

"Sorry," he offered. He could already feel the warm swimming sensation of the wine going to his head, or maybe it was the painkillers starting to kick in.

"I read about the Inquiry," Connie informed him. "I could never understand why, or make any sense of what happened that night. But it was the day you heard they'd rejected your testimony, wasn't it? You were lashing out."

"I'm sorry. I really am." Wallace's cheeks flushed with shame. "It tore me up. They called me a liar, but I didn't care about myself. It was those poor people, those children—no one would ever know the truth of what happened to them."

Connie shook her head and Wallace knew exactly what she was thinking: his righteous crusade had destroyed their relationship and it had all been for nothing. There had been no justice, no resolution, just an angry trail of shattered lives. He felt a pressing need to change the subject.

"This wasn't anything to do with the Inquiry," he protested. "I haven't contacted any of the investigators for over a year. This was something else. A guy broke into my house and tried to kill me. Then he found me in hospital and tried again."

Connie considered him and then drained her glass. "More?" she asked, turning for the bottle.

"I'm so sorry, Connie," Wallace said as he gently took hold of her arm. "I didn't mean to hurt you."

"I know," she said. "But you did."

He searched desperately for something to say, but Connie's demeanor shifted before he found the words. She suddenly shook her head and smiled sadly.

"That's enough reminiscing. Why don't I order us a pizza from Il Baccio?" she suggested with forced humor. "And then you can tell me exactly what's been going on."

Wine and pizza. Connie opposite him on the Anatolian rug. Watching her carelessly tease a loose strand of hair. Simple pleasures. Two bottles in and Wallace felt immune to his troubles. Connie had listened intently as he told his tale. Now and again his voice would start to break as he recounted the horror of his experiences, and every so often Connie would ask a searching question, but Wallace never got the feeling she was trying to trip him up. Finally, when he'd shared the account of his escape and his decision to approach her for help, they both fell silent. He watched her carefully, waiting for her to say something.

"What did it feel like?" she asked eventually.

Wallace didn't need to be told what she was talking about. He thought for a moment. "It was beyond anything I've ever experienced," he said hesitantly. "I was totally powerless. I felt frustration. Anger. Regret. Mainly regret. The mistakes I've made. The people I've hurt."

The significance of his words wasn't lost on Connie.

"And this tremendous feeling of loss. I would have traded anything for another breath."

She reached out and touched his arm, then rubbed it reassuringly.

"And the worst thing is—" Wallace's voice broke. "And the worst thing is," he continued. "Someday I'm going to have to go through it again."

She leaned forward and hugged him. "It's okay," she said quietly.

Wallace pulled away, and looked her in the eye. "It's not. We think we're in control, but we're not. At some point, I'm going to have to feel myself slip away. It scares me, Connie. It really scares me," he repeated, with the kind of honesty that Doctor Taylor could only ever dream of inducing.

"My mum always said you have to make a choice; you can focus on the destination, or you can enjoy the journey. You can't do both," Connie said. "With time, you'll forget."

Wallace shook his head. The wine and painkillers kept the room spinning a few seconds after his head fell still. "It's part of who I am now. I'll never forget that feeling," he countered. "I thought I was fucked up after Afghanistan, but this . . . I've been . . . I'm just all over the place, Connie."

She leaned forward. Her lingering kiss was the sweetest thing Wallace had ever tasted. She pulled back and smiled.

"We're all just as much the dark space beyond death as we are the light of life," she told him, her words slurring ever so slightly. "You've been freed from it, John. You've experienced something that terrifies us all, and you've come back. You've been freed from all the illusions that bind you. You've lived the moment of death. What else do you have to be afraid of? You can be true."

He looked at Connie, wide eyed. He suspected they were both much drunker than they imagined.

"Sorry, I've been listening to a lot of Alan Watts," she explained.

Wallace hadn't thought about Watts since university. He'd spent more than a few hazy Bristol nights listening to crackling recordings of the old philosopher. "No, don't apologize, it's good," he assured her. "It's all good."

He leaned forward and kissed her. They'd shared a moment too profound to be concerned about complications, and neither objected as they moved toward the bedroom.

10

A bitter coating of furry bile lined Wallace's mouth. He opened his eyes and immediately regretted the decision, as the world assaulted him. The bladed edges of the slatted blinds sheared the morning sunlight. In their inebriated haste to consummate their desires, they hadn't even bothered to close the blinds, and the two large sash windows would have offered anyone in the neighboring buildings a ringside view. A sudden bubble of memory rose from the murky depths of Wallace's hangover and he caught a vision of Connie sitting astride him, the two of them thrusting rhythmically, him pawing at her firm breasts like an enthusiastic teenager. He felt a profound pounding deep within his skull and his collarbone throbbed with the intensity of a thousand tears. Flags of pain semaphored the length and breadth of his body, the violent urgency of each signal being outstripped as new clusters of nerves sparked into life. Wallace needed relief and he needed it fast. He rolled out of bed onto his knees and then pulled himself to his feet. Naked, he staggered toward the kitchen like an unsteady toddler.

Complication, Wallace thought as he leaned against the kitchen counter. He found the painkillers, grabbed a dirty wineglass, and washed two pills down his gullet with a mouthful of cloudy water. *Complications*, he mused. He was here for a reason and that reason was not romance, or its primal, physical cousin. Wallace could not believe that he and Connie had been stupid enough to sleep together on their first night back. Mixing drink with pills hadn't been smart, but intoxication was only part of the story; he'd wanted someone to hold. Or rather, he wanted someone to hold him. And Connie was as good a person as he'd find anywhere.

He returned to the bedroom and pulled on his jeans and T-shirt, looking at the framed postcards that covered two of the walls. Moments of friendship memorialized by monuments from all around the world. He recognized a couple of cards he'd sent. One was a picture of the Croisette sent during a work trip to Cannes; the other was a picture montage of Paris, which he'd bought and given to Connie when they spent the weekend there together. There were dozens of other cards from all over the planet. Friends? Family? Lovers? They created a collage of some of the world's most beautiful places, and each one would remind Connie of an instance when someone else had thought kindly of her. Wallace wondered how many postcards he'd received over the years. It could not have been more than a dozen.

The tiny bathroom was empty and the rest of the flat was still. Wallace shuffled through the kitchen into the living room. Lying on the small dining table, pinned by one of the empty wine bottles, was a note.

Had to get to work early. Big project. Make yourself at home.
Laptop in sitting room. Password is bootle94. Connie xxx.

Relieved to have avoided the awkward morning-after, Wallace returned to the kitchen and looked in Connie's small fridge. Lots of green and red, healthy, useless for a hangover. He needed beige and brown foods: burgers, chips, substances wonderfully high in alcohol-absorbing saturated fats. The best Connie's fridge had to offer was half a block of extra mature Cheddar. He grabbed it and ate straight out of the package.

Chewing the last mouthful of cheese, he went into the living room and saw Connie's Apple laptop on the sofa. He crumpled onto the sofa, then leaned back, propping his head on the arm of the sofa, and rested the computer on his raised knees. Powering up the machine, he entered Connie's password and, within a few moments, was online with the collective knowledge of the world at his fingertips. He started typing in the Google search bar, looking for anything on *staged suicides*.

Wallace considered himself an extremely literate Internet user. He sought creative inspiration in all the weird and wild corners of the web. He spent a lot of time online researching photo shoots, scouting locations, and managing his portfolio, but despite his experience, he was surprised that such a dark search topic still managed to elicit ads. The first two links were for marketing companies promoting their search engine optimization services. Wallace ignored the commercials and focused on the genuine search results. The top links were from a website titled Practical Homicide, an online resource for law enforcement agents run by a US investigative training company. Lower down were a series of news articles about murders that had been staged to look like suicide. A wife hanged by her estranged husband, a husband suffocated by his wife, a woman shot by her boyfriend, and a mother throttled by her daughter. Intimate relationships terminated by the ultimate act of betrayal, each made even more shocking by the prosaic culprits. One murderer was a CEO, another a bored housewife. No masks, no body armor. As he read through the cases, Wallace wondered what could possibly make a person kill someone who loved and trusted them. In addition to the profound betrayal, another common feature shared by all the staged suicides was that the victim and assailant knew each other. Wallace had turned his mind upside down since the original attack in a vain attempt to identify anyone who might have a reason to kill him. The Masterson Inquiry had cleared Captain Nash and his men. Wallace simply wasn't a threat to them anymore. Beyond the soldiers, he struggled to think of anyone with sufficient reason to want him dead. He was a photographer, an observer, and didn't make enough impression on life to have accrued enemies.

He continued running through search results for the next hour, sifting case after depressing case of murder dressed as suicide. The number of people killed by their loved ones was simply staggering, and Wallace felt as though he could spend an eternity reading these tragic tales without getting any closer to his would-be killer. His first search had led him into a blind alley. Simon Mackay, his tutor at Bristol, and something of a celebrity within photography circles, had always said creativity was not about getting the right answers, but asking the right questions. All Wallace had to do was find the right question.

He tried searching for *suicide murder*, but that only yielded an endless stream of news articles about murder suicides. He skimmed a couple of articles. A family wiped out by a father with debt problems, a young guy murdering a group of college girls before turning the gun on himself. Unlike the staged suicides, which seemed coldly premeditated, Wallace got the sense that these crimes were committed in the unbalanced heat of the moment.

He tried *unexplained suicides* next but got a series of articles on a sudden, inexplicable rise in the number of suicides in the United States. He was surprised to learn that there were more suicides than homicides in America. You were twice as likely to kill yourself as you were to be killed by someone else. Darkly fascinating, but another blind alley.

It was one thirty when the phone rang, and Wallace let it go to the machine.

"Hi, I'm not here right now, but leave a message and I'll get back to you soon," announced the recording of Connie's voice.

"John, if you're there, pick up," Connie said after the beep.

Wallace wavered, uncertain whether he was ready to talk.

"Is anybody there?" Connie mimicked a spooky medium.

He leaned over and picked up the cordless phone. "Hello," he croaked.

"How are you feeling?" Connie asked.

"I've been better," he replied.

"I'm not surprised. We got through a lot of wine. And I saw the pills in the kitchen," Connie told him. "Sorry I had to cut and run, but we've got this big project on . . . you know how it is. Besides, it spared you any awkward morning cuddles."

"You wouldn't have wanted any. Trust me," Wallace replied honestly. "I wasn't fit for human consumption."

"That I can believe," she giggled. "I'll be back around seven. I'll make you something healthful and fortifying."

"Does it involve lentils?"

"My secret weapon," she said lightheartedly. "And no more boozing."

The line went quiet, but they were both eager to prove how much last night didn't matter and started talking over each other.

"I found your note," Wallace began.

"Were you still in bed?" Connie asked simultaneously.

"No," Wallace replied lightly. "I'm searching the web, looking for some sign of the guy."

"Any luck?" she asked.

"Just lots of dark stories about people killing each other."

"Have you run a description? It's where the police always start."

"No, I haven't done that yet," Wallace admitted, almost slapping his forehead at the illumination of his stupidity.

"Like I said, no more boozing," Connie joked. "I'll see you later."

And with that she was gone. No awkward references to the previous night, no searching questions that tried to ascertain each other's feelings.

Wallace could no longer ignore his gnawing gut or the rising pain in his collarbone. He went to the kitchen and fixed himself a salad and a mayonnaise sandwich on spelt bread. Dessert was a couple of Paramols washed down with a glass of orange juice. After a quick trip to the tiny bathroom, he returned to his position on the sofa.

His next search was for *murder suspect body armor mask*. The search results were dominated by stories of the Aurora cinema shooting in Colorado. Wallace tried *suicide body armor mask*. The screen filled with a random collection of results. An article on gunshot wounds, another on how jogging in a gas mask may cause panic, a link to a movie called *Rampage*, and a Wikipedia entry on Ned Kelly. Wallace flicked through to the second page, which was similarly eclectic, and then on to the third. Halfway down the page of ten search results was something of interest: a forum post on a website called Suicide Methodology. Wallace clicked and was taken through to a discussion thread started by a user called Screw The Trolls. The subject of the thread was weird suicides and Screw The Trolls had got the ball rolling with the tale of a man who had chosen to drown himself in a septic tank. Wallace scrolled through various accounts of the sick and unusual ways people had chosen to end their lives until he reached a post by a user called Death The Romantic.

A couple of months ago I heard about a guy who'd killed himself in his garage. Hanged himself. Boring as fuck, right? But the wife says he was offed. Guy kept saying a dude in a mask tried to kill him. Armored up like Batman. Not a weird exit, but a weird story.

Wallace felt a powerful surge of instinct telling him that this was a possible lead, and he scoured the rest of the page. The posts immediately following were full of pointed remarks that instructed Death The Romantic to stay on topic. Wallace clicked Death The Romantic's name and was taken through to the user's profile. One hundred and eighty-three posts, and Wallace read them all. There was no further mention of that particular case, but Wallace built a picture of this person. Death The Romantic claimed to be female and spent the majority of her time trying to console and advise would-be suicides against taking the final step, but when they demonstrated how determined they were, she would give simple practical instruction on how to end a life in the quickest, most painless way possible. She'd been an active user for three years and her most recent post was six days old.

Wallace wondered what would possess a person to trawl the bulletin boards of a suicide advice site for three years and put themselves in such close proximity to some of the most desperate people on the planet. Just a couple of hours on the site had made him extremely uncomfortable. He read the musings of individuals resolved to kill themselves, he saw responses from twisted voyeurs, some of whom actively encouraged death in the most hateful ways, and he observed the glee with which some of the voyeurs greeted news of a suicide. Then there were the messages of hate directed at the site, posted by religious groups and individuals who disagreed with the existence of such an easily accessible, comprehensive manual of self-inflicted death. This was a dark community at the edge of society, one that would never have existed without the Internet, and one that he did not want to be exposed to any longer than necessary. Based on what he'd seen, Wallace felt some sympathy for the opponents of the site; suicide was an insidious pestilence that could take root in the correctly cultivated mind. The experiences of the past few weeks had taught him that even a seemingly healthy mind could be unbalanced by traumatic events. The existence of sites like Suicide Methodology were permanent scabs on otherwise fleeting wounds, and as with any scab, there were some people who were doomed to keep picking.

He copied the contents of Death The Romantic's post about the weird story and used it to run a Google search, but the only relevant result was the Suicide Methodology post. With no other obvious options, he created an anonymous e-mail address and used it to register as a Suicide Methodology user. His e-mail address and username were DeathDetective. Once he'd confirmed his registration, Wallace wrote Death The Romantic a private message.

Dear Death The Romantic

I'm new to Suicide Methodology. I read your post on the weird suicide story. A friend of mine claims a masked man tried to kill him a few weeks ago. Could you tell me where you heard the story of the man who hanged himself in his garage? I really want to help my friend and prove that someone is out to get him.

Death Detective

He sent the message and received a delivery confirmation from the forum system. He spent the rest of the afternoon and early evening searching but didn't find anything as promising as Death the Romantic's post. Every fifteen minutes or so, he checked his e-mail account and his "Suicide Methodology" profile, but despite his obsessive, hopeful desperation, there was no reply.

Connie arrived home at seven thirty. She smiled warmly as she walked into the living room. She was wearing sneakers, gray leggings, and a pink tank top.

"Sorry, I'm late," she said as she slipped her knapsack off her shoulders. "It was one of those days. I had to go to the gym and then I ran home."

Wallace looked up from the computer. "It's okay," he replied.

Connie's hair was tied back in a ponytail that only served to accentuate her flushed, sweaty face. Wallace's memory suddenly flashed with an image of that same blushing face contorted in ecstasy.

"How's it going?" she asked.

"Not too well," he responded, suppressing the memory. "I've got nothing so far."

"Well, I'm going to have a shower before I stink the place up too much," she smiled. "Then you can help me with dinner, and afterward we'll see what the Internet can tell us about your man." She picked up her knapsack and left the room.

"Can I do anything?" Wallace called after her.

"Chop up an onion and some garlic," she shouted from the bedroom.

Wallace went into the kitchen. He searched the cupboards, which were full of fair trade organic foods and mismatched dishes, until he found Connie's stash of vegetables. "How much garlic?" he yelled.

"A couple of cloves," Connie replied, startling Wallace with her quiet voice.

He turned to see her standing in the corridor, wrapped in a white towel. Her hair fell over her pale shoulders and the tresses trailed down toward her concealed breasts. She looked stunning, and Wallace was only half aware of himself as he walked over to embrace her and plant a passionate kiss on her lips. Connie put her arms around him, and the towel fell away.

★ ★ ★

Connie lay with her head on Wallace's undamaged shoulder. They were naked under her duvet, both breathless and glowing with satisfaction. Wallace studied Connie as she stared into the middle distance, and realized that he had been a fool to let her go; she was beautiful, good, kind, and smart—a combination most men would kill for.

Connie caught him staring at her. "I wasn't expecting that," she said. "I thought last night might have been a one-nighter. We were both pretty out of it."

He wondered suddenly whether they were making a terrible mistake, but it felt so natural. More than that: it felt right. Connie smiled at him and planted a kiss on his cheek.

"Don't overthink it," she teased as she slipped out of bed. "I'm not expecting wedding bells. Not yet, anyway."

She stepped into the bathroom and shut the door behind her. Moments later, when Wallace heard the shower, he climbed out of bed and quickly got dressed in a fresh pair of jeans and a clean T-shirt. He went into the kitchen and popped a couple of painkillers before carrying on where he'd left off. He peeled two cloves of garlic and an onion and carefully sliced them on an old wooden chopping board. As he concentrated on finely slicing the layered flesh, Wallace found himself relaxing. Aikido stressed the importance of balance, and while it was natural to be moved by the grand moments of life, he had long appreciated the importance of simple, mundane tasks; the little activities that linked life's significant events. Living in the insignificant present and truly concentrating on his simple job brought him a degree of peace.

"Meticulously done," Connie noted as she approached. She'd put on a pair of pale-blue shorts and an oversized turtleneck. "I'd expect nothing less from one of the world's leading obsessives . . . I mean artists."

She winked and Wallace smiled back at her, relishing the easy domestic familiarity.

"What else?" he asked.

"Nothing," Connie insisted as she rooted in one of the cupboards. "I'll take it from here."

He took Connie at her word and leaned against the counter and watched as she produced a stainless steel bowl. She emptied in a couple of cans of broad beans, a handful of flat leaf parsley, some cumin seeds, and salt and pepper, and then puréed the whole lot with a food processor. When it was reduced to a green paste, she added the onions and garlic and a sprinkling of flour.

"Ta'amaya," Wallace noted.

"One of the only good things you brought back from Afghanistan," Connie responded casually, but Wallace could see that she instantly regretted giving voice to the observation.

"It's okay," he said, putting his hand on her back. "You're not far from the truth."

She smiled at him gratefully as she filled a frying pan with olive oil. Wallace watched her form the paste into little discs and fry them. While they were sizzling, Connie got out a couple of plates and covered them with whole-wheat wraps that she filled with salad. When the ta'amaya were done, she placed three of the fritters on each plate and drizzled tahini over the contents before rolling the wraps into neat tubes.

"Let's eat," she said, handing Wallace his food. She led them into the sitting room and they sat at the small dining table.

Facing the window, Wallace could see a group of Hasidic Jews leaving the synagogue opposite. Even though he couldn't understand the thought process that enabled people to surrender themselves to ancient fairy tales, he envied them their certainty. In their final moments they would have no doubts about where they were going. He took a bite of his wrap and was rewarded with a powerfully fresh umami taste.

"Well?" Connie asked expectantly.

"Good," he admitted. "Really good. For vegetarian food."

"Pig!" Connie laughed.

They spent the rest of the meal talking, conscientiously avoiding anything too deep. Connie's work at Suncert provided the perfect topic—endless politicking, a cast of strange, eccentric characters, and the all-encompassing, eternal pursuit of profit—giving them the illusion of a meaningful conversation without any of the tricky substance.

* * *

After dinner, Connie took the plates to the kitchen. Wallace could hear her putting them in her half-sized dishwasher as he picked up the laptop and placed it on the dining table. He brought the machine to life and typed in Connie's password.

"What's a bootle?" he called out.

"Bootle was my first cat," Connie replied as she entered the room. She joined Wallace at the table and immediately noted the website he was on: "Suicide Methodology."

Wallace registered the concern in her eyes. "It's a lead, nothing else," he said as he logged on to the forum, where a tiny yellow flag indicated that he had a message. He went to his private mailbox and saw a reply from Death the Romantic.

Hi DD

Welcome to SM. Sorry to hear about your friend. My day job involves logging coroners' reports, so I get to see a lot of strange things. I've attached the relevant verdict. Hope it helps.

DTR ☺

Wallace clicked the paperclip symbol and Connie's computer downloaded and opened the attached PDF.

Miranda Miles LLB

HM Coroner for the County of Staffordshire

INQUEST TOUCHING THE Death of Stewart Huvane

Narrative Verdict

Mr. Stewart Huvane died from asphyxiation after he hanged himself in his garage. At the time of his death, Mr. Huvane had been receiving psychiatric counseling after an earlier attempted suicide, also by hanging. Mr. Huvane claimed to have been attacked by an unknown assailant wearing a mask and body armor. Police inquiries found no evidence of an assailant and Mr. Huvane was sectioned. After treatment, Mr. Huvane was released into an out-patient program. His case officer, wife, and psychiatrist testified that Mr. Huvane continued to exhibit signs of paranoia and be-came increasingly convinced that someone wanted to harm him. A message posted on social media that was discovered following Mr. Huvane's death seemed to suggest he was having difficulty with a number of personal issues. Following police evidence pre-sented to the court, which found no signs of struggle or intrusion, a verdict of suicide is returned.

Wallace typed *Stewart Huvane Staffordshire* into the Google search bar and received a handful of results from local newspapers.

"Look at that one," Connie advised, pointing to the third link down the page.

Wallace clicked and opened an article from the *Staffordshire Star*, a local paper. Dated June 23, the article was topped by a photo of Stewart Huvane, a slight man with receding gray hair and luxuriant sideburns. Huvane had the rosy glow and stupefied smile of a man who'd had too much to drink. He had his arm around some unknown person who'd been cropped out by the picture editor. Huvane was standing in front of a pub bar that was covered with empty glasses.

LOCAL MAN CLAIMS
VICTIMIZATION CAMPAIGN
By Graham Parkes

Leek resident Stewart Huvane has sensationally claimed he was the victim of an assassination attempt. Huvane was recently found by his wife, Cynthia, hanging from the rafters in their Leek home after she'd returned home early from a dinner engagement. In an effort to clear his reputation, Huvane, a livestock farmer, has given an exclusive interview to the *Staffordshire Star*.

"Cynthia was out," Huvane said. "I was watching TV. There was a knock at the door. I went to answer and the next thing

I knew, I blacked out. I came round in the barn with a bloody noose around my neck and this fellow in a black mask was hoisting me onto the rafters."

Huvane credits his wife with his survival. "If Cynthia hadn't been feeling ill, I wouldn't be here today," he said. "Everyone thinks I tried to top myself, but why would I want to do that? I've got a great life."

Staffordshire Police have refused to respond to Huvane's allegations, stating that it is Force policy not to comment on ongoing investigations.

Wallace felt a wave of relief. It seemed that the same man who had attacked Stewart Huvane had tried to kill him.

"That sounds like what happened to you," Connie observed.

"Yeah," Wallace replied as he stared at the image on-screen and wondered what on earth he had in common with a farmer from Leek.

11

Wallace stirred when he felt someone touching his head, and opened his eyes to see Connie leaning over him. She was made up, her hair was done, and she was dressed in a dark-green pantsuit.

"Hey," she said gently. "I wasn't sure whether to wake you."

Wallace sat up, ignoring his collarbone, which was no longer screaming but merely shouting pain. His brain took a moment to click into gear.

"You sure you're doing the right thing?" Connie asked with genuine concern.

After the revelations of the previous night, she had tried to talk him into going to the police, but Wallace remained convinced that the safest course was for him to gather more evidence. A newspaper article that outlined the ravings of a perceived lunatic would not be sufficient to open a criminal investigation, and Wallace reminded her that police betrayal had led to the second attack on him. Until he knew more about what was going on, he couldn't be sure who to trust. As long as he stayed off the grid, there was no way for either the police or the killer to find him. After extracting a promise that he would be careful, Connie had accepted his plan to investigate Stewart Huvane's death himself.

"I'll be okay," Wallace reassured her. "Thanks."

Connie tilted her head the way she always did when she was puzzled.

"Thanks for everything," Wallace continued.

"Don't overdo it," she cautioned lightheartedly. She opened her dresser drawer and produced an envelope that she tossed on the bed. "This is for you."

"What is it?" Wallace said, tearing the flap. He saw the familiar image of the Queen's face staring up at him.

"You'll need money, right?" Connie said.

"I can't take this," Wallace protested. "It's too much."

"There's a thousand pounds," she replied. "It's no big deal. I know you're good for it."

"I'll pay you back," he promised.

"I know," Connie said, glancing at the Wedgwood alarm clock on her bedside table. "I've got to run." She leaned forward and kissed him. "Make sure you call me. And be careful."

With that final instruction, she left the room, and, moments later, Wallace heard the front door slam shut. He got to his feet, took a couple of painkillers, and headed for the shower.

Wallace forced himself onto the packed 08:46 from Stoke New-ington to Liverpool Street. Rush hour had never previously both-ered him, but after two attempts on his life, the proximity of others invading his personal space in a confined compartment made him anxious. In addition to the psychological toll the journey exacted, Wallace endured sixteen minutes of physical discomfort. Every time the rattling train started, stopped, or clattered over a junction, one of his neighbors would collide with him and trigger shooting pain from his collarbone.

Released into the bustle of a London morning, he found a T.K. Maxx off Camomile Street. In addition to the clothes Connie had bought him, which were in a thick tote bag, Wallace selected a couple of casual tops, walking boots, a jacket, and a knapsack. He caught the tube to Euston and purchased an off-peak return to Stoke-on-Trent. He checked the large clock that hung over the concourse: 10:23. With seventeen minutes until his train, he paid a visit to Boots and stocked up on civilizing essentials: toothpaste, toothbrush, shower gel, and deodorant.

The train north offered a stark illustration of what life could be like when there weren't eight million people competing for space and resources. A dozen travelers peppered a passenger car designed to carry six times that number. Wallace chose the seat nearest the door so that he had a complete view of the car. Nobody could sneak up on him and he could see anyone coming. Not paranoid, Wallace reassured himself, just prudent. When the train pulled out of the station on time, he relaxed into his seat as they started their journey through an architectural history of London. The Georgian terraces of Camden were followed by the converted redbrick warehouses of Islington, then came the Victorian streets of West Hampstead and Finchley, before the postwar semidetached houses of Wembley and Harrow slipped past, and the train finally started to gather real speed as the twentieth-century retail park in Watford came and went in a blur and they shot into open countryside.

As he hurtled north, Wallace tried to think of connections he might have to Stewart Huvane. He had never been to Leek. He had never heard Huvane's name before and could not recall anyone ever mentioning it. Wallace's family was too small and withered to have overlooked any relations, no matter how distant. He was an only child, and before they died his parents made sure he had a full family tree. More of a weed than a tree: a second cousin in Canada and another in South Africa. Wallace had never seen or spoken to either. He had drifted away from the few friends he had. His work was unpredictable and required a great deal of travel, qualities that put a strain on any relationship, and his failed crusade to get the Masterson Inquiry to accept the truth of his testimony had completed Wallace's transformation into something of an angry loner.

If he had a connection to Huvane, it was one he was unaware of. As rich green fields rolled by, he considered other theories. His first was that the attacker was selecting victims at random, but if that was the case, why would he risk capture by making a second attempt on Wallace's life? His next theory was that there was more than one killer and that any similarities with Huvane's story were pure coincidence. Another possibility was that his own would-be killer had chanced upon Huvane's outlandish description and used it as inspiration for a costume.

Wallace tormented himself with theories for the entire eighty-five-minute journey north, but the only thing he was able to conclude was that there were more possibilities than certainties and he needed evidence if he was going to get any answers.

The train drew into Stoke-on-Trent at six minutes past twelve, and Wallace grabbed his knapsack and disembarked. The large red-brick station had a glass roof supported by an intricate wire lattice, a grand Victorian structure that spoke of more prosperous times. No more than a dozen people left the train, and around an equal number boarded, heading north to Manchester. The meager numbers did not merit such an impressive building, and Wallace guessed that whatever rationale there had once been for the impressive station was lost to history. He followed the signs for the taxi stand, which was situated down the street from the old station.

"Where to, pal?" the driver asked, as Wallace slid onto the backseat.

"The *Staffordshire Star*," Wallace replied.

Crumbling old buildings lined the main road that led away from the station. Some of them were abandoned and derelict. Farther along, the city had been razed to create wide open spaces for car dealerships, megastores, and prefabricated hotels. Rather than renovate and improve, the past had been destroyed to make way for a cheap, functional future. It was as though the place had given up on its history.

The *Staffordshire Star* occupied a small, white two-story building in Stoke's museum quarter. Wallace paid the taxi driver and went inside to find a modern lobby where a tattooed Goth sat behind a large reception desk.

"Hi, I'm here to see Graham Parkes," Wallace said, as the painted man looked up. "I'm an old friend."

"Does he know you're coming?" the Goth asked.

"No. I was in the area and thought I'd surprise him," Wallace replied.

"And your name?"

"Huvane. Stewart Huvane," Wallace gambled.

"Take a seat," the Goth instructed. "I'll see if I can find him."

Wallace walked over to a seating area that was lined with framed images of some of the newspaper's more memorable front pages. As he pretended to scan the headlines, he kept glancing at the receptionist, who was on the phone. After a couple of minutes the Goth came over.

"Hi," he began, "Graham is out on a story. He said he might be a while, but if you want to leave a number, maybe he could give you a call."

"I lost my phone," Wallace replied with a half-truth. "I'll just wait," he added firmly.

"He might be a while," the Goth repeated.

"That's okay," Wallace countered. "I've got time."

He planted himself on one of the molded chairs, which were all linked to form a circular bench. The Goth hesitated, unsure how to handle the situation, but then reverted to his training.

"Can I get you something? A tea or coffee, maybe?"

"I'll have a tea, thanks," Wallace replied. "Black, weak, no sugar."

He read the newspaper, occupying himself with stories of money raised for a heavily disabled child to go on a dream holiday, an overweight local who'd shed half her body weight on a new miracle diet, and a local entrepreneur's dream to revitalize Stoke as a Silicon Valley for the West Midlands. When he'd finished the paper, Wallace drank his tea and waited. The Goth would occasionally glance over with growing resentment in his eyes, as though Wallace's continued presence was a serious inconvenience. For a little over two hours Wallace watched the comings and goings of staff and visitors, until finally a balding, middle-aged man entered. When he glanced at Wallace and then scurried over to the Goth for a huddled conference, Wallace knew the man was Graham Parkes. After a minute or so, an uncertain Parkes approached.

"Are you here for me?" he asked. "I'm afraid I don't remember you."

Parkes's bare pate gleamed under the recessed ceiling lights. Wallace placed him in his mid to late fifties. He was mildly overweight and had the gray skin of a man who spent too much time indoors. Underneath a dirty coat, he wore a cheap crumpled shirt and shiny black nylon trousers.

"We've never met," Wallace replied as he stood and offered Parkes his hand. "I'm investigating a man called Stewart Huvane."

Parkes declined any physical contact with a dismissive wave. "Never heard of him," he said. "Listen, I'd love to help, but I'm up to my neck in it and I'm on deadline."

"A few months ago you wrote a story about Huvane," Wallace continued. "He was a farmer who claimed someone had tried to kill him."

"Oh, that guy," Parkes recalled. "Strange fruit."

"He's dead," Wallace said.

"I'm sorry," Parkes responded. "Was he a friend of yours?"

"No, but I think he was right. I think someone tried to kill him," Wallace replied, as Parkes eyed him with suspicion. "I'd like to take a look at your notes," he continued.

"Notes?" Parkes asked with a smile.

"Your notes of the interview," Wallace clarified.

"See this building?" Parkes inquired. "You probably think it's a pretty decent little place, but until a couple of years ago we used to occupy an entire office block in the city center. Now, every moronic Tom, Dick, and Sally thinks they can be a journalist because they've got a blog. In the last five years this paper's reporting staff has shrunk from forty to four. So if you think I've got time to keep track of every kook I talk to, or keep notes of my interviews, you're mistaken. I'm not a reporter anymore. You want to know what I really am?" Parkes paused. "I'm a filler," he continued. "It's my job to fill the space between the ads that keep this sinking ship afloat. My only hope is that we stay above water until I'm old enough to retire, because God knows the world doesn't need someone with my skills anymore. I wish you well, friend, but I can't help you." He turned and began to walk away.

"Can you at least tell me where he lived?" Wallace called after him.

Parkes stopped. "What was his name again?"

"Stewart Huvane."

"Huvane Farm, out past Leek. I remember thinking that only a narcissist would name his farm after himself," Parkes said before continuing on his way.

The Goth looked at Wallace with the half-smile of pity people reserved for those caught in embarrassing circumstances. Wallace ignored it. He had a lead.

"Thanks for the tea," he called out to the Goth, before picking up his knapsack and leaving the building.

Wallace regretted not having asked the taxi driver to wait. A cool wind negated the warmth of the late afternoon sun, which beat down on his shoulders as he knocked on the farmhouse door. The only response was the steady bark of an unseen dog. The deep timbre suggested that the signs that peppered the farmyard were correct to advise visitors to "Beware of the Hound." Other than the ferocious-sounding canine, the old gritstone farmhouse did not appear to be occupied, so Wallace backtracked through the farmyard. The scree and concrete surface was cracked and potholed and in as much need of repair as the tumbledown outbuildings that surrounded the farmhouse.

Wallace walked up the drive and off the property, taking care to follow the posted instructions to close the gate behind him. Flakes of rust came away in his hands, which he brushed clean as he continued up the gravel track to the blacktop road. The track was flanked by ancient dry-stone walls, and the fields on the other side of them were bleak, a mix of hardy short grass and gorse bushes; perfect land for sheep. Dozens of the puffy white animals dotted the landscape. Wallace climbed up the shallow slope that led to the road, and when he reached the blacktop, he stopped and admired the view that had so impressed him from the back of the taxi. Huvane Farm was tucked off a tiny country road that cut into the Peak District National Park. The road itself ran along the flank of a hill, about three quarters of the way from the summit, and offered a commanding view of the smaller hills and valleys immediately below, and the flat plains and pastures beyond. The patchwork of fields was peppered with farm-houses, tiny white sheep, a handful of horses and cows. Ancient oaks rose out of the land, and in the distance a large reservoir glistened under the falling sun. It was a truly grand landscape that would be worth a return journey once he had his old life back.

Wallace chewed down a couple of painkillers, hitched his knap-sack over his good shoulder and set off for the hostel he'd spotted on the taxi ride out to Huvane Farm. With no guarantee that Huvane's wife still lived at the farm, and the impending sunset, he thought it prudent to find a bed for the night. He guessed it was about a three-mile walk back to the hostel, and it was all downhill, so he strode on, just an ordinary hiker seeking refuge.

The occasional weathered wooden post informed him that the road cut across a number of public footpaths, but he didn't meet another soul during his forty-five minute hike. The only sounds he heard were of nature: the autumn wind breathing gently in his ear; sheep blathering to one another; birds tunefully warning of the com-ing winter. Wallace couldn't remember the last time he'd gone so long without seeing another person. Born and raised in West Hamp-stead, he had the city in his blood. As he walked through the peaceful countryside, he wondered what long-term toll the bustling metrop-olis had exacted. He couldn't explain it, but he felt calmer, more at peace with himself. He longed for his camera. He was seeing the world with new eyes and ached to record his visions. The landscape before him held no cares, and had stood more or less unchanged for eons. It reminded Wallace that he was less than small and insig-nificant; he was nothing, and the world around him would endure, unchanged by his presence or his passing. He felt strangely freed by the thought: nothingness brought with it a freedom that any sense of self-importance could only deny.

He arrived at the hostel just after six. The manager was a gruff, bearded man who introduced himself as Mark. The hostel was quiet—November was not a good month for ramblers—so Wallace got a four-bunk room to himself for just ten pounds. Mark showed him the men's shower room and toilets and explained that the front door was locked at ten sharp. Stereos weren't permitted and any inconsiderate behavior would be dealt with harshly. Satisfied that Wallace couldn't claim ignorance of the rules, Mark stalked away to his office. Wallace found a pay phone just off the recreation room, deposited the two-pound minimum charge, and dialed. He listened to the ringing tone a few times and had prepared himself to leave a message when his call was answered.

"Hello?" Connie said.

"Con, it's me," Wallace spoke softly in an effort to avoid being overheard.

"John! I've been worried about you. You need to get a phone," Connie advised.

"I'm fine," he responded. "The farmer's wife wasn't home, so I'm going to stay overnight and see if I can get hold of her in the morning."

"Where are you?" she asked.

"The Roaches Hostel. It's a little bunkhouse just outside Leek." There was a brief silence that Wallace felt compelled to break. "Please don't worry about me, I'm fine. I miss you."

Connie was silent, and Wallace wondered whether this was due to shock or dismay.

"I miss you, too," she finally replied. "But I'm still at work, and I've got to get back to the meeting from hell. Be careful."

"Will do."

Connie hung up and Wallace put the receiver down. He wandered into the deserted recreation room and found local takeout menus fanned out over a pine coffee table. He sacrificed another two pounds to the avaricious telephone and ordered a pizza. Forty minutes later, alone in the recreation room, he tucked into a greasy, doughy Sicilian with tuna, anchovies, and capers. He could only eat half of the giant disc and left the rest near the tea station. Congealed pizza would make a functional if somewhat unappetizing breakfast.

The clock in the recreation room said quarter past eight, but Wallace was tired and didn't know what the next day held in store, so, with a belly full of fish, dough, and cheese, he sauntered down the quiet corridor and went to his room to collect his toothbrush. After a quick visit to the communal bathroom, he returned to his room and locked the door. With the prudence of someone who'd recently had multiple brushes with death, he placed his knapsack in front of the door as an early warning system and elected to sleep fully clothed. He climbed aboard one of the lower bunks, swallowed a couple of painkillers, and laid his head against a skinny foam pillow. The bunk was six inches too short and the mattress an inch too thin, but Wallace didn't care. He fell asleep quickly but then spent a fitful and troubled night being assailed by vivid dreams of Connie and his would-be killer.

12

Wallace woke to the strong smell of bacon frying. The pain from his collarbone had diminished to a dull ache, but he took a couple of Paramols to subdue it further. Downstairs, he discovered Mark standing over a stove at the far end of the recreation room. The tiny kitchen area was flanked by a large twelve-seat rustic dining table that was blemished with the pockmarks of thousands of meals.

"I found your pizza," Mark said as Wallace approached. "Man can't live on that rubbish. You need proper food."

Wallace looked at the bacon, sausage, and eggs frying in a blackened old pan. "Thanks," he said gratefully.

"No bother," Mark said. "There's only one of you. I couldn't rightly let you sit watching me eat. Get me some plates. Down there."

He gestured at an ancient cupboard with a chipped laminate door, and Wallace reached in and produced a couple of mismatched plates.

"There's tea by the kettle," Mark said, as he served their breakfasts and took them to the table.

Wallace collected a couple of mugs of strong, milky tea. He never normally took milk, but he wasn't about to undermine his host's generosity. He passed Mark a mug as he sat down.

"Other one's mine," Mark informed him. "I take a lot of sugar. Keeps me smiling."

Wallace swapped the mugs, looking for any evidence that Mark had just made a joke, but his host was as gruff and deadpan as ever.

"You from London?" Mark asked as he ate. The question seemed loaded with all kinds of prejudice.

Wallace nodded.

"What you up here for?"

As he chewed a mouthful of egg and sausage, Wallace considered how best to answer the bearded man. A lie might result in a swift cooling of their nascent relationship. "I need to talk to Mrs. Huvane," he said eventually. "Thanks, by the way. This is great."

"No bother. It's all local," Mark said, as though there was never any doubt his food would be anything but great. "You want to talk to the woman about her husband, I'm guessing."

"Yeah," Wallace said. "I think he was telling the truth."

Mark sat back, his scowling, weathered face impossible to read. "Probably," he said at last. "All that nonsense that came out after he died. Someone wanted to get him."

"What nonsense?" Wallace asked.

Mark resumed eating. "Not my business. Talk to the wife. If she'll see you."

"I tried yesterday. There was no answer."

"She doesn't come out much," Mark explained. "Not since it happened. But she was in there. Probably didn't like the look of you. I'll run you up after breakfast. See if that makes any difference."

"Thanks," Wallace said.

"No bother," Mark replied.

When they'd finished eating, Wallace grabbed his knapsack and paid for his bunk.

"Can I give you something for breakfast?" he asked.

"No," Mark replied as he led Wallace out to his Land Rover Defender. "I didn't feed you for money. You needed food, I gave it t'you."

Wallace climbed into the passenger seat. Mark clambered in beside him, sparked the old four-wheel drive to life, and drove away at a lumbering pace. Wallace had to jump out a couple of times to open and close gates, and they covered the three miles to Huvane Farm in less than ten minutes. Mark drove down the gravel track and stopped at the farm gate, which was as Wallace had left it. The only difference was the huge dog that leaped up at them and barked ferociously, startling Wallace, who took a step back.

"Don't mind him," Mark advised. "He'll have your arm off, but as long as you stay this side of the gate, he can't get you."

The dog was truly formidable; Wallace thought it was a bullmastiff. Muscles rippled all over its large frame and its slavering jaws snapped open and shut with sobering ferocity.

"Cynthia!" Mark yelled. "Call your beast off! Man here wants to talk to you!"

Wallace looked past the dog to the farmhouse. There were no signs of life.

"Don't be difficult, Cynthia!" Mark yelled over the dog's deep barks, as he turned toward Wallace. "Say something, man," he suggested. "State your case."

"Mrs. Huvane!" Wallace called toward the house. "I want to talk to you about your husband!"

Nothing moved but the relentless dog. Mark looked at Wallace and signaled defeat with a shake of his head, but something caught Wallace's eye. Across the yard, the farmhouse door opened and a ruddy-cheeked, rotund woman with blonde hair filled the frame. She held a large-bore shotgun, which was leveled in their direction.

"What's he want to talk about?" she called to Mark.

"I think your husband was murdered," Wallace yelled back.

Cynthia studied Wallace for a moment and then lowered her shotgun.

"Ronnie! Come!" she commanded, and the giant dog stopped barking and complied immediately.

"She'll see you," Mark noted, as he turned toward his vehicle.

"You not coming?" Wallace asked, nervously eyeing Cynthia and her canine guardian.

"Nope. This is between you and her," Mark stated simply, without breaking his stride.

Wallace approached the gate, released the latch, and kept his eye on the dog as he stepped into the yard. Ronnie tracked Wallace but made no attempt to move. Wallace heard the sound of the Land Rover starting and looked over his shoulder to see it drive off. He turned toward the farmhouse, where the gun-toting widow waited with her wolf.

"Come in," Cynthia instructed.

Up close, Wallace could see that she wore her troubles on her face. Craggy worry lines were etched into her skin and dark shadows ringed her eyes. Wallace glanced nervously at the dog.

"Don't worry about him," Cynthia said. "He won't hurt you. 'Less you cause trouble."

"Big dog," Wallace noted. "Is he a bullmastiff?"

Cynthia chuckled darkly. "Namby dog for blowhards, the bull is. Ronnie's an English mastiff. All two hundred and twenty pounds of him."

Wallace looked at the beast with newfound respect. The dog weighed more than him.

"Come on," Cynthia said impatiently. "Let's hear what you've got to say."

She stood to one side, and Wallace edged past her and the dog and found himself in a small hallway. Sunlight glared off red ceramic floor tiles, illuminating a rustic staircase that was lined with photographs of Cynthia and Stewart Huvane. Taken over a number of years, the photos featured the happy couple in different locations around their farm.

"This way," Cynthia commanded. She led Wallace through the hall into a large farmhouse kitchen. "You can sit or you can stand. I'll be seated."

She moved toward an imposing farmhouse table. Beyond it a large, squat cookstove lay flush against the wall. Copper pots hung from a rafter that cut across the room, and oversized matte red tiles covered the floor. The windows offered views of open fields that sloped down to ancient woodland. The kitchen would have been like something out of a farmhouse catalog had it not been for the memorial portrait that stood at one end of the table. A framed formal photograph of Stewart stared at Wallace. Pinned to the top right corner was a small black wreath.

"We still talk to each other," Cynthia explained. "He's still with me."

"I'm sorry for your loss," Wallace said meekly. He'd never been particularly good around death. He couldn't remember much of the month after his own parents died, but Wallace did recall the feeling of distraught awkwardness that had overwhelmed him. He put his knapsack down and looked at the memorial portrait for as long as possible in a futile attempt to avoid her gaze.

Cynthia rested the shotgun against the edge of the table and grunted something indecipherable as she sat down. She looked at Wallace expectantly and when he didn't react, she added, "Well, go on then."

Wallace took his eyes off the photo and was about to speak, when Cynthia commanded, "Come, Ronnie!"

Ronnie trotted over to his mistress, his claws clicking against the hard floor. He sat behind her and rested his huge head on the bench. Cynthia scratched the top of Ronnie's skull and stared at Wallace with growing impatience.

"I think your husband was murdered," Wallace began.

"You've said that," Cynthia sniped.

"And I think the man who killed him tried to kill me," Wallace continued. "Twice." He noted a shift in Cynthia's mood, and her impatience seemed to turn to hostility.

"So you're one of them, are you?" she asked. "One of them pigs?"

Wallace was puzzled by the response.

"Well, you can just get out!" Cynthia exclaimed. "Get out!"

"Mrs. Huvane, I have no idea what you're talking about," Wallace protested.

"You knew Stewart?"

"I've never met your husband," Wallace replied.

Cynthia fell silent. She studied Wallace and then said, "You weren't part of what was going on?"

"Like I said, I have no idea what you're talking about," Wallace responded. "Maybe if you explain."

Cynthia looked at the photograph of her husband and welled up.

"You stupid bastard!" she cursed. "You stupid, stupid man!" The troubled old woman took a moment to compose herself and then turned to Wallace. "After he died, the police found a suicide note on Stu's Facebook profile. I didn't even know he was on Facebook.

He said he couldn't take the lies anymore and that he'd been living a double life," Cynthia's voice cracked at the memory. "They also found videos. Lots of videos. Stewart had been driving down to Cannock Chase to meet people. Strangers . . . for sex. They were like animals . . ." Cynthia trailed off. "And I never knew! I never knew. We were married thirty-two years. How could he keep something like that secret from me?"

Wallace shook his head, but Cynthia wasn't really looking for an answer from a stranger.

"The police accepted it was suicide," she continued. "But I thought it was one of the sick perverts in the videos. Or maybe some woman's husband. When I saw what they did—some of those women—the things they did with all those men. I could have killed for it." Cynthia fell silent and the only sound in the kitchen was Ronnie's deep breathing. The huge dog had fallen asleep.

"I'm very sorry for your loss, Mrs. Huvane, but I wasn't part of what your husband was doing. I've never been to Cannock Chase, and I can assure you that I'm not involved in any of that sort of activity," Wallace said.

"So what are you here for?" Cynthia brimmed with hostility.

"The description of the man your husband said attacked him. The way he tried to kill him. That was exactly what happened to me," Wallace replied.

"I should've done more!" Cynthia cried out suddenly. "I shouldn't have listened to that bloody doctor! Stu needed me and I let strangers talk me into thinking he was crazy."

"If it's the same man, I've encountered him twice, and believe me, Mrs. Huvane, there was nothing you could have done," Wallace said in an attempt to comfort the distressed widow.

"I could've killed him," Cynthia noted quietly, glaring at her gun.

"Can you tell me what happened?" Wallace probed gently.

"The first time, I'd gone to play bridge at the Johnson Farm, had a bit of dinner with them first, but I felt poorly and came home early," Cynthia recounted. "I found Stu hanging . . ." She broke down and cried, but after a minute or so, she continued, "I forced him to go into therapy and I was with him all the time in case he tried again. They said he was better, but four weeks after the first attempt, I woke up and he wasn't in bed. I knew something was wrong; he never gets up before me. I went into the garage and I found him. I tried to get the police to investigate, but they wanted nothing to do with it. No way could an intruder get into the house without me hearing, they said. When they found the suicide note and the sex videos, they wrote Stu off completely. And they wrote me off too. How well could I know my husband if I hadn't cottoned on to this double life of his?"

"I'm sorry," Wallace said. It was an inadequate response, but it was all he could offer.

Cynthia stood, tore a couple of sheets of paper towels from a dispenser by the large double-door fridge, and used them to dry her eyes. "I found something after he died," she told Wallace. "Something you'll want to see."

Stewart Huvane's study was a mess. His small leather-topped oak desk was covered in paper, farm equipment catalogs, and invoices. Shelves lined all three walls and were crammed with binders full of documents. An old photo was propped up against the window. It showed a smiling young Stewart Huvane standing beside what looked like his first tractor.

"I tried to clean it up," Cynthia explained as she and Wallace entered, "but it's hard. Every time I get started . . ." she trailed off momentarily. "Well, I have to stop."

"I can only imagine," Wallace sympathized.

Cynthia surprised him by getting to her knees. She shuffled under the desk and pulled a red metal filing cabinet forward. The cabinet was on wheels, so it slid out easily. Cynthia fished behind the cabinet and produced a cardboard file box. She stood up, placed it on the desk and stepped back as though the box was dangerous.

"I found it a couple of weeks ago," she said. "There didn't seem to be much point giving it to the police. They've already made up their minds." She continued toward the door. "I can't look at it again," she said with tears in her eyes.

Wallace watched Cynthia leave and heard muted sobs as she walked downstairs. He turned his attention to the box. Scrawled across the purple lid in black marker was the word "Private." He pressed the plastic button on the side of the box, which released a catch inside. He lifted the lid and was immediately greeted by a grainy photograph of a woman on her knees giving a man a blow job. The scene was lit by car headlights, and Wallace could see other men and women standing around the intimate couple. Underneath the photograph was a handwritten note.

Stu,
   Thought you might like this one. Came out well didn't it? Until next time.
   Kisses
   Sally

Wallace took the photograph and note out of the box and found another seedy picture beneath. This one showed a woman, possibly the same one, kneeling on all fours on the hood of a car, while a man penetrated her from behind and she fellated another.

Stu,
   The thought of you both inside me always gets me wet.
   Kisses
   Sally

Wallace picked his way through the box. There were dozens of notes and images. Early in his career he had worked fashion shoots. Some models required careful coaching in order to feel comfortable performing in front of a camera. Others were brazen and, no matter how little they wore or how outrageous the setting, would exhibit themselves with no sign of discomfort. The images in the box all featured the same woman—likely to be Sally—in a variety of sexual encounters with a number of different men, and Wallace recognized her eager exhibitionism. She was not lost in the moment, but instead posed for the camera, almost goading it to capture her in a depraved sexual adventure. Some of the photos were taken during the day, but most happened at night, and there were usually a number of onlookers. Wallace found Stewart Huvane's face staring back at him in a couple of pictures. The jolly farmer was either smiling excitedly, or grimacing in sexual ecstasy.

When he neared the bottom of the box, the contents changed dramatically. It started with an e-mail exchange between Stewart Huvane and an artist called Wynn Goldman. The first e-mail came from Huvane.

Dear Mr. Goldman
    I write to inquire whether you would undertake a commission of a single piece of artwork based on my design.

Yours expectantly
Stewart Huvane

The next e-mail was a reply from Goldman saying that he did indeed accept such commissions. The two men then exchanged e-mails agreeing a fee before Huvane sent Goldman his brief.

Dear Mr. Goldman
    The individual I would like you to draw wore a black face mask, like the one worn by Anthony Hopkins in Silence of the Lambs, but not exactly like it. A bit like a cycling mask, or a military combat mask.
    He wore body armor over his chest like the new Batman, but not as sophisticated. A step up from what the combat types wear when paintballing. Also black. Black trousers, black gloves and boots, with black goggles over his eyes, and a black coat with purple lining.
    If you have any questions, let me know. I look forward to seeing your drafts.

Yours sincerely
Stewart Huvane

There then followed a series of exchanges when Goldman started sending Huvane his draft images. There were about a dozen rough illustrations, each one slightly more refined than the last. Huvane commented on every iteration, changing the shape of the mask, the body armor, and the image gradually evolved into a piece of finished artwork. Wallace caught his breath: it was an almost perfect representation of the man who had tried to kill him. Huvane had paid an artist eight hundred pounds to produce an exceptional illustration of his murderer. Wallace was unsettled by the sight of his own assailant, but excited by the prospect of real evidence. He had what he needed to go to the police. He put the illustration back in the box, closed the top, and took it with him when he went downstairs.

He turned the situation over as he passed the photos of Stewart and Cynthia that lined the staircase walls. Happy lies. The truth was miserable and sordid, and he needed to figure out a way to convince Cynthia to let him take part of that dirty reality away with him. He couldn't begin to understand what the old woman must be feeling, having spent so many years living what she thought was a simple, wholesome life. To discover that her cherished husband had a secret existence that betrayed their life together. To carry the guilt of knowing that he was murdered while she slept. Anger, sorrow, frustration; whatever her emotions, they would be devouring her. There was no correct way to approach Mrs. Huvane, Wallace concluded as he entered the kitchen.

Cynthia was in the far corner, stooped over a dog bowl, filling it with a can of jellied meat. Ronnie had already started to gobble the chunks greedily. As she stood, Cynthia caught sight of the cardboard file box and nodded sadly.

"I thought you'd want it," she said quietly. "I haven't known what to do with it. I thought about burning it, but fire can't cleanse what's in there. The police helped me take down the suicide note and destroy the videos. Damage was done by then, though. I can't show myself in town anymore." She looked around the kitchen. "Time to move on, I suppose."

Wallace coughed and shifted awkwardly. "The woman—" he said, but he didn't get a chance to finish.

"Sally Harris," Cynthia cut him off. "A hundred and fourteen Mercer Avenue, Stone. I hired a man to find her. Never had the courage to confront her, though. I just want to take a pill. Forget it all happened. Remember the man I knew, not the one in there."

Wallace felt the gloom of intense sadness as Cynthia stared at the box. It spread like a heavy black storm cloud and filled every inch of the kitchen. They stood silently for a moment, until Wallace crossed the room and put his arms around this woman he hardly knew. There was no resistance. Cynthia simply slumped against him and sobbed into his shoulder.

"It's okay," he murmured. "It's okay."

They stood there for what seemed like an age, until Cynthia composed herself enough to break his embrace.

"Well, that's enough of that," she said in an artificially brusque tone. "I've got a lot to do. Farm doesn't run itself. You'll see yourself out."

"Thank you," Wallace said, as he stepped toward his knapsack.

Cynthia said something inaudible. He slung the bag over his shoulder and nodded at the sad old woman as he moved toward the front door.

"Good luck," Cynthia called out to him.

Wallace turned to see her silhouetted against the kitchen window, her canine guardian standing loyally beside her. "And to you, too," he replied.

"Well, go on then!" she commanded.

Wallace stepped outside to be greeted by a bright-blue sky and crisp, cool air. Relieved to be free of the misery inside, he shut the door and started for the road.

13

It was quarter to eleven by the time Wallace made it back to the bunkhouse. He found Mark bent over a wheelbarrow full of stones, painstakingly selecting one that would best fit a hole in the dry-stone wall surrounding the building.

"Needs some attention," Mark explained, when he saw Wallace watching him. "Did she talk to you?"

Wallace nodded slowly.

"You got what you came for," Mark observed. It wasn't really a question.

"Kind of," Wallace replied.

Mark furrowed his brow.

"Can I use your phone?" Wallace asked.

"Go on, then." Mark indicated the door.

Wallace entered the bunkhouse and headed straight for the recreation room. He fed the pay phone and tried Connie. It went to voice mail. "Hi, Con," he said. "The farmer commissioned an artist to draw a portrait of the killer, so I've got a picture, but I still can't find any connection to me. I'm going to a place called Stone to follow another lead. I'll try you later today."

He hung up and used his remaining credit to order a taxi. The dispatcher told him it would be a ten-minute wait, so he headed back outside to find Mark still searching for the right stone. He stood nearby and kept an eye out for his cab.

"You leaving?" Mark asked.

"I need to find this man," Wallace explained. "People think I'm crazy."

"Like Stu," Mark noted without looking up. Stones clanged against the metal barrow as he continued his search.

"Is she going to be okay?" Wallace asked, gazing toward the high rocks of the Roaches.

Mark glanced up at the peaks and shrugged. Wallace couldn't even begin to imagine how a person could recover from the ordeal that had wrecked Cynthia's life.

"Here we are," Mark said, holding up a stone. "Takes time, but it's worth doing right."

He spun the stone in his fingers. He lined it up with the hole and pushed it in. It wasn't a perfect fit, but with some careful manipulation and pressure applied to its neighbors, Mark managed to make it seem so. Satisfied with his work, he wheeled the barrow farther down the wall, a little closer to Wallace, and stopped alongside the next hole. He began the selection process again, rooting around the wheelbarrow for perfection.

Wallace watched him work. If he had simply wanted a way to delineate his property from the road, a wooden fence or a brick wall would have sufficed, but it became clear to Wallace that the stone wall was more than a boundary marker: it was meditation. What seemed like manual labor appeared to nourish the gruff man. There was no frustration in his search; in fact he seemed serene as his rough hands worked their way through the stones. His movements were repetitive. He picked through the stones until he found one that might work. He lifted it out of the barrow and eyed it like an assayer valuing a diamond. He would check it against the hole, and if it failed to measure up, the stone would be carefully replaced at the far end of the barrow. The seemingly haphazard walls that crisscrossed the countryside grew in beauty now that Wallace knew the meticulous care with which they were created. The cracks between the rough gray stone ran in every direction like wild veins and reinforced the wonderful disorder of the wall as a living work of art.

Mesmerized by Mark's work, Wallace mentally framed dozens of stunning macro photographs of the stonework and didn't notice the taxi when it rolled up ten minutes later. The driver honked his horn, which only irritated Wallace and Mark, who glowered in the direction of the cab.

"Thanks for everything," Wallace said as he approached Mark and offered him his hand.

"No bother," Mark said. His hand was covered in dust and felt rough and gritty. "Hope you find what you're looking for."

The journey to Stone took a little under an hour. Wallace tossed down a couple of painkillers en route and noted that he was running low; only four pills remained. He flipped through the contents of the file box for part of the journey, but concentrating on anything in a moving car always made him feel nauseous, so he gave up and put the file into his knapsack.

Mercer Avenue was a long street in a large housing development that marked the edge of town. The road was lined with detached, redbrick "executive" houses that spread to within inches of their boundaries. The cab stopped outside number 114, which showed more signs of wear than any of its neighbors. The development was probably a little over ten years old, and while most of the houses showed evidence of refurbishment and repainting, 114 looked like it hadn't been touched since it was first built. Wallace paid the driver a surprisingly reasonable thirty pounds and walked up the short, narrow path to the red front door. There was no bell, so he rapped the brass knocker. After a moment, he saw movement through the frosted picture window at the top of the door, and a distorted shadow stalked toward him. The door opened and Wallace was met by the face he'd seen in the photographs.

"Hi," Sally Harris said with a smile.

"Hello, Ms. Harris," Wallace replied.

"It's actually Ms. Norton," Sally corrected. "Divorce."

"The moment I tell you why I'm here, you're going to want to slam the door on me," Wallace continued. "But I really need your help."

Sally's smile fell and her right hand gripped the edge of the frame. "I don't do that anymore," she said curtly. "No matter what you've heard."

As she moved to shut the door, Wallace put out his hand to stop her.

"I haven't heard anything, Ms. Norton," he said. "I'm here about Stewart Huvane. I think he was murdered, and I believe the same man who killed him is trying to kill me."

Sally looked at Wallace and smiled wryly. "If he was still alive, I'd have killed him myself," she said. "You'd better come in, duck. We wouldn't want the neighbors getting the wrong idea."

She stood to one side and allowed Wallace to enter. He stepped into a small hallway that was almost completely devoid of furnishings. The hallway carpet ended abruptly at the foot of the stairs; bare planks led to the upper floor. A chipped mahogany occasional table with a broken leg leaned precariously against a wallpapered wall. Wallace knew it was wallpapered because a large strip had been ripped clean off, exposing jagged shards of plaster.

"He cleaned me out," Sally explained as she led Wallace inside. "But I got to keep the house."

The sitting room was covered with old, garishly patterned floral wallpaper. An ancient gray fabric sofa was pushed against one wall and a table with a large, empty birdcage stood against another. Net curtains hung over the windows, but there were no fabric drapes. No television, no photographs or ornaments. If this was where Sally took visitors, Wallace wondered what the rest of the house looked like.

"Pretty rough, huh?" Sally observed as she walked over to the table and picked up a box of cigarettes and a lighter. "But life's more than stuff, right? As long as you've got your health." She popped one of the cigarettes into her mouth and, after half a dozen attempts with the lighter's rusty ignition, managed to get a flame.

The cigarettes might explain the excessive lining of her face, which made her look older than she probably was. Wallace placed Sally in her midforties, but the lines nudged her up a few years.

She had wavy shoulder-length hair with a cheap peroxide tint. Her rounded curves were crammed into a summer minidress that looked a size too small. Wallace couldn't help but notice little crushed honeycombs of cellulite at the top of her thighs.

"What's your story, then?" Sally challenged between drags.

"Do you know anyone who might have wanted to kill Stewart Huvane?" Wallace asked.

"Not until after the videos went public," Sally replied. "Would have been at least a dozen people on the list then. Stu was a harmless old codger. He used to party. But we all partied. There was no jealousy or any of that bullshit."

"What about a husband or boyfriend? A wife?"

Sally shook her head. "Nah," she said. "Listen, when that idiot posted those videos, a bunch of marriages fell apart—including mine. Nobody got killed. It's not worth it, is it? Over a few random cocks." She smiled slyly and her eyes flashed with mischief, satisfied that she'd shocked Wallace with her bluntness. "I'm guessing you've seen the videos."

Wallace shook his head. "Just some photos."

"It's a real shame," Sally continued. "Killed the scene round here. No one wants to get caught. I'll probably move on," she observed, looking round the room. "If I can find anyone to buy this shithole."

Wallace watched her for a moment. She cut a sad figure outlined against the wallpaper's faded flowers. "Well, I'm sorry to have troubled you," he said as he started for the door.

"No trouble, hon," Sally replied. "There was one thing that has always bothered me about those bloody videos, though. I have no idea how Stu got hold of them. I uploaded them to Blue Vidz and made them private."

Wallace paused by the door, a little surprised.

"Well, I wasn't about to let those idiot blokes do it," Sally said. "Not with what was at stake. I sent them passwords, but none of them could access the original copies. They could just stream low-resolution versions. Enough to bring themselves off, you know? The videos Stu posted were originals. High resolution. Good enough to pick out each and every pube."

Wallace grimaced inwardly.

"Stu could barely send an e-mail, so you tell me how he managed to get those bloody videos?" Sally challenged.

"Maybe from your computer," Wallace suggested.

"He's never been to my house," Sally replied. "I kept my hobby and my home life separate, for obvious reasons." She gestured at the empty room. "If Stu was killed," she continued, "I reckon whoever did it posted those videos. Like I said, Stu was a harmless old codger. Even if he had wanted to kill himself, he wouldn't have ruined all our lives in the process."

Wallace had offered to wait outside, but Sally said that a strange man hanging around outside her house would only give the neighbors more gossip. So, he sat on the tatty sofa and waited for his taxi while Sally busied herself in another room. It was an uncomfortable, odd ten minutes, but the taxi eventually arrived and the driver sounded the horn. Wallace hurried into the hall as Sally came down the stairs.

"Thanks," he said.

"Good luck, hon." Sally blew him a smoky kiss.

Wallace let himself out and walked down the path to the waiting cab. He climbed in the backseat and instructed the driver to take him to Stoke Station.

Thirty minutes later, he was on a fast train to Euston. He'd asked the taxi driver to stop at a newsstand and had run in to buy a pen and pad. Once on the train he'd started writing. In neat, careful script, he transcribed everything he'd learned during the previous couple of days. He recounted conversations to the best of his ability, noted names, and annotated footnotes where elements of the narrative dovetailed or needed to be cross-referenced. By the time the train arrived in Euston, an hour and a half later, Wallace had twenty-nine pages of handwritten testimony. He slipped the pad into the file box and disembarked.

★ ★ ★

Wallace tried Connie from a pay phone in Euston Station, but got her voice mail. He hung up without leaving a message, crossed the concourse, and walked a couple of blocks west to Euston Square. From there he caught a Circle Line train to Edgware Road, and at 4:18 p.m. presented himself to the receptionist at Paddington Green Police Station.

"I'm looking for Detective Sergeant Bailey," he said.

The civilian receptionist studied Wallace; he didn't look like a drunk, lunatic, or hardened criminal. "Is he expecting you?" she asked.

"No," Wallace replied. "But he's going to want to see me. Just tell him John Wallace is waiting outside."

He backed away from the receptionist, who suddenly became suspicious. She looked at her colleague, who was busy trying to decipher the rantings of a Russian who'd been pickpocketed. Wallace smiled at the young woman and nodded confidently as she picked up the phone.

He didn't have to wait long. It took less than three minutes for Bailey to emerge from the station with a couple of burly uniformed officers in tow. He scanned his surroundings and caught sight of Wallace, who was standing beside the open door of a black cab that had stopped in the mouth of Newcastle Place.

"Come on, mate!" the cab driver said impatiently.

Wallace handed the man another twenty-pound note.

"Another minute," Wallace said. "I need to see what my friend's going to do."

He turned his attention to Bailey, who was fast approaching with his two brutish colleagues. Wallace shook his head emphatically and pointed at the two uniforms. He made to get into the taxi and was gratified when the detective understood his meaning. Bailey turned to the two officers, instructed them to stay back, and continued his approach alone.

"I thought we could take a ride," Wallace said to Bailey when he was within earshot. "I've got something to show you."

Bailey turned to the uniformed men and signaled the cab license plate. "Come on, then," he said.

"Hackney," Wallace instructed, as he and Bailey climbed into the cab.

Wallace slid onto the bench seat, and Bailey sat on one of the rear-facing jump seats. Bailey slammed the passenger door and the taxi pulled into the traffic. Wallace looked through the rear window and saw the two uniforms talking into their radios as they ran back to the station. He turned to face Bailey.

"I'm really sorry about before," Wallace started. "How are you?"

"I'm not here for a health check," Bailey replied. "You've got sixty seconds before I stop this cab and arrest you."

Wallace noticed the cab driver's ears prick up, so he switched off the intercom. He felt Bailey tense as he reached into the knapsack for the file box.

"I found someone who was killed by the man who attacked me," Wallace said. He opened the file box and found the illustration Stewart Huvane had commissioned. "He was a farmer named Stewart Huvane," he continued. "He claimed that this man tried to hang him in his barn, but the local police didn't believe him. They referred him for psychiatric care."

He was gratified to see the similarities strike home; Bailey was genuinely interested.

"About a month later the killer went back again. While Huvane's wife slept in the upstairs bedroom, Huvane was hanged in his garage. The police wrote it off as suicide after they found a note and videos that linked Huvane to an underground sex ring. After the first attempt, Huvane commissioned this image from an artist he found online. This is the man who attacked me. He's killed before and if we don't stop him, he's going to kill again."

Bailey took the illustration and studied it.

"It's all in here," Wallace said, indicating the file box. "E-mails, photographs, and I've written up notes of everything I've found. Take it," he said. "If you read it and don't think I'm telling the truth, you can arrest me. I'll tell you where I'm staying."

Bailey studied Wallace for a moment before asking, "What happened the night of your escape? Did he come for you again?"

Wallace felt a buzz of elation as he heard the question; Bailey already suspected he'd been telling the truth. "He dragged me into a medical storeroom and tried to inject me with something. Morphine, I think. We fought and I escaped. Are the two guards okay?"

"They were pretty messed up, but they'll live," Bailey reassured him, as he accepted the file box. "Okay," he said at last. "I'll keep this between us for now. If what you're saying checks out, I'll help you make things right, but if this is some crazy fantasy, you're going back to the Maybury."

"Deal," Wallace responded, offering his hand.

"I wouldn't do that," Bailey cautioned. "A big part of me just wants to put a cuff on it."

Wallace nodded sympathetically and withdrew his hand.

"What's the address?" Bailey asked.

"Flat four, ninety-one Cazenove Road, Stoke Newington."

"Stop the cab!" Bailey instructed, tapping on the partition.

The taxi pulled to a halt on St. John's Wood Road. Wallace couldn't believe how close he was to his flat; he could have walked to it in less than five minutes. But there was no way he could return until the man who'd tried to kill him was in custody.

"I'll be in touch," Bailey told him. "Make sure you don't go anywhere."

"I won't," Wallace reassured him.

Bailey stepped out of the taxi, taking the folder with him.

Wallace activated the intercom. "Stoke Newington," he instructed.

Bailey slammed the door shut and glowered at Wallace as the taxi drove on.

Wallace sat back and relaxed as the pounding adrenaline ebbed away. There was nothing he could do but hope the policeman was as smart—and as trustworthy—as he seemed.

14

Wallace was seated at the dining table, hunched over the laptop, when Connie arrived home. He rose and gave her a warm hug, which she returned with a kiss.

"How did it go?" she asked, as she stepped away and slipped off her heels.

Wallace was mesmerized by her long legs, which were encased in sheer black tights. Or were they stockings? He took her by the hand. "Let's talk later," he said, as he led her toward the bedroom.

Connie was covered in a glistening sheen of perspiration. She lay against Wallace's right shoulder and looked up at the ceiling as he admired her flawless skin and beautiful curves.

"I missed you," she observed.

"I missed you, too," Wallace said honestly.

"You're just grateful for a bed," Connie joked.

"No," he said seriously. "I never should have let you go."

"You didn't let me go. I couldn't handle it," Connie said. "You were a mess."

"I'm sorry," Wallace interjected with a twinge of guilt.

"It wasn't just you," Connie assured him. "I'd been doing the same thing my whole life. Finding people who need fixing. Trying to save them. I was in a real state after we split, so I went to see a psychologist. He helped me make sense of what happened. I knew how screwed up you were going into the relationship, but I thought I could make it work."

"I wasn't always screwed up," Wallace replied. "And I'm not now. This whole thing, it's made me see things differently. Ever since my parents died I've spent my whole life trying to push people away. And when I did care about something . . . about the Inquiry, those kids . . . it almost destroyed me. When I was hanging there at the end of that rope I saw you. I realized . . . I don't know . . . I realized I'd lost the best thing that ever happened to me."

She kissed him tenderly and they lay silently in each other's arms.

"So what did you find up north?" she asked eventually.

"I'm reasonably sure Stewart Huvane was killed by the same man who tried to kill me. I just can't see a link between us. The killer might have selected us at random. Huvane was into dogging. A suicide note and a bunch of videos were found on his Facebook page, but if he didn't commit suicide, then the killer probably posted them. I spoke to one of the women Huvane was meeting for sex. She says he was useless with a computer—"

Wallace stopped suddenly.

"What?" Connie asked.

Wallace was lost in thought.

"What is it?" she pressed.

"He didn't leave," Wallace said. "After he hanged me, the killer didn't leave. He was still in my flat. Why?" His mind sparked as it made connections. "You doing anything tomorrow?" he asked.

"It's Saturday," she replied with a shrug.

"Good," Wallace said emphatically. "I need you to go to my flat."

"What for?" she asked in surprise.

"We've got to get my laptop," Wallace replied.

Saturday morning in St. John's Wood was usually a quiet affair. There were very few vehicles cutting across the intersection of Hamilton Terrace and Abercorn Place, so Wallace had a good view of Connie as she crossed the street and headed toward his building. As he stood on the opposite corner of Abercorn Place with his hood pulled firmly over his head, Wallace felt a mix of emotions: anger that he'd been so violently torn from such a comfortable life, gratitude that he'd survived the savage assaults, and joy at his reconciliation with Connie. He watched her walk up the path to his building. When she reached the front door, he saw her press one of the intercom buttons.

"Hello?" came a voice.

"Mrs. Levine?" Connie asked.

"Who is this?" the voice said with more than a hint of distrust.

"My name is Constance Jones," Connie replied. "I'm a friend of John Wallace. If you look out of your window, you'll see him on the corner."

The intercom fell silent and Connie waved to Wallace. She saw him look up to the first-floor window and wave. A few seconds later, Connie heard the intercom crackle to life.

"He looks different," the voice observed.

"He's in disguise," Connie explained. "In case the building is being watched."

"We don't want anything dangerous here," the voice cautioned. "First this suicide. Then all the police traipsing around the place. It's not good for the neighborhood."

"Mrs. Levine," Connie interjected, "John says you have a spare key to his place. He wants me to get a couple of things."

Silence.

"Then we'll be gone," Connie assured her. "I promise."

Silence. Then the buzzing sound of the latch unlocking. Connie pushed the front door and stepped inside.

She was on edge as she hurried up the stairs. If the place was being watched, she was putting herself in danger. *He'd do the same for you*, Connie told herself. *Or would he really?* she thought darkly. *He let you go.*

When she rounded the final flight of stairs, she saw Mrs. Levine's suspicious face peering out of the narrow crack between the door and the frame. Connie could see the chain was on.

"Here," Mrs. Levine said, proffering a set of keys through the crack. "Take them."

Connie hurried forward. "Thanks," she replied, as Mrs. Levine dropped the keys into her hands.

"Wish him well," Mrs. Levine requested. "But ask him not to come back until all this trouble has passed. We're too old for it."

Mrs. Levine shut the door, leaving Connie alone on the landing. *You don't get to pick your family or your neighbors*, she thought as she hurried up the next flight of stairs. With the exotic dancer living on the top floor, Connie had always thought of Wallace's building as a bohemian artists' commune. It was reassuring to know there was a timid, normal retired couple living beneath him.

Her face fell when she reached the landing outside Wallace's flat. In addition to the normal locks, there was a police padlock and a caution notice. She approached the door and tried the Chubb dead-bolt. It was unlocked. She then slid the key into the Yale latch and opened it. The door gave about an inch before it was reined in by the police padlock. Connie pushed at the door, but the padlock was firmly attached and held fast. She thought about getting Wallace, but she had no idea what lay behind the door. If the killer had staked out the place, at least she had a chance of explaining away her intrusion. Bringing Wallace would only endanger them both. She hurried back downstairs, took a deep breath, and knocked on Mrs. Levine's door. She sensed movement on the other side and saw the spyhole go dark.

"It's her," came a hissed whisper.

"Find out what she wants." This whisper was deeper; a man's.

"Pretend we're not here," Mrs. Levine hissed.

"She knows we're here. You just gave her the keys," the man whispered with a sense of exasperation.

"And I can hear you," Connie said loudly.

"You and your big mouth!" Mrs. Levine hissed before she opened the door. "What do you want?" she asked Connie.

Connie shifted from side to side, plucking up the courage to finally ask, "I don't suppose you have a crowbar I could borrow?"

"Push it, don't pull it!" Mrs. Levine instructed.

Her husband, a short, spry fellow in his early seventies, was pull-ing against a claw hammer that was wedged between Wallace's front door and the frame.

"Okay, then!" Mr. Levine retorted. "Have it your way."

Connie put her hand to her mouth to conceal a smile as Mr. Levine shifted position. He leaned against the hammer's handle, and there was a slight splintering sound.

"Let me help," Connie offered. She couldn't tell whether the Levines had insisted on coming upstairs because they didn't trust her with their hammer, or whether they were driven by a desire to keep tabs on her. Maybe they were just being neighborly?

"I'm okay," Mr. Levine said firmly.

"Let her help!" Mrs. Levine exclaimed. "It's the Sabbath. You shouldn't be doing anything."

"This is an emergency," Mr. Levine replied curtly. "If I don't get some peace, I might kill somebody!"

Connie chuckled at the spirited exchange.

"Did you say something, dear?" Mrs. Levine asked sharply.

"Nothing," Connie responded meekly. Mrs. Levine might be a short woman, but that didn't diminish her presence.

"Let me get set properly," Mr. Levine said. He took a step back and stared at the hammer, which was suspended by the pressure applied between the door and the frame. If it were possible to metaphorically roll up one's sleeves, that's exactly what Mr. Levine did as he prepared himself for the next push. The little man stepped forward, grasped the handle with the determination of a Samoan weight-lifter, and pushed with all his might. His face went red, a throbbing vein appeared on his forehead, and he grunted and groaned like a drunken lover. Finally, there came the crack of splintering wood, and the padlock separated from the frame. The door swung open, and Mr. Levine hurtled forward. He was only just able to keep his balance.

"There," he said breathlessly. "I did it."

"Well done," Mrs. Levine acknowledged. "Now let's get you home before you have a stroke."

"Thank you so much," Connie said gratefully. "You really didn't have to."

"What are neighbors for?" Mrs. Levine asked as she steered her red-faced husband to the top of the stairs.

"Tell John he can buy me a cognac," Mr. Levine advised.

"Don't you dare," Mrs. Levine chastised.

"What? A man's got to have his vices," Mr. Levine responded as they disappeared down the stairs.

Connie heard them banter all the way into their flat. She envied their easy familiarity, the rhythm of their relationship. *Maybe one day?* With that optimistic thought running through her mind, she entered Wallace's flat.

Wallace had told Connie what happened, but nothing prepared her for the devastation in the living room. The main beam had collapsed, bringing down much of the plaster ceiling and some of the masonry above. The window was covered with a clear plastic sheet that had been taped over the jagged hole. Shards of glass were everywhere, either scattered by the impact or distributed by the many people who must have come and gone since Wallace made his escape. Fingerprint dust covered almost every available surface.

Connie backed out of the room and went down the corridor that led to Wallace's bedroom. The immaculate, hardly used kitchen lay off to her left. Beyond it, to the right, was the guest bedroom, and Wallace's studio was the next room on the left. Connie entered and immediately saw that the forensics team had also been in here; fingerprint dust was everywhere. It covered the beech chest of draftsman's drawers that Wallace used to store his larger prints. It speckled the black flight cases that housed his cameras and lenses. Dust also marked all of the large framed photographs that lined the walls. There were eight of them; four mounted on the long wall and two on each of the flanks that ran out to the side of the building. The photographs were of Victorian industrial machinery. They were beautifully lit and perfectly composed, but Connie had never liked them. Of all the pictures he'd ever taken, Wallace had chosen to adorn his walls with soulless machines rather than people or places.

Wallace's laptop was where he'd said it would be; on his large partners desk next to his huge high-resolution screen. Connie didn't recognize the machine; Wallace must have replaced his old one after they split. She hurriedly unplugged the power cable and deposited it and the laptop into a vintage leather satchel she found beside the desk. Mission accomplished, she hurried from the room with the satchel under her arm. Her heart leaped when she saw a silhouetted figure in the corridor ahead of her. Connie tried to cry out, but her throat refused to obey the command.

"Hello?" a tentative voice said. The figure stepped into the light from the kitchen and Connie saw it was the dancer who lived above Wallace. Lexi? Leona?

"Did I scare you?" she asked. "I'm sorry. I just heard all this noise."

"It's okay," Connie replied, her heart pounding almost to the point of bursting. "John asked me to get some things. I'm a friend."

"I know," the woman responded. "I recognize you. Been a while, though."

"You know how it is," Connie said. "Anyway, I'd better get going."

She started down the corridor. The woman turned and headed for the front door, leading Connie all the way.

"Is he okay?" she asked.

"Yeah," Connie replied.

"When's he coming back?"

"It's hard to say."

"Send him my love," the woman said, as they stepped onto the second-floor landing.

"I will," Connie said as she pulled the door firmly shut. She used Wallace's key to turn the Chubb deadlock, and, satisfied that his flat was secure, hurried downstairs.

Wallace paced the corner, growing more concerned with each passing minute. He and Connie had agreed that he'd come in if she hadn't emerged after fifteen minutes, but it wasn't until she'd entered the building that he realized he had no way of telling the time. No watch, no phone. He cast around until he remembered the large church at the top of the terrace. The square Norman-style tower had a clock, which seemed accurate enough. When it reached the allotted fifteen minutes, Wallace started across the road, only to be greeted by the sight of Connie hurrying from the building with his soft leather satchel under her arm. She dodged a car and scampered across the road.

"I did it," she said proudly. "Your neighbors send their regards."

Wallace hugged her and looked back at the building to see the Levines watching from their living room window. Then, above them, he saw Leona.

"Come on, let's go," he said as he took Connie's hand and led her up Abercorn Place toward St. John's Wood tube station.

"What do we do with this?" she asked, indicating the satchel.

"I need to know if it's been tampered with," Wallace replied. "What are your detective skills like?"

"Pretty crappy," Connie said honestly. "But I may know someone who can help."

They crossed the street and hurried on to Grove End Road. Wallace used the excuse of trying to read the plaque on Sir Lawrence Alma-Tadema's house to turn around and check if they were being followed. Apart from a black cab that shot past without slowing, the street behind was empty, but Wallace didn't relax until they were on the tube heading back to Connie's place.

15

When they arrived in Stoke Newington, the November sun was strong enough to trick them into thinking it was a spring day. Connie suggested they go out for lunch, so they trekked up Stoke Newington High Street with its boutique shops and small, independent cafés and restaurants. They found a table at the Blue Legume, which Wallace thought was a terrible play on words, but the quality of their food earned them forgiveness. He ordered a cheeseburger and fries and Connie asked for a falafel burger with a side of spinach. Wallace kept his legs on either side of the satchel and made sure his feet were touching it at all times. With Detective Sergeant Bailey finally taking him seriously, he felt optimistic that he'd soon have his life back.

The tables in the Blue Legume were tightly crammed together, so there was no opportunity to discuss anything sensitive. Instead, Connie asked him about the films he'd worked on since they'd split. Had he met any famous people? *Yes.* Were any of them divas? *No.* Connie's face animated with excitement as he talked. He'd worked on so many films, with so many stars, that he was inured to the supposed glamor. It was just a job working with normal, flawed human beings, some of whom happened to be sensationally famous. He couldn't help but smile at Connie's starstruck enthusiasm.

"You're laughing," she said accusingly.

Wallace shook his head and his smile broadened. "I'm not laughing," he said. "I'm smiling. And I'm only smiling because I think you're great."

Connie tilted her head bashfully and replied with a coy smile of her own.

After the meal, they held hands and walked back to Connie's place. The tall, old trees that lined Cazenove Road were beginning to shed their leaves, and a team of street cleaners brushed them off the pavement toward a mechanized road sweeper. Wallace and Connie moved at a languid pace, a fixed distance behind the sweepers, and, for a few indulgent moments, Wallace imagined the path was being cleared just for them.

As they approached Connie's building, he saw a face he recognized peering at him from the window of a Vauxhall. Bailey climbed out of the car and walked toward them.

"He's police. Don't mention the laptop," Wallace said quietly.

Connie nodded.

"Mr. Wallace," Bailey said, "I thought we'd agreed you weren't to go anywhere."

"Man's got to eat," Wallace replied. "Detective, this is Constance Jones. Connie, this is Detective Sergeant Bailey."

Bailey offered his hand and Connie shook it.

"I need to talk to you," Bailey said to Wallace. "Privately."

"Let's go inside," Connie suggested.

As Bailey followed Connie toward the front door, Wallace glanced up the street. Part of him wished he and Connie could just keep following the sweepers down the newly cleared path.

Bailey sat with his back to the window. He had pushed his chair away from the dining table to give himself the space to cross his legs, and one elbow rested on the back of the chair. Wallace recognized the self-assured, relaxed pose of someone accustomed to being in charge.

"Can I get you a drink?" Connie offered.

"I'm okay," Bailey replied. "Thanks."

"John?" Connie asked.

"Nothing for me, thanks," Wallace answered.

Bailey looked at Connie expectantly.

"Do you want me to leave?" she asked.

"I'd like her to stay," Wallace said emphatically. "Connie knows everything."

Bailey's eyes narrowed, but he didn't say anything. Connie sat next to Wallace, opposite the policeman.

"So your story checked out," Bailey began. "I asked enough awkward questions to convince Staffordshire Police to reopen the Huvane investigation. And my commanding officer has agreed to allocate resources to bring this guy in."

Wallace felt a flood of relief and turned to see Connie smiling at him.

"We just have one problem," Bailey continued. "We've got no idea why this man targeted you and Huvane. Like you said in your notes, there's no connection. We also don't know how he found you in the Maybury. The fact it happened after I gave them your real name may mean he was able to access records, but that's just guesswork."

Bailey fell silent and stared at Wallace, who had a strong suspicion he knew what the policeman was thinking.

"You want to use me as bait," Wallace said.

Bailey didn't respond.

"No," Connie interjected. "He didn't say that. You didn't say that."

"He's right," Bailey replied calmly. "We could spend months trying to track this guy down. Or we could give him what he wants. My commanding officer has agreed to a specialist firearms command unit that will provide round-the-clock protection: six SCO19 officers working in teams of two. We'll have a couple of unarmed officers providing additional support at all times. And I'll take one of the shifts. You'll be completely safe."

Wallace considered the proposal.

"You can't do this, John," Connie protested. "Let them take their time to catch him. Just stay here. Nobody knows about us. This man, this killer, will never find you here."

Wallace smiled at her. "And what if they never find him?" he asked.

"Then you can just stay here," she said sadly. She wasn't even fooling herself with her wishful thinking.

"I can't stay hidden forever." Wallace turned to Bailey. "I'll need a weapon."

"I'll see what we can do," Bailey replied.

"How would it happen?" Wallace asked.

"You're a wanted criminal. We'll have a unit arrest you somewhere public, probably a train station. They'll bring you in, process you, and ship you back to the Maybury," Bailey answered.

"Will they know?"

Bailey shook his head. "No. We'll bill the SCO19 officers as additional security to ensure you don't escape again, but we won't tell any of the staff what's really going on."

"So I'll be a patient?" Wallace inquired. The thought of returning to Doctor Taylor's sessions tied a knot in his stomach.

Bailey nodded.

"How long?" Wallace asked.

"I don't know," Bailey conceded. "But my CO has cleared funds for two weeks. So we'll have to reevaluate if it takes any longer."

Wallace looked at Connie, who shook her head and pleaded with her eyes. He nodded apologetically. "Okay," he said finally. "When do we do it?"

"My car's outside," Bailey said as he stood.

"No, not today," Connie protested.

"Give us a moment," Wallace requested.

Bailey nodded and gave Connie a sympathetic look. "It was nice to meet you," he told her. "He'll be safe. I promise."

Connie stood up, but she didn't respond until Bailey left the room and she heard the front door slam shut.

"This is crazy," she blurted out. "It's so dangerous. You're more likely to get shot by one of them."

"I can't just hide, Connie," Wallace replied quietly.

She shook her head and turned away from him in exasperation. He walked over and put his arms around her.

"I've got to do this," he said firmly. "I won't let anything bad happen, I promise."

"You can't make that promise," she said angrily.

"Con, I have to get my life back," he explained.

Connie turned to face him and Wallace could see that she'd finally accepted this was an argument she couldn't win. "You make sure you stay safe," she commanded. "I'm going to visit you every day."

"You can't," Wallace said. "Right now, nobody knows about you." He could see frustration cloud her face. "Help me," he offered. "Take my computer to your friend and find out if it's been tampered with."

"I wouldn't call him a friend," Connie said, her mood easing slightly. "So, how will I know you're okay?"

"I'll ask Bailey to phone you."

"Go, then," she instructed. "Before I start getting emotional."

Wallace could see that it was already too late; her eyes were welling up, and when he kissed her, he felt warm tears on his cheeks.

"I'm sorry," Connie said when they separated.

"It's okay," he assured her. "I'll be back before you know it."

He stepped away and retreated toward the door. Connie looked beautifully fragile and sad and he wanted nothing more than to stay with her and hold her, but he didn't. Instead, he turned his back on her and hurried from the flat under a cloud of oppressive sadness that swelled as he descended the stairs. It was a depressing contrast to the lunch they'd shared earlier. He promised himself that he'd come back, and, as he walked along the garden path, he looked up at Connie's flat and saw her standing at the window. She gave him a sad wave and wiped her eyes. Whatever his future held, Wallace knew that he wanted Connie to be part of it. He hurried out of the garden and saw Bailey leaning against his car.

"Everything okay?" the detective asked.

"Fine," Wallace replied. "Let's go."

Bailey didn't say much to Wallace as they drove west; instead he spent most of the time on his phone, coordinating with his team. They agreed on the concourse at Euston Station as the location for

Wallace's arrest. Someone named Superintendent Cross told Bailey that SCO19 had been put on standby, ready for Wallace's transfer to the Maybury. Wallace felt reassured by the level of preparation going into his staged capture.

"When do I get a weapon?" he asked, as they passed St. Pancras.

"In the hospital," Bailey replied. "Anything you have on you now is going to get confiscated. As far as everyone else is concerned, this is a real bust."

Wallace reached into his pocket and produced a little over seven hundred pounds, which he showed to Bailey. "I'd better leave this with you," he suggested.

"Put it in the glove box," Bailey instructed.

Wallace held back twenty pounds, which he stuffed in his pocket, before opening the glove compartment and tucking the rest of the cash underneath the owner's manual.

"Sorry," Bailey said, catching Wallace by surprise. "You must have been going nuts in there. You shouldn't have had to find the evidence yourself."

"I appreciate the sentiment, but I think we're probably even," Wallace replied. "I worked most of my frustrations out on you."

Bailey rubbed his jaw, recalling the assault.

"Just make sure you catch the guy," Wallace said.

"We will," Bailey responded with confidence. "We're almost there. I'm going to turn into Gordon Street. When I stop, jump out and go straight to the station. The arresting officers will be there in about ten minutes. Just hang around where they can see you."

Wallace looked puzzled.

"You've been all over the Met briefing sheets. You're a wanted man," Bailey explained.

"Great," Wallace observed sarcastically, as Bailey turned the corner.

The car pulled to a halt in a red-zone loading area and Wallace jumped out.

"See you soon," Bailey called out, as Wallace slammed the door. He started walking toward the station and looked back to see Bailey drive south.

Wallace lifted his hood and joined a small crowd of pedestrians waiting to cross the busy junction on Euston Road. After a minute, the lights turned red and the green man illuminated. He walked across the road and up the diagonal path that cut between two imposing office blocks. He entered the station and crossed the large, black-tiled concourse. He didn't know whether it was nerves or real pain, but his collarbone had started to throb, so he went into Boots and bought another pack of Paramols. He lied to the cashier and told her it was his first time on them. He paid for the pills and took two as he exited the shop. He'd been on them for more than the recommended three days, but suspected this would be his last opportunity for a dose. With his impending hospitalization, he'd be back on a cocktail of mind-numbing medication very soon. He saw fluorescent yellow tops across the concourse and drew closer until he saw two uniformed officers, one male and one female. Wallace dropped his hood and walked nonchalantly toward them.

The woman spotted Wallace first. He was about thirty feet from them when he saw the flash of recognition. Wallace pretended not to notice, but saw the stout policewoman nudge her gangly colleague. Satisfied that they were moving toward him, he looked up at the departures board.

"John Wallace," the policeman said, "you are under arrest."

Simultaneously, Wallace felt a forceful pair of hands grab his forearms. A knee went into his back, and he was forced down to the ground. He cried out in genuine pain.

"Calm down!" the policeman ordered. "Get down!"

Wallace was pushed flat on his stomach.

"Arms behind your back!" the policeman commanded.

Wallace complied, and when he turned his head in an effort to see what was happening, he caught sight of Euston's travelers backing away. A few had their phones out and were filming the arrest. Wallace felt a smaller hand on his head, turning it back toward the floor.

"Look down," the policewoman instructed.

Heavy cuffs coiled around Wallace's wrists, biting tightly.

"I'm going to help you up," the policeman informed Wallace. "Your hands are shackled, so you will not be able to properly support yourself in the event of a fall."

A hard tug on his biceps indicated it was time to rise. With both officers' assistance, Wallace struggled awkwardly to his feet.

"This way," the policewoman directed.

Another tug informed Wallace which way to go, and he was frog-marched through the station, with the officers flanking him closely.

"You do not have to say anything. But it may harm your defense if you do not mention when questioned something which you later rely on in court. Anything you do say may be given in evidence," the policeman recited. "Do you understand?"

Wallace nodded as they led him out to the covered walkway that ran between the station and Melton Street. There, waiting near the pedestrian crosswalk, was a police car, its blue lights pulsing rhythmically.

Processed and packed into a cell within an hour, Wallace had to remind himself that he was incarcerated voluntarily. But the police officers who brought him in, the custody sergeant. and his colleagues didn't know that, so Wallace was given the same dehumanizing treatment as every other suspected criminal. His meager belongings had been taken, along with any items of clothing he could possibly use to harm himself—in Wallace's case, his shoelaces. He'd been asked a number of intrusive questions about his personal life, his health, and his background, and finally, when they'd taken everything they desired, he'd been led to the cellblock; a long corridor lined with eight red metal doors on either side. Wallace had been thrust into the third one on the left, which contained a melamine bunk and toilet, no natural light, and no stimulus whatsoever. It made his cell at the Maybury seem like a luxury suite.

Wondering how many unhappy people had spent countless miserable hours here, Wallace sat down on the bunk and waited.

He lost track of time. Bailey knew he was in custody, so why was he taking so long? Frustration rose like a hot tide, engulfing his body in its angry swell. Acting as bait was difficult and dangerous enough; he didn't need the added stress and discomfort of being treated like a normal prisoner. He stood up and started pacing. He could feel the confinement getting to him and dark thoughts wormed their way up from the fertile corners of his mind. This might be a ruse to get him back into custody. Bailey probably hadn't even looked at what was in the folder. Worse still, this was a trick to lure him to the killer. The second attack had taken place after Bailey had given the hospital his real name. What if Bailey was in league with his assailant? Wallace took a deep breath and tried to disperse the darkness clouding his mind, but he struggled; he had good reason to be paranoid.

Metal struck metal, and the clanging sound startled him. Wallace turned to see the cell door open. Bailey stood in the doorway with the custody sergeant at his shoulder.

"Mr. Wallace, you're to be transferred to the Maybury Hospital," Bailey said. "Follow me, please."

Bailey led Wallace out of the cellblock and down a corridor that was capped by a large metal door. The policewoman who had arrested Wallace held the door open, and Bailey ushered him outside. They emerged into a parking lot that was filled with police cars, vans, and bikes. There were a few unmarked vehicles, but most of them bore the familiar orange-and-blue checks. Bailey pulled him toward a waiting police van, its rear doors gaping like the jaws of a trap. Wallace climbed aboard to find the arresting policeman sitting on one of the two benches that lined either side of the vehicle. Bailey pushed Wallace toward the opposite bench and then sat next to the arresting officer. The policewoman slammed the rear doors shut. The last rays of the dying sun shone through the windows, which were laminated with one-way plastic. Cargo secured, Bailey rapped the divider that separated the holding area from the driver. The engine roared to life and, a moment later, the van started moving.

"I could have run him down, sir," the policeman said to Bailey.

"It's personal. I want to make sure he gets taken care of," Bailey replied, rubbing his chin and fixing Wallace with a menacing stare.

Was this part of the act?

The policeman smiled slyly, satisfied with his superior's response.

The rest of the journey passed in silence. Wallace wasn't a human; he was a criminal and merited none of the courtesies most people took for granted, like conversation or concern. This suited him fine; he was used to solitude. Even on a film set, he was an outsider; a voyeur chronicling the lives of others.

Bailey wore a watch, which enabled Wallace to see that the journey south took exactly one hour and thirty-eight minutes. They arrived at the Maybury Hospital at quarter past seven. Wallace felt a dry lump climb into his throat when the van doors opened and he saw Doctor Taylor and Keith waiting for him. He resisted the powerful urge to shout the truth of the situation, and allowed Bailey to lead him out of the van.

"Welcome back, John," Doctor Taylor said with a smile. "Keith will see you to your room."

Keith's fingers took tight hold of Wallace's upper arm and pulled him toward the main entrance. The windows Wallace had smashed hadn't been repaired yet; just covered with long pieces of plywood.

"Never works," Keith advised. "Running away just lets us know you're a long way off being better."

Wallace wasn't paying attention to him. He craned his neck to see what Bailey was doing.

"I'd like to talk to you about the additional security, Detective Sergeant Bailey," Taylor said as he approached Bailey. "I really don't think it's necessary."

Wallace didn't hear any more. Keith pulled him inside the building, where a square-jawed man with burning eyes sat behind the reception desk. One of the cops, maybe? The man eyed Wallace with intense hatred as Keith produced a key card and swiped it through the reader. The security door opened and Wallace felt a wave of panic. He was back, trapped, helpless and without the weapon Bailey had promised him. He was totally reliant on the strength of others for protection.

Keith led him through the canteen. The other inmates were having dinner, and Wallace couldn't help but feel he was their cautionary tale, proof positive that escape was a futile endeavor. He locked eyes with Heather, who looked as sad as ever. When she smiled sympathetically, Wallace wished he could tell her—tell them all—that he was back voluntarily as part of a special mission to catch a killer. But who'd believe a tale like that in a place like this? Rodney shook his head slowly as Wallace was paraded past, the pathetic man registering his disapproval of the escape attempt. Fat Bob waved, and even Button offered a flicker of recognition at the return of his TV buddy.

Satisfied that enough eyes had seen Wallace, Keith pulled him out of the room and led him to the shower block. Wallace stripped and went into one of the cubicles, where he washed with the red gel. His bruises had lost some of their anger and were starting to fade. Only his collarbone still had the rainbow tie-dye discoloration that now looked worse than it felt. Keith smacked the cubicle door to signal that Wallace's time was up. He turned off the shower and stepped outside to the depressing sight of the hospital's pajamas and Crocs placed in a neat pile on a bench that ran the length of the room.

"Get dressed," Keith instructed. "Food's waiting in your room. You're on special measures."

Wallace smiled inwardly. They thought it was punishment to deprive him of the company of his fellow inmates, but it was a relief. The less he was exposed to the damaged people who shared his incarceration, the more chance he had of keeping himself positive.

Once dressed, he followed Keith to his cell. It was the same one he'd escaped from. Inside, sitting on his old bunk, was a tray with a sandwich, an apple, a slice of cake, and a carton of pineapple juice. It looked like the contents of a child's picnic box, but it was food, and Wallace approached it eagerly.

"Good night, Mr. Wallace," Keith said before he shut the door. Wallace heard the spring-loaded lock click securely into position.

Welcome home.

Connie ordered pizza from Il Baccio, but it wasn't the same without John. She couldn't believe how close they'd grown in such a short space of time. Without him there, her mind started playing to her insecurities. Maybe their intimacy was simply the product of his trauma. Maybe as time passed, Wallace was cooling on her. Maybe that's why he had jumped at the detective's proposition. Wallace had always been difficult to read and lived in his own head most of the time, something that had infuriated Connie when they were together. She had learned to recognize the signs: a distant look, a total lack of engagement with anything or anyone around him. Entire conversations could be lost on him because he simply wasn't there. Instead he was confined to his own mind, trying to give life to a creative concept or, as was more common during their relationship, trying to solve a difficult problem. The problem that occupied him for the duration of their relationship—convincing the Masterson Inquiry of the truth of his testimony—was one that could never be solved. Wallace had turned in on himself, destroying their relationship and almost destroying himself in the process. *He says he's moved on*, Connie told herself, *but maybe he knows that's exactly what you want to hear*. With doubts plaguing her mind, she went to the 1970s Habitat unit she'd picked up at a yard sale and opened one of the crooked doors. She was greeted by her small DVD collection and selected *Magnolia*. It was the only film that would adequately reflect her mood.

Wallace had finished his meal hours ago and was lying on his bunk counting speckles in the ceiling when he heard the door open. He assumed it was Keith coming to collect the tray but was surprised to see Bailey. Keith loomed at the policeman's shoulder.

"Give us a minute," Bailey told the heavy orderly.

Keith wavered; the visit was already a serious breach of protocol, but Bailey shot him a look he couldn't disobey. When the orderly stepped away, Bailey hurried forward and pulled something from his jacket pocket.

"I didn't forget. Keep it hidden," Bailey said as he handed Wallace a small rectangular object wrapped in black cloth.

Wallace unfolded the material and saw the electrical pincers of a stun gun. Not a Taser, but at least it was something.

"Thanks," he said.

"What for?" Bailey looked puzzled. "I never gave you anything. We don't know who this guy is or how he's tracking you. Keep your eyes open, and trust no one but me." He stepped away and turned toward the door. "And if you ever give me any more shit, you'll be rolling out of here in a wheelchair!" he yelled for the benefit of Keith, who was undoubtedly eavesdropping in the corridor beyond.

Bailey backed out of the cell. "You can lock him up," he instructed Keith, before stalking down the corridor.

Sporting a beaming smile, Keith entered and picked up Wallace's tray. "You listen to the nice policeman. There's a couple of guards who'd like to help him put you in that wheelchair." He smiled as he tapped Wallace on the head with the plastic tray.

Wallace resisted the desire to electrocute the orderly with the stun gun that was under his left thigh; it was intended for bigger prey. Instead, he simply smiled blankly at Keith, who left the cell and slammed the door shut behind him.

Wallace pushed the stun gun into the back of his trousers and lay down to count the speckles in the ceiling.

16

Connie felt washed out when she woke the following day. She wondered what she was doing to herself. When she'd left John, the loss had hit her hard enough to knock her into therapy. She'd opened her home, her bed, and her heart to the man far too easily, and there was no guarantee they had any sort of future together. The dark cloud was still there, raining doubt onto her fertile imagination. *Just roll with it*, she told herself as she clambered out of bed.

Once showered, she pulled on a pair of old Levis, a sleeveless floral blouse she'd found in a vintage shop in Islington, and an over-sized gray sweater. Shoes were her weakness, and she picked out a pair of Aubrey boots that she'd treated herself to in Kurt Geiger.

She sat at her dressing table and looked in the mirror. She knew she was blessed with great skin, which required very little maintenance. Mascara, eyeliner, and lipstick were her cosmetics of choice. Once they were applied, she brushed her hair back into a loose ponytail and put on her boots. She went into the living room and picked up Wallace's laptop bag. Slinging the satchel over her shoulder, she grabbed an apple and left the flat.

Sunday trains were few and far between, so Connie caught the 73 from the corner of Stoke Newington High Street. She climbed the stairs and took a seat at the front of the upper deck. The bus wound through the back streets of London and took just under an hour to deliver her to Victoria Station.

As she left the bus, Connie checked her phone for the text message she'd received from Riley Cotton. He had responded to her inquiry at 4:03 a.m.—Connie knew the exact time because the message alert had woken her up. She hadn't seen him for years but was surprised to discover that the address he'd given her was in Pimlico. Riley had obviously come a long way from the days when he was programming customer applications for Connie. A Java developer and amateur hacker, he was cocksure to the point of abrasive arrogance, even by the standards of the IT industry. He was difficult to work with and terrible at interviews, so Connie was pleased that he'd landed on his feet. She wandered along Victoria Street, looking for number 68.

She walked past the building a couple of times in an effort to see whether there was a 68a, or somewhere else that looked like a residence. Surely this had to be a mistake. Number 68 Victoria Street was a huge glass-and-steel skyscraper, at least twenty stories high, and was the headquarters of a number of financial and legal firms. She tried calling Riley but got no answer. She checked the text to see if she'd misread it, but it definitely said 68. Connie could see a security guard sitting at a desk watching something on his tablet. She approached the main entrance, a carousel door, and tried it. Locked. The guard looked up and waved her to one of the side doors. When she approached, the guard buzzed it open, and watched her as she crossed the lobby.

"I'm sorry," Connie said. "I think my friend gave me the wrong address."

"What's his name?" the guard asked.

"Riley. Riley Cotton," she replied.

"Eighteenth floor," the guard said with a smile. "Take the second lift on the right." He pointed Connie in the direction of a bank of elevators and nodded encouragement when she stared at him in puzzlement.

She crossed the gleaming black marble floor to the waiting elevator, stepped inside, and pressed the button marked 18. The elevator was tiled with cream marble and lined on two sides by dark wood and on the back by a full-length mirror. Connie surmised that Riley had invited her to meet him at his office. He had always been a show-off, keen to rub any achievement in the faces of those around him.

The elevator doors opened and Connie stepped into a large lobby. There was no corporate logo, just the same cream-colored marble floor and wood-clad walls. An unmanned reception desk stood at one end of the lobby. Next to it was a set of solid wood double doors. Connie walked over and rapped her knuckles against them. No response. She tried the handle, but the door was locked. She looked around and started to wonder if this was a practical joke—she wouldn't put it past Riley to harbor a grudge over some perceived slight that occurred years ago. She heard a noise behind her and turned to see Riley Cotton open the double doors.

"Constance Jones!" Riley exclaimed. "Welcome to my humble home."

She saw that Riley had undergone a significant image change. Gone were the cargo pants, long hair, and expletive-strewn T-shirts. In their place were dark jeans, a short-sleeved checked shirt and a crew cut.

"Hi, Riley," Connie responded as she approached.

"You look hotter than ever," he said enthusiastically. He leaned forward to hug her and planted a kiss firmly on her cheek. Connie had never seen him so full of life. The transformation from cynical, miserable computer troll was unsettling.

"Come in. Come in," Riley instructed. "Check this place out."

Connie stepped through the double doors and was greeted by a superb view of London. She'd often tried to peer into Buckingham Palace Gardens from the top deck of the 73, but the buses were never quite tall enough. The eighteenth-floor windows offered a view, not only of the gardens, but of the palace beyond. Glass seemed to stretch endlessly, showcasing London in all its splendor: the mall, the Houses of Parliament, the Thames, and all the glorious architecture in between. Connie drifted toward the windows and then realized that there was something very odd about this office. It wasn't an office at all. The open-plan space was about two hundred feet long and a hundred feet wide. It had been divided into loosely designated zones. There was an expansive living area with a couple of large sofas, a huge television, and a coffee table. Behind a partial screen was a king-size bed and two large chests of drawers. Two clothes rails hung nearby, laden with suits. Farther along was an exercise area, with a treadmill, rowing machine, a multigym, and a free-weights section. In the far corner of the space was the only visible partition, a temperature-controlled server room that was sealed off by glass walls. This was no joke; Riley had turned a twenty-thousand-foot open-plan office into his home.

"Good, isn't it?" He smiled broadly.

"I . . . I don't even know where to start," Connie spluttered. "What is this place?"

"It's my pad," Riley replied slowly. "It's—where—I—live."

"Why?" she asked.

Riley tapped the side of his nose. "Do you know how many important computers are within a mile of this location? Government, security services, banks, hedge funds, corporate headquarters."

She looked at him with horrible realization. "No, you wouldn't be that daft," she challenged.

"I don't know what you're talking about," he said innocently. "I'm a computer consultant with a small, exclusive client base."

Connie eyed him suspiciously.

"A client base that pays exceedingly well," Riley bragged. "Want to test the bed?"

Connie shouldn't have been shocked; Riley had always been crass. But her dismay must have shown on her face.

"I was only kidding," he explained. "Bed's been tested plenty. You wouldn't believe how easy it is to score when you've got a Ferrari."

This is exactly where the world went wrong, Connie thought. A socially inept misfit like Riley had become exceedingly rich, and he'd almost certainly made his money doing something highly illegal. The old adage that good things happen to good folk was a lie people told themselves to feel better about life. Good things happen to folk who can rob or cheat their way to them.

"I'm glad to see you're doing so well," she lied.

"Yeah, well, after my last stint working for you, I decided I couldn't be a wage slave anymore," Riley said. "Imagine spending what little time we get on the planet serving Omnimegacorp, so that some gray-skinned fat oligarch can buy another yacht. Fuck that. So I sat down and figured out the quickest way to get rich. Money buys everything, right? Love, freedom, and a shitload of stuff. Well, we're living in the information age, and I worked out that the best place to be is slap bang in the middle of the information superhighway. Directing traffic, so to speak."

"As long as you know what you're doing," Connie cautioned.

"Got to be in it to win it, Constance. And if I do get caught, I get a slap on the wrist, a few months in a country club prison, and a job with MI6 when I get out. How terrible!"

"Well," Connie started on the purpose of her visit, "I was wondering if you could do me a favor. I need you to run a diagnostic on a machine."

"Does this look like PC World?" Riley feigned outrage.

"It may have been tampered with," Connie continued. She was happy to see Riley's eyes spark with interest, and she slipped the laptop case off her shoulder.

He put his arm out, and Connie handed over the satchel.

"Okay, Constance," he said. "I'll run a diagnostic for you. Be a fun little workout."

"Can I give you anything?" she offered.

Riley raised an eyebrow and smiled. "Ten minutes between the sheets," he suggested.

It was Connie's turn to raise an eyebrow, but she didn't smile.

"Just a smile, then," Riley suggested.

Connie forced a fake smile. "Thanks," she said. "Give me a call if you find anything."

"You want to stay for brunch? A drink?" Riley pleaded.

"I can't. I have to be somewhere," she lied as she hurried toward the door.

"Some other time," Riley suggested.

"Yeah, maybe," Connie replied vaguely as she opened one of the double doors and stepped into the lobby. "Take care of yourself, Riley."

"See you soon, Constance Jones," Riley said, before slowly shutting the door.

Connie called the elevator, urgently pressing the button over and over. She was relieved when the doors pinged open and she stepped into the escape pod that would take her away from Riley and his creepy lair.

17

Sunday had taken its toll on Wallace. Special measures at Maybury meant that he was chaperoned by Keith at all times. The orderly accompanied him everywhere, standing outside his shower cubicle, posting a watchful eye from the corner of the men's bathroom, and looming like a globulous shadow at his shoulder during meals. Keith's only respite from guard duty was during Wallace's session with Doctor Taylor, who sat there spewing theories and suppositions that were based on the lie that Wallace had tried to kill himself. Wallace desperately wanted to grab Taylor and shake him until he accepted the fact that he was wrong; Wallace was here voluntarily with the support of the police, who were out to catch the man who had tried to kill him. Instead, he sat quietly and listened to the doctor drone on. Taylor interpreted his silence as denial and prescribed another pill to add to the cocktail of medication that was supposed to help Wallace return to reality. Wallace was already struggling to combat the numbing effects of the first dose Keith had given him after breakfast.

After his session with Taylor, Keith had taken Wallace for a walk in the gardens. Other inmates ambled, shuffled, and trembled along the paths that crisscrossed the grounds. The cold November air cut through some of the narcotic haze as Wallace wandered the grounds and thought of Connie. The tall trees reminded him of the view from her living room window, and he longed to be back in her flat with her wrapped in his arms. Later, he sat alone in the crowded canteen and ate dinner with Keith looking on. After the meal, Keith administered another dose of pills, with the new one—some kind of sedative—prescribed by Taylor. Denied television, Wallace was offered a range of improving books in the recreation room: recognized classics such as *Pride and Prejudice, Wuthering Heights,* and *The Count of Monte Cristo*. With a sense of irony, he selected the latter but couldn't really concentrate and had only reached the part where Fernand and Danglars plot against Dantès when Keith told him it was time to return to his cell.

Wallace changed in the shower block, carefully concealing the stun gun in his palm as he put on his pajamas. Once dressed, he followed Keith to his cell. As he shuffled slowly along the corridor, the walls seemed to curve and bubble and the floor rose and fell in waves. Whatever Taylor had prescribed to return him to sanity was having the opposite effect. He only just made it to his cell before the world became a gelatinous mass of shapes and colors. He tried to say something to Keith but heard a drooling mess of sound. He staggered over to his bunk and collapsed. The last thing he remembered was hearing the cell door shut behind him. The tumbling lock stopped with a sudden snap that seemed to echo for eternity as Wallace fell into oblivion.

Sound. Darkness. Movement. Wallace floated up from the murky realm of unconsciousness and became aware that he was not alone. He was facedown on his bunk, his wet cheek pressed into a pool of stinking vomit. Someone was behind him. Wallace reached his arm round to his back and fumbled for the stun gun inside the waistband of his pajama trousers. Without knowing what he would find, he turned and swung his arm up. His eyes registered a shape in the darkness: *it was the killer.* Wallace's masked assailant stood over him holding a syringe that was pressed into a vial of liquid. The man must have been surprised to see Wallace move and didn't have time to properly parry the blow. Wallace struck his assailant's neck and pulled the trigger, and the stun gun unleashed over one hundred thousand volts directly into the man's body. He fell to the floor, shaking violently, and Wallace hauled himself to his feet.

"Help!" Wallace cried weakly. The word barely carried; his throat had been stripped raw by acidic bile. He swallowed and took a deep breath. "Help!" This time his cry echoed along the corridor.

He heard movement behind him as his assailant stirred. Wallace lunged with the gun, but the masked man blocked the blow and tried to grab his arm. Wallace ran from his cell and tried to pull the door closed behind him, but the lock had been deactivated and wouldn't catch. Wallace saw gloved fingers reach around the edge of the door and felt a forceful tug. He held onto the handle with all his strength, but the man on the other side was too powerful. Wallace could see the outline of his masked face through the gap between the door and the frame. The opaque goggles prevented Wallace gauging his assailant's emotions, but he knew the man was angry and determined to finish his murderous task. A piercing sound cut through the building as the main alarm was activated.

"Move!" a familiar voice yelled.

Wallace turned to see Bailey sprinting down the corridor. Behind him were two tall men in orderly uniforms. Both men were pointing black pistols in Wallace's direction.

"Move, now!" Bailey shouted again.

Wallace felt the pressure on the other side of the door subside, and he peered into the gap to see nothing but darkness. He let go of the handle, but the door didn't move, so he turned and scrambled down the corridor toward Bailey. The detective ushered Wallace behind him and waved the two armed police officers forward.

Wallace looked behind him to see an orderly and two security guards approaching.

"Stay back," Bailey commanded above the persistent sound of the alarm. The three men hesitated. "And you," Bailey told Wallace. "Stay right back."

The two firearms officers crept toward Wallace's cell. The heavier one stayed on the near side, while the other, a gaunt officer with a pinched face, moved swiftly to the far side of the door. Both men held their pistols a few inches from their chests, pointed in the direction of Wallace's cell. The heavyset officer raised three fingers to signal the start of a countdown. The first finger dropped, and his colleague nodded seriously. The second finger fell and the cell door swept open. The masked assailant sprang from the darkness beyond and rushed the large officer. Wallace saw a blur of movement as the masked man lashed out with rapid punches and kicks. The efficiency and discipline of movement were hallmarks of an expert martial artist and in less than a breath, the masked man had snatched the pistol from the stunned officer. He turned swiftly and shot the gaunt policeman. The bullet caught the man in the throat and he dropped his gun and clutched at his neck, screaming a hoarse, wet cry as blood gushed from the wound. Wallace was sickened by the sight and saw Bailey's face cloud with dismay as the masked man turned to the large policeman and shot him twice in the head.

"Run!" Bailey issued the command and started pushing Wallace before his colleague's limp body hit the floor.

Wallace was mesmerized by his attacker, and turned his head to see the man bent over the gaunt policeman, who had fallen to his knees. The masked man picked up the second pistol, and used it to shoot the wounded policeman in the temple.

"Come on!" Bailey cried as he grabbed Wallace and urged him to speed up.

Behind them, Wallace saw the masked man turn in their direction. The first security door was fifteen feet away. One of the guards was fumbling with a set of keys. Wallace could hear them jangling nervously over the nagging pulse of the alarm. The second guard looked down the corridor, and the orderly tugged at the door handle. Wallace turned to see the masked killer level the pistol in their direction. *Ten feet to the door.* A look of relief crossed the first guard's face as the lock gave. A loud crack echoed off the walls and something whipped by Wallace's cheek. Relief turned to horror as the guard registered the pain of being shot. The bullet tore through his right arm, into his chest. The orderly pulled the door open and yanked the wounded man toward it. Another crack, and the guard's head cratered. The man dropped instantly, and fragments of skull, matted hair, and blood flew in all directions. *Five feet.* The terrified orderly let the dead man fall, and turned to run. The second guard tried to follow, but a third crack sounded and the bullet caught him in the back.

Wallace and Bailey were at the door. Bailey pushed Wallace over the fallen man, and then jumped through the doorway. When they were on the other side of the door, Bailey reached round and grabbed the fallen guard. Wallace followed the detective's lead and leaned forward to help pull the wounded man to safety. Another crack and the bullet caught the guard in the leg. The man screamed in agony as Wallace and Bailey pulled him clear. The security door swung shut behind him, and Wallace heard the satisfying sound of the lock catching.

"Can you walk?" Bailey asked the guard above the sound of the alarm.

The man didn't respond. Wallace looked down to see the guard's eyes rolling back in his head. While Bailey checked the man's pulse, Wallace stood slowly, and cautiously peered through the small panel window in the door. The masked attacker was striding down the corridor toward them, and was no more than twenty feet from the door. Wallace realized with sudden, gut-wrenching horror that he could see something hanging on the other side of the door: *the keys*.

The window shattered as a bullet cut through it. Wallace heard the high-velocity projectile slice the air beside his head. He was so shocked he hardly registered the flying glass, which scored a crisscross pattern of scratches on his face.

"We've got to move!" he shouted to Bailey.

"He's not dead," Bailey said. "We've got to bring him with us."

Bailey stuck a hand under the guard's left arm and Wallace put one under the man's right. Pulling together, they dragged the unconscious guard toward the next security door. The guard's feet trailed behind them and his leg wound left a bloody ragged line in their wake. Wallace could see the orderly up ahead. He was frantically hitting the door.

"Help!" the orderly yelled.

"Where are your keys?" Bailey called.

"In the staff room!" the orderly replied, his fists hitting the door furiously. "Help!"

"Check his pockets," Bailey ordered, as he and Wallace reached the door.

They dropped the unconscious guard and both began ferreting in the man's pockets. Another crack and Wallace felt an impact above him. The orderly fell to his knees, retching as his hands grabbed at his chest. A pulsing pool of crimson spread across his white tunic, growing with each beat. Wallace would never forget the look the orderly gave him as he registered his own death. It conveyed the same mix of terrible emotions Wallace had felt hanging at the end of a rope. The orderly fell forward onto the unconscious security guard. Another crack and a bullet hit the door. Wallace looked up to see his assailant striding toward them, taking aim with one of the pistols.

"Got them!" Bailey yelled. The detective leaped up and tried the first key in the door. It slotted in perfectly, and turned. "Come on!"

Bailey grabbed Wallace and pulled him up and through the door. Another crack and Wallace felt the strength ebb away from the hands that held him. He fell onto the other side of the door, which slammed shut. As he pulled himself to his feet, Wallace saw that Bailey had been hit in the abdomen. Blood was spreading across his sky-blue shirt. Black blood, possibly from the liver. Wallace registered someone pulling on the other side of the security door. Bailey held up the keys, and smiled weakly. One of the keys had been snapped and Wallace knew that the other end was lodged in the lock.

"Let's go," Bailey said.

Wallace helped Bailey to his feet and slung the detective's left arm over his shoulder. They set off toward the canteen. Moments later, Wallace heard another gunshot and shattering glass. He turned to see a gloved hand reaching through the panel window and searching for the latch. Wallace cast around the corridor, his eyes scanning for something he could use to vent his rage. He suddenly remembered his previous escape.

"Wait here," he told Bailey. Before the detective could react, Wallace slipped out from under the man's arm, crossed the corridor and grabbed a large, red fire extinguisher. He raised it as he rushed toward the door. The gloved hand had made contact with the lock and was beginning to turn the latch, when Wallace started his swing. The door opened as the fire extinguisher arced through the air. Wallace heard himself roaring with a bestial fury as he put all his strength into the blow. The edge of the metal base connected with the masked attacker's wrist and the side of the extinguisher smashed into his hand with so much force that the door slammed shut. Wallace felt a rush of satisfaction as he heard a muffled howl and saw the crippled hand hastily withdraw through the panel window. He dropped the fire extinguisher and ran back to Bailey, grabbing the detective as fresh gunfire came from the panel window.

"Good work," Bailey said weakly, before suddenly crying in pain. Wallace felt the instant drag of weight as the detective went down. He hauled the man round the corner, into the corridor that led to the canteen. He turned and saw with dismay that Bailey had been hit again. Blood was spreading across his shirt.

"Come on!" Wallace shouted, but Bailey was going nowhere. A sheen of sweat covered the wounded man's face. His breathing was shallow and irregular and his eyes glassy.

"Fucker," Bailey said weakly. "You make sure you get him."

"Come on, we can make it," Wallace urged.

Bailey fumbled for his pocket. "Take my car," he said, his voice taking on a hollow, rasping sound as his lungs fought for every breath. "Kye Walters," he added weakly. "File."

"What?" Wallace asked, trying to focus on Bailey's soft words.

"Kye Walters," Bailey reiterated impatiently. "The Monkey Puzzle. Salamander. He'll help. Salamander. Get him." Bailey's head fell onto his left shoulder and his eyes rolled back.

Wallace shuddered as the policeman's life ebbed away, but he had no time to mourn. He reached for Bailey's pocket and pulled out the detective's car keys. He peered round the corner and saw the killer's other hand turn the latch. The door swung open as Wallace got to his feet and started sprinting.

He burst into the canteen to be greeted by two orderlies and a security guard running toward him.

"Get out!" Wallace yelled.

The orderlies barely had time to exchange skeptical looks before the killer ran into the canteen and fired off two shots. One of the orderlies went down. Wallace passed the other two shocked men and raced for the exit. He heard gunshots behind him, but didn't turn to see what was happening. He made it to the security door that separated the canteen from the administration block and ran into another guard. He grabbed the man and dragged him back through the door, which was swinging closed.

"Hey!" the guard yelled.

"There's a guy with a gun!" Wallace shouted in reply.

Wallace felt the man's resistance abruptly stop and when he turned, he saw why: the masked killer was running up the corridor behind them. One hand held a pistol, the other hung limply by his side.

The guard started running with Wallace and the two of them rounded the corner by the dispensary. They raced up the corridor toward the final security door that led to the main lobby. The guard had his key card in hand. Wallace heard another crack and there was a tumble of arms and legs beside him. The key card flew forward and landed by the door. Wallace looked down at the fallen guard, who was splayed in a rag-doll pose, a gaping wound in the back of his skull. Wallace heard a couple of shots as he lunged for the key card. Wood splintered as bullets struck the door. He swiped the card and the reader flashed green. He felt something sear his arm, but he ignored the screaming pain, barreled into the door, and sprinted across the lobby.

Wallace prayed that his luck would hold. He aimed for the edge of one of the pieces of plywood that covered the lobby window frame and charged it with his shoulder. He hit the temporary covering at full speed and felt satisfyingly out of control as it came away from the frame. There was a splintering sound and crushing pain, and Wallace found himself outside the building. He scanned the parking lot and saw Bailey's car. As he sprinted toward it Wallace looked behind him and, through the hole in the plywood, saw the killer taking careful aim. Wallace suddenly changed direction and rolled as the crack of gunfire sounded across the parking lot.

He got to his feet and pressed the central locking button. He yanked open the driver's door, fumbled the key into the ignition, and turned it. The starter screamed as Wallace held it longer than necessary, but he didn't care; he slammed into reverse and hit the accelerator. A bullet shattered the rear window and pierced a hole in the windshield, just to the left of Wallace. He thumped the gearshift into first and stomped on the accelerator. The car roared forward, raced down the drive, smashed through the hospital gate, and swung onto the main road. Behind him, Wallace could see distant blue flashing lights. He held his foot on the accelerator for a couple of blocks, and kept checking his rearview mirror. He saw two police cars turn into the grounds of the Maybury Hospital, but he wasn't being followed. Satisfied that he was safe, he slowed down and tried to drive like a man who wasn't running for his life.

The adrenaline that surged through his veins dissipated and was replaced by a numb emptiness. He looked at his right arm and saw a bleeding gash where a bullet had taken a slice out of him just below the shoulder. Wallace felt the car oscillating and realized it was because he was shaking so violently. He pulled into a bus stop and looked in the mirror, desperately willing himself to keep it together. The sight of his reflection, the memory of all the men he'd seen killed, and the knowledge that his ordeal was far from finished overwhelmed him, and Wallace broke down. He opened the door and staggered from the vehicle. He only made it two steps before he vomited by the back wheel. His body heaved violently as though trying to expunge the events he'd just experienced. Satisfied that he had purged himself, Wallace stood upright, only to be greeted by the sight of a night bus trying to pull into the stop. The driver gestured angrily and sounded the horn. Feeling totally drained, Wallace just waved weakly, climbed back into Bailey's car, and drove into the night.

18

Connie rolled over to pick up her ringing phone, her eyes trying to focus as her brain was shocked into consciousness. The display showed an unknown number. It also showed 05:08, an uncivilized time for any conversation. "Hello," she answered.

"Connie, are you okay?" Wallace asked, his voice alive with palpable concern.

"I'm fine. Where are you? What's going on?"

"He came," Wallace told her. "They're all dead."

Connie heard the panic in Wallace's voice as his words ran into one another.

"Are you sure you're okay?" he asked.

"I'm fine," she replied emphatically. "Where are you?"

He didn't reply.

"Are you okay?"

"I don't know what to do," Wallace responded weakly.

"Let me come and get you," Connie suggested. "We can go to the police."

"It's too dangerous," Wallace insisted. "I don't know who to trust."

"You can trust me, John."

The line went silent.

"I know," Wallace replied finally.

"Let's meet somewhere," Connie said. "Somewhere public and safe. The Millennium Bridge, opposite Tate Modern."

There was a moment's pause.

"When?" Wallace asked finally.

"As soon as you can get there," she said. "I'm leaving now."

"Okay," Wallace conceded.

"I love you, John," Connie said.

"I love you, too." Wallace's voice quivered with emotion.

Connie hung up and hurriedly climbed out of bed.

Wallace replaced the receiver and exited the glass coffin that encased the pay phone. He looked up and down the quiet street and couldn't see any obvious signs of danger. Bailey's car was parked on the other side of Station Road in a pay-and-display space. The Vauxhall was pointed toward Norwood Junction train station. The trains weren't running yet, but Wallace knew he'd be a fool to continue driving Bailey's car. The police, the killer—everyone would be looking for it. He crossed the street, which was lined with small shops, real estate agents, and a taxi office.

He began his preparations to abandon the car by opening the trunk. Inside was a carryall that contained a first aid kit, a flashlight, a telescopic baton, and a change of clothes. Bailey was about the same size, so Wallace stripped out of his Maybury pajamas and slipped on a pair of jeans. He used the first aid kit to treat the deep gash the bullet had cut into his arm, before putting on a hooded top and a pair of sneakers. He pushed his pajamas into the carryall, slung it over his good shoulder, and slammed the trunk shut. He moved on to the inside of the car and first explored the back, where he found a midlength black coat on the rear seat. He checked the pockets and found half a packet of gum. He draped the coat over the carryall and moved on to the front. Some antibacterial gel, an ice scraper, and some old pay-and-display parking receipts in the side pockets.

Wallace opened the glove compartment, looking for the cash he'd secreted there two days earlier. He was greeted by the sight of a manila folder that had been squashed into the small space. The folder was marked "Huvane Logs." He opened it and found a thick sheaf of documents. The top sheet had a scrawled name and phone number: *Christine Ash, 212 555 3781.* The other sheets were covered with website addresses and dates. Some of the entries had been circled, and Wallace recognized a name—Kye Walters, the name Bailey had said as he lay dying. He put the folder in the carryall and reached under the owner's manual for the bundle of cash. He thrust the money into his jeans pocket, tossed Bailey's keys on the front seat, and slammed the door. He walked away from the car feeling like a tomb robber, but consoled himself with the thought that Bailey wouldn't be needing any of this stuff. Wallace had no idea what the future held and had to scavenge whatever he could lay his hands on.

He walked into the taxi office and approached the gray-faced controller sitting in a small cave behind a glass window.

"Where to?" the controller's voice crackled from a speaker at the side of the window.

"Clapham Junction," Wallace said into the microphone.

"Two minutes," the controller replied.

"I'll be outside," Wallace told the sick-looking man. If there was trouble he did not want to be cornered in the tiny space of the cab office.

Connie had been standing on the narrow bridge for over four hours. She kept scanning the oncoming pedestrians in both directions. As Monday morning wore on, the crowds of people grew thicker and morphed from individual commuters to groups of tourists. The squat mass of Tate Modern dominated the south bank of the river, and to the north, in between the gleaming glass of the riverside office blocks, she could see the distinctive dome of St. Paul's Cathedral. She had called in sick, resolving to spend the day on the bridge waiting for Wallace. The Maybury killings had made the news and Connie kept checking her phone for BBC London's latest reports. To her dismay, police were seeking escaped inmate John Wallace in connection with the deaths.

At ten forty-five, she saw Wallace approaching from the north. He was wearing a blue hooded top, jeans, and sneakers without any socks. He had a green oblong bag slung over his shoulder. But the thing that stood out most was his face; underneath fresh wounds, he looked haunted. Anxiety and fatigue marked him, and if it hadn't been for his hood, every single person he passed would have read the signal loud and clear: here was a man in deep trouble. Connie wanted to run to him, but she couldn't risk drawing unnecessary attention, so she walked slowly in his direction. She put her arms around him and felt tears spring as she squeezed him close to her.

"John, I'm sorry," she began.

"I know," Wallace said, pulling away from her. He looked up and down the bridge, his eyes cutting through the crowd, searching for danger. "So am I."

"The police are looking for you," Connie said. "It's all over the news."

"We need to find somewhere safe."

"My place?" Connie suggested.

Wallace shook his head. "Detective Bailey probably told his superiors where he found me. We've got to go somewhere else."

Somewhere else was a seedy hotel in Bayswater. They'd taken a taxi to Paddington and then walked the back streets of West London until they found somewhere that looked desperate enough to accept cash. The receptionist, a thin man of Middle Eastern origin, had not even bothered asking for identification. The wry smile he gave when Wallace filled in the registration card with the names Mr. and Mrs. Turner, suggested that he suspected Connie was hired pleasure. Wallace peeled a hundred pounds from his shrinking supply of cash, and the receptionist handed him a key and directed them to their accommodation on the third floor of the white stucco building.

The room was foul. The threadbare paisley carpet looked like it had been laid in the 1980s and was so dirty that it was hard to distinguish pattern from stains. Cracked, peeling paint flaked from the frame that lined the lone dirty window. Filthy green wallpaper was marked with ancient damp stains. Wallace checked the tiny bathroom. The tiles were chipped and the grout covered in black mold. The heavy toilet and sink were ringed by rusty limescale. Farther into the small room lay a tiny double bed that sagged in the middle. It was covered by a cheap purple spread, stained and ragged. Wallace put the carryall down on the rickety desk and slumped into a creaking wooden chair. He ran his hands through his hair. Connie walked over and touched his shoulder lovingly. Wallace took her hand for a moment and then released it, feeling utterly defeated.

"What happened?" she asked as she sat on the edge of the bed.

"I woke up and he was in my cell. I don't know if the doctor prescribed something too strong or if the killer was somehow able to dose me, but I never even heard him come in. If I hadn't come round . . ." Wallace trailed off. "Detective Bailey had given me a stun gun, so I used it. It gave me time to escape, but I couldn't lock the door behind me, so I held the guy in my cell until the cops arrived. Bailey called me over and these two big policemen with guns went to my cell. The guy—the killer—he came out and attacked them. He went through them, grabbed one of the guns and killed them both. We all ran, but Detective Bailey and I were the only ones who made it. Then he was hit—twice."

Wallace broke down at the memory and his voice cracked as he continued, "I watched him die and—"

"He's not dead," Connie interrupted. "I've been listening to the news—Bailey's in a coma. They've got him in intensive care."

"But he . . ." Wallace trailed off in disbelief.

"He's alive," Connie said emphatically.

Wallace felt a wave of relief wash over him. "Bailey mentioned a name," he said, reaching for the carryall and pulling out the manila file. He tossed it to Connie. "I found this in his car. The name he's circled; that's the one he mentioned—Kye Walters."

Connie examined the folder and its contents as Wallace finished his story.

"After Bailey was shot, he told me to take his car. I ran. The guy killed at least another three people, but I made it out. I ditched the car at Norwood Junction. That's where I called you. I took a cab to Clapham, then a bus to Victoria, then I got the tube to Euston, then walked to Euston Square and took the tube to Moorgate—I'm sorry it took me so long, but I had to make sure I wasn't being followed."

"John, I'm so sorry," Connie said. "Are you okay?"

"I don't know," he replied, breaking down.

She stood up and embraced him. Wallace recoiled in pain.

"What?" Connie asked with concern.

"I was hit," he explained, indicating his arm.

"Let me see," she instructed.

Wallace sat on the edge of the bed while Connie applied a fresh bandage to his wound.

"It's stopped bleeding," she told him.

"I'm sorry I got you into this," he said sadly.

"It's going to be okay," she assured him.

With the dressing complete, Connie backed away and gave Wallace space to put his shirt back on. While he straightened himself out, she examined the folder he'd found in Bailey's car.

"These are Stewart Huvane's server logs. They show the websites he visited in the weeks before he was killed. The ones that have been circled all have the same name in the domain address: Kye Walters."

Connie produced her phone and typed one of the addresses into the browser. Wallace crossed the room and studied the folder. After a few moments, Connie's phone displayed an article from a local news site, the *Cold Spring Bulletin*. The article was accompanied by a photograph of a smiling teenage boy. The caption beneath identified him as Kye Walters. Connie scrolled down and she and Wallace read the headline: "Suicide Shocks Cold Spring. Local Teen Selling Drugs Online."

"It says he was selling crystal meth on the Satin Road. It's an illicit online marketplace, a successor to the Silk Road," Connie summarized as she scanned the article. "His mum found him hanging in his bedroom. His note, posted to Facebook, said he couldn't live with the shame of his drug dealing any longer."

"Another suicide. Another set of shocking revelations," Wallace mused. "No wonder Bailey was interested in this."

"Any idea what this number is?" Connie asked, signaling the scrawled digits on the top sheet.

Wallace shook his head.

"Let's try it," Connie suggested. "It's American. Two-one-two area code is New York." She tapped the number into her phone.

They waited as the call connected. Wallace could hear the faint sound of someone speaking.

"Voice mail," Connie explained. "'You have reached Special Agent Christine Ash of the FBI, please leave a message,' et cetera. Should I leave one?"

Wallace shook his head. "Not until we know who to trust," he said, and Connie hung up. "Did you take my laptop to your friend?"

She nodded. "Let me try him." She tapped in a number and the call rang out to voice mail. "Riley, it's Connie. Let me know how you're getting on with that machine. I really need an answer." She hung up and looked at Wallace. "He keeps his own time," she said apologetically. "What do you want to do now?"

"Detective Bailey mentioned something else; the Salamander Monkey Puzzle," Wallace said.

Connie typed the words into her phone and ran a Google search. Her phone displayed a set of random results, and she scrolled down. "I can't see anything with an obvious connection," she observed. "But there is a pub called the Monkey Puzzle in Paddington. Might have been his local. It's not too far from here."

Wallace nodded slowly. "Let's check it out," he said.

"Riley, it's Connie. Let me know how you're getting on with that machine. I really need an answer." Riley heard the words replayed by his voice mail. Favors were a pain in the bloody arse, he thought to himself.

He rolled out of bed and bent over to pick up the boxer shorts he'd been wearing the previous day—they looked clean enough. He slipped them on and walked over to the living area. The laptop bag was lying on the small couch. He sat next to it and took the machine out. A Dell; the mark of someone with no imagination. He switched on the laptop and interrupted the start-up process to cut into the boot menu. He rose with a sigh and carried the computer to his server room, where he input a six-digit code on the keypad and heard the room exhale as the pressurized door opened. He pulled it wide, and, as he stepped into the cooler environment, goose bumps

formed on his skin and his nipples hardened. Riley loved feeling the
cold on his body. He shut the door behind him and heard the hiss of
the pneumatic seal pressurizing.

He walked into the center of the server room, where his worksta-
tion was concealed by the servers that were humming and whirring
all around him: his little army of drones mining the world for salable information. He placed the laptop on his neatly organized metal
mesh desk and reached into one of the cubbyholes on the shelf above.
He pulled out a USB drive and connected it to one of the ports on
the machine. A green light on the drive flashed and then flickered as
one of his custom-made cracking programs started working on the
laptop. Riley tapped the desk with his fingertips. He cycled through a
dozen iterations before the laptop screen changed color and the Windows start menu came to life. His cracking program had bypassed
the Windows password and he now had full administrator access to
the machine.

Riley brought up the DOS command prompt and pulled up the
system registry. He looked at the pattern of behavior and saw that
the machine had not been active for over a month. There was nothing
unusual in the registry: browser, e-mail, word processing programs
activated by the user, with a bunch of background processes running
automatically on start-up. Riley reached into another cubbyhole and
produced a large freestanding hard drive marked "Shadow Stalker."
He plugged the USB 3.0 cable into one of the Dell's ports and opened
the file window, which displayed a single executable file called Shadow
Stalker. Riley double-clicked it, and a black DOS-like window opened,
only this one instantly began cycling through hundreds of thousands
of files on the laptop. Riley left his program to do its work and exited
the server room. It was coming up to lunchtime and he had a feeling
it was Monday. If he got dressed, there was a chance he'd catch the
blonde from the tenth floor buying her tuna, sweet corn, and mayonnaise ciabatta at the sandwich bar across the street.

19

The weak November sun lit London's busy streets as Wallace and Connie navigated the swarm of pedestrians that moved in every direction around Paddington Station. Wallace wore his hood up, concealing his face from all but the most determined observers. He and Connie held hands and could have passed for any carefree couple.

"Was Detective Bailey based around here?" Connie asked.

Wallace nodded toward Edgware Road. "Paddington Green Station," he replied. "This was his patch."

"Salamander could be a person," Connie observed.

Wallace nodded. He'd thought as much when Connie had discovered the pub.

Connie's phone directed them off Praed Street. They cut along Norfolk Street, which was lined with three-story Georgian townhouses that had been converted into hotels, which looked as though they might be cheaper than the one Connie and Wallace were staying in. Left onto Sussex Gardens and they found the Monkey Puzzle on the corner of the next block. The beer garden was concealed by an ivy-covered wall, and the pub itself was situated at the base of a low-rise, brown-brick apartment building. It looked like the sort of residence local councils threw up all over Britain in the early 1980s. Connie and Wallace climbed a small flight of tiled steps that led up to a gate, but it was locked, so they continued down Southwick Street to the pub's main entrance. A green sign above the door identified the pub, and one beside the door informed passersby that the

Monkey Puzzle was the home of good food and real ales. Large picture windows revealed little; the interior looked dark and gloomy.

They entered a surprisingly traditional pub: the floor was laid with a wild paisley carpet; the furniture was all deep browns and reds; and stained-glass dividers separated sections of the lounge and threw a kaleidoscope of light about the place. The only mark of modernity was the color of the walls—a brilliant white, which helped brighten the place. There were a handful of customers in the pub and a few in the beer garden; midafternoon on a Monday was hardly peak drinking time.

"How do we do this?" Connie asked quietly.

Wallace looked over at the bar. A tall, tattooed man with a shaven head stood behind it. He leaned against one of the drinks coolers and stared into the middle distance. As Wallace approached, he focused with practiced hospitality.

"What can I get you?"

"Two Cokes," Wallace replied.

"Ice and lemon?" the barman queried as he reached for the glasses.

"Yes," Wallace said. As the barman prepared the drinks, he continued, "I'm looking for a guy called Salamander?"

The barman glanced up at Wallace, who was sure he saw a flicker of recognition, but shook his head. "Never heard of him, mate," he replied, pushing the brimming glasses onto the bar. "That'll be four-forty."

Wallace handed over a five-pound note and passed Connie her drink.

"A mutual friend suggested we should talk to him," Connie tried.

The barman shook his head again and handed Wallace his change. "Sorry," he said. "Wish I could help you," he added as he backed away from them and returned to his position by the fridge.

Connie sipped her drink. "What now?" she asked.

Wallace was at a loss.

"Let's go back to the hotel," she suggested. "I'll try Riley again."

Wallace looked around in frustration and caught the eye of a man who was studying him from across the bar. The man had jet-black hair that sat atop the jowly, pasty face of an alcoholic. His pale, pock-marked skin was scarred so badly that it was difficult to guess his age, but the black beady eyes that gazed at Wallace suggested the man had lived an eternity.

"We need to get out of here. I think that guy just recognized me," Wallace said quietly. "Finish your drink."

Connie glanced at the scarred man and immediately reverted to Wallace. "He's coming over," she said.

Wallace looked in the man's direction and saw him lumbering toward them. He wasn't tall, maybe five feet seven, but he was broad and his squat neck and wide shoulders reminded Wallace of a bull. "Let's go," he said, taking hold of Connie's hand, but he was too late; the Scarred Man had positioned himself between them and the exit, and was now closing in. "Get ready to run," Wallace advised as he prepared himself to fight.

The Scarred Man drew close. "You're too fucking dumb to be cops," he observed, looking them up and down derisively. "What d'ya want with Salamander?"

"A friend sent us," Wallace replied.

"Who?"

"Detective Sergeant Bailey."

The Scarred Man thought for a moment. "Bailey?" he asked.

Connie smiled and nodded.

"Come back tonight," the Scarred Man instructed.

"Do you know Salamander?" Wallace asked.

"Don't be a fucking retard all ya life," the Scarred Man advised with more than a hint of aggression.

"Let's go," Wallace said to Connie. He took hold of her arm, pulled her gently toward the door, and led her into the hazy sunlight.

"What time is tonight?" Connie asked, as she pulled her jacket tight in an attempt to fend off the cold air that bit her neck.

Wallace smiled nervously. "I have no idea," he said. "But I'm not going back in there to ask for an appointment. Come on."

"Where to?"

"The hotel," Wallace said. "Let's see if we can get hold of your friend."

Riley Cotton strolled along Victoria Street with the satisfied gait of a man who'd spent the afternoon in the company of two fine, fun-filled Australians. He'd seen the blonde in the sandwich bar. Some might call it stalking, but Riley regarded it as attentiveness. He knew what sandwich she had on which day, he noticed when she added anything new to her wardrobe, and he noted her weight loss and occasional weight gain. The blonde had looked particularly fine that afternoon; she'd been wearing a pair of skin-tight jeans and a blue sweater that clung to her chest like an old friend. Riley had often fantasized about the blonde, but he still didn't know her name. He choked every time he got within ten feet of her, and today was no exception. His head brimmed with erotic images of the two of them together, her inno-cent face twisted in the throes of lust. But no matter how tempting the possibility, Riley could never work up the courage to approach her. Instead, as she had done so many times, the blonde excited pas-sions that had to be satisfied by others, so Riley had shuffled out of the sandwich bar and strolled off toward the Churchill Gardens housing development.

Most of the redbrick council development was now in private hands, and flats that had once been available to the poor and helpless were now bought and sold for hundreds of thousands of pounds. Riley had found the Australians through an online escort agency. Tara and Michelle—he wasn't sure those were their real names—charged him three hundred an hour, and unlike the blonde, the two profes-sionals elicited no inhibition. Tara was a tanned brunette with an athletic body and a gorgeous smile. Michelle was a fake blonde. She stood a couple of inches shorter than Tara, at about five feet six, and had fuller curves. As a customer, Riley suffered from none of the shyness of a lover, and he was most forthright in instructing the girls what to do to him and each other. Their two-bedroom, second-floor flat became his domain and he lived out his wildest sexual fantasies for three hours until he left, almost a thousand pounds lighter.

It was quarter to five when Riley entered his building. The sun had dropped below the rooftops and lazy fingers of light were reaching through the gaps between buildings, casting the world in a hazy red glow.

"Afternoon, Vimal," Riley said to the short Indian security guard behind the front desk.

"You're looking happy, Mister C," Vimal observed impishly. "Good trip down under?"

"You know how it is," Riley replied. He had scored some grass from Vimal a few times and had once pointed him in the direction of the Australians in the smoke-fueled bonhomie of a buy.

"I do, Mister C, I do," Vimal leered.

Riley crossed the lobby and stepped into the waiting elevator, hit the button for the eighteenth floor, and turned to study himself in the mirror. His expensive black suit and fitted shirt made his disheveled appearance look roguishly glamorous. His tousled hair, his stubble, and his bloodshot eyes were all offset by the quality of his tailoring. No wonder the Australians always said he was their favorite client. When the elevator doors opened, Riley walked across the eighteenth-floor lobby to the double doors and tapped his four-digit code into the keypad. The doors buzzed, and Riley pushed one open, triggering the alarm system, which started squawking and continued making the nagging sound until Riley fed the deactivation code into the keypad. The large room fell silent, save for the distant, quiet murmur of the server room cooling system. Outside, Riley could hear the muffled sound of London traffic as rush hour began in earnest. The sun had fallen quickly and the city was starting to sparkle with flecks of artificial light.

Riley headed over to the server room, hoping that his hack had yielded information that would conclude his favor for Connie. He entered his security code and stepped through the pressurized door. As he rounded the corner, he was dismayed to see a set of warning windows open on his main terminal. He hurried to his desk and pulled out the retractable metal shelf that held his master keyboard and tablet. The first window informed him that a device was

attempting to access the Wi-Fi network. Riley picked up the tablet
stylus and moved the window to reveal that the main terminal had
identified another attempt. Beneath that window was another. And
another. And another. Riley felt his stomach tie itself into a knot as
he checked the machine Connie had given him. His hack had completed its search of deleted files and discovered that someone had
altered the system registry. There were a number of entries relating
to a Facebook domain that had been removed. More worrying was
the concealed program that ran on start-up and activated a simple
ping that tried to access local Wi-Fi.

Riley switched back to his main terminal and brought up his Wi-
Fi system. He had layer upon layer of protection and used encryp-
tion systems that were beyond those used by the most secure banks.
There was no way Connie's laptop could have accessed his network,
and when he checked his network connections, the new laptop
wasn't listed there. Ever paranoid, Riley went back to the notification
windows and checked their properties. The last alert had happened
at three p.m. It made no sense for the attempts to have suddenly
stopped. Riley used the main terminal to bring up his Wi-Fi network
and logged into the traffic system to look at the data packets being
transferred. He sorted the packets by machine tag, and there, to his
horror, he saw a machine identifier he did not recognize.

He looked down at Connie's laptop with terrible realization.
Someone had installed an automated program to hack the nearest
Wi-Fi network whenever the machine was powered up. Someone
had concealed the existence of the hack from both the host machine
and the network. Riley's machine had only logged the attempts
because he was a paranoid nut who knew more about computers
than anyone he'd ever met. But whoever did this probably knew
more than him, which meant NSA or someone even more dangerous. Either equated to big trouble, so Riley picked up the laptop
and dropped it on the floor. He stood up, lifted his chair and thumped
the heavy metal wheels onto the device until it was dead. He checked
his Wi-Fi log and saw that the alien data packets had stopped. If the
hard drive wasn't too badly damaged, he could boot the disk in a

safe environment and try to reverse-engineer the program. He had no idea what information was being sent—but a program that could bypass his security and conceal itself during operation would be tremendously valuable.

As Riley stooped to pick through the debris, he heard the hiss of the pressurized door. Puzzled by the sound, he stepped forward only to be greeted by the terrifying sight of a masked man rounding the bank of servers. The large, muscular figure was clad in synthetic body armor and wore a mask that covered his mouth and nose, with a pair of opaque goggles above that. The tails of a long black coat trailed behind the fearsome figure. Riley guessed that this man, or an associate, was responsible for the Wi-Fi hack and that the small data packets were simple identifiers to enable the programmer to locate the originating machine. It was an elegantly simple, highly sophisticated bugging program.

"I don't—" Riley began. He stopped talking as the masked man raised a gloved hand to reveal a pistol.

"Please," Riley begged, but the masked man ignored him. He pulled the trigger and the gun fired a dart that hit Riley square in the chest. Riley felt a sudden heaviness permeate his body. He tried to turn toward his desk, but his legs failed him, and his eyes rolled back in his head moments before he hit the floor with a heavy thud.

20

The gentle hum of the cooling fans roused Riley. His eyes were polluted with the grit of a thousand hangovers. His head felt raw and it seemed as though he could feel his brain grating against the inner lining of his skull. Every muscle in his body ached and his testicles and groin felt swollen and tender. His body had reacted badly to whatever substance had knocked him out. He tried to focus on the blur of lights and colors. He shook his head slowly, provoking a sudden stab of pain in both temples, which made him wince and clench his eyes tightly shut. He tried to raise his hands, but they were restrained. When he opened his eyes and looked down, his predicament slowly came into focus.

He was bound to his chair, his arms and legs tied with electrical cord, and, when he looked up, he could see a figure moving between the server racks. The main lights were off, so the armored figure was faintly illuminated by the blue and orange server LEDs, his shadow cast on Riley's precious machines. Riley turned his head very slowly, wary of drawing attention to himself. His eyes stopped at his desk, and his mobile phone. He looked down at his legs. Straining, he could just about push them to either side of the struts that kept the chair on its wheels. Articulating his ankles allowed him to apply pressure with his toes and nudge himself slowly toward the desk. He was about three feet away and each movement brought him an inch closer. Riley focused on the phone and with each push rotated his body so that he would be in the best possible position to reach it. The desk was almost level with his arms; the biggest challenge was going to be the fact that the phone was about a foot or so away from the edge of the desk.

"Riley Cotton," a gravelly voice said softly. Riley stopped and turned to see the masked man standing behind him. "Where is John Wallace?"

The fearsome figure gestured toward the broken laptop on Riley's desk. Riley's mind whirred like the drives of the servers that surrounded him. He tried to compute the best way to handle his assailant and searched for anything that might give him an advantage. Nothing physical; the man was covered in dark body armor. His opaque goggles and mask betrayed nothing of his face. The accent was almost impossible to place; just an Anytown mid-Atlantic twang.

"I don't know," Riley answered honestly. "A friend brought it in. She wanted me to find out if someone had tampered with it." He guessed that he'd found the person responsible for the locator embedded in the machine—or rather, that person had found him. Riley shuddered as the masked man approached, but the figure continued on toward his desk and picked up his precious phone.

"Name?" the man asked.

"Constance Jones," Riley replied. "My passcode is—"

But the mask cut him off, "I know your code. I know everything about you, Riley."

The words cut into Riley with more violence than any pain caused by the aftereffects of the tranquilizer. Information was his business, and his clients paid huge sums for the knowledge he gleaned from computers around the world, but they paid even more to ensure that their identities remained private. Riley had no doubt that the man in front of him could overcome any of his security measures, and he realized that his entire operation was exposed.

"I have money," he offered.

"So do I," the mask replied, as he scrolled through the contact list on Riley's phone. "Tell her the truth. Tell her you discovered evidence of tampering. Someone altered John Wallace's Facebook page, then deleted all the changes. Tell her to come. Tell her to bring her friend."

Riley knew better than to argue. This well-equipped, highly trained man would get what he wanted, so why risk making him angry with false bravery? He smelled a strong synthetic aroma as the man drew close. It was coming from the man's body armor. Riley felt his phone pressed up against his ear and heard the familiar sound of ringing at the other end.

"Hello?" Connie said. "Riley? Now's not a good time. Can I call you back?"

Riley could hear the hubbub of a crowd so loud that it almost drowned out Connie's words. She was somewhere busy; an airport or train station.

"I found something," Riley replied, raising his voice. "The machine has been tampered with. Someone made changes to John Wallace's Facebook page. I found a load of stuff I need to show you."

There was a pause, and all Riley could hear was the sound of the crowd. "Is he with you?" he asked. "You need to bring him. You need to—" He broke off when he felt the sudden pressure of pain. The masked man was digging his gloved fingers into the flesh beneath Riley's neck. Riley realized that he was coming on too strong. He looked up apologetically. The mask betrayed no emotion, but the talons loosened their grip and the pain subsided.

"I'm in the middle of something right now," Connie replied. "I'll come over later. Pay you a little midnight visit."

"Sounds good," Riley said. "I'll see you later." He looked up at the mask and nodded, and his captor hung up. "She's coming," Riley told the man. "Later."

The mask looked down at him. "Then we have time to talk," he said. "You're going to tell me everything you know about Constance Jones and her friend John Wallace."

"That was weird," Connie observed as she skipped to catch up with Wallace.

They were in front of Paddington Station on their way back to the Monkey Puzzle, and the late-evening crowds swirled around them, with more than one traveler snarling at their cardinal sin of pausing in the middle of a busy London thoroughfare.

"What?" Wallace asked.

"Riley says he's found something," Connie replied. "But he was being very un-Riley. Normally he'd drag me through a round of questioning to make me feel small and stupid and then rub my face in his vastly superior intellect. He didn't even take the bait when I said I was coming over for a midnight visit. He'd always have a smutty reply for a remark like that."

Wallace's face clouded over. "You think he was scared?"

"Maybe," Connie replied. "It's hard to tell. It's so noisy here."

"Let's do this and then figure out how we handle Riley," Wallace suggested.

Connie nodded, and the two of them set off for the Monkey Puzzle.

It was eight fifteen and the streets were thronging with Londoners freed from their daily toil. Crowds gathered outside pubs and the chill November air made it difficult to tell the hard-core smokers apart from the loyal friends keeping them company in the vapor-inducing cold.

The Monkey Puzzle cast a golden glow into the night. From a distance, the soft light that spilled from the windows offered an inviting contrast to the harsh yellow streetlights that surrounded the building. As they approached, Connie and Wallace saw that the pub was packed. They entered and pushed their way through the crowd, which was a real slice of London; laborers in their overalls stood in small groups alongside suited office workers. Connie and Wallace caught the edges of conversations as they moved toward the bar: the relentless rise of London property values; the lameness of *Doctor Who*; whether the hottie in the corner was up for it.

When they reached the bar, Wallace saw three staff, all women. The barman who had served them earlier was nowhere to be seen. He scanned the crowded room and caught sight of a familiar, scarred face standing near a set of carpeted stairs, above which hung a sign that read "Saloon Bar." The Scarred Man nodded at Wallace.

"Come on," Wallace instructed Connie. They moved slowly round the bar, forcing their way into spaces that didn't exist. After a minute, Wallace found himself level with the scarred face. The black, narrow eyes looked glassy, but the man didn't have a drink in his hand. Maybe the glazed effect was permanent?

"Keep an eye," the Scarred Man said to a skinny, rat-faced youth who stood on the other side of the staircase. The pockmarked face turned to Wallace and said, "Come on."

The Scarred Man started up the stairs and Wallace and Connie followed. As they topped the first flight and turned to climb the second, Wallace saw that the rat-faced youth had moved and was now standing in the middle of the staircase, blocking the path of anyone foolish enough to attempt the climb.

At the top of the second flight of stairs stood one of the largest men Wallace had ever seen. At least six feet eight, it wasn't just the man's formidable height that struck Wallace; standing square on the top step, he eclipsed whatever lay behind him. The man was at least three feet wide. A tattoo of a red skull covered one side of a bulbous shaven head, which protruded from a pale-blue hooded Adidas top. The matching blue tracksuit bottoms and navy sneakers made Wallace think the man had modeled himself on a sky god whose mission was to guard the heavens. In truth, given his size, the guy probably had limited wardrobe choices. As the Scarred Man neared the top of the stairs, Red Skull stood to one side, revealing a stained-glass door behind him. A brass plaque bore the words "Saloon Bar." The Scarred Man pushed the door open, and Wallace and Connie passed through the shadow of the giant and followed him inside.

The saloon bar was a mirror image of the ground floor, except for the fact that it was almost empty. The tattooed barman who had been downstairs on their earlier visit leaned against the counter and watched Wallace and Connie as they entered. Seated at the far end of the room, next to one of the windows that overlooked the beer garden, was a thin man with short black hair and dark brown skin. Wallace guessed he was of Indian or Pakistani descent and put his age somewhere in his late twenties. The man wore dark-blue jeans, weathered brown boots, and a black hooded top. He typed busily on his iPhone and didn't give Wallace or Connie a scrap of attention.

The Scarred Man turned on Wallace and grabbed his shoulders, forcing him to a halt. Wallace felt huge, powerful hands lift his arms and turned to see Red Skull holding him for a search. The Scarred Man frisked Wallace, paying particular attention to his legs and torso. Satisfied there was no threat, the two men moved on to Connie. Wallace thought she looked tiny against the giant. The Scarred Man showed no embarrassment at laying his hands on a strange woman and searched her with the same detached efficiency Wallace had experienced. Satisfied that Connie also posed no danger, the Scarred Man led them forward.

"Come on," he instructed.

Wallace and Connie followed him toward the windows, where the man Wallace assumed was Salamander sat, engrossed in his phone.

"Sal, these are the guys," the Scarred Man said, confirming their host's identity before backing away to join Red Skull by the bar, where the barman served them both: a pint for the giant, a large measure of Scotch for him.

Salamander still hadn't looked up.

"Detective Sergeant Bailey sent us," Wallace tried.

Salamander's only response was to hold up the index finger of his left hand in a dismissive gesture that signaled patience. Wallace looked at Connie, who shook her head ever so slightly.

Finally, Salamander looked up. Unlike the dull, dead eyes of his scarred associate, his brown eyes betrayed warmth and intelligence, which meant he was probably a lot more dangerous. "Haybale sent ya?" he asked. "But he didn't come himself, which means ya shady."

"He's in hospital," Wallace said flatly. "In a coma."

Salamander's eyes narrowed as he absorbed the statement, and Wallace got the sense that he was trying to gauge the honesty of the man he'd only just met.

"How?" Salamander asked.

"Shot," Wallace replied. "Trying to save me. He told me to find you."

"Was it that gunplay at the nuthouse?" Salamander inquired. Wallace nodded.

"I heard about that, but I had no idea Haybale was caught up in it. Fuck." Salamander shook his head and looked down at the ground, but there was no hiding the fact that the news of Bailey's shooting had affected him deeply. "Who was the shooter?"

"I don't know. He wears a mask. He's killed at least six people now," Wallace replied.

"We have no idea why," Connie added.

Salamander looked at Connie as though noticing her for the first time.

"Are you a friend of Detective Sergeant Bailey?" she asked.

"Used to be, back in the day. Runnin' round Streatham like a couple of fool kids," Salamander added. "Before he became a cop. We catch each other now and then, but it's tough. Let's just say we ain't got the same interests. But he's still my bro. Bring me a name and I'll take care of it."

"Okay," Wallace replied. He could feel Connie's dismayed eyes on him.

"John," she objected. "We need to go to the police."

Salamander sucked his teeth and shook his head. "Ya know how many times I've been in jail?" he asked. "None. Law's for fools. Ya don't go to the law, ya come to me. Bailey told you. He may be a cop, but he knows where ya get justice for something like this. Ya come to me, ya hear?"

"Okay," Wallace reiterated firmly, more for Connie's benefit than the man seated opposite him.

"You don't know why Bailey sent you here," Connie objected. She eyed Salamander. "Does the name Kye Walters mean anything to you?"

Salamander looked blank.

"Bailey had a file on him," Connie explained. "Maybe he thought you knew something about him. American boy. He killed himself."

"Never heard of him," Salamander replied. "Bailey sent ya here for one reason. Come back when ya got the name. Ted knows where

I am." He nodded toward the Scarred Man at the bar. "You can go now," he added quietly.

Wallace backed toward the door and gently pulled Connie with him. Her face was still twisted in surprise and disgust, but she had the sense not to say anything until they were at the bottom of the stairs. The rat-faced youth stood aside and let them launch themselves into the sea of customers.

"I know what you've been through," Connie chided as they pushed their way toward the door. "But this isn't the right way to handle it. You're not a killer."

Wallace turned suddenly. "Now isn't the time!" he exclaimed in louder tones than he would have liked. He felt nearby eyes fall upon him and sensed a lull in adjacent conversations. "Let's go!"

He grabbed Connie's hand and pulled her through the crowd. They swept through the pub, the people ahead of them parting more readily in the face of a discordant couple. When they spilled out through the doors into the cold night air, Wallace turned to find Connie welling up.

"It's murder, John," she protested as she wiped her eyes.

"It's self-defense," Wallace countered. "Besides, it's not our call. Bailey sent us to this guy, and he was police."

"He'd just been shot!" Connie yelled. "You have no idea what he was thinking!"

"Let's get the name and then figure out what to do," Wallace suggested.

Connie looked into his eyes, searching for his true feelings.

"Whatever happens," Wallace assured her, "I don't want to lose you." He leaned down and kissed her, ignoring the dull ache of his collarbone and the more urgent pain of his shoulder wound as he pulled her close to him.

When they parted, Wallace saw that Connie was more at ease, and, as they turned toward the main road, she took out her phone and placed a call to Riley.

21

Summarizing his relationship with Connie had been a brief affair. Riley had told the masked man that she had once been his boss on a dull programming project at the Suncert Corporation. He didn't know anything about John Wallace; Connie kept her private life very much to herself. When he had run out of facts, he even confessed his romantic longings for Connie, but his captor seemed less than interested and returned his attention to the servers, so Riley relaxed a little. Sensing he was out of any immediate danger, Riley was more concerned about what the masked man was doing to his machines.

When Connie's call came, the mask was deep in the coldest part of the server room, and it took him five rings to get back to Riley. The masked man picked up the phone and held it to Riley's ear.

"Connie," Riley said. "So, are you coming over or what?" He smiled up at his captor, making a demonstrable effort to cooperate.

"Give me the exec summary," Connie instructed.

"No can do," Riley replied. "There's a load of stuff I need to show you." For a few long moments he heard nothing but the sound of traffic passing at the other end of the line.

"Okay," Connie said at last. "We're on our way."

When the line went dead, Riley looked up at the masked man and said, "They're coming."

Wallace could see that Connie was troubled.

"Problem?" he asked, as she put the phone in her pocket.

"Riley's being strange," she replied.

"Do you trust him?" Wallace asked.

"Not really," Connie answered honestly.

"You think he could sell me out?"

"Selling information is what he does," she told him.

Wallace looked around for inspiration and his eyes drifted back to the pub. "Wait here," he said and started toward the building, but Connie caught his arm.

"No, John," she said. "I'm probably just being paranoid."

"We can't be paranoid enough. I'm going back in. See if Salamander will sell us some protection," Wallace assured her. "Nothing more."

"I'm coming with you," Connie said firmly as she followed him.

Wallace almost walked into Salamander as he came through the exit, closely trailed by Red Skull and the rat-faced kid. Red Skull grabbed Wallace and swung him against the wall.

"Let him go," Salamander ordered. "He's not dangerous. Are you?"

The question was directed at Wallace, who shook his head. Red Skull released his steel grip and took a couple of steps back.

"I want to buy protection," Wallace began. "I can give you a couple of hundred now."

Salamander smiled and looked at his associates, who couldn't help but smirk at Wallace's naivety. "Ya gonna be a gangster now?" he laughed.

"No," Wallace replied.

"Good," Salamander said. "Ya ain't got what it takes. What d'ya need protection from?"

"We're going to see someone who may know the name of the man who shot Bailey," Wallace said. "But he's not the most straightforward guy. He may have sold us out."

Salamander looked at the rat-faced kid. "Take Danny," he said, before adding with a chuckle, "no charge."

Wallace looked at the scrawny kid and then at the giant standing next to him.

Salamander must have sensed his disappointment at not getting Red Skull. "Danny's useful, mate," he advised. "He'll look after

ya." He started walking toward a black Mercedes that was parked
farther down Southwick Street. Clearly the subject was not up for
discussion.

A muscled black man with a shaved head leaned against the bon-
net, but he bustled into action and opened the rear passenger door as
Salamander approached. Red Skull smiled at Wallace before leaving
to join his boss in the back of the Merc.

"So, Danny, is it?" Wallace asked, turning toward the rat-faced
kid.

Danny eyed him sternly. "Everyone reckons that gorilla is hard,
but I could have him," he spat. "Come on then, show me where the
trouble is."

The cab ride lasted about twenty minutes. Nobody spoke, but,
as they traveled through the city, Wallace watched the thin young
villain opposite him. Danny sat with the exaggerated confidence
of an aspiring alpha male. Legs spread wide, perhaps an evolution-
ary throwback to maximize the possibility of a female catching
the scent of his musk. His left arm stretched along the top of the
backseat, his hand just behind Connie's head. Wallace felt foolish
and inadequate; not only because he'd allowed this young kid to
force him onto one of the rear-facing, fold-down jump seats, but
because he'd insisted on asking for protection in the first place.
The experiences of the past few weeks had stimulated his paranoia
to such an extent that he felt safer in the company of a fresh-faced
thug who looked as though he was hardly old enough to shave.
Danny would never have asked strangers for protection. His confidence might be exaggerated, but it was real. Wallace could see
the promise of violence in the kid's eyes. He offered none of the
outward threat of Red Skull, but Wallace could sense an unhinged
danger that probably was more vicious than anything the giant had
to offer. Wallace felt even more foolish when he contemplated that
they were going to see a computer hacker who used to work for an
insurance company. At best, Danny's skills would be redundant;
at worst, volatile.

Wallace was surprised when they arrived at number 68 Victoria Street. He'd expected a house or an apartment block, not a large steel-and-glass office building. He paid the cab driver and turned to see Connie knocking on the side doors. Inside, a security guard looked up at her with a flash of recognition and buzzed them in.

"Hello, again," the guard called across the lobby as they entered. "Just go straight up. He's expecting you."

The doors of the nearest elevator opened and Danny, Connie, and Wallace stepped inside. Connie pressed the button marked "18" and the doors closed.

"Seems pretty sleepy. What kinda trouble you expectin'?" Danny asked with a smile.

Wallace felt more foolish than ever.

"Zombie accountants," Danny smirked, rubbing salt in the wound.

"How many armed policemen did he kill?" Connie asked Wallace pointedly.

"Two," Wallace replied.

"Cops don't have these," Danny noted with more than a hint of satisfaction as he unzipped his hooded top to reveal a pair of machine pistols concealed in snugly fitted holsters.

Wallace and Connie stared at the guns, aghast.

"You said you needed protection," Danny remarked defensively.

The elevator slowed and then stopped. The doors opened and they stepped out onto the polished marble floor of the deserted lobby. Wallace and Danny followed Connie toward a set of double doors. She knocked on one and they waited.

When there was no response, Danny rapped harder. The lack of progress didn't sit well with him, and he reached for the door handle.

"It'll be locked," Connie advised, but the moment she said the words, the handle yielded at Danny's touch.

The three of them exchanged glances, and Danny produced one of his guns; a small pistol with an elongated ammunition clip. Wallace could see the letters "VBR" stamped on the barrel. Danny pushed the door open and led Wallace and Connie into the room.

Wallace was surprised to see that the vast open-plan space beyond had been converted into someone's home. A living area, kitchen, bedroom—all the things that might be found in any normal dwelling, all spread out over thousands of square feet of commercial office space. Beyond the incongruous domestic furnishings, the lights of London glittered beneath them.

"Someone lives here?" Danny asked in disbelief. "Must cost a fucking fortune."

"Where is he?" Wallace asked Connie, who shrugged.

"He's probably in the server room," she replied.

Danny started toward the bedroom area, which was separated from the rest of the room by a partition, while Wallace followed Connie toward a large glass-walled room full of computers that was located in the far corner of the building.

"This doesn't feel right," Wallace said. "We should leave."

Connie was undeterred. "Riley Cotton is an arsehole," she told him. "He used to take great pleasure playing practical jokes when he worked at Suncert. He once replaced the milk in every fridge in the building with wallpaper paste."

They neared the glass walls, and Connie peered through them.

"There he is," she said, pointing to a figure seated in the center of the room.

Wallace could only see segments of the man, his view obscured by thin computers mounted on floor-to-ceiling racks. Shins, a forearm, part of the back of the man's head. He was working at a computer.

Wallace jumped when Connie banged on the glass.

"Riley, you idiot," she said. "Open up." She pulled at the door handle, which gave way, releasing a gentle hiss of escaping air.

"Nobody's 'ome," Danny noted from the other side of the large space.

"He's over here," Wallace informed the young villain before following Connie into the server room.

Machines hummed and tiny lights blinked all around them as Connie led Wallace through the short maze of racks. When they rounded the corner that led to the heart of the server room, Connie stopped in her tracks. The color drained from her face, and when he followed her eyeline, Wallace realized why. Riley Cotton was dead. He was seated in an operator's chair, his head sagging back over the headrest. His hands lay in a wide pool of viscous blood that had coagulated over the mesh of his desk. Riley's arms had been slit vertically, from the wrists down to near the elbow. His skin was pale, bled of color, and his glassy eyes stared up at the ceiling as though searching for heavenly help that would never arrive.

"Oh, God!" Connie cried.

Movement. Something dark on the other side of the farthest server rack. Wallace recognized the armor and was stricken by terror. Unable to speak, he grabbed Connie's arm and pulled at it. Connie looked up at him and, seeing the panic on his face, followed his gaze to the black armor-clad figure rounding the corner. Terror gripped her, too, as she realized they were trapped with no way to escape.

22

Wallace saw a pistol in the man's gloved hand and his flesh froze. Their only way out was past this terrible figure—this murderer—who loomed like an ominous shadow no more than fifteen feet away. If he could just rush the man—

The gunshot shocked Wallace. There was no preamble. No sporting chance. No explanation. The loud crack unleashed a pain that would never end. Wallace knew the moment he looked round and saw Connie clutching her chest that the image would haunt him forever. Thick dark blood spread across her top. Another crack and Wallace saw Connie jerk backward as the bullet tore into her breast. She fell, her eyes wide with shock. She hit her head on the wheels of Riley's chair but did not pass out—the pain and anguish she felt were too powerful to be overcome by unconsciousness. Wallace dropped to his knees beside her. He was vaguely aware of movement behind him, but it didn't matter, none of it mattered; he would welcome death.

The world around him was leached of color and became faded and vague, and silence sucked away every sound, creating a terrible, startled stillness. Wallace's desperate mind scrabbled to cling to the agony of every hopeless moment, and the seconds turned to hours. As each instant became an unbearable eternity, he was unable to focus on anything other than Connie. He lifted her right hand and pushed it over her first wound, and then took her left hand and placed it gently over the second. Even as he went through the motions, Wallace knew there was nothing that could be done. Blood was soaking

Connie's top in steady waves—the first bullet had torn an artery. Her gray hands grew cold and weak as the life drained from her. Wallace couldn't see properly for tears. He wiped his eyes and looked down at Connie's beautiful face. Her soulful eyes brimmed with shock, and her lips shuddered with each gasping breath. He touched her cheek and, as his fingers left an ugly smear across her face, he realized that his hands were covered in blood.

Wallace tried to talk, but grief throttled him, choking his throat with such force that every breath became a shuddering effort. Connie's loving eyes looked up, pleading, searching for hope, but there was none. Wallace felt movement and realized that it was his hands, patting ineffectually at Connie's wounds. His head was light, his body disconnected, as his mind raged against a world that destroyed such innocent beauty. Anger turned to grief as he saw Connie weaken further, her eyes becoming distant as the spark of her soul drifted toward darkness. He thought of all the lost moments they would never share, the little tendernesses she would never give him, and the love that swelled in his chest that she would never feel. He fought against the overwhelming grief, determined that Connie should know love as she breathed her last.

Try as he might, Wallace simply could not speak, but he regained control of his fussing hands and willed them to be still. His right hand trembled as he brought it up to Connie's face and stroked her cheek. The gentle sensation surprised her and she looked at Wallace in bewilderment. He felt tears streaming down his cheeks as he watched Connie struggle with her fate. He recognized the storm of emotions that flashed through her dying mind, and it was precisely because he had already experienced the moment of death that Wallace knew the anguish and torment Connie was suffering. Above grief, fear, anger, and sorrow rose impotence, and, try as she might to cling to life, Connie's efforts were futile.

Wallace longed to save her, but he knew the only thing he could do was let her know how much she was loved. He leaned forward to kiss her, but before his mouth reached hers, he saw that she was gone. One moment Connie's eyes were alive with dismay, the next they were blank and empty. Despair consumed Wallace. Connie's death had come so quickly that they hadn't even exchanged a single word. He was stricken by the realization that he hadn't even said good-bye. Betrayed by a voice that had failed him, he had been robbed of the chance to tell Connie how much he loved her. Fury snapped him back to reality and, as the world came rushing in, Wallace remembered that the vile man who had extinguished his beautiful love stood no more than fifteen feet away.

23

Enraged, Wallace turned, but stopped suddenly when he felt hot metal pressed against his temple. The masked figure that had filled his life with so much misery stood above him, pushing the pistol that had killed Connie against the side of his head.

The gunshots robbed Wallace of any chance of peace, and he felt Connie's killer shudder and fall. Looking beyond the prone man, he saw Danny standing at the end of the rack of computers, smoke drifting up from the barrel of his machine pistol. Wallace wanted to grab the gun and give furious vent to his rage, but his body wouldn't comply. His limbs were leaden, unable to do his bidding. It wasn't until Danny hauled him off the floor that Wallace was able to move, and even then it was only because the skinny kid was dragging, pinching, and kicking him out of the room. Each physical assault was like a charge from a cattle prod, stimulating Wallace's unwilling limbs into unwanted action. He looked down at Connie's receding body. He couldn't leave her like this. She deserved better.

"We've gotta go!" Danny shouted, pulling at Wallace, continuing his assault, dragging him back inch by reluctant inch.

Wallace looked down and saw his assailant lying flat on his back. His left arm had been torn by a number of Danny's bullets, but Wallace's murderous desires were left unrealized by the bulletproof body armor that encased the man's torso. Even now, as Danny hauled him from the room, Wallace could see the dark figure moving as he caught his breath and recovered from the shock and momentum of the bullets that had hit him.

"For fuck's sake! Come on!" Danny yelled.

Wallace saw the murderer reaching for the pistol, which had fallen inches from Connie's lifeless feet, and, as fear jolted his body back to life, he stopped burdening Danny. As their assailant raised his pistol, Wallace and Danny rounded the maze of servers and fled through the exit. Glass panels exploded as the wounded killer opened fire. Danny wheeled round and sprayed a short burst of shots in the general direction, and the remaining panels shattered. Danny pulled out his second pistol and unleashed another volley of bullets, which had the desired effect and stemmed the murderer's gunfire.

Wallace sprinted toward the double doors, drawing level with Danny. They were no more than fifty feet away when cracks of gunfire came from behind them. Wallace felt searing pain and his leg gave out from under him. As he fell, Wallace saw the vile figure rising behind the server racks, firing between the columns of computers.

Danny returned fire as he heaved Wallace to his feet. "Fuck the pain!" he commanded. "Come on!"

Wallace ignored the sound of rapid gunfire and hauled himself to his feet. Each step sent a jolt of stabbing agony up from his ankle to his neck, and his body screamed at him to lie down and accept his fate, but he refused. Anguish and anger fought the pain and fueled him with sufficient willpower to propel him toward the door.

When Danny changed clips, the masked man's gunfire began afresh. As the bullets whipped past them, Wallace turned to see Connie's killer silhouetted in the doorway of the server room, his masked face lit up by intermittent muzzle flashes.

Danny slammed the clip in and started shooting, filling the air with acrid gun smoke. Rather than dive for cover, the figure ran toward them, but his determined audacity worked against him and he caught a bullet in his chest that sent him flying backward. The momentary respite was all Wallace and Danny needed, and as their attacker scrabbled to his feet, they swept out through the double doors. Danny ran for the bank of elevators and pressed the call button, but Wallace grabbed him and pushed him toward the fire door on the other side of the lobby. As they bundled against the bar-latch, bullets peppered the wall around them. Danny and Wallace burst through the door and slammed it shut behind them. They sprinted down the stairs, jumping, falling, and colliding in a frenzied mess of movement. They'd cleared one story when Wallace heard the fire door slam open above them. Gunfire echoed throughout the stairwell and Wallace felt the sting of debris as bullets pocked the brickwork around them.

Wallace's leg screamed at him as he and Danny tumbled down the stairs. They were riding their luck with every step and needed to get out of the stairwell—fast. Wallace stopped at the door marked "14" and pulled it open. Danny followed him through, and they raced across the lobby of a deserted accountancy firm.

"Shoot it!" Wallace yelled, as they barreled toward the glass doors that offered entry to the accountants' offices. Danny sprayed the doors and the glass shattered. They bundled through as their attacker burst out of the fire door behind them and started shooting.

Ignoring the bullets that sliced the air around them, Wallace and Danny ran into the accountants' offices, which, unlike the floor they had just come from, were divided into individual spaces.

"We're trapped," Danny noted.

Wallace shook his head.

"This way," he said, running right, toward the south side of the building.

They weaved their way through a maze of cubicles, past tiny spaces where lucky people got to spend their mundane days. Bullets shattered glass partitions all around them, but their speed and the darkness served to make them difficult targets. The surrounding space changed, and the office opened up into some sort of canteen. Ahead of them loomed huge floor-to-ceiling windows.

"Shoot it!" Wallace instructed.

"*What?*"

"I think the next building is only a couple of floors below us," Wallace explained.

"You think!" Danny exclaimed.

The air crackled with gunfire. Danny whirled and sprayed the space behind them. Wallace saw his assailant among the cubicles, about thirty paces away.

"Shoot it!" Wallace bawled.

Danny turned and shot the window, which shattered but didn't break. Wallace sprinted toward it, praying that his memory was correct. The glass gave way as his body hurtled into it. The noise was staggeringly loud as each tiny fragment snapped away from its neighbor to create a sharp cloud of glass that fell with Wallace into the night sky. As he tumbled, Wallace realized that his memory had failed him; the adjacent roof was more like three stories below. Thirty feet. Survivable. Wallace turned as he plummeted, and saw Danny falling above him, his eyes wide with terror.

Wallace landed heavily on his feet and the pain almost pummeled him into unconsciousness. His wounded leg screamed at him, the agony invading every cell in his body. Danny, who had fallen and rolled to his feet nearby, was already running toward him. Oblivion would have to wait, as Danny's determined hand grabbed Wallace and yanked him toward a small structure that protruded from the otherwise flat roof. Bullets snapping at their heels, Danny shot at the door that blocked their escape. Sparks flew as Danny's bullets chewed at the lock. He grabbed the door handle and pulled. Wallace turned to see their assailant standing in the shot-out window above them. The man had a bead on Wallace and was taking his time to ensure the accuracy of the shot. As Danny pulled the door open, Wallace saw his killer squeeze the trigger, but nothing happened. From the irritated way the man lowered his weapon, Wallace could tell that he was out of ammunition. Sirens blared in the distance, and Wallace stared up at the figure that had robbed him of so much.

"Come on!" Danny screamed, trying to force Wallace through the door.

Wallace resisted Danny's efforts and glared at Connie's killer. It was only when the masked man backed into the shadows that Wallace allowed Danny to pull him through the doorway to safety.

PART TWO
Limbo

24

Wallace only realized it was Christmas Day when he staggered down to the liquor store and found it closed. A handwritten sign decorated with badly drawn Christmas trees informed him that the shop would reopen on Boxing Day. Wallace looked around, his eyes scouring the concrete wasteland that had been his home for more than a month. The Old Kent Road was quiet. A couple of cars drifted lazily along the otherwise deserted road. Anyone with even the most tattered social connection had better things to do than troll the streets of South East London on Christmas Day. With his mood darkening, Wallace turned and limped along the dirty wide pavement until he reached the corner of Dunton Road. Even the behemoth Tesco superstore lay still, its massive parking lot completely empty. Wallace reached into his pocket for the key to the miserable guesthouse, a large building that had been created by joining two Victorian townhouses together. The brickwork was stained black and the once white window casements were gray and cracking. The place looked as though it hadn't been touched for over thirty years, a filthy reminder of a London long past.

Inside, a narrow corridor ran from the front door to the foot of an uneven set of steep stairs. There were two rooms on either side of the corridor. Sconce, the degenerate caretaker, lived in one, but Wallace had no idea who lived in the other. The occupants of the building were a private bunch, which wasn't surprising given that they would all have some sort of connection to their landlord, Salamander. When they had fled Victoria Street, the night of Connie's murder, Danny had described it as a "safe house." The phrase carried connotations of intrigue far beyond the reality of this tatty old wreck.

Wallace slowly climbed the stairs, which were clad in a carpet that looked like it had never been cleaned: decades of dust, grime, and filth lay beneath his feet. When they first arrived, Wallace had been in such a state of shock he didn't notice his surroundings. Blinded by despair, he was simply glad of somewhere private to vent his grief. He knew better now. When he woke crying with the echo of his recurring nightmare cascading around his skull, he took comfort in his grim surroundings. He didn't deserve anything good, and part of him wanted to die in this filth.

When he reached the second floor, Wallace walked past the two doors that led to rooms at the rear of the building before approaching his own. There was another door directly opposite his, but he had never seen his neighbor. Wallace occasionally heard sex noises through the tissue-thin walls, but had never put a face to such intimate sounds.

He slid his key into the scratched lock and opened the door. His room was a depressing throwback to the 1980s. Everything was floral: the peeling wallpaper, the shabby lampshade, the patched armchair, even the stained bedspread. But the flowers that had once been bright and colorful were worn and moldy. The ceiling was yellow from years of smokers, and there was a stale smell of decay in the air, as though something had died here a very long time ago. An analog television with a wire coat hanger for an antenna offered no connection to the digital world. Judging by the ringed stains on top, other guests had used the television much as he did: as a place to put glasses. Or, in Wallace's case, a single glass. A straight pint glass that had probably been pilfered from a pub by a previous tenant. When he'd first arrived, there had been two glasses, but Wallace had broken one during a binge. If it happened again, he'd have to start drinking from the bottle.

The night they'd arrived, Danny couldn't wait to leave. Whether it was discomfort around Wallace's inconsolable grief or the kid's inherent desire to be rid of any connection to the evening's crimes,

Danny had virtually thrown the keys at Wallace. He'd been dragged back a couple of hours later by an irate Salamander, who also arranged for someone to come and take care of Wallace's leg wound. The man Salamander sent had a twisted sense of humor and called himself Doctor Death.

Over the next few weeks, Wallace learned that the man, who was in his mid-fifties, was really called Alastair Timson and had lost his license to practice in the 1990s for some serious indiscretion. He scratched out a living as a physician to those who did not want the attention of mainstream medicine. People like Wallace, who wanted to avoid awkward questions about the bullet wound that had torn through his calf muscle and the other one that had sliced into his arm. Wallace also discovered that Doctor Death was an inveterate drinker. Dosed with diazepam and codeine, Wallace watched the doctor polish off an entire bottle of Scotch each evening. Wallace lay in bed and watched as the disgraced physician sat in the filthy armchair and rambled on about the miseries of the world. By the end of the night, none of what he said made any sense, but Wallace didn't mind. The foul cloud of despair emanating from the doctor helped make him feel worse, which was fine; Wallace couldn't dig a hole deep enough for his misery.

The drug-fueled dreams of that first week were the darkest nightmares Wallace had ever experienced. He kept seeing Connie. The final moments as her life slipped away. The horror of her loss overwhelmed him, and the beautiful simplicity of suicide beckoned. Doctor Death was as sloppy and careless as could be expected of a disgraced alcoholic. He left Wallace with far more pain relief than was necessary. An overdose washed down with the dregs of Doctor Death's liquor would have been an easy end. But no matter the level of deranged torment Wallace felt, he could not bring himself to do it. Even at his darkest, when his eyes burned with all the tears he had wept, and his throat was raw with lament, Wallace knew that death was cowardice—he owed Connie more than that. He owed her justice.

Every wave of grief was followed by tumultuous eddies of swirling rage that animated Wallace with purpose. After the first week, when he was steady enough to stand, he explored the area and discovered the liquor store around the corner. Tesco was too clean for someone like him, but the small shop with its ancient stock of cheap beer, wine, and spirits was perfect. It was there that he'd seen the tabloid headlines screaming about a serial killer at large in London. One of them had carried a photograph of Connie on its front page, and what little emotional façade Wallace had been able to construct immediately crumbled and he fled the shop, distraught. He hadn't returned until the following day when the papers had moved on.

Wallace spent the last of Connie's cash getting drunk. He sat in the filthy armchair and watched shoppers flock to the giant supermarket opposite. In his drunkenness, he found some relief from the torment, and the combination of cheap vodka and his pain medication made life feel unreal and distant. He had spent three weeks drinking and brooding, and with each swell of grief there now came a slurred promise that he would find Connie's killer and exact justice. Even in his inebriated haze, Wallace knew that the word rang hollow. There was no price the killer could pay that would ever make up for Connie. She would never have justice.

One night—Wallace couldn't remember exactly when—blind drunk, he had been overcome with a sense of duty and finally plucked up the courage to use the phone number Salamander had found. Danny had delivered a burner phone so that Wallace could stay in touch with his boss, and Wallace had used it to call Australia. He felt every inch the miserable drunken fool when he heard Peter and Sandra Jones's cheery message.

"G'day, you've reached the Joneses," they said with the faintest Australian twang. "We're not here right now. Leave a message after the beep."

Wallace heard the beep, but there simply weren't words to express his confused thoughts, so, after a few muted sobs, he hung up. Wallowing in the misery of isolation, he knew he had no right to intrude on those people. He didn't pull the trigger, but there was no doubt in his mind that he was responsible for their daughter's death. They'd almost certainly been notified by now and were probably in London dealing with the consequences of his fatal decision to involve Connie. Wallace sobbed some more before vengeful resolve took over. *You can't bring her back*, he told himself, *but you can punish the man who killed her.*

It was during his third week that Wallace had shared his purpose with Salamander, who lived in a world of blood and vengeance and sympathized with the sentiment. Salamander's sympathy did not stop him from charging 100 percent interest on monies loaned to Wallace. But Wallace didn't care—he would have given everything he owned to get to the man who killed Connie. As it was, he borrowed twenty thousand pounds from Salamander, with a promise to return double that amount within a year. Salamander took five hundred back immediately; the price of a forged passport. Wallace spent another eight hundred on an Air France ticket to New York. Both items lay in the drawer of the rickety bedside cabinet. Danny had dropped the passport off three days ago, along with intelligence that Salamander had obtained from a source inside the Metropolitan Police. Bailey was stable, but still in a coma. In addition to the Maybury killings and Bailey's shooting, Wallace was now wanted for questioning in connection with Connie's and Riley's murders. Until Bailey came out of his coma, there was no way to prove his innocence, and Wallace could not afford to gamble on the wounded policeman's recovery.

Danny had congratulated Wallace on his scraggy stubble and disheveled appearance—anything that could put distance between him and the clean-cut photograph that would doubtless be posted on every police and port authority bulletin board was good. Wallace hadn't bothered to tell Danny that he'd simply lost interest in shaving and that his disheveled appearance was the result of a hazardous mix of insomnia, booze, and prescription medication. Danny had assured him that the counterfeit passport was bulletproof. The kid had given Wallace a phone number that he could use to reach Salamander if he needed help. And then, with a final "good luck," Danny had swept from the place with an ill-concealed eagerness to be away from the troubled, damaged man opposite him.

Wallace crossed the room and slumped into the filthy armchair. He looked out the dirty window at the deserted supermarket opposite and tormented himself with familiar thoughts. He enumerated the ways in which he could have prevented Connie's death. From not approaching her in the first place to insisting that they arrange to meet Riley somewhere public. All the things that hindsight screamed at him. Eventually, when the burden of guilt became too much to bear, he stood and limped over to the bedside cabinet. There, in the drawer, resting on his new passport and airline ticket, were his pills. He swallowed three diazepam with the dregs of a bottle of Scotch and returned to his chair.

As the easy warmth of the psychoactive sedative caressed his mind, Wallace consoled himself with the thought that in a week he would be on a plane to New York on the trail of Connie's killer.

"What the fuck is he doing?"

The words were angry and urgent, and tore through the dark fog that menaced Wallace's mind. He opened his eyes to find Doctor Death leaning over him. An agitated Salamander paced nearby while, across the room, a concerned Danny smoked a cigarette. Wallace tried to move but immediately felt a crashing wave of nausea.

"He's back," Doctor Death advised Salamander. "Can you understand me?" he asked Wallace, who nodded as he fought back the sudden urge to vomit.

"Ya think I need another body? Well, ya wrong! I don't need any more fucking heat!" Salamander growled as he rounded on Wallace. "What the fuck are ya playin' at?"

Wallace was genuinely perplexed and the feeling must have shown.

"Were ya trying to kill ya'self? Or did you miscount?" Salamander continued. "Bailey didn't send ya to me to die!"

"I took three," Wallace rasped, his throat rich with bile.

"You took twelve," Doctor Death informed him. "If Danny hadn't found you . . ."

"I thought I'd check in on him," Danny explained to Salamander. "I felt sorry for the bloke, not having anyone, and it being the holidays."

"I took three," Wallace protested, as the reality of the situation finally dawned on him.

"Fuck!" Salamander yelled. "Yer a fucking mess, mate. Ya keep bangin' on about revenge, but ya too busy gettin' fucked to do anything. I bet ya don't even know what day it is!"

Wallace looked toward the window and saw daylight fringing the curtains. "Boxing Day, the twenty-sixth," he said confidently.

Salamander shot Danny and Doctor Death a disappointed look. "It's the twenty-eighth. The twenty-eighth of December. Ya been out three days. I've listened to ya sob story, I've lent ya money, I even bought your fucking ticket, but I ain't seen shit to tell me ya gonna do something. All I seen is a man who wants to die."

Three days, Wallace thought. He knew the drink and drugs had insulated him from reality but hadn't realized they'd disconnected him entirely.

"Do ya want to get the fucker who killed ya girl?" Salamander pressed.

Wallace looked him in the eye and nodded emphatically.

"Okay, then," Salamander continued. "No more drink, drugs, or pity. Danny's gonna hang around, make sure ya get cleaned up, and when ya ready, he'll get ya out of the country. Deal?"

Danny didn't seem too pleased with the new arrangement, but Wallace looked up at Salamander, full of resolve. "Deal," he said decisively.

PART THREE
New York

25

The Explorer pulsed rhythmically, its fourteen-year-old engine threatening to cut out as the revs dropped dangerously close to zero at the tail of every combustion cycle. As the heavy SUV started to shudder, the fuel injection system would compensate for the additional air that was being sucked through the cracked manifold and the engine would growl back to life. With almost 200,000 miles on the clock, the Ford was nearing the end of its life, but the old wreck suited Wallace perfectly. Parked alongside the treacherously glassy sidewalk outside the East Point Café, the Explorer drew no attention. Its black bodywork was covered with gray crystalline patterns left by salted snow, and its New York State plates had four months left to run. The rear window sported the ghostly outlines of long-removed stickers, and the fuel cap was covered by a circular version of the Stars and Stripes, all of which helped sell the illusion that the vehicle was the property of a long-settled local.

Wallace had purchased the old Ford from Seth, a bald man with a brilliant white smile. Seth ran Five Star Auto Sales, a ramshackle operation located on Liberty Avenue, a couple of miles from the De-Lux Suites, the seedy airport motel that Wallace had been shown shortly after arriving at JFK. Seedy, run-down, ramshackle: these words had become hallmarks of Wallace's new existence. He had no credit cards, no identification—other than a forged passport in the name of William Porter—and he was wanted in connection with a number of murders. Wallace had to be careful to avoid the mainstream and instead selected places that were so grateful for his business that they would not question the source of his cash. He had secreted the money he'd borrowed from Salamander in a leather belt, which he'd worn around his waist when Danny had put him on the Eurostar from London to Paris.

He'd caught the train on New Year's Day, traveling with Parisian revelers who'd been in London for the huge riverside fireworks display the previous night. Danny had suggested that New Year's Day would see a high proportion of sleepy, hungover immigration officers, and that the Eurostar's late start would see a high volume of passengers crowded onto fewer trains. The gamble had paid off; the William Porter passport held up, and Wallace boarded the train without incident. For all his rat-faced bravado, Danny was a smart little thug, and Wallace was grateful to have had him around.

The train journey had proved to be more difficult than Wallace had expected. It was his first prolonged exposure to people in weeks. An elegantly disheveled couple sat across the table from him. Tired and drained by their New Year experience, they held hands and whispered to each other in French, their heads bowed together like a pair of cooing doves. The adjacent table was occupied by four young men who were part of a larger group of twelve that had taken the tables ahead and behind. Grubby and hungover, the men spoke quietly, occasionally breaking into loud ribaldry when recalling an embarrassing incident from the previous evening. Seeing these people going about their easy existences made Wallace long for Connie.

As the train cut through the Kent countryside, he leaned against the window and closed his eyes. He'd had three hard sober days under Danny's supervision but could still feel the residue of painkillers and alcohol, which magnified the effect of the train's gentle rocking and soothed him into a sad sleep. He dreamed terrible nightmares of Connie's death, his hands covered in her blood. The jolt of the train passing over a junction startled him awake, and, momentarily bewildered, he thought he saw Connie coming down the carriage to take her place in the vacant seat beside him. But his cruel senses returned, and Wallace realized that the woman was a stranger. As the train sped through the Picardie countryside, the stranger smiled at him and walked on, exiting through the doors that led to the next compartment.

Wallace had felt lost and alone when he arrived in Paris, but he did not allow the storm of emotions to cloud his sense of purpose. He found an Internet café near the Gare du Nord and located a gîte in Sarcelles, a suburb near the airport. He used a pay phone and his moderately proficient French to call the owner, Vincent Gassot, and book the accommodation; a small studio at the bottom of Gassot's garden. He had taken a taxi to Sarcelles, passing mournfully through the vibrant city where he and Connie had once spent such a wonderful, passionate weekend. Gassot was a graying university professor who lived alone. Wallace presented him with the forged passport and explained that he was on a two-day layover before he flew out to New York. The studio was a converted garage and offered very basic accommodation, but it had its own entrance, which suited Wallace just fine. He paid in advance, which had pleased the bookish Gassot.

The following day, Wallace located an Internet café and completed his ESTA Visa Waiver application, giving New York City's YMCA as his intended residence. He also purchased a knapsack, clothes, toiletries, and a cheap digital SLR camera. The strongest lies were built of half-truths, and Wallace had resolved that if challenged, William Porter, an amateur shutterbug, would explain his presence in the United States as a photographic holiday.

Charles de Gaulle Airport had tested Wallace's nerves. Airlines were on high alert for the holidays, and he had no idea how widely his photograph and details had been circulated. As a murder suspect, there was every chance he had madde Interpol's alert list. He had photographed enough actors to know that trying too hard was fatal to any performance. The most powerful portrayals were grounded in an easy truth, so, rather than try to appear relaxed, Wallace had thought about Connie. Grief overwhelmed him, and his deep sadness was both genuine and palpable. The French immigration officer had returned his passport without comment, and an usher instructed him to proceed through security. Wallace was relieved not to be selected for a full body scan, as he was carrying close to eighteen thousand pounds in his belt, which was over the money-laundering limits imposed by the United States.

The flight had been unremarkable and had arrived into John F. Kennedy International Airport at three p.m. The surrounding countryside was blanketed with thick snow, and dirty great piles of the stuff had been shoved to either side of the slick runway. Inside the terminal building, Wallace had joined the snaking immigration line, and gave quiet thanks that he had never been to the United States before. Seated in small cubicles that ran the width of the arrivals hall were a dozen immigration officers, each of whom took photographs and fingerprints of every single visitor.

"First time to the States, Mr. Porter?" the immigration officer had asked him. The poker-faced man's name tag identified him as Efren Luiz.

"Yes," Wallace replied, as the fingerprint scanner captured an image of his digits.

Wallace had waited for what seemed like an age while Luiz studied the screen on the other side of the counter.

"Purpose of visit?" Luiz asked at last.

"Holiday," Wallace replied with relief.

"Vacation," Luiz said firmly as he stapled Wallace's visa waiver into the passport. "Welcome to America, Mr. Porter."

Wallace had asked the cab driver for a budget motel near the airport and had rejected the first option as too wholesome. The second choice, the De Lux Suites, had looked suitably seedy and earned the cab driver a generous tip. Wallace paid for three days in advance and used the time to acquire a vehicle and plan his trip north. Locked alone in his room, he also fought the painful effects of withdrawal. Determined to regain control of his mind and body, he resisted the urge to find a nearby pharmacy or seek out one of the many brightly signed liquor stores. Instead, whenever cravings threatened him, he performed his aikido drills over and over until he was too exhausted to do anything other than collapse on his king-size bed. The martial art that had brought discipline and routine into his teenage life now performed a far more profound function and prevented him from being swept back into the dangerous spiral from which he'd emerged.

Wallace had decided against public transportation because it increased the number of people he would come into contact with. Although he was taking a risk driving without a license or insurance, he thought that as long as he assiduously adhered to the speed limit there was little chance of being stopped by the police. After trudging the slushy streets to check out the used car dealers in the neighborhood, he had settled on Five Star Auto Sales as somewhere that wouldn't demand too many answers. The Explorer had cost three thousand dollars, which Wallace obtained by exchanging small sums of sterling for greenbacks in half a dozen different banks. The ever-smiling Seth had been unperturbed by the cash or by Wallace giving the De Lux Suites as his address for the registration transfer. He simply waved happily as Wallace drove the lumbering old wreck off the lot.

With an iPad purchased from Best Buy and the motel's pay-by-the-hour Wi-Fi, Wallace was able to research Cold Spring, Kye Walters's hometown. Situated on the east bank of the Hudson River, just over an hour's train ride from New York City, Cold Spring was described as an upscale village that attracted tourists and wealthy New Yorkers tired of city living. Photos of the village made it look picturesque and inviting, with twentieth-century redbricks dominating the architecture. But there were also New England–style clapboard houses with slate roofs and grand three-story brown-brick townhouses that added to Cold Spring's traditional charm. It was not the sort of place Wallace would immediately associate with a teenage meth dealer.

Aside from the local news articles Connie had found, there didn't seem to be anything else on Kye Walters. Wallace read them over and over, each time growing ever more convinced that the man who had tried to kill him had also murdered Kye. On the face of it, there was no obvious connection between him and the previously untroubled eighteen-year-old high school student who had suddenly taken his own life, revealing a shameful secret existence as a meth dealer in a suicide note posted on Facebook. But the unexpected suicide and subsequent sordid revelations also fit the pattern of Huvane's death.

Wallace had checked out of the De Lux Suites and traveled north on US Route 9, through the snow-covered landscape of New York State, until he found the Country Comfort Motel, five miles north of Cold Spring. There were a couple of guesthouses in town, but Wallace wanted to put some distance between himself and Cold Spring: a stranger asking difficult questions might attract the attention of local law enforcement.

The Country Comfort Motel was an aluminum-clad box that had been divided into a dozen units. The owner, a chubby, middle-aged, heavily made-up woman named Martha, had given Wallace number 8, a one-bedroom unit on the ground floor with a studio living room/kitchen and a tiny faux-marble bathroom/shower combo. After he'd deposited his luggage, Wallace had returned to the wood-paneled reception area and explained to Martha that he was a film-maker researching a documentary on suicides. Eager to oblige her foreign guest, Martha had volunteered Kye Walters before Wallace even mentioned his name. With the hushed tones of a gossip's false compassion, Martha told Wallace everything she knew about Kye and expressed surprise that Kye's mother, Robyn, didn't leave Cold Spring as a result of the scandal. According to Martha, Robyn was a single mother who lived in a tumbledown mobile home on a gnarly lot on the outskirts of Garrison, a tiny village a few miles south of Cold Spring. Apparently Robyn still managed the East Point Café on Main Street, which was how his rasping Ford Explorer came to be parked in the heart of Cold Spring the following frozen January morning.

Wallace sat in the warmth of the SUV and rehearsed how he would approach the bereaved mother. Condensation clouded the windows of the East Point Café, which was located on the ground floor of one of the many redbrick buildings that lined Main Street. Wallace could not see inside, but he watched as a handful of loyal customers braved the cold and stopped for morning coffee and pastries on their way down to the train station, which was located by the Hudson, at the western end of the street. The last of the customers, a trim man in an expensive suit, parked his gleaming silver SUV directly ahead of Wallace and left his engine running while he went inside to collect his order. Emerging minutes later, the man carefully crossed the icy sidewalk and nodded a greeting at Wallace before getting into his car and driving toward the station. Wallace waited a couple of minutes, and when he finally felt there was a lull in the rhythm of the café's morning trade, he switched off the Explorer's engine and stepped out to be greeted by the bitterly cold winter air.

26

"Sorry about the view," the bubbly blonde called across the empty café, indicating the misted windows.

"At least it's warm," Wallace observed, pulling the door closed behind him and stamping his feet on the thick rug to shed the snow that clung to his heavy boots.

"You visiting?" the blonde asked.

Wallace nodded.

"What can I get you?"

For all his rehearsal, Wallace was at a loss. He assumed this effervescent, friendly blonde was Robyn Walters and suspected that he was about to ruin her day. She was younger than he expected; Wallace guessed she was mid to late thirties. Her long blonde hair was tied in a loose ponytail revealing a warm, unblemished face. She was naturally beautiful, with smooth skin and a country-fair smile. Only her eyes hinted at sadness. They were a striking green, but unlike her lips, they weren't smiling. Instead, they seemed to be peering beyond Wallace, as though searching for something they would never see.

He walked to the counter. The café walls were lined with framed postcards of local landmarks and old monochrome photographs of officer cadets at West Point. There were ten heavy rustic tables arranged in neat rows, with four high-back chairs at each. The blonde stood next to a pastry display, and behind her was a large Italian espresso machine and a door that led off to the kitchen. Wallace leaned against the counter and bought time by studying the pastries.

"What'll it be?" the blonde asked. "We do a mean apple Danish."

"I'll take one of those," Wallace replied. "And a mocha."

"Coming right up," the blonde said brightly, turning toward the chrome espresso machine. Wallace watched as she ground the beans into fine powder and then filled the double basket before securing it to one of the group heads.

"Are you Robyn?" he asked finally. She paused for a moment, and then pushed a small paper cup under the basket. When she turned around, the friendly effervescence had been replaced by cautious suspicion.

"What d'you want?" she asked coldly.

"I'm looking for Robyn Walters," he replied.

"Like I said; what d'you want?"

"I want to ask you about Kye," he said softly, but the moment he spoke the words he saw the blonde's face harden. She turned back to the espresso machine and studied the slow stream of brown ink intently.

"I'm sorry. I know this is difficult," Wallace continued. "Please. Someone tried to kill me."

The blonde spun around suddenly. "Listen, mister!" she spat. "You don't have any fuckin' idea what difficult is!"

"Mornin', Robyn," a voice called from the door. "Everything okay?"

Wallace turned to see a large, middle-aged bear of a man in a thick winter coat. The bear stamped his boots on the mat and removed his hunting cap to reveal a tight crop of close-cut hair.

"I'm good, Saul," Robyn lied. "Just getting this guy his coffee."

She turned for the paper cup and placed it on the counter. Saul joined Wallace, looming over him by a good four or five inches.

"Best coffee in the state," Saul observed, as Robyn used a pair of tongs to claw a Danish into a bag. "You visiting?"

When Saul unzipped his coat to reach for his wallet, Wallace saw that his imposing neighbor wore the black jacket and insignia of the Putnam County Sheriff's Department.

"Just staying for a couple of days," Wallace lied. "I'm on holiday— vacation as people keep telling me. I'm heading up to Niagara Falls."

"Nice part of the world." Saul's reply was light and easy, but Wallace got the sense that the huge man was studying him.

"That'll be five-sixty," Robyn announced as she deposited a paper bag in front of Wallace.

"Thanks," he said, pulling a ten from his wallet.

"That your truck out front?" Saul asked.

"The Explorer?" Wallace responded, and Saul nodded. "Yes, it is."

"Rental?" Saul probed.

"No," Wallace answered. "I did the math, and it was cheaper to buy an old banger than to rent. And this way I get the authentic experience, right?"

"Right," Saul said halfheartedly. "I didn't catch your name."

"William Porter," Wallace replied.

"Four-forty," Robyn said, handing Wallace his change.

"Thanks." He dropped a dollar in the tip jar, and picked up the coffee and Danish. "Nice meeting you both," he said as he backed away from the counter. He turned for the door and felt Robyn and Saul watching him as he moved casually toward the exit.

"Hey!" Saul called out. Wallace froze in his tracks and turned to see the huge man lumbering toward him. "You forgot this." Saul handed Wallace the brown leather wallet that he'd left on the counter.

"Thanks," Wallace smiled with relief.

"You take care now," Saul counseled as Wallace opened the door and stepped outside.

Feeling nothing but relief as the raw air stung his cheeks, Wallace carefully crossed the sidewalk and climbed into the Ford. Glancing over his shoulder, he saw Saul watching him through a freshly wiped patch of glass. Wallace smiled and nodded at the sheriff with the heavy realization that he could never risk returning to the café. He'd have to find another way to persuade Robyn Walters to talk about her son.

Pink juices ran down Wallace's chin and he instinctively sagged back to prevent them from falling onto his shirt. He reached for the dispenser and grabbed a couple of paper napkins that he used to mop his mouth and the tiny puddles that had fallen between his thighs onto the high stool. The towering burger was rich and flavorsome, the thick patty topped with crispy bacon, blue cheese, and pickles, all of which was enclosed in a brioche bun. But it was too big to be eaten without creating a sticky mess. He glanced around the Hudson Burger Joint and saw that he wasn't the only one struggling; the place was packed with diners and, despite the variety of techniques being employed, every single one of them was finding it difficult to fit an oversized burger into a standard-sized mouth, but the taste more than compensated for the mess, and Wallace tried to take another bite.

"Everything okay?" the genial barman asked.

Wallace nodded, and the barman continued preparing a tray of drinks. The Hudson Burger Joint was a lively restaurant across the street from the East Point Café. Wallace sat at the bar—the waitress had called it a counter—and watched through the window as a small but steady procession of returning commuters stopped for their final fix of caffeine. After the morning's encounter, Wallace had returned to the motel. Checking online, he discovered the East Point Café closed at seven p.m. He spent a restless afternoon impatiently flicking between television channels, and eventually, when his thoughts began turning to drink, he performed two hours of aikido drills. After showering, he had driven into town and parked the Explorer around the corner, a block west from the East Point Café. At six thirty, he had left the stifling warmth of the Ford and stepped into the freezing night. He walked past the café and saw Robyn was still inside. He'd rightly gambled that a small café running a twelve-hour day would not incur the extra cost of shift workers. He had selected the Hudson Burger Joint because of its position; the quality of the food was an unexpected bonus.

The large clock on the wall behind the bar said seven fifteen when the East Point Café's lights went off. Moments later, Robyn Walters emerged in a long woolen coat. As she locked the door behind her, Wallace threw twenty-five dollars onto the bar, grabbed his coat, and hurried out of the restaurant. He reached into his pocket and pulled on a thick ski hat. He was grateful for the ominously dark clouds that swelled the night sky. Without moonlight he was just a dark shadow on the other side of a wide street. He watched as Robyn headed east, and when she turned onto Kemble Avenue, the next block up, Wallace realized he had a decision to make: try to follow her on foot or go for his car. He opted for the latter, and hurried west as fast as the icy conditions would allow. He reached Rock Street, jumped in the Explorer, gunned the engine, and quickly pulled onto Main Street. When he turned onto Kemble Avenue, Wallace was relieved to see Robyn two hundred yards away, opening the door of a small dark car. He pulled into a parking space and killed his lights. Leaving the engine running, he waited until Robyn pulled out. The first flakes of snow started to fall as he followed her out of town.

There was very little traffic, so there was no way for Wallace to try to use other vehicles to conceal his presence. By the time they made it to the Bear Mountain Highway, their cars were the only ones on the road. He simply had to hope that after a busy day Robyn would not notice she was being followed, and even if she did, the bright glare of his headlights would make it impossible for her to identify the vehicle. The windshield wipers were waving furiously and Wallace was glad that Robyn had slowed to just over twenty miles per hour. The thick falling snow was making the road treacherous, and he could feel the Explorer starting to slide around as its wheels fought for grip. The Ford's beams took on clearly defined, tight conical shapes as bulbous flakes reflected most of the light. Up ahead, Wallace could just see the bright-red taillights of Robyn's small car as it moved slowly south.

After fifteen minutes, Robyn signaled left and pulled off the highway onto Indian Brook Road. Wallace followed, turning onto a potholed track that cut through a large pine forest. He had always heard how vast America was, but nobody had ever mentioned the wilderness. Here, not more than fifty miles from one of the world's biggest cities, was an ancient wild woodland complete with coyotes, deer, and black bears. Even though he was only a few miles outside town, the sheer scale of the expansive wilderness that stretched out toward the Atlantic made him feel isolated and vulnerable. He kept his eyes on Robyn's car as it bounced around the narrow road over a newly laid blanket of snow that made the potholes impossible to detect. The Explorer took a couple of jarring knocks as it slowly climbed the steep hill, winding its way farther into the forbidding landscape. Occasionally the forest would be broken by a house, but for the most part Wallace drove with nothing but tall, imposing trees lining his route. There was no doubt Robyn would have noticed the trailing vehicle, but Wallace hoped she'd think he was one of her neighbors. After another fifteen minutes snaking up the hill, she finally turned into a driveway. Wallace glanced into the property as he drove slowly past and saw Robyn's car pull to a halt next to an old pickup truck that was parked in front of a small mobile home.

He drove fifty yards farther on before pulling into a turnout. He killed the lights and engine and stepped out. The fresh snowfall had formed a soft blanket over deeper, ice-crusted drifts that crunched under every step as Wallace walked back toward the trailer. The falling snow and thick forest created a muffled silence that made his crackling footsteps seem even more pronounced. He reached the driveway and peered toward the property. The trailer had a flat snow-covered roof and was situated in the center of a small parcel of land, surrounded by high trees. The lights of Robyn's car were dark and there was no one around, so Wallace started up the drive.

"Take another step and I'll blow a fuckin' hole in your head." The man's voice was quiet and full of menace.

Wallace turned to his left and noticed a figure in the trees. The man stepped forward and Wallace saw that he wore an army surplus jacket, jeans, and black boots, and in his hands he carried a high-caliber hunting rifle.

"I got 'im!" the man yelled toward the trailer. "Call the cops!"

"Please don't," Wallace said as he saw Robyn in the doorway with a phone to her ear.

"Shut the fuck up!" the man commanded, prodding Wallace with the barrel of the gun.

Almost a full foot shorter than Wallace, the man had a weathered face topped by a mop of dark hair that ran into a neatly clipped beard. His narrow eyes had a hardness that might have concealed a killer, but Wallace did not care; he could not risk getting taken into police custody. He instinctively stepped sideways and grabbed the barrel of the gun. There was a sudden crack and Wallace felt his palms scream with the pain of explosive heat as the rifle discharged. The gun recoiled, but Wallace didn't let go. He registered his adversary's look of shock as he tugged at the barrel and pulled the rifle out of the man's hands.

"Dad!" Robyn yelled, as Wallace flipped the weapon and brought it level with the man's chest. He drew the bolt back, sending another round into the chamber.

"Don't do anything crazy," Robyn's dad counseled, his voice edged with fear.

"Put the phone down!" Wallace shouted at Robyn. He watched as she slowly took the phone away from her ear. "I just want to talk."

Wallace tried to play down the gun, but even though it was no longer pointed at anyone, it was there in his hands and Robyn and her father kept giving it nervous glances. Wallace stood in the center of a large, dilapidated living room. A couple of bowed and bulging couches covered in stained fabric formed a right angle in the western third of the room. The apex of the couches was directly opposite a huge old television, which rested on a chipped table. The eastern third of the room was taken up by a laminated dining table and chairs, all from the previous century, all peeling. Robyn and her father sat on two of the chairs, their palms flat against the tabletop.

Pressed against the wall between the doorway to the kitchen and another that led to the bedrooms was a large dresser that was covered in cheap ornaments and photographs. There was a photograph of Robyn's father that looked like it had been taken when he was in his late twenties, his arm around an attractive woman, who Wallace guessed was Robyn's mother. The next picture seemed to confirm the supposition: it was a wedding photograph of the father with the same woman. There were a series of photographs of Robyn as a child, and then others of her as a young woman with a baby. Wallace could not see any images of the child's father, nor were there any pictures of Robyn's mother once the child arrived. The child in the pictures matured into a young man, who Wallace recognized from the articles that Connie had found; it was Kye Walters.

"I'm really sorry to have to do this," he began.

"You're not a reporter," the father noted. "So just who the hell are you?"

"Take it easy, Dad," Robyn cautioned.

"Must be a gun in the room, 'cause you ain't called me Dad since . . ." Robyn's father trailed off. "Well, it's been a long time."

"Take it easy, Hal," Robyn said sourly.

Hal glared at Robyn and looked as though he was about to speak, but his face softened as he caught sight of a photograph of Kye and he fell silent.

"I need to know what happened to Kye," Wallace said at last.

Robyn glowered at him, her eyes brimming with burning resentment.

"Go fuck yourself," Hal said bluntly. "You any idea what we've been through? Frankly, that round you got in there might be a blessing." He stared pointedly at the rifle.

"I'm sorry for your loss, I truly am, but someone tried to kill me," Wallace replied. "This man, he tried to hang me. I've followed his trail and it's led me here."

"Like I said; go fuck yourself," Hal growled the words. "Don't start tryin' to put your craziness on us."

"I'm not crazy. This man didn't just try to kill me, he's killed other people," Wallace protested. "He killed my . . ." He choked on the words before he finally said, "He killed a good friend of mine. Please help me."

Hal snorted and shrugged, unimpressed by Wallace's plea.

"You think this guy might've killed Kye?" Robyn asked quietly. Wallace nodded.

"Don't go buyin' into any bullshit, Robyn," Hal said.

"Why? You worried you won't be able to pin what happened on me?" she asked testily.

"What're you talkin' about? Pin what on you?" Hal challenged his daughter.

"Just 'cause I don't rise to the bait doesn't mean I don't see it," Robyn replied. "How many times you said something about how it was my fault he was on that damned computer all the time? That if he'd been your kid you'd have had him out landscaping and working people's gardens instead of hanging out with his friends?"

"Friends? They got him into that shit," Hal objected. "And even if they didn't put the drugs in his hands, they created the hunger. Gotta have a car, new clothes, new phone, new this, new that. God knows I ain't never had two beans, but I don't have shit because I don't need shit. Once the hunger was there, the boy was always gonna find a way to feed it."

"What d'ya want to know?" Robyn asked Wallace, her words a direct challenge to her father.

"Fuck!" Hal exclaimed in a long drawn out breath.

"Fuck you, Hal!" Robyn yelled. "I've carried my boy's bones. There isn't a day goes by that I don't blame myself. Curse myself for not knowing my son, not know what he was doing, what was going on in his head. Hate myself for not being there when he . . ."

The three of them waited in silence while Robyn caught her breath and composed herself.

"If there's a chance," she said quietly. "Any chance, no matter how small, that Kye didn't kill himself, then I wanna hear it."

Hal stared at Wallace and then looked at his daughter. Wallace could see him wrestling with Robyn's words, and finally the old man nodded.

"When did it happen?" Wallace asked.

"Two years in April," Robyn replied.

"How?"

"I found him out back," Hal said quietly. "Hanged in the woods."

"The newspaper said there was a note posted to Facebook," Wallace said.

"Newspapers!" Hal exclaimed. "Nothing like a small town scandal to get them all excited. Once it came out that Kye'd been dealing drugs, they were all over us like coyotes."

"There was a man in England who was supposed to have killed himself," Wallace said. "After he died the police found a note and videos on Facebook that revealed the man was a pervert."

"You think it's a vigilante?" Robyn asked.

Wallace shook his head. "I haven't done anything wrong. It doesn't make sense. The man in England claimed he'd been attacked a month prior to his murder. Did Kye ever talk about a stalker or anything like that?"

Robyn shook her head. "What makes you think there's a connection?"

"The policeman investigating my case found details of Kye's story on the dead man's computer," Wallace replied. "It seems the victim, this farmer from the middle of nowhere, thought there might have been a link. Was there anything unusual in the weeks leading up to Kye's death?"

Robyn's expression was unchanged, but Wallace was sure he saw doubt flicker across Hal's face.

"Please," Wallace said. "Anything. It doesn't matter how small."

"There was a letter," Hal said flatly, his eyes cast at the ground. "There was a letter from his school."

"What letter?" Robyn asked coldly.

"Couple of months before . . ." Hal hesitated. "Before it happened, I found a letter in his bag. I'd go through his school bag every couple of days because he had a habit of letting old sandwiches fester. I found this letter addressed to parents."

Robyn shook her head and glared at her father.

"I was just as much a parent to the boy as you," Hal protested. "Anyway, I opened it. Some kind of public service announcement from the school warning parents to be vigilant about the signs of depression. It listed half a dozen case studies of kids who'd committed suicide in the state in the past year."

Hal paused and Wallace could sense Robyn's hostility building as her father started to break down.

"I never told you. I never told nobody," Hal whimpered, his voice cracking at last. "I thought I'd put the idea in his head. I thought I was the one . . ."

"What did you do?" Robyn asked, her voice brimming with anger. "What did you do?"

"I showed him the letter," Hal replied weakly. "I thought I was doing the right thing; treatin' him like a man. It was a mistake. The moment he saw the case studies he froze. He said something about the girl."

"What girl?" Wallace asked.

"There was one girl on the sheet," Hal said. "It was the girl. Something about her cut into him. He clammed up pretty quick, but I knew something was wrong. I asked him about it, but he put on a front and told me it was nothin'. But it wasn't nothin'. He was never the same again. You never noticed it. Maybe 'cause I was with him when it happened, I could see it in his eyes. It was like there was a sadness hanging over him."

"You dumb son-of-a-bitch!" Robyn yelled. "Why didn't you tell me?"

"I couldn't," Hal said pathetically. He stood and shuffled toward Robyn, his arms held out limply. "I couldn't have my little girl thinkin' that I put her son in the ground."

He tried to move in for a hug, but Robyn pushed him away. "I carried it for so long," she said quietly. "You let me carry it! You let me think it was my fault!"

"I couldn't tell you," Hal protested. "I didn't want you to hate me."

Robyn leaped out of her chair and slapped and clawed at Hal, who simply stood and took the punishment. Wallace pushed his way between them, and when Robyn realized her blows were no longer connecting, she stopped.

"Get out!" she screamed. "Get out!" She grabbed the rifle from Wallace and pointed it at her father. "Now!" she bawled.

Hal looked sadly at Robyn through tear-filled eyes before turning for the door and staggering out into the bitterly cold night. Wallace hesitated for a moment, but knew there was nothing he could do or say to help this angry, damaged woman.

"I'm sorry," he said, heading for the door.

"Hey!" Robyn called after him. "If you're right and you find the motherfucker, you tell me, you hear?"

He turned toward Robyn, who stood trembling as tears spilled down her cheeks. "I will," he promised.

Hal leaned against the tailgate of his pickup and took out a cigarette. Wallace approached slowly and the old man looked up. Thick snow had already soaked his hair and face, and he looked lost, cast adrift by powerful, dark emotions.

"I'm sorry, Mr. Walters," Wallace offered helplessly.

Hal could only shake his head.

"Do you remember the girl's name?" Wallace asked. "The girl in the letter?"

Hal tried to answer, but the words wouldn't come. "I'll never forget it," he said at last. "Erin. Erin Byrne. The way Kye looked at her name, it was like he knew her."

Hal smoked his cigarette, the burning tip flaring brightly as he inhaled. He turned back to his truck, his head bowed in private misery. Wallace stepped away from the distraught man and walked through virgin snow down the driveway and out onto the silent road.

27

The children's feet dangled above an unnaturally deep valley. Silhouetted against the warm glow of the setting sun, the girl had her right hand wrapped around one of the long ropes that secured her swing to a huge, sweeping branch that arched some forty feet above her head. Although the silhouette concealed the girl's features, the way her head tilted toward her raised left hand suggested that she was supposed to be talking. A boy sat in the adjacent swing, both hands on the ropes, his head slightly cocked as though he was listening. The tree that held them was impossibly large, with branches that spanned the width of a rocky gorge that led off to a distant golden horizon. The image took up the entire rear wall of the Canopy lobby and was a blend of photographic manipulation and original artwork to create a striking illustration of a place that could not possibly exist in the real world. The lighting and colors were exquisite and the figures of the children perfectly proportioned and posed. The perfection of the piece was its only flaw, and, while Wallace had to admire the skill of the artist, he did not connect with the artwork's artificiality. *True beauty is blemished*, he thought.

Even though the digital painting was striking, it could not compete with the view of the city skyline offered by the expansive windows that ran the length of the room. Thirty-two floors up and seven blocks from Central Park, the northeast-facing windows offered an arresting perspective of Manhattan. Wallace could not help but be impressed by New York City. Years of watching American television and studying the cityscapes of photographers such as Berenice

Abbott, Walker Evans, and Joel Sternfeld could not have prepared him for the towering height of the buildings that cast all else into shade; massive monuments to human ingenuity.

As Wallace stood and walked to the window, he could feel the receptionist's eyes tracking him, but she returned to her computer screen when she saw that he was simply admiring the view. He looked out, peering along the wide artificial canyon created by Sixth Avenue, one of the city's five-lane thoroughfares, toward Central Park. Thick snow covered the trees and shrouded the natural heart of the city. Unlike the merry sprawl of London, Manhattan was a showpiece of order and efficiency, the island parceled up into neat blocks by the city's grid system of roads, the granite bedrock facilitating the construction of massive monoliths that could ingest thousands of people at a time. Wallace looked beyond the park; somewhere, many miles past the high buildings on the other side, was the wilderness that he'd left six days ago. He suddenly found himself thinking about Hal and Robyn Walters, stuck up that rutted track. He hoped they'd been able to reconcile—if Kye was a victim of the same killer, there was nothing either of them could have done to prevent the boy's death.

After he'd left the Walters' trailer, Wallace had returned to the motel and researched Erin Byrne. There was a lot of material on the high-profile Byrne family and Erin's tragic death. A sixteen-year-old high school student, Erin had taken her own life just over two years ago on a dark September night. According to her supposed suicide note, which had been posted to Facebook, Erin felt the world would be better off without her ugly worthlessness. The coroner's report said she had died from asphyxiation caused by hanging. Erin's father, Steven Byrne, and her older brother, Max, had returned home from a football game to discover her body in her bedroom, but neither could resuscitate her, and paramedics pronounced Erin dead at the scene. Erin's mother, Philicia Byrne, was at a Democratic Party fund-raiser the night of Erin's death, and she and Steven separated soon afterward in a hostile, public, and expensive divorce.

Steven Byrne was a third-generation immigrant, the grandson of Dublin-born Donal Byrne. An accomplished pianist, Donal founded the successful music publishing business that made his fortune. A deeply honorable and patriotic man, Donal believed he owed his adopted country a debt of opportunity that could never be repaid. After fighting for the US Army during the Second World War, he joined the US Army Reserves and instilled an ethos of public service in his family. His legacy was still in effect: before founding the digital security company that made him a billionaire, Steven Byrne completed eight years' service in the First Ranger Battalion, followed by four years in military intelligence, after which he continued to serve as a reservist until he turned forty, some twelve years previous. After Erin's death and his divorce, Steven focused on his company, Erimax Security. Named after his two children, the company had become one of the preeminent providers of digital security, and Steven's 60 percent share translated to a net worth of over four billion dollars.

Twelve years older than Erin, Max had tried to follow in his father's footsteps and had served three years with the 75th Rangers before being discharged over a disciplinary issue. Wallace couldn't find anything on the nature of the disciplinary problem, but Max didn't suffer; he walked straight into a job at Erimax and showed considerable aptitude for his father's business. After Erin's death, Max suffered a breakdown and was sent to a psychiatric hospital for treatment, but Wallace couldn't find out whether he was still there.

Following the divorce, Philicia started the Canopy, a charity dedicated to preventing youth suicides. The Canopy website provided extensive information on education, outreach programs, and advice for parents, teachers, and other interested individuals. It was clear to Wallace that Philicia had poured herself into a crusade to stop youth suicides, but if Erin's death was also the work of the serial killer, then all this philanthropy was built on a lie. People like the Byrnes were normally extremely hard to reach, but the Canopy gave Wallace a way in.

He turned away from the window and walked back across the cream-colored marble slabs to the huge digital illustration. He drew close to the two children on the swings and wondered whether they were meant to symbolize Erin and Max.

"It's a brilliant piece," a woman's voice came from behind him. "It highlights the precariousness of life."

Wallace turned to see a young African-American woman with a warm face, bright eyes, and black shoulder-length hair. She wore a smart brown pantsuit.

"I'm Marcie, Mrs. Byrne's assistant," she said, offering her hand.

"William Porter," Wallace replied, gently clasping it.

Marcie turned toward the illustration. "Two children on swings," she said. "Nothing more innocent and childlike. But all the girl has to do is let go with that one hand and she'll slip away forever. We want to make sure that every child has both hands on the rope." She paused for a few moments and studied the picture before continuing, "If you'll follow me, Mrs. Byrne is all set for you."

Wallace tailed Marcie into a corridor flanked by a glass wall, which offered a view of an open-plan office and the city beyond. There were a dozen people in the spacious office, all busy at their big desks. The interior wall was lined with four more illustrations by the same artist featured in the lobby: the silhouette of a teenage girl at the top of a cliff, peering at a distant horizon; the same girl at the top of a high mountain looking at a twin-mooned starry night sky; standing on a rocky outcrop next to a high waterfall; walking in the ruins of an overgrown, once great city. Each image put the girl in an impossibly unreal but breathtaking landscape, but unlike the image in the lobby, in each of these pictures the girl was alone.

Marcie led Wallace through her office toward an inner door on the other side of the room. Standing on the sleekly contoured desk that was set flush against the far wall was a photo of Marcie being hugged by a beamingly happy man.

"My fiancé," Marcie explained, before giving a cursory knock and opening the inner door. "Can I get you anything?" she asked, as she stood aside and allowed Wallace to enter.

"I'm fine," he replied. "Thanks."

Wallace stepped into a spacious office. A four-seater couch seemed small pressed against the back wall. The coffee table immediately in front of it held large, expensive books. Beyond the table were two modern high-back armchairs that faced a huge desk, which was covered with neatly ordered rows of documents. Behind it, seated in a black leather chair, was Philicia Byrne, her head bowed and her brow crumpled in deep concentration.

"Let me know if you need anything," Marcie said to her boss.

"Thanks, Marce," Philicia acknowledged without looking up.

Marcie pulled the door closed behind her. Wallace looked at Philicia and questioned her fund-raising techniques. In order to get the meeting, he'd presented himself as a potential donor interested in making a six-figure contribution to Canopy. He wondered whether all prospective patrons were ushered into Philicia's presence without so much as a greeting. His research told him that she was forty-eight, but she looked younger. Long black hair tumbled around her shoulders in delicately layered waves. Her unblemished skin was subtly tanned and her cheeks had a fleshy fullness that belied her slender frame. Wallace had worked with enough models to know that if Philicia's cheeks were the result of surgical fillers, they had been expertly and expensively done.

He looked around the office. A bookcase lined the length of the opposite wall, broken only by another door. The shelves were carefully adorned with hardcovers, curios, and a few photographs. Wallace stepped forward and saw that there was a framed photograph of Erin Byrne. It was beautifully lit, and behind the girl was a distressed red background of the sort that one only finds in photographic studios. Erin had her mother's dark hair and smooth skin. Her wide eyes exuded longing and her full lips were ever so slightly parted as though she was about to whisper a secret. Her delicately featured face exposed the familiar vulnerability of countless teenagers lost in a search for meaning. Next to the photograph of Erin was a picture of her brother, Max, clad in his military dress uniform, looking every inch the brave, confident hero.

The door in the bookcase suddenly opened, startling Wallace. He stepped back to see a powerfully built man enter. The fabric of the man's expensive suit stretched at the shoulders, across the chest, and around the thighs, and Wallace sensed the rippling power of the muscles beneath. The man drew close to Wallace as he crossed the room. He was two inches taller and looked down at Wallace as he passed, his hard blue eyes overtly hostile. A crew cut and deliberate swagger suggested ex-military or police, and Wallace was suddenly on edge.

"Jacob works for me," Philicia said. "He'll be joining us."

Wallace looked around to see Philicia eyeing him from across the room. She was still seated and there was no offer of a greeting. Jacob stared at Wallace as he stationed himself beside one of the armchairs.

"Have a seat," Philicia instructed Wallace, and Jacob reinforced the invitation with a nod of his head.

"You do really great work here," Wallace observed as he sat. He needed to get control of the situation but was unnerved by Jacob, who remained at his shoulder and eyeballed him.

"Let's cut the crap. We both know you're not here to make a donation," Philicia said sharply, her amber eyes narrowing as she looked at Wallace with undisguised hostility. "What did you say your name was?" she asked, glancing at a piece of paper. "William Porter?" she continued. "Immigration shows a man with that name entering the United States two weeks ago. A Putnam County sheriff ran an RTCC search on that name last week." Wallace's face must have betrayed his dismay, because Philicia added, "We make it our business to know everything about everyone who sets foot in this office. Jacob used to work for my ex-husband. He is very good at cutting through bullshit. So why don't you tell me what you really want, before Jacob starts cutting through you?"

"Someone tried to kill me," Wallace replied slowly. "He tried to make it look like suicide. I've found two suicides that I think were murders, and the last one I found, a boy called Kye Walters, had a link to your daughter. I don't know what that link was, but if we find it, it might help us identify this killer."

Philicia looked at Wallace in disbelief and then glanced up at Jacob. "You think my daughter was murdered?"

Wallace nodded.

"I don't know what you think you've found, Mr. Porter, but my daughter took her own life." Philicia leaned forward and glared at Wallace with venomous anger. "Don't ever try to contact me again. Jacob will show you out."

Jacob took hold of Wallace's arm and hoisted him to his feet.

"Please, Mrs. Byrne," Wallace pleaded, "I know this is hard, but you have to believe me. Someone tried to kill me, and I think that same person might have killed your daughter."

"How dare you!" Philicia snapped to her feet and swept across the room to confront him. "How dare you say such things?"

"I've seen what this man can do," Wallace said softly.

"You don't know what we've been through," Philicia snarled, her pitch oscillating wildly. "Don't come in here with your lies!"

"Please, Mrs. Byrne," Wallace protested, "Maybe there was something you missed. Your husband, your son—maybe they saw something. Something tiny. It might seem insignificant."

Philicia looked as though she might strike Wallace, but instead she turned her back on him. "My son is sick. He will never be the same. And my husband . . . Steven . . . can you imagine coming home to find your child dead? Can you imagine the guilt? His life's over. He's just going through the motions."

Wallace watched as Philicia's body shook with the force of her grief. He suspected her words would apply equally to herself. "I'm sorry, I truly am, but I need your help."

"If I ever see you again, I won't hesitate to call the police," Philicia warned. "Get him out of here."

Wallace didn't resist as Jacob pulled him toward the door.

28

The Explorer was parked in an underground lot on Fifty-Fourth Street. Wallace didn't know what an RTCC search was, but he'd been through too much to take any risks. He was certain that the diligent sheriff would also have run his license plate, so the SUV would be tied to his William Porter identity. *The car's dead*, Wallace thought as he pulled his knapsack out of the trunk. *So is the motel.* He'd been staying in a Best Buck Motor Inn on Atlantic Avenue in Brooklyn. It was the least salubrious of his American digs, but the manager asked no questions and the other residents were too busy shooting up or selling their bodies to concern themselves with what a crazy Englishman was doing in their squalid part of the world. Wallace left the car keys on the driver's seat, slammed the door shut, and headed for the exit.

He emerged from the parking garage and hailed a cab. When he'd been looking for somewhere to stay, a couple of places had shown up in Manhattan, but Wallace had rejected them as too grim. One of them, the Fresh City Hotel, was located by the Bowery Mission near the southern tip of the island.

"You sure you got the right place?" the cab driver asked.

"I'm on a budget," Wallace explained as he slid along the backseat.

"No one's on that much of a budget," the cab driver observed wryly as he pulled into the slow-moving traffic.

The frozen city pulsed with life. As they drove south through Times Square, Wallace watched warmly wrapped tourists carefully pick their way along the icy sidewalks. Small groups stopped for photos in front of the huge advertising displays that had become synonymous with New York. Wallace envied every single one of the smiling fools. Under different circumstances, he knew that he would have been one of them. In Paris, Connie had gone to great lengths to pose a ridiculous photograph that appeared to show Wallace holding the Eiffel Tower in his hands. He remembered Connie's beautiful face, smiling brightly as she showed him the preposterous image. He felt his stomach knot at the memory and tried to push it from his mind, but her face was always there, the conclusion to every thought, the punctuation to every sentence, the sharp needle at the end of every thread. At least this memory had her smiling, not covered in her own blood, aghast with horror.

The cab drove on, past Union Square and south along Broadway, skirting the eastern fringe of Greenwich Village, which was lined with traditional redstone and brownstone buildings that offered a sense of history lacking from the uptown monoliths. When they reached a rutted redstone on the corner of Fourth Street, the Yellow Cab swung left and rolled on through the slush. At the intersection with the Bowery, Wallace finally became conscious of why his surroundings seemed so different; he could see the sky. The high towers of steel and glass had been replaced by small three- or four-story buildings, and, as they headed south on the Bowery, the majesty of New York vanished. A few blocks on and they were in a Chinatown that could have been located anywhere in the world—a mishmash of small buildings new and old, covered in brightly colored signs daubed with Chinese hanzi and the odd English word.

"Your budget awaits," the cab driver said as he pulled to a halt and nodded to his left.

Wallace looked across the Bowery and saw an all-night pharmacy and a restaurant called the Fireball Kitchen. He was about to quiz the cab driver when he noticed a small sign above a doorway between the pharmacy and restaurant. The sign said "Fresh City Hotel," or at least it was supposed to; the "F" and the "C" were missing, so it read "resh ity Hotel." Wallace paid the driver and hurried across the street.

The Chinese man behind the thick Plexiglas screen hadn't bothered to open Wallace's passport. He'd taken three days' rent in cash, handed Wallace a key, and sent him up three flights of stairs to a room that was barely large enough for the shabby single bed that resided within. The carpet was covered in fluff, hair, and dirt, and the bedclothes and drapes were stained and fraying. The small window overlooked a storage yard that was piled high with old kitchen equipment, but it was nailed shut so there was no chance of any fresh air to combat the stench of rot that permeated the room. A tiny bathroom lurked behind a plastic screen door, and when Wallace turned on the light he saw a fat cockroach scurry down the drain. He ignored his filthy surroundings, pulled out his iPad, and sat down on the bed to begin figuring out his next move.

Wallace had to wait for a week to get a table at Jean Mata. The restaurant was located on the fortieth floor of a building on Beaver Street and the panoramic windows offered far-reaching views of Brooklyn, Bay Ridge, and Staten Island. Two Michelin stars ensured that a meal for one cost almost as much as a week's rent at the Fresh City Hotel, but the restaurant catered to the Wall Street crowd, who wouldn't give a five-hundred-dollar lunch bill a second glance.

Wallace had discovered that Erin's brother Max had been committed to a psychiatric hospital five months after her death. He had no idea what the brother's mental condition might be or whether he'd be a reliable witness, so Steven Byrne was his best bet. Reaching a billionaire was no easy task. He researched Byrne, but the man's private clubs and philanthropic endeavors offered no obvious point of access, so Wallace had staked out the Erimax Building. He never actually saw Byrne arrive, but every morning shortly after eight, two black Range Rovers pulled into the building's garage. Privacy glass prevented Wallace from seeing the occupants, but he guessed one of them was Byrne. The Range Rovers usually left around seven p.m. Wallace had instructed a cab driver to tail them on the second night and followed them to an underground parking lot located beneath an expensive Park Avenue apartment building.

On the third day he had identified his most promising opportunity. Accompanied by three bodyguards, Steven Byrne left the Erimax Building on Exchange Place and walked two blocks to have lunch at Jean Mata. When Steven did exactly the same thing on the fourth and fifth days, Wallace realized that it was a lunchtime routine. He had spent six hundred dollars on a dark gray suit, a twill shirt, a woven silk tie, and brogues so that he wouldn't look out of place when he made his reservation in person. He had taken care to be in the busy restaurant at the same time as Steven and noted that the billionaire sat alone, with two of his bodyguards positioned at an adjacent table, while the third stood at the long bar and kept an eye on the entrances.

It had been a frustrating week waiting for a table, but Wallace had spent it going over the evidence and doing his aikido drills. When the day finally came, he was so eager that he arrived at the restaurant early and had been at his table for fifteen minutes before Steven Byrne entered. The maître d' offered an effusive flow of compliments as he showed Steven to his usual table. Next to the small, slight maître d', Steven looked particularly tall and powerful. He was around six-one and seemed in great shape. His jet-black hair was close cut, but not shaved, and unlike his praetorians, Steven didn't wear a suit, instead favoring a more casual look: a black jacket, a black turtleneck, and black jeans. As he drew closer, Wallace could see that Steven had a strong, pronounced jawline and a lean face. The billionaire took his seat, and, as the maître d' withdrew, his bodyguards stationed themselves as they had done before: two at the adjacent table and the third at the bar. Wallace made his move before any of them had a chance to settle. He was six tables away, near the entrance to the kitchen. The restaurant was packed, but it took him no time to cross the short distance and take a seat in the vacant chair at Steven Byrne's table.

Steven's intelligent eyes widened with surprise.

"Mr. Byrne, I need to speak to you about your daughter," Wallace said hurriedly. He glanced at the two nearest bodyguards, who were already on their feet.

"It's okay." Steven surprised Wallace by immediately waving the men off. "I want to hear what he has to say."

As the two imposing men returned to their seats, Wallace looked at Steven and saw that his initial surprise had been replaced by curiosity. His brow furrowed ever so slightly, but he said nothing as he studied Wallace.

"I think your daughter may have been murdered," Wallace began. "A few months ago, a man broke into my home and tried to kill me. When I was hospitalized, he tried again and killed a number of people in the process. He murdered my . . . he murdered a friend of mine," Wallace continued. "I followed a trail of killings from the UK to the US. Your daughter is the next on that trail. She was linked to the previous victim."

"How?" Steven asked earnestly.

"I don't know. That's why I'm here," Wallace replied. "Does the name Kye Walters mean anything to you?"

Steven shook his head slowly.

"Can you remember anything about Erin's death? Anything at all?" Wallace pressed.

"Like what?"

"Stewart Huvane, the first victim, told people he'd been attacked before the killer managed to finish him off," Wallace explained.

Steven was lost in silent thought as he considered his daughter's death. Finally, he shook his head. "I can't think of anything," he replied. "I wish I could. In many ways it would make it easier to come to terms with her passing."

"But . . ." Wallace became aware of someone standing beside him and suddenly stopped talking. He looked up to see the obsequious maître d' with two heavyset security guards at his shoulder.

"I'm sorry, Mr. Byrne," the maître d' said with a slight bow. "Is this gentleman bothering you?"

"It's okay, I think he's finished," Steven replied with the gracious condescension of the exceedingly powerful.

"I haven't finished," Wallace protested. "There's got to be something. Please!"

Byrne eyed Wallace with pity.

"If I'm right, if your daughter was murdered and you do nothing—"

"Don't you dare accuse me of doing nothing!" Steven growled, his raised voice drawing concerned looks from the surrounding diners.

"Would you like me to have this gentleman escorted from the building?" the maître d' asked.

Wallace could feel Steven's growing hostility as he slowly nodded.

"If you please, sir," the maître d' said to Wallace. The two security guards stepped forward and one of them placed a hand on his shoulder.

"You're making a mistake," Wallace cautioned. "You owe it to your daughter."

"Let's go!" the first security guard said, grabbing hold of his arm and hoisting him out of his chair.

Wallace realized that he had drawn far too much attention to himself and that things were running out of control. Neither Steven nor his wife had reacted well to his theory, and who could blame them? Without any evidence, these grieving parents would just view Wallace as a deranged opportunist. He needed to defuse the situation, to regroup, and to find a way to convince Byrne that his daughter had not killed herself. If her death followed the same pattern as the others, there would be evidence linking her to another victim or directly to the killer; he just had to find it.

"Okay," he said as he stood. "I'm going."

"I'll need to see some ID," the security guard instructed, tightening his grip on Wallace's arm. "We're going to need to file a police report," he advised Steven, "so we have a record in case he ever bothers you again."

Wallace felt his chest tighten and his stomach broil with panicked acid. "I'll just go," he tried nervously. "I promise I won't bother you again," he assured Steven.

"Let's see it," the security guard commanded. "Or we'll just hand you over right now."

"Look, I don't have anything on me right now. My passport is at my hotel, but my name is William Porter, and I—"

Before Wallace could say anything else, the maître d' cut in, "I think we should call the police, sir."

Steven looked from the maître d' to Wallace and nodded. "Call it in," he said.

Wallace simply couldn't risk being caught and knew that he had to act fast. He punched the first security guard in the face, knocking him cold. As the restaurant filled with outcry, he saw that Steven Byrne's bodyguards were already on the move. The nearest two were on an intercept course and the third had left the bar and was already halfway to the table. Wallace suddenly felt a heavy hand grasp his shoulder and pull him round. He allowed himself to be turned and, using his assailant's force to add momentum to the blow, struck the second security guard in the face with his elbow. The impact sent the man thudding to the ground.

With the building security guards incapacitated, Wallace now faced Byrne's bodyguards. The first man swung for Wallace, but he ducked the blow and brought the top of his skull up into the body-guard's chin. The second bodyguard came for him, but he barreled forward, sending them both crashing into a neighboring table. Wallace got to his feet and saw the third bodyguard blocking his route to the elevators. He started running toward the kitchen, colliding with staff, bouncing off fleeing diners, and rolling over tables in a panicked mess.

As he neared the kitchen doors, Wallace had the wind knocked out of him when the third bodyguard hit him with a flying tackle. Wallace landed on his back, with the bodyguard on top of him. The powerful man was agile and quickly rolled to his feet. Struggling for breath, Wallace was slower, and he paid a heavy price: the body-guard kicked him, catching him in the ribs as he tried to stand. Wallace's vision flared with spinning sparks of pain, and he knew he couldn't take many more hits like that. As the bodyguard came in for a second kick, Wallace blocked the strike and flung his right leg out in a sweeping blow that knocked the man off balance. Wallace saw the other two bodyguards coming toward him, and knew he had no chance against three men. He rolled toward the fallen bodyguard and drove his fist into the man's groin with every ounce of power he could muster. It was the dirty move of a street brawler, but it was effective; the anguished cry of pain told Wallace that the third bodyguard would no longer pose a threat.

He got to his feet and stormed through one of the free-swinging doors into the kitchen. He collided with a group of chefs who had been drawn by the noise. A couple of hands made feeble attempts to grab him, but shock and momentum were his allies and he pushed through the group toward a fire exit. As he raced past the stainless steel appliances he heard a commotion behind him and turned to see the remaining two bodyguards follow him into the kitchen, no more than twenty feet off his pace. A heavyset, middle-aged man in whites emerged from a small office and ran straight into him. Wallace pushed the man aside, forcing him back into the office, but the collision broke his stride and enabled the first of the bodyguards to reach him. The bodyguard punched him in the neck and slammed him into a workbench. He grabbed Wallace's hair and pushed his head down onto the metal countertop. Wallace felt another set of hands on his shoulders; he was pinned down.

"Keep fighting," one of the men said in an accent that oozed with thick Southern sarcasm. "So we can keep hurtin'."

Wallace lashed out with his right foot and felt a satisfying crack as he caught one of the men's shins. He felt the pressure on his head lighten and brought his body up as quickly as he could. Pain snapped the back of his head as it connected with something, but as he spun round, Wallace saw that his opponent had come off worse: he'd cracked the second bodyguard's nose into a bloody mess. He popped a punch at the first bodyguard's face. The blow connected and Wallace followed up with a cross that sent the man reeling. Wallace kicked him in the gut and, as the first bodyguard slammed into the wall, turned and ran for the fire exit.

He burst into a stark concrete stairwell and bounded down the steps three at a time, and as the staircase snaked round and back on itself, he looked up and saw the two bodyguards barge through the fire door and steam after him. Wallace bounced between the black metal railing and the whitewashed walls as he devoured the stairs. Ten floors down, and he misjudged a jump. He landed badly, and had to roll to avoid putting his weight on a precariously positioned ankle, then tumbled down the next flight of stairs. He bounced to a halt against the far wall of the next landing, and, before he could get to his feet, was set upon by the two bodyguards.

The bodyguard with the broken, bloody nose drove a kick into Wallace's gut. The other man punched him in the face, smacking him onto the hard concrete. Wallace scrambled to his knees and barged his shoulder into the man's legs, knocking him off balance and sending him tumbling down the next flight of stairs. He stood up and took a glancing blow to the head as the bloodied bodyguard tried to put him back down. Fighting in close, confined quarters presented perfect conditions for aikido, and with the panic of his initial flight subsiding, Wallace remembered his years of training. When the bodyguard swung a punch, he blocked and caught the man's wrist between both hands. In a single fluid, forbidden movement, Wallace snapped his hands in different directions and heard the crack of the bodyguard's wrist breaking. The man's face went white with pain and he instantly dropped to his knees, cradling his broken arm. Wallace turned, ran down the stairs, and collided with the first bodyguard, who was hauling himself to his feet on the next landing. Wallace punched the man, dazing him, before grabbing his head and smashing it against the concrete wall. The first bodyguard dropped like a dead weight and Wallace sped on, bounding down the stairs until he reached the ground floor.

Breathless and sweaty, but certain he was no longer being followed, Wallace tried to compose himself before stepping onto the street. He waited a few moments in the cold concrete corridor until his hands had stopped trembling and then stepped through the fire exit.

"Don't move!" a powerful voice commanded.

Wallace stopped in his tracks, dismayed by what he saw ahead of him. The street had been closed to traffic and the only vehicles he could see were four cars in the familiar blue-and-white markings of the New York Police Department. Ranged around them were eight pistol-toting police officers. He glanced down the street and saw a small crowd of onlookers standing in the snow, waiting to see whether someone was going to get shot. Wallace had no intention of giving the audience any macabre entertainment. He put his hands high above his head.

29

Christine Ash tapped her pen impatiently as the members of the Disciplinary Review Board filed back into the room. Assistant Director Randall did not look at her as he took his seat, but Ash couldn't tell whether that was a bad sign, or whether Randall was just being his usual misanthropic self. The other board members—five suitably senior agents who spent six months hearing appeals—studiously avoided Ash's gaze. The signs weren't good, and Ash gave her attorney, Isla Vaughn, a concerned glance.

"Looks bad," Ash whispered, inwardly reminding herself that she'd known the risks when she'd taken the shot.

"Let's wait and see," Isla replied quietly.

The two women attracted the ire of Edward Omar, the Review Board's legal counsel, and his glare yelled silence.

The committee members sat behind a long table on a raised dais that was only six inches off the ground, but the slight elevation made it clear to everyone where the power resided. The room had no windows and the walls were covered with soundproof insulation. Ash and her lawyer sat at a small table opposite the committee, and Ed Omar and his assistant sat at a duplicate that flanked them a few feet away. A dozen chairs lined the back wall, but only one was occupied. Ash's boss, Assistant Special Agent in Charge Hector Solomon, had watched the final day's proceedings with the impassive mask of a seasoned poker player.

"Agent Ash," Randall began, "the Disciplinary Review Board has considered your appeal. Last year, on July sixth, you shot and killed

Marcel Washington, the leader of the Hopeland Family, an organiza-
tion implicated in murder, racketeering, drugs smuggling, and gun
running. Your superior, Assistant SAIC Hector Solomon, impressed
upon you the need to capture Washington alive; however, in your
report, you claimed that when your team raided the Dover Plains
compound, you confronted Washington, who produced a weapon,
and that you were forced to shoot him. Despite the efforts of attending paramedics, he died at the scene. Upon learning of the death of
their leader, six members of the Hopeland Family refused to surrender and instead opened fire on your team, killing Special Agent
Valerie Templeton. All six members of the Hopeland Family were
eventually shot by your team. Three of them subsequently died."

Randall paused and stared directly at Ash. Templeton had been a
heavy loss, and Ash still struggled with the burden. If she'd played
things out differently, maybe Templeton would still be alive . . . Ash
suppressed the thought; it didn't lead anywhere good.

"Due to the seriousness of the incident, the Office of the Inspec-
tor General and the Internal Investigations Section concluded a joint
inquiry into your and your team's actions leading up to the shoot-
ings. While the investigation supported your account of events and
considered it a clean shooting, the OIG and IIS investigators could
not rule out the possibility that your judgment fell short of the standard required of a Supervisory Special Agent. As a result, the investigation panel recommended that you be suspended for three months,
during which time you were to receive professional training and
counseling, and that you be demoted two ranks to Special Agent. You
filed an appeal and this Disciplinary Review Board was convened to
consider it. It should be noted that you have served the suspension
and completed the mandated training and counseling, and that this
appeal applies only to your demotion."

Randall looked to his left and right and received a couple of slight
nods of encouragement from his fellow board members. "Having
considered the evidence and submissions from the OIG and IIS, this
committee finds that there are no grounds to overrule the original
disciplinary measures and that this appeal should be denied," he said.

"The board is confident that, if you learn from this tragic experience, the same diligence that earned you such rapid promotion will ensure a swift return to your former rank, Special Agent Ash."

Ash felt a flush of humiliation, but she was determined not to be anything other than courteous and professional. "Thank you, Assistant Director Randall. I'd like to thank you and the other board members for considering my appeal with such great care and attention."

"Sorry," Isla said softly as she patted Ash on the arm.

"It's okay," Ash replied as she got to her feet. But it wasn't okay; her career had just regressed five years.

Ash switched on her cell phone as she hurried along the fourth-floor corridor, desperate to get out of the Hoover Building, away from the scene of her humiliation.

"Ash!" Hector called out behind her.

She turned to see her boss approaching. At five-ten, he was only a couple of inches taller than her, which gave Ash an inch advantage in her heels. Hector was beaming a perfect smile of sympathy. Everything about him was elegant and refined, from his perfectly coiffed dark hair to his gleaming black brogues. His mixed heritage had blessed him with a light tan, and he had the good judgment to know that it was enhanced by a crisply pressed white shirt and dark-blue suit.

"I spoke to Randall," Hector said as he caught up with Ash. "He really wanted to find a way, but—"

"They didn't have a choice," Ash interrupted.

"You know how it is," Hector observed.

Ash nodded. "Can't fight the machine."

"Listen, I'm going to talk to Alvarez, see what he's got for you."

Ash sighed. Alvarez was her contemporary, one of her rivals, and her mind clouded with dirty shame at the thought she'd now have to report to someone who, until a few months ago, had been her equal.

"You know how to do this, Ash," Hector added. "Some good cases and you'll make rank in a couple of years. Maybe less."

Two years to recover lost ground while her peers advanced, despite the fact that everyone agreed it had been a clean kill. Washington was a scumbag and Ash knew better than most what a man like him did to people, but the hard lessons of her brutal past didn't count for anything; they couldn't count for anything. Ash could never explain the real reason why Washington deserved to die. They would never understand. As it was, there had been enough question marks over the shooting for her judgment to be challenged, and it had been found wanting. She felt a surge of angry frustration but knew better than to show it.

"I'll report to Alvarez tomorrow," she replied.

"Great," Hector smiled. "I gotta run. There's some people I need to see while I'm here." He patted Ash on the arm and hurried along the corridor.

Ash watched him stride on, certain he'd spend the afternoon shaking the right hands and smiling at the right faces in an effort to increase his chances of taking over the New York office when SAIC Harrell finally retired. Special Agent in Charge Hector Solomon; it had an inevitable ring to it.

Ash checked her phone, saw that she had a missed call, and dialed her voice mail.

"Special Agent Ash, this is Detective Pinelli, Fifth Precinct," said the recorded voice in deep, gnarly tones. "We picked up a John Doe perp on an assault charge. British guy. No ID, no record, and he ain't talkin'. Says he'll only speak to you, so I was wonderin' if you could come down to the Fifth and maybe help us out."

Ash hung up. She knew one Brit and the chances of him getting picked up on an assault charge were slim. This was probably some nut who'd got hold of her name at random, but, as a newly demoted foot soldier, she had a responsibility to check it out. Her flight out of Dulles wasn't until eight p.m., and she had planned to spend the evening wallowing in pizza and margaritas, a final commiseration before she started this unwelcome retrograde phase of her career. The perp would have to wait until morning.

Wallace could hear the police station coming to life. Distant shouts bounced off the white cinder block walls. He'd spent two nights in a nine-by-five cell. A stainless steel sink and toilet unit protruded from one wall. A bunk ran the length of the other. A thick metal door had bars cut into it so that the custody officers could peer in and check on their prisoners. A heavyset custody sergeant known to his colleagues as Dozer had passed an old copy of the *New York Times* through the bars, providing Wallace with some small distraction from the dark thoughts that preoccupied him. He'd spent most of the first night lost in flailing depression, his mind spinning into dangerously dark territory, wondering about the dangers of the American justice system. Exhausted, he'd managed to sleep most of the second night, waking to the early morning sounds of one of the precinct janitors cleaning out the adjacent holding cells, filling the air with the caustic stench of bleach.

Detective Pinelli, the squat Italian New Yorker running his case, had warned Wallace that they could only keep him in custody for seventy-two hours, after which he'd be transferred to Rikers Island, where he'd be held until he could be identified and processed for trial. Wallace had no idea whether it was the truth or whether Pinelli was simply threatening him in an effort to get him to divulge his name, but he'd heard of Rikers through countless movies and TV shows, and, despite the jail's notorious reputation, he was not about to relinquish the safety of anonymity.

He heard footsteps approaching and turned to see the rotund Dozer swagger into view.

"You got a visitor," the custody sergeant announced through the bars.

Wallace's handcuffs were secured to an anchor point on the table, which in turn was bolted to the floor. He sat in one of two cheap chairs that faced a matching pair on the other side of the small, windowless room, which couldn't have been more than eight feet square. The floor was covered in thin carpet tiles and the walls were lined with white wood paneling. Wallace had been waiting long enough to lose track of time. His wrists ached and he felt nagging discomfort in his upper back as he hunched forward to keep his forearms on the table.

The solid blue door opened and Pinelli entered, followed by a white woman in her late twenties. She was slim and slightly taller than the NYPD detective. She wore practical flat shoes, a pair of black trousers, a tan pullover, and carried a long coat, which she slung over the back of one of the chairs. Her light-brown hair fell straight around her shoulders. She had a tiny, almost button nose, and a wide mouth with thin lips. Her cheeks and nose were covered with delicate freckles. At first glance, she seemed fragile, but her eyes gave her away. They were beautiful wide ovals with pools of amber brown nestled in the center, but there was a hardness to them that Wallace had come to recognize as the cynical mark of every police officer he'd ever met.

"I'm Special Agent Christine Ash," the woman said. "Detective Pinelli says you want to talk."

"I'd like to see some identification," Wallace replied. Pinelli rolled his eyes and Ash sighed, but Wallace didn't care how paranoid he sounded. Ash pulled a leather wallet from her coat pocket and flipped it open to reveal her FBI identification.

"You want to tell me your name?" Ash asked as she sat opposite Wallace.

"This needs to be a private conversation," he said, looking pointedly at Pinelli.

"Motherfucker," Pinelli remarked. He shook his head at Ash, who nodded. Pinelli stared at Wallace with undisguised hostility as he backed out of the room and closed the door.

"So?" Ash said finally.

"I found your name in a file given to me by Detective Sergeant Bailey," Wallace replied. "Do you know him?"

"Pat? Sure. We met at an International Tactical Law Enforcement conference a few years back," Ash said.

"Did he call you recently?" Wallace asked. "In the last few months?"

Ash nodded.

Wallace sensed a change in her demeanor; she was beginning to take him seriously.

"A couple of months ago," Ash acknowledged. "He asked me to look into something."

"A suicide," Wallace noted. "Kye Walters."

"I told Bailey what the local PD report said; it was a tragic case but there was no evidence of foul play."

"Kye Walters was murdered," Wallace said flatly. "He was murdered by the same man who tried to kill me."

Ash hesitated, her head tilting ever so slightly as a look of puzzlement crossed her face. "Murdered?"

Wallace nodded.

"And how do you know that?" Ash asked with more than a hint of disbelief in her voice.

"I've followed the killer's trail all the way from London," Wallace replied.

"Does Bailey know about this?"

Wallace nodded. "The murderer almost killed him. He's in hospital in a coma."

Ash watched Wallace, but gave no indication of her thoughts.

"He believed me. He's the one who gave me the files on Kye Walters," Wallace continued. "The killer hangs his victims. He then publishes a suicide note online. The note reveals a shameful secret that supposedly drove the person to take their own life."

"Why didn't you take this information to the police?" Ash challenged him.

"I saw this man gun down two police officers. He's tried to kill me three times. Nowhere's safe from him," Wallace replied.

Ash studied him for a moment, and he began to relax as it became clear that she was taking his story seriously. She leaned forward and spoke slowly, "See, Detective Pinelli is a very thorough man. Among other, more routine searches, he also checked the Metropolitan Police's list of wanted fugitives and found your mug shot somewhere near the top. We know that your name is John Wallace."

The cool delivery of Ash's words did nothing to lessen their impact, and Wallace felt as though he had been kicked in the gut. *They knew his real name.*

"We know that you are an escaped psychiatric patient currently wanted by the Metropolitan Police in connection with a series of murders, including the attempted murder of Detective Sergeant Patrick Bailey. What I can't understand is why you'd tell us about your crimes. Maybe you thought we Americans are too stupid to do our jobs properly," Ash mused coldly.

"I didn't kill anyone!" Wallace attempted to stand, but his cuffs caught against the anchor and he fell back into his seat.

Ash stood and knocked on the door. "The people you attacked are pressing charges," she said, as Pinelli rolled into the room.

"I didn't attack anyone," Wallace protested.

"There are dozens of witnesses who say otherwise," Ash countered. "You are going to be transferred to Rikers Island, where you will be held pending a trial. If convicted, once you have served whatever sentence you are given in the United States, you will be extradited to the UK to face the charges brought against you there."

Wallace thumped his fists against the table. "You have to listen to me! Someone tried to kill me! He killed Connie!"

"Good luck, Mr. Wallace," Ash said quietly. "I hope things work out for you."

Wallace felt a dark storm of despair sweep over him as Ash turned away. She left the room and Pinelli followed her, flashing a dark smile as he pulled the door shut. As Wallace heard the sound of the bolt snapping into the frame, he looked down at his hands and realized they were shaking.

30

Ken Pallo stumbled out of the theater and almost fell over Giselle, his hot young companion. Pallo chuckled at the euphemism; companion was so much more acceptable than whore. Giselle giggled back at him, her unfocused eyes shining wide. Fueled by coke and some mighty trippy OG Kush, they were both soaring higher than any kite. Pallo grabbed Giselle's firm ass, making her yelp with impish delight. A couple of passing suits frowned, but Pallo didn't give a rat's fuck. What was the point of being in the movie business if you couldn't grab ass and get high? Giselle had been stroking his dick through his pants for much of the movie, which earned them icy looks from the cold bitch seated on the other side of him. He'd met her before—Nina or Nita or some such—she was the wife of a middling studio executive. A perma-tanned, gray-suited cog called Josh who helped keep the big greasy wheels turning. With the amount of money he'd sunk into the picture, Pallo probably could have cowgirled Giselle right in front of NinaNita, and the thin-lipped nobody would have just had to sit there and smile for the money shot.

Giselle pulled Pallo forward. She skipped on, a lithe figure in her gold-sequined minidress and matching stiletto heels. Pallo kept hold of her hand, her tiny fingers folded in the fleshy cushion of his palm, but his body wasn't designed for rapid flight, and he stumbled, pulling Giselle back so that she landed flat on her ass in the entrance to the Academy lobby. Pallo burst out laughing and people turned to sneer at the brouhaha. *Pompous fucks*, Pallo thought as he caught the disapproving glances, *it's a movie premier, not a fucking wake*. Giselle looked muddled for a moment, as though she was trying to figure out why her legs were sprawled in front of her, and then she grinned. Pallo offered her his hand. At five feet six and two hundred and fifty pounds, there weren't many things his body was good for, but impersonating an anchor was one. He didn't budge as the tiny girl, who couldn't have been much more than a third his age, pulled herself up.

He led Giselle into the large, marble-clad lobby and scanned it for familiar faces. The vast room was humming with the garbled noise of a couple hundred people: needy writers shuffled around, their pleading eyes desperately searching for approval from one of the many puffed-up producers; brightly polished agents stalked through the lobby, their feral eyes searching for any opportunity to poach hot talent; faded directors wandered about the place, desolately combing it for any crumbs of good fortune; and bubbly publicists guarded their star clients with phony smiles and false promises served up to cynical members of the Hollywood press. All around the room hot wannabes pressed themselves on power, their eyes brimming with the promise of lustful bargains to be struck. Studio executives danced around in a series of beaming, insincere interactions. Pallo was in the rarest of all groups; the money men. Imperious figures, they rarely moved. Eventually most of the hustlers in the room would drift into their orbit and try very hard to prove that they weren't angling for a buck.

"Ken!"

Pallo turned and saw Johnny Urban approaching. Urban was one of the movie's producers and something of a legend in the Hollywood community. Pallo had heard a rumor that Urban murdered his first boyfriend. Strangled him after he came at Urban with a knife. Even though he'd been a participant in many deaths, Pallo had never killed anyone. The thought of choking the life out of someone excited him, and Pallo stroked the nape of Giselle's neck, fantasizing about what would come later.

"What a fucking movie!" Urban proclaimed. "We're already getting awards buzz."

He slapped Pallo on the shoulder in friendly bonhomie. The blow was so slight that Pallo struggled to believe the murder rumor was true. Urban was short and skinny and looked like he'd have trouble crushing a soda can, let alone squeezing the life out of a crazed lover. Only in Hollywood could the aphrodisiac of power overwhelm all else. It didn't matter how short, ugly, bald, or murderous Urban was; this weedy nerd never ran short of hot young twinks. There was one on his arm, a perfectly bronzed young blond in a light linen suit.

If it hadn't been for Giselle's hand all over his crotch, Pallo wouldn't have enjoyed the movie at all. Too much talking, not enough explosions. But Urban's pictures had a track record of making money and Pallo had deliberately chosen to invest in a highbrow drama slate. A few serious award-winning movies would help counterbalance his more licentious business interests, and his private peccadilloes.

"I loved it," Pallo lied. "You've done a great job."

"Thanks, man," Urban smiled. Neither of the middle-aged men bothered to introduce their hot young mates.

"Hey, Bob!" Urban called over Pallo's shoulder. "We gotta go say hi," he explained, as he patted Pallo on the shoulder and swiftly moved on to the next hollow conversation.

Pallo felt the happy effects of his buzz dissipating. There were no familiar faces in sight, just an assortment of hostile eyes. Pallo knew he wasn't going to win the vote for prom king. The Hollywood community disapproved of the way in which he'd made his money, but his background wasn't the source of the hostility; it was pure sour grapes that he'd invested with Johnny Urban and not them.

"I'm sobering up," he said to Giselle. "Let's get the fuck out of here."

Pallo woke to the familiar sensation of tiny hooves galloping deep within his chest. At fifty-four he knew he was running out of track. His pasty, bloated body told the tale of a life lived fast and hard. He belched and raw acid burned his throat. The hooves beat their irregular rhythm and Pallo knew he needed something to bring him down. He was getting too old for coke, but it helped him claw onto a youthful vitality that was long past. He sat up and looked down at Giselle's perfectly smooth curves. Her neck bore the faint red imprint of ligature marks, and Pallo glanced at the woven silk noose that hung over the side of the bed. Girls like Giselle got extra for giving life to his fantasy: five hundred bucks to compensate them for having to wear a scarf until the marks faded.

Giselle was deeply asleep, her face pressed against his six-hundred-thread linen, but that didn't stop Pallo using his finger to trace the curve of her firm tits, along her soft belly, and down between her thighs. Giselle stirred, and Pallo felt the painful ache of a nascent erection. He knew a blast of powder would kill the pain and give him the juice for another fuck, but he was worried his heart wouldn't take it. Ten years ago, maybe, but now . . .

Pallo grabbed the noose and hauled himself out of bed onto the teak floor, which felt cool as he crossed his large bedroom. He unwound the noose, placed the woven rope in the top drawer of his dresser, and turned toward the panoramic window to look at the dark Pacific Ocean, which crashed against the Malibu sand as puffball clouds shrouded the moon. The view was worth every cent of the twenty-two million the place had cost. Pallo quietly closed the bedroom door behind him and crossed the landing to the marble steps leading down into the vast oceanfront living room. He was halfway down the stairs when he felt a draft and realized that the ocean's roar was much louder than usual. He looked across the room and saw that one of the retractable glass panels was open. He and Giselle were so fucking blasted that he had forgotten to lock up properly.

He ambled round the back of the stairs to the chef's kitchen that he never used and opened his medicine drawer. He produced a pack of beta-blockers and swallowed a couple with a glass of water. *Keep the beast alive a little longer*, Pallo thought as he crossed the living room to the control terminal that operated the retractable panels. He pushed the "secure" button, which was supposed to close every window and panel in the building, but nothing happened.

"Fuckin' thing," Pallo seethed as he moved toward the faulty panel. The crashing roar of the ocean filled his ears as he stepped onto the wooden deck that ran around the whole house. None of his neighbors' lights were on. The only lights he could see came from a house about a mile up the beach—it might have been the old Griffin place—so he didn't have to worry about anyone catching a peek of his hairy ass as he crouched down and checked the panel runners. With the ocean filling his ears, Pallo pushed his fingers into the metal groove that was scored into the deck to enable the glass panels that made up the living room walls to move freely. His finger caught on something sharp that was wedged under the runner of the faulty panel.

"Fuck!" Pallo hollered as he whipped his finger to his mouth. He stood and was about to go inside when he sensed something behind him. He turned to see a masked man step toward him, his arm raised. Acrid fluid sprayed from a small aerosol in the man's hand, and Pallo immediately felt the world turn heavy and distant. He didn't even have time to panic as his legs gave way and he blacked out.

Cold static. Pain flowing over his body. Not pain. Fluid. Water. Pallo made sense of the signals and he was assailed by the world as sensations flooded his mind. He was on his back, lying in shallow water. Intermittent spray flecked his face as the Pacific waves rolled in. The air was infused with the sour, briny stench of the sea, and the crash of rolling breakers filled his ears. There was darkness above him. Something solid that obliterated the sky. Pallo turned his head and saw a forest of thick wooden columns. The pier. He was beneath Malibu Pier. He looked along the beach and could see his house half a mile away. He longed for the softness of his bed and the warmth of Giselle and tried to roll onto all fours, but realized that his hands were bound. He pushed his head back and saw his masked assailant. The man wore a long coat. Pallo could see flashes of dark armor beneath it, like SWAT gear. The guy was standing on a packing crate, his back to Pallo. He jumped off the crate, splashing Pallo with water. Pallo blinked, and when his eyes finally cleared, he saw something hanging above him. It took him a moment to realize what it was; looped over a structural support, a hangman's noose swung in the breeze.

"No!" Pallo yelled, as his masked assailant drew out the slack so that he could pull the noose down. "Fuck you! You can't do this!"

"I know about Next Life," the masked man revealed. "I know what you do when you think no one is watching."

The exposure of his darkest secret filled Pallo with terror and he thrashed about in the water, but his efforts were futile; with his arms bound behind him, he could hardly move. He tried to keep his head bucking from side to side, but his frenetic struggle proved fruitless and the masked man slipped the noose under his chin and pulled it snug around his neck.

"It's easier if you stand," Pallo's assailant said in a voice that was just loud enough to be heard above the waves.

"Fuck you!" Pallo spat. He felt the rope bite into his neck as the masked man began pulling on the other end. Pallo tried to curse, but the words choked in his throat as the noose hugged ever tighter. He was shocked at the ease with which the man was able to hoist him out of the surf. Within moments he was dangling beneath the pier, his feet swinging above the foaming water. Pallo should have been panicking, but the beta-blockers kept him calm, and his defective heart thumped a steady rhythm. As the rope crushed his neck and his lungs burned with a scorching lust for air, Pallo felt his arms fall limp as his bonds were cut. His hands instinctively rushed to his throat and clawed at the rope, which was lost in massy folds of flesh. *So this is what it feels like*, he thought, as tendrils of darkness whipped the edges of his mind. The masked man walked round and stood in front of him, his opaque goggles concealing any emotion he might have felt as he watched his victim die.

"Who?" Pallo tried to say, but there was no sound as his lips moved, just a fierce burning in his throat. There were countless names that might have put him at the end of the rope. He'd spread way too much pain in pursuit of his own warped pleasures. As the cool January breeze gently swung him, Pallo turned away from his killer and gazed up at the heavens.

Twisting at the end of a fucking noose, he reflected. *Justice is one ironic bitch.*

Pallo smiled, as death finally took him.

31

"Good morning." Arturo Alvarez smiled as he breezed past Ash's cubicle. *My boss*, Ash thought glumly as she considered her shriveled career. Alvarez was on his way to a twelve-by-twelve corner office with a view of Broadway and the city beyond. She was stuck in a four-by-four cubicle in the heart of the building. Windows were a distant privilege that she'd have to earn all over again. At twenty-nine, Ash was four or five years older than most of the peers that had boxes next to hers.

"Mornin'." Parker, Ash's bright-eyed, boy scout neighbor, looked as though he was tempted to salute as he stood up and called after Alvarez, who wheeled round midstride, nodded a half-smile, and then continued toward his office.

Ash shook her head at Parker's terrible ass-kissing. Still, suck-up Parker still had a better assignment than Ash; he was on the Domestic Terrorism Task Force working the Foundation, a militant anticapitalist network that had surfaced two years ago and had been implicated in a cyber attack on the First Atlantic Bank and Square Pillar Trading, an online brokerage. In both cases the Foundation had attempted to devastate the companies with a total shutdown, but, while the attacks had crippled the firms for a few hours, they were ultimately unsuccessful. The Foundation had dropped off the radar in recent months, but the Bureau had picked up cyber chatter that suggested it was about to gear up its activities.

Ash longed to work such an interesting case but had instead been assigned historic profiling. She tried to tell herself that she'd been stuck with a bunch of cold cases because the other teams were over-resourced, but she knew that wasn't true. Historic profiling was the type of assignment given to rookies straight out of Quantico; Alvarez was trying to make a point, maybe even trying to sideline a potential rival. But the truth was Ash was no longer Alvarez's rival. Washington's death had knocked her back to the starting blocks. Alvarez was way ahead; she was now racing dumbasses like Parker.

Ash looked down. Pushed into the corner, where her desk met the felt-lined panels of her cubicle, was the framed photograph of Ash with her mother. They were both smiling in the California sun, standing high in the Santa Monica Mountains, the hazy City of Angels sprawling out behind them. It was the only photograph Ash had of her mother, and whenever she was feeling blue, it reminded her of what some people had to endure. *Don't be afraid, baby.* The last words her mother ever said to her, and Ash repeated them to herself almost every day.

The phone on her desk rang. "Ash," she answered.

"Special Agent Ash?" a man's voice said. He was somewhere loud and busy. "My name is Scott Herson, I'm with the Public Defender's Office. I've got a client, real pain-in-the-ass guy by the name of John Wallace. You know him?"

"We've met," Ash replied.

"So he's not totally nuts," Herson observed. "That's good to know. He's refusing to talk to me until I give you a message, so do with it what you will. He says you should check out Ken Pallo."

"The porn guy?" Ash asked.

"Yup," Herson replied. "Wallace says it's the same killer."

"Okay, thanks," Ash said as she wrote "Ken Pallo" on a scrap of paper. "Hey, Scott, how's he doing?"

"Who? Wallace?" Herson's disembodied voice dripped with unmistakable condescension. "He's in Rikers. It's the closest thing New York has to hell. You know how he's doing. Listen, I gotta go."

"Thanks," Ash tried to say, but Herson had already hung up.

Ash turned to her laptop and googled Ken Pallo. Dozens of sensational headlines filled her screen. *Porn King Snuffs It. Porn Mogul*

Swinging. Suicide Takes Porn King. Most of the articles used the same image, a wide landscape photograph of Malibu Pier with Pallo's body hanging beneath it. Pallo had killed himself three days ago, but Ash had only caught the sound bites. As she read the details, she wondered how Wallace could think this was anything other than suicide. Pallo, a multimillionaire mogul who owned five of the world's top ten porn sites and was alleged to have been worth more than two hundred million dollars, posted a lurid suicide note to Facebook in which he cataloged his drug addiction and terrible exploitation of the young men and women who worked for him. Wallace was nuts; there was nothing to this. Ash scrolled down the *New York Post* article. Under the picture of Pallo beneath the pier, there was another photograph of the pasty-looking fat man at a movie premiere the night he killed himself. He had his arm around a gorgeous young brunette in a gold dress and both of them were smiling at the camera, their wide, glassy eyes reflecting the lights that surrounded them. Something about Pallo made Ash hesitate. The look in his eyes was one she'd seen before: self-obsessed, greedy, and narcissistic, it reminded Ash of her father, and she knew that people like that rarely gave anything up, least of all their own lives.

She couldn't see any harm in checking out Pallo's death. It was probably a snipe hunt, but it beat shuffling through old files of the long dead.

32

Wallace looked at the kaleidoscope of colors and wondered how much longer he could stay alive. It wasn't just the physical threat; he was acutely aware of the toll Rikers was taking on his mind. He hadn't slept properly since his incarceration three weeks ago. He'd spend much of the night awake, worrying what the next day would bring. Eventually, exhausted, he'd pass out for a couple of hours and his subconscious would assault him with a vivid montage of violence: Connie's death, the attempts on his life, and the attacks he'd experienced at the hands of Smokie.

Each morning, Wallace would wake, his eyes burning with ever-increasing exhaustion. Sleep deprivation, hunger, and relentless stress had shredded any excess fat, and as he looked down at his badly bruised torso, Wallace knew that he would soon become dangerously emaciated. There was no obvious solution, and it needed to be obvious because his mind was struggling to simply make it through the day. He spent most of the time feeling light-headed, the world sliding around him precariously, taunting him with the sensation that it might spin violently out of control. His reactions were sluggish and his soul was steeped in the dirty lethargy of depression.

Food would be the obvious answer, but that was how the beatings had started. On his fourth day in Eric M. Taylor Center, the bleach and cinder block detention building that was now his home, Wallace had his first encounter with Smokie, the noxious product of a depraved life. He was a recent addition to the Murdering Taylors, or MTs, the block's offshoot of the Bloods, which was run by

Ole Creepy, a savagely scarred, one-eyed man. Smokie couldn't have been much more than thirty, but he had the hard eyes and unstable temperament of an experienced killer. Wallace could tell that Smokie was ambitious and that he was looking for an excuse to challenge Ole Creepy for leadership of the thirty or so Bloods who made up the MTs. Some as young as sixteen, they all shared a wild propensity for violence.

Seated alone in the block's vast canteen, Wallace had intended to eat quickly and then hide in a quiet corner of the dayroom, but Smokie rolled up with six of his psychopaths. It had all started so quietly. Smokie didn't say a word as he helped himself to a hash brown from Wallace's tray. Wallace turned and looked up to see the muscular young black man staring down at him with glaring insolence. His hair was closely cropped and his arms and neck were covered in a strange combination of military tattoos and murderous gangland ink. Smokie and his gang all wore white tops, dark trousers, and the standard-issue Rikers flip-flops. Smokie grabbed a piece of turkey and then nodded to his associates, who proceeded to strip the rest of the food from Wallace's tray. Wallace looked over at Ole Creepy, who sat three tables away. It was hard to read the knotted scars that crisscrossed his face, but Wallace got the sense that Ole Creepy didn't approve. When the food was all gone, Smokie stared coldly and only walked away once Wallace had lowered his gaze. They hadn't spoken a word, but there was nothing that needed to be said; Wallace belonged to them.

That night Wallace had spoken to his cellmate, a twenty-six-year-old Dominican meth dealer called Pablo Matias who had spent two years in Rikers awaiting trial. Pablo had the face of a man twice his age. His skin was pulled tight over pronounced cheekbones, deep fissures crept from the corners of his eyes, and his mouth was ringed by craggy pout lines, the legacy of too many pipes. Pablo's listless eyes had showed no emotion as he'd explained Wallace's situation. Without gang affiliation, Wallace was unprotected and fair game. Word on the block was that Smokie was a hotshot looking to make a name for himself within the MTs. The gang was splitting between those who wanted a new leader and those loyal to Ole Creepy. Pablo got the sense that this wasn't about Wallace at all. He was a pawn in a much larger game. This was about leadership of the Murdering Taylors. Smokie had staked a claim on Wallace as a challenge to Ole Creepy's authority. If an MT member wanted to make someone theirs, they had to get Ole Creepy's permission to ensure that they didn't upset Rikers' delicate gang power balance. Smokie hadn't sought any such permission and had simply signaled that Wallace was his. He would start with food, move on to sex, and when he had finally taken all he wanted from Wallace, it would end in violence. Rikers was no place for false hope, so Pablo gave his bleakly honest diagnosis: no other gang would offer Wallace protection; he was too much of an outsider.

The following day, Smokie had taken Wallace's breakfast, lunch, and dinner. Wallace sank into desperation. When he'd seen news of Pallo's death on the dayroom TV, he'd convinced himself it was his ticket out. He'd given Scott Herson a message to convey to the FBI agent who'd locked him up. Anyone with half a brain would see the pattern, but nothing had come of the tip, and frustration had turned to unfathomable despair.

On the fourth day, they had taken all Wallace's food and then Smokie and his gang had accosted him in the dayroom, surrounding him with promises of sexual violence.

"Leave him be!" Ole Creepy's words had echoed off the walls.

Smokie had backed away from Wallace and sidled up to the mutilated leader of the MTs with ill-concealed contempt.

"Get out of here!" Ole Creepy commanded Wallace, who didn't need any further encouragement and ran from the dayroom as fast as his weakened legs would carry him.

Unable to sleep, his stomach gnawing with two days' hunger, Wallace had made the mistake of going to the authorities. On his way into the canteen for breakfast, he had spoken to Will Grover, one of the section supervisors, who had smiled warmly but dismissed Wallace's "settling-in problems." When Smokie and his gang came to take his breakfast, Wallace had yelled for Grover, but the tall guard in the black uniform simply stood on the high gantry that ringed the large room and kept his head turned studiously away. That night Wallace had learned the nature of his mistake. Pablo told him that Grover and the other guards had a deal with the Bloods. Ole Creepy and his crew helped keep order, and in return the guards did not interfere with them.

The violence had started the following day. Smokie and a dozen of his followers had jumped Wallace on the way back to the cells.

"Creepy ain't gonna save you!" Smokie yelled as he beat Wallace. "Time for some new blood."

Smokie and his men kept the brutality away from Wallace's face, and, once they got him to the floor, had buried him beneath a barrage of kicks. Two Department of Corrections officers had finally managed to pull Wallace out of danger and haul him into his cell. The beatings had continued daily, and although they were never enough to put Wallace in the infirmary, they gave each day a grinding haze of pain.

Wallace pressed his hand against the worst of his angry bruises and winced. He pulled his sweatshirt down and noticed that Pablo was watching him from the top bunk. There was sadness in his eyes. It was not the first time he'd seen Rikers destroy a man, but it was the first time he'd shared a cell with the victim. Wallace nodded at his cellmate. The only reason he was still standing was because Pablo had been sneaking small scraps of food back to the cell for Wallace to eat in secret.

"Maybe today will be better," Pablo said as he rolled down from the bunk and stood over the toilet.

Wallace looked away as his cellmate took a leak. The gunmetal-gray door was covered with the marks of previous inmates, runic records of others whose humanity had been chipped and scored away by this diabolical place. Wallace heard the familiar sound of the Klaxon, followed by the electromagnetic buzz of the locking mechanism on the cell door. A moment later the door slid open to reveal the two-story atrium beyond. Wallace stepped out onto the metal mesh balcony that ran the length of the block, and Pablo followed him.

They filed along, following thirty of their neighbors toward the stairs. Ole Creepy was near the front of the line, with a couple of his loyal followers in tow. Three DOC guards shepherded the group down the stairs and into the corridor that led to the canteen. At an intersection halfway along the corridor, they were joined by another group of prisoners from the cells on the opposite side of the block, and when Wallace caught sight of Smokie, he immediately realized that something was very wrong. Smokie jacked forward, breaking ranks, and rushed straight for Wallace. He was followed by a dozen Bloods, all eager for violence. The three guards responsible for Smokie's group held back the prisoners who hadn't run, and Wallace's guards focused on restraining his neighbors, allowing him to be swept down the corridor at the head of Smokie's violent gang.

Wallace saw Ole Creepy and three of his men break free of the guards and sprint toward him.

"Don't you fucking do it, Smokie!" Ole Creepy yelled, his gravelly voice echoing off the walls.

Wallace felt himself forced through a door, and, propelled by the momentum, he tumbled into one of the block's processing rooms where prisoners were mustered before being led to different sections of the facility. He rolled to his knees and Smokie surged forward, launching a vicious kick to his gut. Wallace felt something rupture and his stomach spasmed, forcing up a gob of blood that he coughed onto the melamine floor. Wallace ignored his wretched innards and tried to push himself to his feet, but was beaten back by a bombardment of blows. Smokie's gang hit and kicked him with such ferocity that Wallace stopped thinking about anything other than survival. He curled into a ball, trying his best to protect his head. The Bloods were hitting him so hard and fast that Wallace could not register any individual strike; he was lost in a storm of powerful violence. Then, as suddenly as it had begun, the onslaught ceased and Wallace looked up to see Ole Creepy and his followers holding Smokie and his men.

"Get back!" a Department of Corrections guard yelled, as he and two colleagues entered the room. They started peeling inmates off the fight, and their interference gave Smokie an opportunity. He pulled free of Ole Creepy's grasp and rushed at Wallace. Smokie swung hard and punched Wallace in the face. The DOC officer caught Wallace, preventing him from falling to the floor, where he would have been even more vulnerable. The guard pushed Smokie back, and the murderous gangster sidled back to his men, strutting in front of them, stamping the ground like an angry bull.

"You ain't the first buck I had to put down," Ole Creepy cautioned. "Every line on my face marks a grave."

That's when Wallace saw it. A young Blood who'd only just entered the room slipped Smokie a shiv. None of the guards noticed it, but the moment Wallace saw Smokie advancing, he knew that death was in the air.

"He's got a knife!" Wallace yelled.

Wallace's cry was like a starter's pistol; it triggered a chaotic bout of violence that engulfed the entire room. The guards were thrown around as Blood fought Blood in a final battle for leadership. Through the mayhem, Wallace saw Ole Creepy square up to Smokie, but the old gangster was outclassed. Smokie lashed out, his hand snapping like a whip, the jagged blade of the shiv piercing Ole Creepy's torso over and over again. Crimson spread across Ole Creepy's top and he dropped to his knees clutching his chest. He looked up at Smokie, his face twisted by hatred. Wallace was certain the old gangster tried to say something, but the words never came and he toppled forward, dead.

Ole Creepy's murder had an instantaneous effect. The MTs ceased their feud and fell silent as they looked at Smokie. As the DOC officers composed themselves, Smokie concealed the shiv up his sleeve.

"Everyone against the wall," the nearest guard commanded when he caught sight of the growing pool of blood oozing from Ole Creepy's body.

"Fuck that!" Smokie yelled. "Blood ghost!"

Wallace could only guess at the meaning of Smokie's words, but the MTs in the room forgot their differences and surged forward, targeting him.

"Move!" the guard commanded. He bundled Wallace toward the only safe place: a holding room that was normally used to segregate violent inmates from the general population. The guard yanked the door open, thrust Wallace inside, and turned to try and stave off the horde of murderous Bloods.

Wallace collided with the far wall as the door swung shut. He turned and saw Smokie's evil face peering through a picture window and the vicious gangster snarled as he pulled at the handle. The door opened a few inches, then suddenly slammed shut as a guard managed to pull Smokie away. Wallace paced frantically, bouncing off the walls of the tiny room. Adrenaline was the only thing that prevented him from collapsing under the excruciating pain, and as he heard the sounds of the melee outside, he had to suppress a powerful urge to scream.

The door was forced open and then snapped shut. Wallace couldn't see any faces at the window, but he could hear the guards yelling, "Get back!"

Then came the sound of a body hitting the door, and Wallace saw the back of a guard's head as it cracked the picture window. The guard slid down with the unmistakable slump of unconsciousness, the door opened, and two Bloods rushed in. The door slammed shut behind them and there were renewed sounds of struggle from beyond it. Wallace squared up to the two intruders, a short, vicious-looking man with no teeth, and a rangy giant with empty eyes. He swung for Toothless and felt a satisfying crunch as the man's jaw dislocated. The giant lunged for Wallace, who ducked and delivered a pair of punches to the man's gut, but the blows only served to increase his anger, and the giant delivered a vicious kidney punch that winded him and gave his assailants the opportunity to each grab an arm. Toothless offered him a twisted, bloody smile as he resisted Wallace's attempts to break free. He and the giant held fast as the door opened to reveal Smokie. The gangster produced the shiv and brandished it as he approached.

"It's time, motherfucker," he growled. "Time to pay."

Wallace tried to scream as Smokie stalked forward, but fear gripped his throat and choked his cries. Smokie was six feet away, his eyes blazing with murder. At four feet, he bared his teeth in a savage snarl, and Wallace saw the sharpened Plexiglas blade streak back as Smokie prepared to strike. Wallace shut his eyes and prepared to join Connie.

The scream was deafening. Wallace opened his eyes to see Smokie on the floor, convulsing violently. Two thin wires ran from his back to a Taser in unit supervisor Grover's hands.

"Let him go!" Grover ordered, and the two men holding Wallace released their grip. Grover turned his attention to Wallace. "You okay to walk?"

Wallace nodded uncertainly, his whole body palpitating in time with his racing heart.

"Good," Grover said quietly as he stood aside to let two guards into the room. The men grabbed Wallace and hauled him toward the door.

33

Pain plagued Wallace as he was pulled through the building. He knew that the confines of the infirmary were even more dangerous than the block and that Smokie and his people could easily reach him there, so he tried to give no hint of his injuries. When they reached the grille gate, one of the guards misjudged the distance and Wallace collided with the frame as he was pushed through. His ribs shrieked, his head throbbed, and tears welled in his eyes, but as the world warped and wavered and his mind grappled with the onslaught of agony, Wallace resisted the urge to double over. The guards led him along whitewashed corridors as pain pushed fearful thoughts into his mind. *Maybe these men were taking him to his death? Somewhere quiet where Smokie could finish the job?* The whispered legends and his own tormented experience of Rikers had convinced Wallace that it was a savage place where hope was suffocated by cruel reality. Sudden awareness cut through the bewildering pain and Wallace realized that he was in an unfamiliar part of the block. With no other prisoners or guards in sight, this windowless section was unusually quiet. On one side of the corridor, every twelve feet or so, a gray door broke the dirty white wall. The guards led Wallace to a door at the very end, and by the time they stopped outside, he was utterly overwhelmed by pain and fear. He could see the door; he could feel his heart pounding and his chest heaving with shallow, rapid breaths; he could smell the guards' sweat as it overpowered their cheap cologne; and he could hear the sound of the door opening, but the sensations seemed as though they were being experienced by someone else. He felt his mind disconnecting from reality, adrift in a furious ocean of despair as the guards led him through the doorway.

Holy fuck. The words flared in Ash's mind the moment she saw the Englishman being ushered into the room. She looked across at Parker, who was seated at the table in the center of the deposition room, and saw that she was not the only one shocked by Wallace's appearance. His skin was stretched taut over his skull, giving his face deathly definition. Dark shadows circled his sunken eyes. Ash tried to catch his gaze, but he walked blankly into the room and slumped in the chair opposite Parker. Ash had encountered that blankness before and recognized that Wallace was broken. She moved away from the wall and took a seat at the table as the Department of Corrections guards left the room.

"Mr. Wallace." Ash paused. Wallace hadn't acknowledged her or Parker. Instead, his attention was focused on blood splatters that covered the front of his white sweatshirt. His eyelids fluttered erratically, and Ash could see him straining to focus.

"Mr. Wallace," Ash tried again. This time Wallace looked up, but his gaze was unfocused and distant. "The information your attorney gave me checked out."

Wallace looked directly at Ash and gave a weak, twisted smile.

"I'm sorry it took so long," Ash offered apologetically.

Wallace's smile fell, and his eyes rolled back in his head. Neither Ash nor Parker had the chance to react as Wallace's unconscious body tumbled out of the chair and his head hit the floor with an emphatic thud.

34

Bonnie Mann looked down at the faded green baize and tapped her cards with her bitten, stubby fingers. The king of spades and the nine of clubs. No room for maneuver, but the dealer's face card was the five of hearts. The odds were on her side, Bonnie thought as she waited for her neighbor to make his play. He was a drunk, fat cowboy whose face looked as though it had been carved by years of degeneracy, and he was showing a double deuce. As he split his hand, Bonnie looked around the rotten old casino and caught sight of her reflection in the huge gilt mirror hanging beside the blackjack tables. She couldn't kid herself any longer; the life she'd lived had taken a heavy toll. Her skin was puffy and pale, possibly a side effect of the antidepressants she'd been prescribed. She mixed the pills with alcohol in an attempt to silence her worries, but the regimen hadn't succeeded and she spent most working days troubled by her financial woes and obsessing over strategies to win back the money she'd lost. Bonnie's once impressive cascading golden hair had been cut into a short crop on the advice of a twenty-buck stylist, who had said it was the only way to minimize the patchy hair loss. Gone were the thousand-dollar dresses. Instead, she was wearing a pair of Walmart jeans and an old Stussy top she'd found in a Goodwill store. She thought of what she'd done to herself, the relationships she'd wrecked and the money she'd lost, and turned away from the mirror. She felt fiery shame engulf her and stared at her cards in a studious effort to get her emotions under control.

She regretted the day when her colleague, Lilly Ashby, introduced her to 808. Bonnie had started slow, making light, manageable bets with the online casino, but then a terrible thing happened: Bonnie won. A spin of a digital roulette wheel and one hundred and fifty bucks on number seventeen had become four thousand five hundred dollars. Working in tech, Bonnie was making good money, but there was something instantly addictive about the thrill of winning. She upped her stakes and started playing more frequently. She branched out from roulette to blackjack and at one point she was more than fifty thousand dollars up. Whenever she recalled that flawless run of wins, she felt aggrieved at her stupidity. If only she'd banked the money and quit, she wouldn't be stuck hustling in the only casino in Vegas desperate enough to give her a marker. But she hadn't quit. Instead, she started losing, and, in chasing her losses, she'd squandered her home, her husband, her job, her pension, her savings—everything that she ever gave a shit about.

When she could no longer get credit online, she'd come to Vegas and started gambling in the real world, desperate to try to recover something. She only ever lost more. She knew she was sick, but she couldn't stop herself. Work had faded into insignificance, and she'd been fired for gross negligence when they'd discovered the three-thousand-case backlog she'd concealed. Bonnie called it a backlog, but the truth was that she knew she'd never deal with any of those cases; gaming had taken over her life. She knew she should be ashamed, but she didn't care, she only wanted to beat the ugly monster that had stolen so much from her. She looked in the mirror, well aware of the true identity of the monster, but it was one that she couldn't face. Instead, she blamed bad luck, and so she sold all her things, dresses, jewelry, shoes—anything and everything that could raise more than a dime. She borrowed money from friends and family, telling herself that it wasn't stealing because she would pay it back when her luck turned, but she lost it all.

As the cash dried up, the reputable casinos started turning her away, and Bonnie worked her way down the Strip, until only the Element would give her credit. She was at the marker's limit and knew that she had only one way of paying out if she didn't win tonight. The last of her chips, some five hundred bucks, lay scattered in front of her cards. All her desperate dreams rested on the king of spades and the nine of clubs. Even as the light of false hope crept into her mind, Bonnie knew the outcome was inevitable. She wondered whether she'd known it the day she'd taken her first spin of the wheel.

The cowboy busted both hands and the dealer flipped his hole card to reveal the six of diamonds. Bonnie knew what was coming, and had started to turn away before the ten of clubs hit the baize. She walked quickly, aiming straight for the gleaming lights of the Strip that glowed brightly beyond the Element's gloomy and decrepit lobby.

"Miss Mann," Rusty said, stepping out from behind a gaudy Wild Streak slot machine. A tall, muscular man with a cruel face, Rusty was one of the Element's senior pit bosses. "We need to talk."

Bonnie turned away from Rusty and almost ran into two heavyset men in dark suits. She'd seen them eject a few troublemakers from the casino and had the feeling that providing additional security was only the start of their duties. Her shoulders sagged as she faced Rusty, and the last spark of hope flickered and died. She wasn't going to escape her marker.

"Sure," she said sadly.

As the two men steered her through the casino, Bonnie looked down at the worn carpet and wondered how a life that had once held such promise could end in such failure. The penalty for a dishonored marker had been made very clear to her when she'd taken out the credit. Rusty swiped a key card and opened a door marked "Employees Only." Once they were out of the lobby, the two men took hold of Bonnie's arms and the pace quickened. She thought about screaming or trying to break free, but she knew that would only result in a more painful punishment.

The men led her down a long corridor, past the quiet casino kitchen and through another set of double doors to a loading area, where a black Buick waited in one of the bays. The men dragged her to the rear of the car and pulled her around to face Rusty.

"You owe us ten grand." Rusty leaned in, full of menace.

"I can get the money," Bonnie pleaded. "It'll just take me a couple of days."

"We don't have to do this very often," Rusty shook his head. "But we both know there's only one way you can pay us back."

"Please don't." Bonnie started weeping. "Please. I'll find the money. You don't have to do this."

Rusty nodded at the man to Bonnie's left. "Leo, why don't you and Eli take Bonnie for a ride?" he suggested as he opened the Buick's trunk.

Leo and Eli forced a struggling Bonnie inside.

"Please," she begged. "I'll do anything."

"Fucking dumbass," Rusty muttered as he slammed the trunk shut.

"Do it in the desert," Bonnie heard Rusty say. She pounded on the trunk and was rewarded with two hard thumps in reply.

"Make all the noise you want," Rusty said through the metal. "Ain't nobody gonna hear you."

Bonnie sobbed as she heard two doors open and close. Moments later the engine rumbled to life and the car started moving. As she whimpered in the darkness, she heard odd snatches of conversation between her two captors, but for the most part they were silent as they drove out of town, and Bonnie spent the long journey lamenting the dark desperation that had driven her to sign over her life insurance policy to a nominee of the Element Casino—a person who acted as a front and collected the payout on the casino's behalf. This was how the rancid casino ensured every marker was paid; it loaned money to people who were prepared to sign away their lives. Bonnie had life insurance worth a quarter of a million bucks. The Element was actually going to profit from her death.

"We got a tail," Bonnie heard the muffled voice of one of the men through the rear seats.

"Pull over," the other man instructed. "See if it passes."

Bonnie felt the car slow. *Please let it be a cop*, she prayed.

"It's slowing down," said the first voice.

"Shit! You think it's a cop?" asked the second man.

Hope burst like a firework and lit up Bonnie's heart. She heard the sound of a vehicle pulling to a halt behind the Buick. A door slammed and there was the sound of approaching footsteps.

"Get ready," said the first man.

The footsteps passed the trunk and moved along the driver's side of the vehicle.

"What the fuck!" the first man yelled. His cry was quickly followed by the sound of two gunshots. Then there was silence. Bonnie wept with relief when she heard footsteps by the side of the car.

"In here! Please! Help!" she cried, smacking the roof of the trunk with her palm.

She heard the latch pop and the trunk opened. It took a moment for Bonnie's eyes to become accustomed to the moonless desert night, but when they focused, what she saw filled her with horror. A man in dark goggles and a face mask loomed over her. He whipped a gloved hand forward and sprayed something in her face. She felt him start to lift her out of the trunk as darkness overcame her.

Cool wind caressed her face. She felt rumbling vibration all around her. Bonnie opened her eyes and immediately screamed. Starlight illuminated the outline of a rock that she recognized as Fort Point, which meant the expansive body of water that stretched out far beneath her was the San Francisco Bay. Bonnie felt heavy, but her muscle control was slowly returning and she looked around. She was surrounded by red-orange metal struts with a long, wide roof above her. Bonnie realized she was on the lower service level of the Golden Gate Bridge, next to the western safety barrier. She sensed movement next to her and turned to see her masked abductor approaching. He had a thick noose in his hands. The other end was attached to a nearby strut. Bonnie recoiled as the man slipped the noose over her neck. She lashed out, but her fist struck the hard surface of the body armor that covered his chest. She tried to tear at his goggles, but he struck her in the face, knocking her head against the hard metal barrier.

As nighttime traffic rolled overhead, the masked man lifted her over the barrier. She came to her senses as he began to lower her over the other side, and she clawed at the barrier, desperately trying to grab the metal lip. Her assailant lashed out, knocking her backward with a punch to the side of the head. Bonnie felt herself falling, but the masked man grabbed the other end of the rope, and her descent was suddenly arrested by the noose closing around her throat. For a moment they were completely still. Bonnie's feet were precariously perched on the edge of the girder that ran along the bottom of the safety rail, her body leaning away from the bridge at a perilous forty-five-degree angle. The only thing that prevented her from falling was the opposing force of the noose around her neck.

"Please!" she begged, her throat straining to expel the word.

The mask and opaque goggles offered no hint of the man's emotions as he fed out some slack. Deprived of tension, Bonnie's legs slipped off the girder and she swung free. She pawed at the rope and thrashed her legs violently as she was lowered below the bridge. Her eyes streamed and the pain in her lungs was unbearable, as was the stark realization that this was the end.

This is what it feels like when hope truly dies, Bonnie thought as she reached the end of her drop. Swinging beneath the bridge, she looked up and saw the blurred silhouette of her killer. He leaned over the guardrail and watched impassively as she took her final few breaths.

Why? Bonnie wondered, but it was a question that was never answered.

35

A powerful staccato of vivid dreams flashed through his mind. Strip lights flying overhead. Unfamiliar faces looming over him, judging him. Hands touching him. Dragging him. Connie. Beautiful Connie, smiling up at him. Then suddenly lost to darkness. Flashing lights. Movement. Faces close to him. A man listening to his chest. Travel, as though he were floating. A long tunnel. A deep hum. Distant voices. Commands. Beeps. Bells. Buzzers. More hands touching him, pulling at his body. The killer standing beside him like a dark monolith. Huvane hanging in his barn. His eyes open, his gaze rich with accusation. Concerned whispers. A woman he recognized but couldn't name. Then darkness. Long, untroubled oblivion.

A breath. Sensation. His head was enveloped by soft warmth. His skin felt smooth and clean, pressed against crisp sheets. Wallace opened his eyes to find himself in a bedroom, his head resting on a pair of thick pillows at the top of a king-size bed. Gray light circumscribed a set of heavy drapes that hung over a large window.

"Hey," a woman's voice said. Wallace looked across the room. His eyes took a moment to focus on the figure in the armchair; it was Christine Ash. She rose and crossed the room.

"We took you to the hospital," she said as she took a seat on the edge of the bed. "You were pretty out of it. Docs said there was no permanent damage. How are you feeling?"

"Okay," Wallace croaked.

Ash reached for a glass of water that rested on the bedside table and passed it to him. He raised himself onto his elbows, and the movement incited bursts of pain all over his body. Wallace guessed he'd been given pain relief, because the discomfort seemed dull and distant, but it was still sufficient to make him wince.

"You've got a couple of cracked ribs," Ash explained. "As bad as it looks, the rest is just bruising. The doc says you've got a few bullet wounds, one old, two new."

"I got the old one outside Kandahar," Wallace said. "The other two came from the guy who's trying to kill me."

"I read your background," Ash said. "Sounds like you went through hell in Afghanistan. Were you telling the truth? About those soldiers?"

Wallace nodded.

"I'm sorry," she offered.

"Don't be. I was lucky."

Wallace took a sip of water before handing the glass back to Ash. He held his hand behind his head as he lowered it onto the pillows. The tendons in his neck were tender with whiplash.

"I had the local field office send an agent down to canvas Malibu Beach," Ash explained. "He found a man named Bruce Morton, who claimed to have been on the beach the night of Pallo's murder. He says he saw your killer. Didn't get a good look, but he says there was a guy in a long coat and mask underneath Malibu Pier. Morton's homeless, and a little unstable, so he didn't come forward because he was afraid the cops would think he had something to do with the murder."

"Thank you," Wallace said gratefully, struggling to control his emotions.

"Don't thank me, Mr. Wallace," Ash replied. "If you hadn't prompted me, there is no way we would have been able to identify the fact that there's a serial killer passing murder for suicide."

"What's going to happen to me? Are you going to send me back?"

"No. This is a Bureau safe house," Ash said. "You've been put into the witness protection program."

"He was in a mask. Body armor. I didn't see anything," Wallace warned her.

"Did he speak?"

"Yes."

"So you'd recognize his voice," Ash said. "And the way he moves. His height, build, the type of armor he was wearing. Apart from Morton, and Bailey, whose recollection is hazy, you're the only person alive who's seen this guy, so for now, you're our best witness. The assistant district attorney is prepared to drop the charges against you in exchange for your cooperation. You won't be going back to jail."

Wallace sagged with relief as he was hit by the realization that he'd escaped the hell of Rikers.

"And I put a call in to London yesterday. Detective Sergeant Bailey came out of his coma a few days ago. The Metropolitan Police have his statement, which exonerates you."

His relief was a potent drug that soothed the raw memory of his experiences in Rikers.

"What you've been through," Ash said. "It would have broken most people. You're a strong man, Mr. Wallace." She put a conciliatory hand on Wallace's shoulder and smiled at him. "I've got to get back to work," she announced as she stood up. "I just wanted to be here when you woke up. You have a rotating guard; two US marshals on duty at all times. If you need—"

She was interrupted by Parker, who burst into the room. "You gotta see this, Ash."

"Excuse me," she said to Wallace, before following Parker out.

Ash chased Parker along the corridor and down the stairs into the open-plan living room. Two US marshals, Perez and Hill, were standing in front of the large television, and Ash didn't get a clear view of what was on the screen until she was almost alongside them. She felt a cold rush of dismay as she saw a woman's body hanging far beneath the Golden Gate Bridge. They were watching an east-facing, wide-angle helicopter shot of the iconic structure. The sun was rising behind the bridge, throwing the body below into solid silhouette. The rope ran about fifty feet up to one of the struts on the service level. There was no traffic on the bridge apart from a stationary fleet of emergency vehicles. Ash could see a group of cops and firefighters making their way along the service level.

"The identity of the woman is unknown," the news anchor reported over the image. "And as we can see from our live coverage, authorities have closed one side of the bridge until they complete the recovery of the body. We're going live to Al Henson, who is on the scene."

A file photograph of Al Henson, an earnest reporter, was superimposed over the shot of the bridge.

"Al, what are you hearing on the ground?" the news anchor asked.

"The woman's body was discovered earlier today, swinging beneath the bridge," Henson's disembodied voice revealed. "The first job for law enforcement is to recover the body and discover who this individual is."

Ash's phone rang and she pulled it from her pocket to see Hector's name.

"You seen it yet?" he asked.

"I'm watching right now," she replied. "If she'd jumped, the drop would have ripped her head off. Rope that long means she had to be lowered."

"Exactly," Hector agreed. "I need to see you."

"I'm on my way." Ash hung up and turned for the door. "Look after him," she instructed Parker. She exited the small, converted redbrick warehouse and stepped onto the icy Brooklyn Heights street.

The Brooklyn Bridge was heavy with rush-hour traffic creeping slowly through the slush. The journey from Hunts Lane to Federal Plaza took twenty-five minutes, and by the time Ash slid her late-model black Ford Taurus into a bay beneath the building, she had figured out how to approach the next phase of the investigation. She'd ask Hector to arrange for local liaisons from the Los Angeles and San Francisco field offices to coordinate the murder investigations. She would ask for Tommy Holt if he was available. He was a good agent based out of LA and they'd worked together before. Ash couldn't think of anyone from San Francisco, but she'd be able to put the word out and get the local recommendations. The New York team would be tasked with investigating the Byrne and Walters deaths, and she'd liaise with the Met about the killer's activities in the UK.

She stepped out of the elevator, swiped her key card, and hurried along the corridor. She passed the thirtieth-floor offices of a dozen senior agents before she reached Hector's, which was located in the northeast corner of the building. Brooke, Hector's middle-aged assistant, stood as Ash approached.

"They're waiting for you," Brooke said before she opened the door to Hector's office. Something about her feeble smile unsettled Ash. Did she sense pity?

Ash knew the answer the moment she entered the room. Hector was leaning against his desk talking to Alvarez, but their conversation came to an abrupt end when they saw Ash. Hector nodded solemnly and Alvarez offered a weakly curled smile, the twin of Brooke's.

"Take a seat, Chris," Hector offered.

"I'll stand," Ash replied.

"How's Wallace?" Alvarez asked.

"Pretty beat up." Ash crossed Hector's office and peered down at the street, where tiny vehicles rolled along like toys. She watched miniature New Yorkers weave their way between gray mounds of snow. If Hector was going to do this, she wasn't going to give Alvarez the satisfaction of seeing her disappointment. The dim noise of distant traffic drifted into the room.

"Arturo's taking this one," Hector said finally.

"I brought this in, Hector. You put me in charge." Ash spoke quietly, keeping her eyes firmly focused on the street below.

"That was before this morning," Hector protested. "Before this thing became national news. We've got murders in at least three states, two countries—"

"Nobody outside the Bureau knows we're dealing with a serial killer," Ash interrupted.

"And how long do you think that will last?" Hector countered. "This thing needs seniority."

"Seniority," Ash sneered. "Alvarez and I came up together."

"Arturo is an SSA, Chris. You're not," Hector countered. "Not anymore."

"No offense, but you know I can run rings around this guy," Ash replied flatly.

"Hard not to take offense at that," Alvarez interjected. "But I'm a big guy, Chris. I know how hard this demotion thing has hit you."

"You have no fucking idea," Ash snarled, wheeling round from the window. "Or you wouldn't have had me profiling."

"It's done." Hector positioned himself between his two subordinates. "This is too big, Chris. Washington needs to see a senior agent running the task force."

Ash swallowed her anger and returned to the window.

"Arturo wants you on the team," Hector said, trying to mollify her.

"Profiling?" she asked sarcastically.

"Wallace knows you," Alvarez replied. "Depose him. When you're done, report to Parker. He's gonna be running the New York investigation."

Ash bit her bottom lip and kept her eyes on the little street far below. There was no doubt Alvarez was trying to play her. He'd lobbied Hector to take charge of the investigation, but that wasn't enough; now he was trying to humiliate her, goad her into a reaction. There was no way she should be working for Parker.

"I thought Parker was already assigned to investigate the Foundation?" she tried desperately.

"A handful of anticapitalist nuts hacking bank accounts?" Alvarez countered. "This has to take priority."

"We good?" Hector asked.

Ash made them wait. She listened to the wail of a siren and studied the clouds in the cold gray sky. Finally, she turned away from the window and nodded. "We're good," she said, but the way she looked at Alvarez left no doubt that they weren't. "I'd better get back to the safe house."

Hector patted Ash on the back and walked her to the door. "I'm sorry, Chris," he said. "You still get to play a part."

"I gotta earn it, right?" she replied with a cold look.

"Hey, Chris," Alvarez called after her. "When you get to the safe house, tell Parker to get over here. I gotta bring him up to speed."

"Yes, sir," Ash responded sarcastically as she hurried from the room.

36

Ash collected her laptop and stuffed it into her bag on her way out of the building. She spent the drive back to the safe house thinking about Marcel Washington, wondering whether she could have played that bust differently. *You did the right thing*, she told herself. *This is just a temporary setback*. Dark clouds glowered over the East River, and the temperature was dropping ahead of the forecasted storm. She turned the Taurus into Hunts Lane and saw Perez look up. He was sitting in the driver's seat of an old Crown Vic that was parked across the narrow street, opposite the safe house. He gave Ash a cursory wave as she drove past. She swung a U-turn, pulled in behind the Crown Vic, grabbed her bag, and hurried across the bitterly cold street into the house.

Parker sat on the edge of the couch hunched over his laptop, and Ash saw he was running searches on the NCIC database looking for hangings that might fit the killer's profile. Hill, the other US marshal, sat in a nearby armchair, his eyes turned toward the television, watching a rerun of *Seinfeld*.

"Alvarez wants you," Ash told Parker.

"I know. He called," Parker said, looking up from his computer. "I'm gonna be running the New York investigation."

Ash wondered why Alvarez had called Parker. Was it because he didn't trust her? Or was he simply trying to stick it to her?

"I thought this was your show," Parker observed.

"Shit happens," Ash responded as casually as she could. "You'd better get going."

"Yeah," Parker said as he put his laptop to sleep and slid it into his bag. "Listen, I don't want this to get weird, but Alvarez said that once you've finished deposing Wallace, you need to report to me."

"I know," Ash concealed her anger. "Don't worry. It won't be weird."

"Great," Parker said with a smile. "Call me if you need anything."

Ash kept the frozen smile firmly fixed to her face until Parker had left the building, and then she turned to Hill, who gave her a knowing nod. His craggy face, heavy jowls, and gray-flecked hair marked him as a man of years, an experienced cop who had been around long enough to know when someone was getting screwed.

"Sometimes you eat the bear," he drawled.

"And sometimes he eats you," Ash finished the saying with a grin. "Ain't that the truth?"

She put her laptop on the coffee table, then went upstairs and quietly opened the door to the master bedroom. The drapes were still drawn, and from the deep, rhythmic breathing, she guessed that Wallace was asleep. She crept into the room until she could see his face in the dim light. His eyes were closed and his lids flickered with the energy of a potent dream. Ash backed out of the room, shut the door, and went downstairs.

She perched on the edge of the couch and fired up her laptop to check for the latest on the Golden Gate murder. The press was still treating it as a sensational suicide, but Hector was right; it wouldn't be long before news of the investigation leaked. The body had been spotted by a fishing charter leaving Pelican Harbor a couple of hours before dawn, and unconfirmed reports had named the victim as Bonnie Mann, an unemployed woman from the Bay Area. Her most recent Facebook post had been a detailed suicide note in which she confessed to a crippling gambling addiction.

"Jerry, the Japanese guys had sake in the hot tub," Costanza's voice yelled from the television. "You gotta get 'em outta the drawers and get 'em down here, or I don't have a focus group to sell the pilot to Japanese TV."

Hill's body shook with laughter. He half-turned to Ash, a little embarrassed. "Seen it a million times, but it still kills me. Sorry."

"Don't worry about it," Ash replied. She remembered hearing *Seinfeld* through the walls of the disciplinary cell. Her steward had been watching the contraband show on a smuggled portable television, but even at age nine, Ash had known ratting him out would have brought more pain than she suffered simply serving out her ten-day punishment. "I can work in the kitchen."

Hill smiled appreciatively and turned his attention to the television as Ash picked up her laptop, crossed the room, and went through the lightweight swing door that led to the kitchen. The house had just enough furniture to make a short stay tolerable. There were no pictures or souvenirs or other junk that would make it seem like a real home, but Ash liked spartan. Apart from a framed photo of her with her mother and a large picture of the Malibu coastline, Ash's own home was equally austere. She took a seat at the circular pine table in the middle of the kitchen, determined to learn everything she could about Stewart Huvane, John Wallace, Kye Walters, Erin Byrne, Ken Pallo, and Bonnie Mann. There had to be something that connected these people, so she leaned over her laptop and started digging.

Wallace was hanging by his neck, the noose pulled tight around his throat. It was all wrong. He was in his flat, dying, and Connie was looking up at him.

"What did it feel like?" she whispered.

Then the world warped and Wallace was Connie. He was looking up at her as she choked to death.

"What did it feel like?" he asked quietly.

Connie opened her mouth to reply, but no words came, just a horrific rasping sound.

Wallace woke with the terrible recollection that he would never see Connie again. His potent nightmares permeated the real world, making him tremble and sweat. He felt a welcome rush of cool air as he rolled out from under the comforter and walked toward the window. The sweat on his torso started to evaporate as he pulled one of the drapes back. He was in a narrow street of old warehouses that looked like they'd been converted into homes. It was dark outside and the yellow light from a streetlight was being peppered by heavy snowfall. There were a few snow-covered cars parked on either side of the street. One of the cars had its engine running and its chassis was moist with melted snow. Wallace could see the shape of a man inside. He looked up at Wallace and nodded. Police guard, he hoped.

Dull aches assailed him as he crossed the room. He wore nothing but a pair of tight black boxer shorts that didn't belong to him. He pressed the main light switch, but the bulb didn't work. He tried the lamp on the dresser and it cast the weak, hazy light of an energy-efficient bulb. He noticed his brogues under the chest of drawers. He'd been wearing them when he'd been arrested. If they'd returned his shoes . . . He opened the top drawer and found a pile of clothes that looked like they might fit him. He riffled through, then went to the second drawer, which was similarly stocked. In the third drawer down, he found his own clothes, and nestled between his folded suit and shirt was his belt. Wallace unfurled it and pulled open the concealed zip. He was relieved when he saw a wad of greenbacks and pound notes; he had his money. He put on a pair of black jeans, a lightweight black long-sleeve shirt, and a pair of black sneakers that he found next to his shoes. He looped the money belt around his waist and pulled it a notch tighter than when he'd last worn it. The thought of his enforced starvation at the hands of Smokie made Wallace realize he had no idea when he'd last eaten. His stomach felt crumpled and empty, but he couldn't say for certain whether he was hungry.

He had the answer when he opened the bedroom door and started to salivate the instant he smelled the rich scent of food that filled the corridor. He walked downstairs and followed the smell through the empty living room into the kitchen. A heavyset middle-aged man in a white shirt and dark trousers was standing by the oven, shoveling a slice of pizza into his mouth. The butt of a pistol poked out from the man's side holster. Agent Ash leaned against the counter on the other side of the kitchen and nodded at Wallace, her mouth full of pizza.

"Hey," Ash said, finally swallowing. "You hungry?"

Wallace nodded.

"Help yourself." She indicated a couple of pizzas lying on oven pans that rested on top of the stove. "Edges got a little burnt."

"Crispy," the man interjected. "Exactly how pizza should be."

He leaned forward and offered Wallace his hand. "Peyton Hill, US marshal."

Wallace shook Hill's hand. "John Wallace."

"Go ahead," Hill advised. "Before it's all gone."

Wallace picked up a slice of pepperoni and took a bite. The pre-packaged processed pizza was possibly the most delicious thing he had ever eaten. The first bite incited Wallace's hunger and he devoured the rest of the slice. He was partway through his second when the kitchen door opened and a young, dark-skinned man with jet-black hair entered. He wore a blue suit, which glistened with what looked like dewdrops.

"Man, it's freezing out there!" the man exclaimed, patting his sides as he hugged himself. "Shift change," he said to Hill.

"John Wallace, this is my partner, Geraldo Perez," Hill told Wallace.

Perez shook Wallace's hand.

"Pizza any good?" Perez asked as he picked up a slice.

"Burnt," Ash replied.

"Crispy," Wallace and Hill said in unison.

Hill laughed. "I like your style, man. You got the keys?" he asked Perez, who tossed them across the kitchen. "Time to count snow-flakes," Hill remarked as he left the room.

Moments later, Wallace heard the front door slam shut.

"I'm going to need to take your statement," Ash said to Wallace. "We'll get started when you're done."

"Could be awhile," Wallace advised, picking up a third slice.

Ash hit the space bar, stopping the voice recorder on her laptop. The clock in the bottom corner of the screen said 22:07. Wallace had been talking for almost two hours, chronicling his story. Ash couldn't help but be impressed by the guy; most people would have been broken by his experiences. He'd choked up when discussing Connie, and Ash could see that the guilt of getting her involved was eating away at him. She'd tried to help Wallace see that the weight of the crime should fall on the killer, but his perspective was twisted by love, and, more than most, Ash knew how dangerous that was.

Wallace stood up, filled a glass of water from the faucet, and drank deeply.

"Have you got any theories yet?" he asked.

"We can't be certain that Bonnie Mann was killed by the same person, but if she was, the killer could be a vigilante attacking people he believes have committed crimes: gambling, perversion, drug dealing," Ash replied.

"I haven't done anything like that," Wallace protested.

"It's one of a number of possible theories," Ash added. "We're looking at whether there have been other hangings that we've missed. More victims might give us a pattern, something to connect you all."

"How long do I have to stay here?" he asked wearily.

"Till we catch the guy," Ash replied, shutting down her computer. "Maybe longer, depending on the trial risk. You want us to call anyone? Family? Work?"

Wallace shook his head, and Ash immediately felt sorry for him. Here he was, having lived through three murder attempts and a brutal stay in Rikers, stuck in WitPro in Brooklyn, an isolated alien in an unfamiliar land.

"Listen, I gotta go," she said as she stood up. "Big day with my new boss tomorrow," she added sarcastically, before pulling her card from her jacket pocket. "Hill and Perez cover nights. They'll introduce you to the guys on the day shift. Marshals are pros. They'll look after you, but if there's anything you need, just give me a call."

"Thanks," Wallace replied as she handed him the card.

Ash picked up her laptop and walked out of the kitchen to find Perez watching basketball in the living room: the NBA All-Star game.

"Who's winning?" she asked.

"One-twenty, one-fourteen, West are six clear." Perez didn't take his eyes off the screen.

Wallace had followed Ash out of the kitchen and seated himself on the couch.

"You're in good hands," Ash smiled.

"He is," Perez replied emphatically. "Now will you get out of here? You're ruining the game." He grinned broadly.

"Stay safe." Ash left the men watching the game and stepped outside to find the snow still falling and her car covered by a thick drift. She waved to Hill, who sat in the warmth of the Crown Vic. Every inch the old-fashioned gentleman, he jumped out and helped Ash clear her car. They were both shivering by the time they'd finished.

"Thanks," she said. "I owe you a drink."

"I'm a married man, Agent Ash," Hill joked. "So I'll take hot sex over a drink any day."

"You ever learn the word harassment?" Ash asked as she opened the driver's door.

"It's my motto, baby," Hill laughed, returning to his car. "I can grab ass with the very best of them."

I'm just one of the guys, Ash thought as she slid into the Taurus. If only they knew.

37

"We gotta get out there an' fight these assholes on the ground," the irate voice said. "Bombin' ain't workin'."

Hill loved late-night talk radio. Hard-boiled common sense that no politician had the guts to articulate. He shifted in the seat to prevent his butt from falling asleep and turned down the heater. Even in a thick snowstorm it was possible to be too warm. He checked the safe house. The lights had gone out just after two a.m., but there was a slight glow from behind the living room drapes; Perez was probably still watching TV.

Hill picked up the radio mic. "Dispatch, this is special unit USM twelve, checking in," he said.

"Copy, USM twelve," acknowledged the male dispatcher sitting seven blocks away in the 84th Precinct.

Hill replaced the radio mic and rolled the window down a crack. Condensation was starting to form at the top of the windshield. The snow was bad enough, he didn't need any additional visual impairment. When he leaned over and used his sleeve to wipe the right side of the windshield, he heard the sound of a heavy stone dropping into a puddle and realized that a bullet had pierced the windshield and buried itself in the driver's headrest. He dropped beneath the dash as two more shots popped through the windshield and hit the seat above him.

Fuck, fuck, fuck, Hill thought as he grabbed the radio mic. "Dispatch, this is USM twelve," he said urgently. "Shots fired. Shots fired. I'm taking fire." Hill couldn't hear the reports, and assumed it was a weapon with a silencer.

"Copy that, USM twelve," the disembodied voice replied calmly. "All units, all units, we have reports of shots fired at two-one-four Hunts Lane. All available units converge on two-one-four Hunts Lane."

Hill pulled his Glock from its holster and peered over the dash. He saw the muzzle flash of a gun coming from the second floor fire escape a couple of buildings away. He ducked as the fourth bullet shattered the windshield, showering him with broken glass.

Perez woke with a start. He wiped a slick of drool from his chin and looked around. The television was playing an infomercial about a portable air fryer. When Perez pulled himself out of the armchair, he heard an indistinct noise, like a snake's hiss followed by a pop. He went for his radio, but there was nothing on his belt—*shit, I must have left it in the john.* Feeling all kinds of wrong, Perez raced to the window and pulled the drapes. Hill wasn't in the car and shattered pieces of the windshield hung in the frame. Perez sprinted to the front door and opened it.

"Pey!" Perez called across the street. His yell was rewarded with two bullets driven into the brickwork around the door. Perez caught the firelight on a nearby fire escape and pulled his pistol. Perez started firing and running at the same time, satisfied that the loud gunshots echoing off the tightly packed buildings would wake the entire neighborhood. He was halfway across the street when the Crown Vic's passenger door flew open. Hill was pressed against the footwell. Perez stopped firing as he slid for cover behind the passenger door.

Wallace prayed the noise came from his nightmare. He rolled out of bed and crossed the bedroom to the window. As he drew the drape an inch away from the wall, he heard the familiar sound of gunfire. He looked down into the street and saw the young marshal crouched behind the car door, shooting at something through the shattered window. Wallace followed the line of fire and saw something on the fire escape of a building at the far end of the street. The familiar dark silhouette vanished as muzzle flare blew out Wallace's night vision.

★ ★ ★

Perez heard the pocked thuds of bullet driving through metal.

"Fuck!" Perez yelled. "APs! We gotta bail!"

Hill looked at him and nodded. Perez could hear the sound of distant sirens.

"We get to the house. We hold it until they get here," Hill commanded. "I'll cover you."

"On three," Perez replied. "One, two, three."

Hill pushed his Glock over the dash and started firing at the fire escape. He turned and saw Perez halfway across the street, shooting wildly in the same direction. With all the gunfire, Hill didn't even hear the shot that tore the side of his neck open and spun his head around wildly. The second shot burst the back of his skull, and he fell, lifelessly hanging half out of the car.

Perez cried out when he saw Hill die, but he didn't stop running. He bounded up the steps to the safe house and rolled through the front door.

Horror gripped Wallace as he watched Hill's gaping skull ooze blood all over the snow. He backed away from the window, grabbed his clothes, and started to pull them on as he fled the room.

Perez heard noise above him. He wheeled around, pistol raised, and saw the witness at the top of the stairs.

"Get down here," Perez whispered.

Machine-gun fire shattered the living room window and splintered everything in its path. The firefight had woken the whole neighborhood and police were now en route. The assailant was no longer worried about noise; he just wanted to get the job done.

As bullets shredded the living room, Perez ran up the stairs, pushing Wallace back the way he'd come.

"Move! Move! Move!" Perez yelled as shots tore chunks out of the stairs.

★ ★ ★

Wallace stumbled and fell onto his back as Perez bundled him clear of the stairs. He could hear sirens getting closer, but part of him knew they weren't going to make it in time.

The gunfire stopped, and Perez hauled Wallace to his feet.

"Come on," Perez said quietly.

The charred smell of gun smoke filled the corridor as Perez led Wallace toward the bedroom, but Wallace pulled him back and nodded toward the tiny bathroom. Perez shook his head.

"No way out."

"Exactly," Wallace whispered. "He won't expect it."

Perez stared at Wallace for a moment before nodding.

They moved quietly and entered the bathroom. Perez pushed the door closed behind them and they stood silently, their ears straining to hear. The sirens kept getting louder, and the house was alive with tiny cracks and snaps as it settled after the onslaught.

The footstep was unmistakable, a heavy tread on broken glass. Wallace looked at Perez, who nodded and raised his pistol to the door. *A creak on the stairs.* Wallace willed the sirens on and held his breath as he heard a footstep at the top of the stairs. He took a shallow breath and waited. There was nothing but the sound of the house and the sirens. Then a footstep and another, moving away from the bathroom, toward the bedroom.

Wallace wanted to scream as Perez pulled at the door. He peered through the tiny crack and then turned to Wallace and nodded. He opened the door and led Wallace across the corridor toward the stairs.

Wallace sensed the presence of the killer before he saw him. He looked up to discover the armor-clad man standing in the bedroom doorway, an assault rifle in his hands. Perez saw him too, and opened fire. His shots went wide, striking the wall, and the killer replied with a volley that hit Perez in the chest and head, killing him instantly.

Wallace sprinted down the stairs and ran through the open door into the street. He kept expecting to hear the sound of gunfire, but it wasn't until he was halfway across the street that it started. The killer

shot at him from the bedroom window, spraying his surroundings
with bullets.

Wallace leaped over the hood of the Crown Vic and rolled onto
the sidewalk on the other side. Bullets tore through the bodywork
everywhere except the engine; the solid block must have been too
dense, even for the armor-piercing rounds. The engine screamed,
hissed, and eventually died, but it didn't allow any bullets through.
Wallace ignored the freezing slush around the car and pressed his
back against the front wheel as the storm of gunfire continued. The
sirens were very close, maybe a couple of blocks away, when
the shooting stopped. Wallace was shaking, his heart pounding, his
breathing rapid and shallow; the fear was so powerful it seemed as
though it might tear his body apart. *Connie*. The word cut through
everything. *Connie*. The thought of her dispelled his terror; if she
could be brave, then so would he.

Wallace knew why the gunfire had stopped. He knew what was
coming. He was pinned down, alone, and he couldn't gamble on the
police arriving in time. He had to prepare himself. He crawled along
the car and pulled the driver's door open. He hoisted himself inside
and saw what he was looking for; Hill's pistol, still in the dead man's
hand. Wallace leaned over and grabbed the gun. He wrenched it from
Hill's fingers and quickly withdrew to the safety of the sidewalk.

The sound of crackling snow told Wallace the killer was on his
way across the street. Quick, rhythmic footsteps hurrying to finish a
job made urgent by the piercing sound of sirens that could not have
been more than a block away. Wallace wanted to shoot for the head,
but he wasn't sure of his aim. He guessed at chest height, corrected
slightly the moment he saw the black horror round the car, and
squeezed the trigger. Four shots hit the killer in the chest, the bullets striking hard, burying themselves deep in his body armor, and
knocking him onto his back. Wallace stood and steadied his shaking
hand as he aimed at the killer's head. He pulled the trigger, but the
firing pin hammered thin air: *empty*. Wallace seethed, wishing he had
just one more shot, but his attacker was already stirring, so he turned
and started running.

38

The sound of the phone cut through the soporific fog of the Ambien. The pills were the only way Ash could steal a few hours' sleep from her nightmares, but they made her waking moments feel heavy and polluted. She leaned across her bed and answered the insistent ringing.

"Hello," she croaked.

"Ash, it's Hector," the voice said. "The safe house has been compromised. Hill and Perez are dead."

"Shit!" Ash replied, as adrenaline kicked aside the vestiges of the Ambien. "What about Wallace?"

"No sign of him," Hector answered.

"I'm on my way," Ash said.

Wallace ran until his legs had been pounded into aching submission, his lungs had been blistered raw by the glacial air, and his clothes were brittle with frozen moisture. Exhausted, he slowed to a walk. The snow-covered street was silent, save for his steps. He'd raced blindly, not paying attention to direction or time, and was now on a long road that was lined with four- and five-story brownstones. Deep powder covered the vehicles parked on both sides of the broad street and cold snapped at Wallace's skin. He realized that he wouldn't last long dressed in a thin top, jeans, and sneakers. Sanctuary beckoned in the form of a flashing neon sign that said "Open." He staggered toward the five-story building, his speed slowing as he shuffled through the snow. His mind filled with a garbled jumble of paranoid thoughts, but he forced them all back with a single thought: *survival*. He started at a noise behind him and turned to see a lone car crawl across the intersection two blocks back. As it drove away, silence settled over the neighborhood, and Wallace moved on.

The "Open" sign was located in the window of the Happy Days Diner, which was situated on the ground floor of the building. Wallace staggered along the sidewalk and almost slipped as he approached the steamy entrance. He steadied himself against the handle and then pulled the glass door open. There was a sudden rush of warm air as he stepped into a small porch that protected the diners from the extreme weather outside. He fumbled, pressing his hand against the glass partition wall for support as he took faltering steps toward the inner door. He pulled it open and lurched against the frame for support.

"You okay, mister?" asked the tall man behind the counter. He had thick gray hair and narrow eyes that watched Wallace with suspicion.

Wallace tried to answer, but a sudden flush of heat overwhelmed him. He tried to tell himself it was a reaction to the warmth of the diner, but the heat grew ever more intense, until it felt as though hundreds of tiny blowtorches were searing his skin. Wallace gabbled unfamiliar sounds as his frozen body burned before he collapsed against a table and blacked out.

Ash shivered in her heavy field coat. The snow had stopped, but a brutal wind ripped through Hunts Lane and whipped an eddy of powder into her face. Hill had called for assistance at 2:47 a.m. Witness reports suggested the attack had lasted no more than five minutes. Ash checked her watch: 03:53, just over an hour later, and the street was packed with people. NYPD had cordoned off most of the street and Parker was working with a squad of officers who were interviewing neighbors. Alvarez had gone to Los Angeles to lead the Pallo and Mann murder investigations, so Hector had been dragged from his bed to put a senior FBI face on the scene. Jordan Wiltshire and a couple of unfamiliar US marshals hovered near Hector, talking in low voices. Forensics were working the house, the street, and the rooftop that neighbors claimed the killer had used as his sniper's nest. There was no sign of Wallace or the killer, but there was a statewide all-points bulletin out on both.

Hector backed away from Jordan and wandered over to Ash. "Jordy's pissed," Hector began. "Understandably so. He's never had a breach," he continued, his breath clouding the crisp air. "He's gonna be looking for a leak."

"He thinks it's us," Ash responded with growing realization.

"Protocols guarantee anonymity. WitPro breaches are usually the result of a lapse by a particular individual."

Ash was about to reply when her phone rang. She didn't recognize the New York number. "Ash," she said, answering the call.

"Special Agent Ash?" an unfamiliar voice asked.

"Yeah."

"My name is Lenny Chaskel. I run a diner on Montague Street. I got this guy here, he's pretty messed up. I was gonna call an ambulance, but I thought he might be diabetic or something. I was checked him over for a medical alert bracelet or an insulin pen and found your card in his pocket. Figured I should check with you."

"You're kidding me," Ash replied, feigning dismay as she stepped away from Hector.

"You okay?" Lenny's voice betrayed his puzzlement.

"I'm fine," Ash said, as an idea formed in her mind.

"What d'ya want me to do?" Lenny asked.

"Don't touch anything," Ash instructed. "I'll be there in twenty minutes."

"Who was that?" Hector asked pointedly as Ash hung up.

"My neighbor. She says one of my pipes burst. Water's pouring through her ceiling," Ash lied. "Do you mind?"

Hector shrugged. "Nothing much we can do till we get the witness statements and forensics. Go do what you gotta do."

"Thanks," Ash said as she walked away. When she was around the corner and out of sight, she broke into a run toward Henry Street, where her car was parked.

Montague Street was two blocks away, and Ash made it there in under a minute. She double-parked outside the Happy Days Diner and hurried inside to find Wallace on his back, unconscious. A thin man with dark hair had his ear to Wallace's chest.

"He okay?" Ash asked.

"He's breathing," the man replied.

She knelt down beside Wallace and pressed her fingers against his neck to find a regular pulse. "I'm Special Agent Ash," she said, as she produced her identification. "You Lenny?"

The man nodded.

"You hear the sirens earlier?"

"Sure," Lenny replied. "He got something to do with it?"

"Someone shot up a federal safe house. Tried to kill him."

Lenny checked the street, suddenly on edge.

"You need to help me get him to my car. And you can never tell anyone he was here," Ash commanded. "You understand?"

Lenny gave an emphatic nod.

"Grab his other arm," Ash instructed.

She and Lenny half-lifted, half-dragged Wallace out of the diner. His feet left deep furrows in the snow as they pulled him across the sidewalk. Ash opened the front passenger door and they hoisted Wallace onto the seat.

"Thanks." She shook Lenny's hand.

"No problem," the bewildered man replied, as Ash jogged round the car.

She jumped in, slipped the Taurus in drive, and cruised away. She looked in the rearview and saw Lenny watching her receding taillights. After a few moments he glanced around nervously and then headed back inside the diner.

Most people had heeded the storm warning and the streets were quiet. Snowplows were out clearing the major expressways. Ash saw one on Tillary Street and another on the Brooklyn Bridge as she crossed the East River back to Manhattan. By the time they reached the island, Wallace was stirring. In the grip of delirium, his head rolled erratically and he muttered incomprehensibly.

"John? Can you hear me, John?" Ash tried, but her questions were lost on her rambling passenger.

They'd reached Chambers Street and were outside the Tweed Courthouse when Wallace woke. He lashed out, catching Ash on the cheek with a glancing blow that dazed her. The car veered across the deserted street and crashed into the large stone terracing that flanked the steps up to the courthouse. The air bags exploded, and for a moment Ash was lost in a confused cushion of soft plastic and abrasive powder. As her air bag deflated, she looked to her right and saw that the passenger door was open. Wallace was pulling himself out of the car.

"John!" she cried.

Wallace looked around, but there was no recognition in his eyes, only fear. Ash opened her door, hoisted herself from the car, slid over the steaming hood, and ran after Wallace. He was exhausted, injured, and moving at a slow shuffle, so the chase was brought to a swift end when Ash tackled him, pushing him down onto deep, soft snow. She lay across his torso and pinned his arms to the sidewalk.

"John! It's me," she yelled. "It's Special Agent Ash."

Wallace struggled weakly against her hold.

"It's Christine," Ash tried, softening her tone.

"I don't care!" Wallace exclaimed. "They're dead. Those men. He killed them. Nobody's safe."

"I know," Ash said. "I'm sorry, John."

"I've got to get away." Wallace renewed his struggle.

"You've been hurt, John," Ash explained. "You need help. I'm taking you somewhere safe. I promise."

Wallace wavered.

"I don't know how he found out where you were, but nobody knows you're with me, and I'm not going to tell anyone. It's the only way to be sure you'll be safe," Ash continued. "You need to trust me."

"Why?" The question perplexed Ash and Wallace pressed home his point. "Why should I trust you? I don't know you."

"I'm taking you to my place," Ash replied. "You'll be safe there."

"No." Wallace shook his head wildly. "No. No. No. I won't be safe. He'll find me."

"Somewhere else then," Ash countered. "We'll go wherever you want."

"Let me go!" Wallace yelled in Ash's face, his hysteria building. "You can't help me. You can't protect me. Get off me! Get the fuck away from me!"

He struggled with renewed fervor, surprising Ash with his strength. He threw her off, rolled to his knees, and was about to get to his feet when Ash lunged at him, lashing out with a punch that connected with the side of his head and knocked him flat on his belly. She grabbed Wallace and rolled him onto his back.

"Seven months ago I shot and killed an unarmed man named Marcel Washington," Ash bellowed. "As he lay bleeding to death, I planted a weapon on him."

The confession had the desired effect; it cut through Wallace's hysteria and strangled every sinew of attention.

"If anyone ever found out, I'd spend the rest of my life in jail," she added quietly. "I'm trusting you with it, and I need you to trust me in return."

Wallace stared at Ash, who crouched over him, holding the scruff of his collar.

"I want to catch the man who did this, John," she reassured him. "I'll do whatever it takes."

Wallace nodded. "We can't stay at your place," he cautioned.

"Okay, I'll just grab some stuff," Ash agreed, helping Wallace to his feet.

The two of them returned to the steaming Taurus, and Ash climbed in and tried the ignition. The engine screeched and squealed, but it rattled to life on the third attempt. Wallace fell into the passenger seat and pulled the door closed.

"Sorry about the car," he said sheepishly. "And your face."

"My bad," Ash replied, rubbing her cheek. "I should've put you in the trunk."

Wallace smiled uncertainly, but Ash was deadpan as she reversed the car onto the road. There was a dull clatter and a strange rattling as the car headed west on Chambers Street. Ash prayed the battered Ford would hold together long enough to get them home.

39

Wallace studied Ash as they pulled into an underground parking garage off Washington Square. She seemed genuine, but Wallace's faith in his ability to read people had been rattled by his experiences. Even if she was telling the truth, everyone Wallace trusted had been hurt or killed, and Ash looked too fragile to survive. Her delicate features flickered between light and shade as she drove beneath the strip lights illuminating the garage, and she must have sensed Wallace watching her because she glanced at him as she pulled the battered car into a resident's spot and brought it to a shuddering halt.

"Come on," she instructed.

Wallace slowly followed her into the elevator. His bones were aching and his muscles throbbed with exhaustion. He caught sight of his reflection in the large mirror that lined the rear wall; he looked terrible. He turned his back on the sunken-eyed, emaciated fellow he'd become and leaned against the mirror, taking some of the load off his weary legs.

"The man you killed," he asked as they rode up to the fifth floor, "why'd you do it?"

Ash looked down uncomfortably. "He led a group. It was a cross between a cult and a gang. Rape, murder, kidnapping; you name it, they did it. I knew he'd work the system, probably get a couple of years and then be out and back in business. Didn't seem right."

Wallace nodded slowly. "You ever kill anyone before?"

Ash stared at him, her face betraying no emotion until the elevator doors opened. "We need to be quick," she advised as she stepped into the corridor.

Wallace followed, almost certain that Marcel Washington wasn't her first kill. She led him into her apartment, which was on the top floor of a redbrick building that overlooked the park opposite.

"I'll be a minute," she said as she turned on a light and disappeared down a hallway that ran off the living room.

Wallace shuffled over to the window. The blinds were up, fully exposing the interior of the apartment to the snowbound city beyond. He looked down, surveying the street and park, and although he didn't see anyone, he still felt more comfortable when he pulled the cord and lowered the blinds over the window. Ash's apartment looked like a soulless hotel room. A plush leather couch dominated the space. Alongside it was a matching recliner and ottoman. Both were pointed toward a small flat-screen television. A tall bookshelf lined one wall, and a large photo of a sunny beach flanked the archway that led to the kitchen. Wallace walked over to the bookshelf, his eye drawn by a photograph that showed a young girl and a woman standing at the summit of a mountain that overlooked a sprawling, smog-covered Los Angeles.

"I'm good," Ash said, entering the room with a black carryall slung over her shoulder.

"Is this you?" Wallace asked.

"Yeah," Ash replied.

Wallace sensed discomfort in her voice. "That your mum?"

"We should go," Ash counseled. "Like you said, this place isn't safe."

Wallace nodded and followed her out of the apartment.

"Gonna be an extra hundred-fifty," the girl behind the desk said. Her name tag identified her as Bethany Fong. "Storage costs," she added by way of explanation.

"For a knapsack?" Wallace asked. The bull-necked man in the back office looked away from his television program and fixed

Wallace with a cold stare. It wasn't worth an argument. "Okay. We'll take a twin for a week."

"Passport?" Bethany asked.

"In the bag," Wallace answered.

Bethany shouted something in Cantonese and the bull-necked man shuffled into the recesses of the office and returned moments later with Wallace's knapsack, which had been found when he'd failed to return following his arrest. The bull-necked man opened the bulletproof screen and passed the bag over the counter with a belligerent grunt. Wallace checked inside and found the William Porter passport in the front pouch. He showed it to Bethany, who gave it a cursory glance.

"Okay, total's twelve hundred," she said.

Wallace counted out some of the money Ash had given him and topped it up with notes from his belt. He put it all in the metal cash container that ran beneath the bulletproof screen, and Bethany rewarded him with a key.

"Two-seventeen, on the second floor," she advised.

Wallace took the key and turned toward Ash, who was leaning against the wall a few feet away.

"Welcome to the Fresh City Hotel," he said.

Ash gave a wry smile as she picked up her bag and followed him past the broken elevator.

A nagging voice questioned the wisdom of what she was doing, but Ash silenced it as she followed Wallace. He trudged up the stairs, each slow step showing the painful legacy of his ordeal. The Marcel Washington shooting had made her cautious, and it didn't suit her. She'd risen quickly because of her unique approach to life and her willingness to take risks. The nagging voice was that of a bureaucrat, a fearful, timid creature who only felt safe working within boundaries. Ash knew that boundaries were an illusion; life was wild and dangerous. Wallace presented the perfect opportunity to rediscover herself and show the Bureau exactly why she was so special.

"This place is a real shithole," Wallace said as he stepped over a puddle of unidentified liquid that pooled in the stairwell doorway. "But it's safe."

Ash followed him into a squalid corridor. He struggled to get the key into a battered old lock but, after a few good shoves, managed to open the door. The tiny room contained two small single beds, a rickety closet, and an ancient television. Every surface looked soiled. A tap was dripping in the adjoining shower room, and a cooling unit hummed in the yard beneath the sealed window.

"The penthouse suite," Wallace observed dryly, as he sat on the bed nearest the window and dropped his knapsack by his feet. He fell back onto the filthy comforter that topped the thin mattress, and within seconds the exhausted man had succumbed to sleep.

40

An unfamiliar rhythmic pulse roused Wallace from his night-mares. He realized it was a phone and opened his eyes to see Ash emerge from the bathroom wearing a tight blue pullover and a pair of jeans. She leaned over her bed and grabbed her phone from the tiny shelf beside it.

"Ash," she said.

Wallace could hear indistinct dialogue.

"He's with me," Ash replied. "He's safe."

Wallace sat up, his heart starting to race at the prospect of betrayal.

"No, we're not coming in," Ash said, as if answering Wallace's concern. "Not until you've figured out how the safe house was compromised."

More garbled words from the caller.

"If you want to make it a direct order, go ahead," Ash advised. "You can write me up for insubordination at the same time. Have you read the deposition?"

A sharp response came down the line.

"Then you know what he's been through. And you know how resourceful the killer is," Ash replied. "We're staying off the grid until his safety is guaranteed."

Wallace heard the caller's tone soften as he launched into a pro-longed speech.

"Thanks. I'm going to ditch this phone and get some burners. I'll check in every twelve hours," Ash promised before hanging up. "You okay?"

Wallace nodded. "I've felt worse."

"That was my boss. Ballistics report that Hill and Perez were killed by five-mill slugs fired from an M27. That's a military-grade automatic rifle."

"So what now?"

"We've been ordered to sit tight until it's safe to bring you in," Ash explained.

Wallace sensed there was more to come. "But?" he inquired.

"Well, I've never been great at following orders," she replied honestly. "Where would you have gone next? If you hadn't been caught?"

"The brother, I guess," Wallace replied. "See if he remembers anything unusual about his sister's death."

The drive out to Cromwell took a little over three hours. When the cab stopped for fuel on the edge of town, Ash ran across the street and purchased three prepaid phones from a Best Buy. They drove on through Cromwell, which was a picturesque little town with a mix of New England timber and grand redbrick buildings, and, in complete contrast to the build 'em high, stack 'em deep sprawl of Manhattan, Cromwell offered space to breathe. Most of the buildings were detached, with enough land between them to plant two or three skyscrapers. According to the cab driver, Connecticut had missed the worst of the storm, so the landscape was covered with long-fallen snow that had turned to ice, with the occasional enthusiastic tuft of grass poking through, fighting for spring. They drove north, past a redbrick church fronted by six tall Doric columns supporting a huge pediment. The bold clash of architectural styles somehow worked to give the church a formidable sense of presence. They rolled up the hill and, about a mile past the church, turned right onto Nooks Hill Road, which was lined with large houses set in sprawling, wooded plots of land. As the cab drove east, Wallace caught glimpses of the expansive homes between the trees. After a couple of minutes, he saw a gated driveway, and a sign beside it that read "Cromwell Psychiatric Center."

It was a little after three when the cab driver stopped beside the intercom and pressed the button.

"Hello?" came a woman's voice.

Ash leaned over Wallace and out of his window. "Special Agent Christine Ash. I need to see one of your patients."

"Identification?" the disembodied voice asked.

Ash held her credentials up to the intercom's recessed lens.

"Follow the road up to the hospital," the voice advised.

After a brief delay, the heavy brushed-steel gates opened and the cab drove through. The smooth driveway wound into a mature wood, where the road was flanked by grand old trees.

"This doesn't feel right," Wallace cautioned.

"The trail led you to Erin Byrne," Ash explained. "You've spoken to the mother and the father. You said yourself this is the next logical step. Maybe the brother can give us a new lead."

After half a mile the wood thinned and gave way to a large parking lot that stretched around a four-story redbrick building. The Cromwell Center reminded Wallace of the Maybury Hospital, and maybe it was the similarity that was making him so uneasy.

A grand building set in carefully landscaped grounds, the Cromwell Center revealed small clues to the true nature of the property everywhere: heavy security doors, bars across windows, and spikes along the top of the perimeter wall all signaled that, like the Maybury, this was a prison for broken minds. Wallace shuddered as he remembered the South London hospital where he'd watched so many people die. If he hadn't fought back, if he'd just lain down after the first attack, they'd all be alive. *Connie.* Connie would still be alive.

"Three hundred and forty-four bucks," the cab driver announced as they pulled up in front of the main entrance.

"Keep the change," Ash said as she handed over four one-hundred-dollar bills. "There's another fifty if you wait."

"No problem," the driver responded happily.

Wallace followed Ash up the stone steps to the entrance, where they found a slim woman in her mid-thirties waiting for them.

"Welcome to the Cromwell Center, Special Agent Ash. My name is Grace Kavanagh," she said. Grace wore a light-gray jacket, a matching skirt, and color-coordinated three-inch heels. She exuded warm professionalism and smiled as she looked at Wallace, expecting an introduction. Her smile wavered when none came. "I'm the chief administrator."

"We need to talk to Max Byrne." Ash's response bordered on brusque.

"Really?" Grace asked. "Are you from the New Haven office?"

"New York."

"Your New Haven colleagues said he wouldn't be troubled again," Grace observed. "They were here yesterday to talk to him about his sister's death."

"We just need to clarify a couple of things."

"He won't be able to help you," Grace warned.

"We need to see him," Ash insisted.

If she was put out, Grace didn't show it. Her smile grew broader. "As you wish. Max is in our secure unit. Follow me."

She led them through one of the heavy double doors into a security booth. They were encased on three sides by thick glass, which Wallace suspected was shatterproof. Grace ran a card through a reader and the inner door opened, allowing them to enter the lobby. A middle-aged woman sat behind the reception desk and nodded at Grace as she passed. Wallace and Ash followed Grace across the flagstone floor, walking beneath large Edward Hopper–style watercolors of lighthouses and beach scenes that hung on bare brick. A thick visitors' book rested on a high plinth, and a sign invited people to use it to share their experiences of the center. The room felt more like the innards of a design studio than a hospital, and Wallace suspected that, just like the Maybury, the trendy modernity would be reflected in the Cromwell's treatment methods. Another card reader guarded a door at the other end of the room, and Grace swiped their way into the corridor beyond.

"Everywhere seems pretty secure," Wallace observed as they walked down the long, windowless corridor.

Grace looked puzzled by the remark.

"So I was wondering how secure the secure unit is," Wallace explained.

"Ah. The secure unit is for our more troubled patients, ones who present a threat to themselves or others. People with a history of violence," Grace replied. "It's called the secure unit because of the special protocols we use to keep the patients safe. I hope that answers your question, Mr. . . . ?"

"Porter," Wallace offered hurriedly. "William Porter. I'm helping Special Agent Ash with her investigation."

The corridor ended with a white mesh gate. Next to it was a small black window, which opened as they approached to reveal a large orderly in a white uniform. He sat inside a tiny room lined with shelves that were laden with file boxes and paperwork.

"Afternoon, Miss Kavanagh," he said. "Gonna need your guests to sign their stuff in."

Ash stepped forward and leaned through the window to sign the deposit sheet.

"Thank you, Special Agent Ash," the orderly said, reading the names Ash had written. "You and Mr. Porter will need to leave any weapons, pens, pins, belts, jewelry, and any other potentially hazardous items with us."

"Seriously?" Ash asked.

"It's for your protection," Grace advised.

Ash shook her head as she removed her pistol from its holster. She popped the clip and placed it next to the gun in the plastic tray proffered by the orderly. She emptied her pockets, depositing a small wallet, a billfold of cash, a phone, and a pen, while Wallace unthreaded his belt and dropped it into the tray with his wallet and the key to their hotel room.

"Thank you," the orderly said. "You can collect your stuff on the way out."

He pressed a button located beneath the adjacent shelf and the lock on the wire mesh gate buzzed open. Grace pulled the handle and ushered Wallace and Ash into the corridor beyond, before using her key card to get them through another security door at the end of the corridor, where they emerged into a large open space that was devoid of people. There were no hard edges in the room; even the pastel blue walls were curved, and where they met the soft rubber floor the natural join had been rounded into a smooth contour. Rubber monoblocs and ramps peppered the room and Wallace could see that they were secured to the floor by smooth, recessed bolts. A curved line of mesh-covered windows hugged the high ceiling and ran the length of one wall, flooding the space with light.

"This is the unit's exercise area. We keep our secure patients separate from the others. They're not allowed outside until they are well enough to join the general population," Grace explained. "Max will probably be in the dayroom."

They followed Grace through an arch on the far side of the room and walked along a pastel yellow corridor that stretched into the distance. A short way down, Grace branched right and led them into a large dayroom that was full of nurses, orderlies, and patients. The twenty or so patients sat on long molded benches that were bolted to the floor. Eight nurses clad in purple smocks and trousers sat or hovered nearby, tending to any patients who required attention, while half a dozen orderlies leaned against the walls, paired in quiet conversation. A television played at the front of the room, shielded behind a thick plastic screen, but Wallace wondered if anyone was actually watching; most of the men and women in the pale-green patients' uniform seemed too detached to register anything.

"This way." Grace led Ash and Wallace toward a shaven-headed, emaciated patient in the back row. A young male nurse sat next to him. "This is Max," Grace said. His eyes were completely glassy, and a stream of drool extended from one corner of his mouth. He'd lost so much weight that Wallace hardly recognized him from the photos in Philicia Byrne's office.

"What's he on?" Ash inquired.

"Antipsychotics, sedatives, muscle relaxants," the nurse replied.

"This is Ethan Moore," Grace introduced them. "He leads Max's team."

"Can he talk?" Ash asked.

"Not really," Ethan revealed. "His sister's death hit him hard."

"Max had a patchy history of mental health problems, but his sister's passing pushed him to a very dark place," Grace explained.

"We've got him on a high-dosage combination. Every time we try to taper him off, he becomes extremely violent. Not sure what's going on in there . . ." (Ethan indicated Max's skull), "but unfortunately this case is more about management than cure."

"How long's he been here?"

"Last month was his second anniversary," the nurse replied as he used a piece of gauze to wipe away some of the drool from Max's mouth.

"Any visitors?" Ash asked.

Ethan shook his head slowly. "No. A friend booked him in, but his folks never visit. I guess it got too hard for them to see him like this. They've already lost one kid."

"He say anything to the New Haven agents?" Wallace saw Ash studying Max, scouring his face for anything that might help them.

"No," Ethan replied. "It took us two days to taper his meds. He was jumpy, but when they started asking him questions about his sister, he became extremely distressed. We were worried he'd get violent, so we had to sedate him again."

Ash turned away from Max in exasperation.

"Is there anything else?" Grace asked.

Ash looked at Wallace, who felt as though she was willing him to think of something. "No. Thanks. You've been very helpful," Ash said at last.

"In that case, I'll show you out," Grace replied.

They collected their belongings from the orderly and followed Grace back through the building. Wallace was relieved when they reached the exit and cold air whipped at his cheeks.

"Here's my card," Grace said, handing it to Ash. "Give me a call if there's anything else you need."

"Thanks," Ash replied. "I appreciate it."

Grace withdrew inside and shut the door behind her.

"What now?" Wallace asked, as they descended the stone steps toward the waiting cab.

Ash pursed her lips and shook her head slowly. "I don't know," she said. "I need to think."

"You know any bad motels?" Ash asked the cab driver as they climbed into the vehicle. "Somewhere cheap. We lost all our money getting mugged by a New York cabbie."

"Very funny," the cab driver said, casting a sardonic grin in the rearview mirror. "Anyone nuts enough to take a New York City cab on a three-hour trip to Hicksville deserves all the mugging they get."

41

The sun was being devoured by the horizon when they reached the Best Value Inn, a run-down motel on the Wilbur Cross Highway. Ash paid the driver his extra fifty bucks before climbing out to join Wallace in the parking lot. They stood and watched the cab pull onto the highway and speed into the distance, and when it was gone, Wallace turned for the motel, but Ash caught his arm.

"There's no such thing as too paranoid," she told him, pointing to a cluster of neon signs some distance away. "Driver's gonna remember a four-hundred-buck fare. I don't want anyone knowing where we are."

Wallace nodded, and the two of them set out along the busy highway. Trudging through the filthy snow-covered gutter, their eyes burned by the glare of oncoming headlights, their ears thrumming with the noise of whirling tires on gritty asphalt, their bodies fighting the fierce freezing wind, they walked on through the fading light. After heading south for half an hour, past a few industrial units and fast-food restaurants, they finally came to a motel that was part of a large national chain. It looked too salubrious and would almost certainly have smiling, well-trained staff who might remember a couple of weather-beaten pedestrians with no luggage. They walked on and, three blocks later, reached the Mount Wilbur Inn. It was a single-level, timber-framed building with a redbrick fascia and tile roof. The timbers were peeling and the paintwork molding. The motel was connected to a tumbledown general store that had a "We Buy Gold" poster in the window. Wallace and Ash left the highway, crossed the potholed parking lot, and entered the motel through a door marked "Office."

"Evenin'," said a thin, gray-haired man with a lined, leathery face. The name badge pinned to his pressed polyester shirt read "Tucker Dale."

"You got any rooms?" Ash asked.

"Sure," Tucker replied. "Double okay?"

"Twin," Ash said. "I'm saving myself."

Tucker smiled as he produced a registration card from a folder. "Fill this in, please."

"You handle this, honey?" Ash asked Wallace. "I need to make a call."

Wallace approached the counter and smiled awkwardly at Tucker as Ash stepped out of the office.

Ash took one of the burners out of her pocket and dialed Hector.

"Solomon," he said.

"It's Ash."

The roar of passing traffic filled the silence.

"You need to turn yourself in," Hector said finally. "I got a call from a researcher at *Nightfile* asking me about Alice Silberstein."

Ash froze, gripped by her hideous past, its dark claws reaching up and tearing at her innards. She doubled over, fearing that she was about to be sick.

"Chris?" Hector asked. "Are you there?"

"Yeah." Ash's forced response was pained and clipped.

"Is it true?" Hector continued.

"I . . ." Ash tried. Despair gave way to bewildered anger. It was impossible, but somehow someone had discovered her secret. "I was a minor, Hector. Those files were sealed. I was under no legal obligation to disclose anything."

"No legal obligation? Every case you've ever worked is gonna be reexamined in light of this. And the Washington kill? Shit, Chris, what did you do?" Ash could sense Hector's concern.

"I did my job. I'm still doing my job." Ash kept her anger at bay and her tone as even as possible.

"No. They're running the story tonight. You need to come in," Hector advised. "You'll be suspended pending a full inquiry."

Ash leaned against the wall beside the office door and put her head in her hand. She felt soiled, her body permeated with the filth of failure. The world became distant and unreal as her mind tumbled further into despair. She knew she was finished.

"You've got to come in," Hector insisted. "Where are you?"

Ash looked at the ugly world surrounding her: the run-down motel, the highway covered in frozen slurry, and the filthy vehicles that roared along it. Success was not found in such squalor, she admitted inwardly. She was not one of life's winners, she thought before she started to speak. "Connecticut, just off the—" She was cut off by Wallace, who slapped the phone out of her hand.

"What are you doing?" he asked agitatedly. "Who was that?"

"Hector," Ash replied, wiping the moisture from her eyes. She watched Wallace pick up the phone and disconnect the call. The phone started ringing almost immediately, so Wallace popped the battery out.

"I trusted you," he protested. He seemed genuinely hurt.

"I know, but I've screwed everything up. I need to turn myself in."

"No. If I go back, I'm dead. This guy has reached me in the hospital, in a safe house, fucking everywhere. This is the safest I've ever been. You might be reckless, but you're also smart enough to stay one step ahead. Who else would walk two miles in the freezing cold on the off chance that a cab driver might tell someone which motel he took us to?" He held Ash's shoulders and gently pulled her toward him. "I don't need witness protection. I need you," he said emphatically.

Ash gave him a weak smile.

"I'm frozen. Let's get inside." He held out the key to their room. "Room twelve. Round the back."

The walls were clad in pine veneer, but age had chipped it to reveal the dirty yellow plastic lining underneath. The beds were bowed and lumpy, but the linen was clean, as was the old carpet. The hard-to-reach corners of the tiled bathroom were lined with antique black mold, but the aged fixtures had all been well bleached.

Ash seemed distracted as she switched on the TV and selected a channel that was broadcasting the last few minutes of a Jim Belushi sitcom. Wallace guessed she wanted something vacuous to take her mind off their troubles. It was clear that her conversation with her superior had not gone well, and she seemed tearful and depressed, but Wallace had no idea what to say or whether he could trust her. She'd been about to give her boss their location, but self-preservation required Wallace to do whatever he could to keep her at his side.

"I'm going to see if I can get us something to eat," he said, looking to buy himself some time to figure things out. "Do you want anything?"

Ash shook her head.

"I won't be long." Wallace hurried through the door and locked it behind him. He couldn't risk leaving Ash on her own for long—she might try to call her boss—but he needed to work out how to encourage her to stay with him and think about what their next move might be. He walked round the motel, past the office, and into the general store, which faced the highway. Glaringly bright strip lights shone on half-empty gray shelves. Wallace didn't recognize any of the brands, but he could tell from the cheap packaging designs that this shop stocked value items. He grabbed some sack-sized bags of nacho chips, a couple of turkey sandwiches from a leaking old refrigerator, and four bottles of Coke. A vacant man in his early twenties took his money and methodically put his purchases in a brown paper bag. Wallace eyed the shelves behind the cashier, which were stacked with branded liquor and cigarettes. He hadn't had a drink since leaving London, but he felt that alcohol might ease the situation.

"I'll take a bottle of Jack Daniels," Wallace told the cashier, who reached for a bottle and pushed it across the counter.

"Anything else?" he asked.

Wallace shook his head.

"Forty-six ninety," the cashier told him.

Wallace handed over a fifty, took his change, and hurried back to the room with the supplies. When he stepped inside, he found Ash pacing in front of the television in a state of agitation.

"Fuck," she said bitterly.

Wallace turned his attention to the screen and saw Ash's face staring back at him. Her Bureau photograph was accompanied by a lower-third title that identified her name and rank, alongside a branded *Nightfile* ID.

"Special Agent Christine Ash was the subject of a recent FBI investigation following the fatal shooting of Marcel Washington." The female reporter's voice was earnest and urgent. The on-screen image changed to file footage of the aftermath of the FBI raid on the Hopeland Family's Dover Plains compound. "Mr. Washington was killed last August during an FBI raid on his property. What makes his death particularly troubling is Special Agent Ash's background."

An elderly African-American woman's face filled the screen. Next to her was a young African-American woman with long flowing hair. Both women looked as though they'd been crying. The lower-third title identified them as Cleo and Donna Washington, mother and sister to Marcel.

"She's got no business being in the FBI," Marcel's mother, Cleo, spoke in strained tones. "She's lied about who she is."

The image returned to the file photo of Ash.

"*Nightfile* has learned that Special Agent Christine Ash was born Alice Silberstein, and that, as a child, she gave evidence against her father when he was accused of her mother's murder. Her father was Nicholas Silberstein, who, it later emerged, was the leader of a notoriously violent cult, the Mulholland Clan. It seems that Special Agent Ash concealed her background from the FBI, so tonight on *Nightfile* we ask the question, when do the private lives of law enforcement agents make them unfit for duty?"

A sudden flash of color and thump of dramatic drum-laden music signaled the transition from the show's intro to its overly theatrical opening credits. Wallace realized he'd been mesmerized by the revelations and when he looked away from the screen, he saw that Ash was badly shaken, so he switched off the television and sat next to her on the bed.

"I saw him do it," Ash admitted at last. She shook with grief as she recounted her long-buried past. "Not the killing, but I was there right after he'd done it. He said my mom had tried to stab him during a fight, but I know there was no fight and no knife. He just shot her. The jury believed him. Social services gave me back to him. Nobody knew what he was really like. I was the only one."

"I'm sorry. I'm so sorry." Wallace placed a reassuring hand on her shoulder.

Ash wiped her eyes and the shaking subsided. "Nobody knew," she said. "I was a minor. My files were sealed."

"Your dad?" Wallace asked.

"Maybe, but he disappeared years ago and I don't believe in coincidences. The timing makes me think it's got something to do with this case," Ash said flatly. "My face is all over the TV, and Hector's gonna have no choice but to put out an APB on us. They'll take us both into custody. Who does that help?"

Wallace saw the sadness in her eyes turn to resolve.

"This story leaking now, it's designed to bring us down," she explained with increasing certainty. "I get suspended, you go back into WitPro, where you become a target." She paused, following her thoughts to their natural conclusion. "The only way to be sure is to find out who tipped off *Nightfile*." She took a moment to compose herself and then gently touched Wallace's hand. "Thanks," she said. "I'll be okay. So, did you get anything to eat?" she asked in a tone that was full of bravado.

"Most people would think they were beaten," Wallace said before taking a bite out of his turkey sandwich. He was conscious he was slurring his words slightly.

"I thrive on adversity," Ash told him. "My life has been one beat-down after another. If I didn't live for the fight, I would have stayed down a long time ago. Sometimes I get low, but that's just me passing through stormy waters, charting my way back to the right course."

"You're pretty self-aware," Wallace observed.

"Maybe it's the Jack," Ash smiled, indicating the Jack Daniels bottle, which was half-empty.

"I'll drink to that," Wallace said, raising one of the plastic cups he'd found in the bathroom. Ash saluted with its twin and they both downed their drinks.

"Most kids got spanked. If I stepped out of line, I got a minimum of a week in a discipline cell. Solitary confinement. Gives you plenty of time to reflect. Really get to know yourself," Ash explained as she took a bite of her sandwich. "What the hell is this?"

"It says it's turkey," Wallace answered, picking up the discarded cellophane wrapper.

"More like dog," Ash drawled the final word so it sounded like daaawg, and Wallace grinned.

He chewed his way through airy bread, wilted lettuce, and leathery turkey and watched Ash as she did the same. She got up and poured him another generous measure of whiskey before returning to sit on the edge of her bed and fill her own cup.

"How'd you get into photography?" she asked.

"I started doing aikido when I was a teenager," Wallace replied. "My instructor wanted some publicity photographs, so I borrowed my dad's camera, and, well, people liked what I did. So I never stopped."

"Your folks live in London?"

Wallace shook his head. "They died."

"I'm sorry," Ash said.

"They were in a car accident just after I finished university." Wallace felt a pang of grief and wondered when he'd last spoken about his parents. "Looking back, I think I had a mini-breakdown. I was working on fashion shoots, but when they died I became consumed by the idea of doing something worthy and important with my life. That's when I started pushing for documentary jobs. Chasing war."

"Were you chasing war? Or death?"

Wallace shrugged, and a wistful smile flickered across his face. "I don't know anymore." He hesitated before adding, "It went badly

for me. I got a war correspondent assignment at *The Times* and was
embedded with the Fourth Battalion of the Lancaster Regiment in
Afghanistan. I was with a unit that had received word of insurgent
activity on the outskirts of Kandahar. They went in ready for a fight,
killed twelve adults and thirty children. It was a birthday party. The
men had been firing AK-47s into the air in celebration. We gunned
them all down. I tried to get out, but the unit commander, Captain
Nash, seized my camera, destroyed the evidence. They put pressure
on me to corroborate their story that some of the men and women
were insurgents who had put the children in harm's way by hiding
out at a suburban family home. I was beaten, my life was threatened,
but I managed to get out of Afghanistan. The government convened
the Masterson Inquiry to investigate what happened. I spent two
years fighting for those people, fighting for those kids, fighting for
the truth to come out. It ruined my life. Almost destroyed me. I met
Connie, my . . . friend . . ."

Wallace took a swig as words failed him and felt warmth spread
across his chest as the dark whiskey worked its way down. "I met
Connie about a year after I got back," he continued. "She was understanding, patient . . . loving." He paused again, struggling with the
words. "But I was fucked up. Obsessed. Depressed. Dark. Two years
ago last September the inquiry threw out my testimony. They came
to the conclusion that I was motivated by a political agenda and a
personal vendetta against Captain Nash, and that my testimony was
the only thing that contradicted the official record and the reports
of all sixteen men in Nash's unit. Those people. Those kids. There
would never be any justice for them. I went out and I got drunk. I
mean really drunk. When I got home, Connie was waiting for me.
I don't even remember the fight, but I know I said I hated her. The
truth was, I hated myself. I'd failed. I felt so powerless. But the damage was done. She'd had enough. Connie and I were finished. It was
one of the worst nights of my life. After she left I drank myself half
to death with regret. I came round in the early hours slumped at my
desk, covered in puke. My laptop, my photographs, everything that
had been on my desk was smashed into tiny pieces."

"I'm sorry," Ash said quietly.

"I suppose I'm just trying to say that we all make mistakes," Wallace explained, before falling silent.

"Yeah," Ash agreed. "We all make mistakes. I guess it's how we fix things that matters. Connie wasn't your fault, and from what you told me, she knew you loved her."

Wallace nodded uncertainly and then looked away. "What about you?" he asked, his tone falsely light.

"What mistakes have I made?" Ash smiled. "I'm starting to think this might be one," she said, holding her cup aloft.

"No, I mean, you're not a typical cop. What are you doing with that badge?"

"It's for my mom," Ash replied. "I joined the Bureau for her. I'm her legacy. I can give her life meaning."

Wallace saw the confident veneer fall away as Ash's eyes filled with the raw hurt that she buried deep within her. He guessed that she didn't open up to many people and was surprised by the honest intimacy. After an endless moment, she picked up her cup and went to the bathroom.

"This stuff is brutal," she said, indicating the Jack Daniels. "I need some water."

Wallace didn't say anything as Ash shut the bathroom door behind her. He reached across the narrow gulf between their beds, grabbed the bottle by the neck, and poured himself another drink.

42

Zach Holz did not regret his decision to walk. The main thoroughfares had been cleared and salted, but Chicago snow wasn't defeated so easily. Huge mounds lined Cityfront Plaza and fed the pedestrian square with a steady stream of slush. Zach's shoes were soaked, the black leather marked with white salt lines. The hems of his tailored pants were leaching freezing water toward his ankles, and if it hadn't been for the thick lining of his Yves Salomon parka, which kept him tucked in a pocket of warm air, Zach's impulsive decision to walk to his hotel would have been a miserable experience. As it was, apart from his wet feet and the intermittent flashes of cold around his ankles, Zach was enjoying his stroll back from the convention. The InterContinental Hotel and Conference Center was located five minutes away from The Langham, but Zach had extended the journey by heading east on Illinois Street and walking a couple of laps of Cityfront Plaza. After two days trapped in a windowless convention hall, breathing the recycled air of hundreds of other cyber security executives, Zach longed for the challenging runs of Foothills Park. Cityfront Plaza was ringed by wispy bare trees and illuminated by street lamps and the interior lights of the surrounding skyscrapers. It was a poor substitute for the expansive Los Altos hills, and Zach paced the small concrete square like a restless lion trapped in a cage.

When his watch told him that his pulse had reached a hundred beats per minute, Zach cut across the plaza opposite the NBC Tower and walked west, past the iconic Tribune Tower. He preferred California's rugged natural beauty, but he could not help but be impressed by Chicago. The soaring peaks of the high towers looked down on a city that gleamed. There was none of the grime of New York or LA; Chicago seemed so clean and new, and, unlike Manhattan, which had to maximize every inch of land, the Midwest could afford to be generous. Wide streets and expansive plazas meant the forest of skyscrapers never felt as though they were overshadowing the city.

Zach crossed Michigan Avenue and headed past the curvilinear Trump Tower to the small crosswalk on Wabash. The illuminated buildings on the south side of the Chicago River reached up toward the cloudless sky, overwhelming the stars with their artificial light. Zach checked his watch; his brisk walk had kept his pulse above a hundred. It was no Foothills run, but it would do. He touched the bevel and his watch displayed the time: nine p.m. Ali and the boys would just be sitting down for dinner. He turned north up Wabash and walked the few yards to The Langham's entrance, which was set at the foot of a gleaming black monolith that towered at least fifty stories above the street.

He exchanged greetings with the uniformed doorman and hurried inside the building. Crossing the lobby to the elevator, he rode it to the eleventh floor, then walked along the quiet corridor toward his suite. His phone squealed and he pulled it out of his pocket: Ali, on a FaceTime call. After a moment, the line connected and Zach saw the faces of his pregnant wife, Ali, and his two sons, Aaron and Reuben, smiling up at the camera.

"Hey, guys," Zach said with a smile.

"Hey, Daddy," Ali, Aaron, and Reuben all replied. They were seated at the dining table and had obviously just finished dinner.

"The boys are going up for their bath, so we thought we'd try you," Ali said.

"I was about to call," Zach responded. "I'm just on my way back to the room. How are my monkeys? Have you boys had a good day?"

"Nah," Aaron said. "Jamie hit me."

"Why?" Zach asked with exaggerated concern.

"We were fighting," Aaron replied with the perfect logic of a six-year-old.

"Oh, you were fighting," Zach said as he slipped his key card into the door. When the light flashed green, he stepped inside. "Did you win?"

"Zach!" Ali protested.

"Yeah," Aaron responded with a broad, gap-toothed smile. "I pounded him."

"Good for you," Zach laughed.

"Zach! Fighting's bad, isn't it?" Ali said reprovingly.

"It's good for the soul to have a little scuffle every now and again," Zach replied. He walked through the entrance hall and dropped his key card on the chaise that ran along one of the floor-to-ceiling windows overlooking the river. He flipped a switch and the recessed spotlights came on, illuminating the hallway and living room.

"You're setting a bad example, Zach," Ali chided him.

"Come on, Ali," Zach protested. "I was never allowed to fight as a kid, and there were times I wish I had. Boys've gotta learn to stand up for themselves."

"Where have you been?" Reuben asked. Two years older than Aaron, Reuben was much more serious and thoughtful than his younger brother.

"I've been at the convention hall, listening to lots of people talking."

"When are you talking, Dad?" Reuben inquired.

"Tomorrow. I'm giving the closing address," Zach replied.

"Isn't Daddy smart?" Ali teased.

"I'm smarter than Daddy!" Aaron exclaimed. "And stronger!"

"I don't think so, Mister," Zach said. "Where's my tiny girl?"

Ali pulled her phone toward her bulbous belly. Somewhere, hidden beneath the bright floral dress, was their daughter, quietly growing in warm darkness.

"Hey, little girl, I can't wait to meet you," Zach cooed. "How was the scan?"

"Everything's fine. She's healthy and she looks great," Ali replied, lifting the phone up to her face. "Only another ten weeks."

"Sorry I missed it," Zach said.

"Don't worry, Reuben took a video," Ali reassured her husband. "There's some great commentary about how gross Mommy's belly looks."

"I can't wait to watch it," Zach responded with a smile.

"What're you doing now?" Ali asked.

"Gonna jump in the shower and then order some room service."

"I'll call you later when I've put the boys to bed."

"Sounds good. Love you," Zach said.

"Love you," Ali echoed.

"Love you, Daddy," Reuben and Aaron yelled at the camera.

Ali smiled at her two enthusiastic boys and then ended the call.

Zach put his phone on the circular dining table before placing his wallet and billfold next to it. He took off his parka and slung it over one of the white leather chairs, then removed his suit jacket and laid it on one of the gray armchairs facing each other across the long glass coffee table. He sat down on the purple couch and proceeded to undo the laces of his now ruined shoes. Once they were off, he removed his sodden socks, and his feet immediately tingled with the warmth of the room. Zach sensed, rather than heard, a hushed sound from the bedroom.

"Hello?" he called loudly as he got to his feet.

He walked past the wet bar and poked his head through the bedroom doorway. The maid must have closed the drapes; he couldn't see the lights of the neighboring buildings. As his eyes became accustomed to the darkness, he saw the outline of a shadow by the bathroom door. His heart leaped as it started moving toward him. Zach took a couple of steps back and was trying to turn to run when a tall, well-built man in a long coat, body armor, and a mask barreled into him. The force of the impact expelled the air from Zach's lungs, and his attacker pushed them on, across the living room, until Zach collided with the large window overlooking the river. His head thumped against the glass, and his teeth snapped against his tongue, sending a very real bite of pain through the surreal situation.

Zach punched at his assailant's stomach, but his fist hit hard armor and the blow simply added to his suffering. A sharp elbow cracked into his collarbone and he was sent crumbling to his knees. His only thought was of his family: Aaron, Reuben, and his beautiful wife, Ali, with their baby girl growing inside her. Zach knew he couldn't afford to stay down, so he forced himself up, grabbed his attacker behind the knees and thrust his shoulder into the man's waist. He pushed forward, his powerful runner's legs pounding the wooden floor. His attacker collided with the edge of the coffee table and the large man fell backward, smashing through the glass.

Zach lunged for the occasional table and picked up a lamp that was set in a heavy crystal plinth. He yanked the lamp free of its cable and brought it crashing down on his assailant's head. The blow landed and knocked the attacker onto his back. As Zach raised the lamp for a second strike, a fist caught him in the gut, sending waves of nauseous pain coursing up into his neck. Another punch forced Zach to drop the lamp, and he doubled over. His dazed assailant drove a fist into Zach's neck, and he yelped in agony and tried to resist the rush of darkness that threatened to overwhelm him. He could not afford to black out. He staggered back, the unyielding floor driving shards of glass into his feet with every step. Zach's attacker pulled himself out of the wreckage of the coffee table and stood upright as Zach hurried toward his phone. As he reached it, a crushing blow flattened his hand against the table, and he felt his fingers crack under the base of the crystal lamp. As he tried to swallow the pain, an arm snaked around his neck and he was pulled backward into a choke hold.

"Please," Zach tried. "Please, I have money."

His broken fingers flopped ineffectually at his assailant's head, while his other hand pulled at the man's wrist. Dazed, dizzy, and deprived of oxygen, Zach simply didn't have the strength to break his attacker's hold, and each breath became more labored.

"Please," Zach pleaded. "My kids."

"Give me what I need," growled the masked man, "and it will be quick."

Tears filled Zach's eyes as he realized that he would never see his family again.

43

Hazy light filled the room, penetrating the paper-thin drapes covering the window. Wallace rubbed his eyes. He'd become accustomed to his aching body, but the gritty residue of a hangover was something he hadn't felt for a while. He sat up in bed and saw that Ash's was empty, the bedclothes pulled back in an untidy pile. The muted television was tuned to CNN, which was broadcasting the image of a hanged man suspended from the window of a tall black building. The caption read "Chicago Hanging." Wallace rolled out of bed and staggered toward Ash's beside cabinet to grab the remote.

"Christine," Wallace called hoarsely. He coughed to clear his throat as he turned up the volume. "You need to see this."

The bathroom door opened, releasing a wispy cloud of steam, and Ash appeared in the doorway, wrapped in a towel.

". . . with authorities unwilling to confirm that these supposed suicides are now the subject of a federal serial murder investigation. Unofficial reports say that the victim's hotel room showed signs of a struggle and that he was murdered by a man that some commentators have dubbed the Pendulum Killer," the male anchor said. "The man, unofficially identified as Zachary Holz, was a resident of Los Altos, California. The Chicago Police Department is expected to make an official statement within the hour, and we're also expecting to hear from the FBI on rumors that there is a link to a series of murders in Britain."

"Shit," Ash observed sourly, as the anchor moved on to a new horror, and Wallace turned the volume down. "Have they mentioned any connection to the other cases?"

"I don't know," Wallace replied. "I just caught the end of it."

As Ash crossed the room toward her bed, Wallace became conscious of the fact that he was only wearing a pair of shorts. He watched a drop of water draw a glistening line down Ash's calf and hurried away from her bed to grab his clothes. As she started combing her wet hair, he pulled on his jeans and took his iPad out of his jacket pocket. He connected to the motel's Wi-Fi network and ran a Google search for Zachary Holz. The screen filled with news reports of the Chicago hanging, and his screen was assailed by sensational reports of the so-called Pendulum Killer. Wallace refined the search with a LinkedIn reference and immediately found the man's professional profile.

"Chief data architect at Facebook," he informed Ash as he returned to the search page and continued to scroll for information. "He was due to deliver the closing speech at the Chicago International Cyber Security Convention. You think his death is connected?"

"Like I said, I don't believe in coincidences," Ash replied. "You better get ready. We're heading back to the city to find out who fed me to the wolves."

She pulled a pair of delicate panties from the pile of clothes beside her bed and dropped her towel as she pulled them on.

Wallace felt his heart pound at the sight of her toned, naked body and quickly diverted his gaze back to the iPad.

"Sorry," Ash said. "I grew up with men, I work with men, I don't even think about . . . well . . . the differences."

He looked up to see her fastening a matching bra. "Don't worry about it," he remarked awkwardly as he stood up. "I'll just get ready."

He hurried into the bathroom.

Primetime Enterprises, the production company behind *Nightfile*, was located on the top floor of a narrow redbrick building on the north side of Twenty-Third Street, half a block west of Fifth Avenue. Wallace had spent the two-and-a-half-hour drive dozing in the back of the cab, dreaming about Ash, fascinated by the carefree ease with which she had displayed her body. He drifted in and out of consciousness, a heavy roll of his head waking him every now and again as the cab navigated the midmorning traffic.

"John," Ash nudged him as they arrived. "You got any money?"

He woke to find Ash holding a thin sheaf of notes. Stunned by sleep, he nodded and unthreaded his belt, then opened the secret pocket to reveal the money within.

"How much do you need?" he asked, his throat hoarse and dry.

"Two hundred."

He pulled out two hundred-dollar bills and handed them over.

"Thanks." Ash turned to pay the driver.

Wallace climbed out of the cab and pulled his belt around his waist as Ash followed him. "This the place?" he asked. "How do we get in?"

"Why don't you take a moment to come to?" she suggested.

Wallace sucked in the cold air and tried to shake the heavy, sluggish feeling that was pulling at his mind. After a moment, he felt the last tendrils of sleep release their grasp. "Okay," he told Ash. "I'm ready."

"You're an acclaimed photographer," Ash said. "It's a news show run by a woman named Kate Baxter. Tell her you've got some photos to sell."

Wallace nodded and put the lie together as they approached the building. To the left of the Thai restaurant on the ground floor was a frosted-glass door that led to the offices above. Wallace found the intercom for Primetime Enterprises and pressed it.

"Hello?" came a voice.

"Hi. My name is John Wallace. I have an appointment to see Kate Baxter."

There was a pause.

"I don't see anything in Kate's schedule," the voice responded at last.

"My agent set it up. I'm over from London." Wallace feigned frustration. "Don't tell me he fucked it up. I've got some pictures she needs to see."

There was another pause.

"Why don't you come up, Mr. Wallace," the voice suggested in a far more genial tone. "Kate would love to meet you."

Ash was a little frustrated by Wallace's lumbering pace as he climbed the fourth and final flight of stairs. She had to remind herself of the ordeal he'd been through; most people would be curled up in a ball somewhere. He'd cried out in his sleep, both in the motel and during the cab back to Manhattan. His screams were so loud that they'd woken her in the early hours, and, during the journey from Connecticut, they'd caused the cab driver to jerk the vehicle to a halt a couple of times. Ash had assuaged the concerns of the driver, telling the man the truth—that her fellow passenger had recently lost someone close to him.

When they reached the landing at the top of the stairs, Wallace pulled at one of the wooden double doors but found they were locked. He peered through the steel mesh covering a small window and waved at a preppy young woman who sat behind a large reception counter. She returned the gesture before pressing a button to open the door.

"Mr. Wallace?" she asked as he entered the lobby, which was decorated in typical new media style: bare brick, reclaimed wood, and expensive abstract artwork. "I'm Sandrine. Kate—" Sandrine broke off when she recognized Ash. "You're—"

"Angry," Ash interrupted. "Don't bother to tell her I'm here," she added as she stormed through the door to the inner office with Wallace trailing behind her. They hurried through an open-plan space where a dozen young New Yorkers worked at paired desks that stretched back almost the entire length of the building. The office was buzzing with conversations and activity, but apart from a couple of puzzled glances, nobody impeded their progress.

At the end of the open area, Ash saw a petite woman sitting behind a driftwood desk in a glass-walled office. The woman was on the phone and turned to look at Ash and Wallace as they approached. Her expression hardened and Ash knew the call was a warning from the receptionist. Ash didn't break stride as she opened the office door and stormed in.

"Kate Baxter?" she barked.

Kate nodded as she stood. She looked like she was in her late twenties and had long, wildly flowing brown hair, styled like a seventies pop star. Her eyes were rimmed with thick eyeliner that offset her lust-red lipstick. She wore tight black trousers, a black turtleneck, and was barefoot.

"Special Agent Ash," Kate began. She walked round her desk and offered her hand, which remained untouched. "We tried to contact you for comment, but we couldn't reach—"

"You did a real number on me," Ash snapped. "My files were sealed under a court order." She saw her words have the desired effect; Kate's face fell. "Whoever gave you the information didn't tell you that," Ash guessed. "And they probably came to you because they knew this two-bit tabloid operation you run wouldn't bother doing proper checks."

"We—" Kate tried, but Ash cut her off.

"Shut up. You're not here to talk. You're here to listen. I'll make you a deal; give me your source and I won't press charges."

"Our sources are—"

"Cut the bullshit," Ash commanded. "Give me a name, or I'll shut you down."

"I don't have a name," Kate admitted as she leaned over her desk and grabbed her iPad. "Just an e-mail."

She handed the computer to Ash, who studied the e-mail displayed on screen.

Baxter
Attached is information that proves Special Agent Christine Ash
is unfit for duty.

Ash opened the attached file to discover a PDF that contained a collection of court transcripts, police interviews, and social service records: her entire childhood laid bare.

Kate eyed Wallace. "Don't you have some connection to the Pendulum case?" she asked.

"What are you talking about?"

"The Bureau's just confirmed these hangings are part of a serial murder investigation, that the deaths of Bonnie Mann and Zachary Holz are linked to a shooting at a hospital in London. The killer's preferred method is hanging, so some Californian stringer dubbed him Pendulum," Kate informed them. "Weren't you originally a suspect in the London murders?"

"You're a fucking vulture," Ash sneered, fixing Kate with a hostile stare.

She wilted under Ash's gaze. "I e-mailed the address a few times but never got a response," she explained awkwardly.

Ash clicked on the "from" field. The sender's e-mail address was zxcv57960@gmail.com.

"I'm sending this to myself," Ash informed Kate as she forwarded the message to her personal e-mail address. "If you ever get another message from this individual, you use my private e-mail to contact me. My address is in your Sent folder. Any contact and you let me know, do you understand?"

Kate nodded as Ash returned her iPad.

"You owe me," Ash advised, prompting another nod. "Come on," she said to Wallace. "Let's go."

44

The Avenue of the Americas belched a steady stream of traffic north. People crowded the sidewalks, compressed into narrow channels beside towering piles of snow. Wallace had spent the past twenty minutes struggling to keep up with Ash, and his body was wrung out. Aching muscles protested every step, and injuries new and old nagged at him, threatening to bring him down altogether, but he didn't say a word to Ash. If she felt Wallace was slowing the pace, she might hand him off to some other branch of law enforcement and pursue the killer alone. Wallace couldn't risk losing the safety of her protection, so he stayed quiet and pushed himself to keep up.

He was glad when Ash stopped suddenly, welcoming the opportunity to catch his breath. They'd just crossed Forty-Seventh Street and had come to a halt outside a diamond dealership. Wallace's relief turned to dismay when he realized why Ash had frozen: a couple of cops were climbing the steps that led up from the Rockefeller Center subway station. Ash grabbed him and pushed him against the green metal railings that surrounded the subway steps. She pulled him close, buried her head in the crook of his neck, and pressed his face down into her shoulder. Wallace felt warm air rise from inside her long coat and smelled sweet jasmine perfume. Relishing the soft touch of Ash's hair against his cheek, he felt a sudden urge to kiss her smooth neck, but he stayed perfectly still as they played a pair of reconciled lovers huddled for protection against a chill in their relationship. He glanced up and saw the policemen walk past. They were no more than three feet away but never gave Ash and Wallace a look. Wallace held Ash, savoring human contact and an opportunity to catch his breath, as the cops crossed the street and headed south along Sixth Avenue. When they were a safe distance away, he tapped Ash on the shoulder and she stepped back.

"Come on," she said before continuing uptown.

Wallace followed, pounding out a few rapid steps to draw abreast. "Where are we going?" he asked, keen to reestablish the professional foundation of their relationship.

"Every now and again, the Bureau uses specialist external contractors," she replied. "I'm hoping one of them can help us. If he isn't in jail."

Kosinsky Data Services was located on the eighteenth floor of a black skyscraper on West Fiftieth Street. Ash and Wallace were buzzed into the airy lobby by a smiling, fresh-faced man with long, curly brown hair.

"Hello," he greeted them with a broad smile. "I'm Todd. How can I help you?"

"Hey, Todd. We're here to see Pavel Kosinsky," Ash replied. "Tell him it's his pretty little nightmare."

Todd's smile faltered.

"He'll know what it means," Ash reassured him.

Todd picked up the phone. "Why don't you take a seat?"

Ash and Wallace crossed the carpeted floor and stood near a trio of rectangular couches that formed a horseshoe.

"What is this place?" Wallace asked, gesturing at their plush surroundings. "Why did you say he might be in jail?"

"Kosinsky completed his PhD at Cal Tech at the age of twenty-four. He's a pain-in-the-ass genius. He hired a bunch of grad students almost as talented as him and started KDS; it's a digital security agency. Part detection, part protection. They operate in the spaces law enforcement can't go."

"I couldn't have put it better myself," a voice boomed from over Wallace's shoulder. He turned to see a tall, slim man in his early thirties with angular features and a shock of thick black hair. "Except for the pain-in-the-ass part. Hello, my pretty little nightmare."

"Pavel Kosinsky, this is William Porter." Ash introduced them as Pavel offered Wallace his hand.

"Really, Chris?" Pavel said. "Are you really going to try to bullshit me? It's nice to meet you, Mr. Wallace, I've read so much about you."

Wallace saw a flicker of discomfort cross Ash's face.

"What? I prefer the British press," Pavel explained, "so I know he was a murder suspect. Some of us remember the faces we see on the news. What the fuck are you doing here, Chris? Your face is all over the news, too. I saw that program," he continued, his tone becoming serious. "They had no business with your past."

Ash nodded her appreciation. "I need your help, Pavel. I need to unlock an e-mail."

"The Washington case had better not bite me on the ass," Pavel said without looking up. He was hunched over a computer at a desk that stood in the middle of an insulated, windowless room. Wallace and Ash had followed him through the building, past the private offices where two dozen bright young computer scientists worked in quiet seclusion.

"Who can work open plan?" Pavel had observed, as he'd led them through security doors guarded by a man in a uniform who stood alongside a biometric scanner. "Machines make mistakes. People make mistakes. But never at the same time."

Once in the secure area, they had passed a large server room, much like the one where Connie had died. Wallace saw her lying between the machines, and even though he knew it was a painful trick of his vicious memory, he had to look away. He kept his gaze on Ash and Pavel, who led him beyond the server room to the secure terminals, which were isolated in insulated clean rooms.

"Pavel helped me get inside the Hopeland Family's operations," Ash told Wallace. "You've got nothing to worry about," she assured Pavel.

"Do you like puzzles?" Pavel asked, glancing up from the screen.

"The password?" Ash guessed.

"Of course not the password," Pavel sighed. "I cracked that some time ago. No, these puzzles."

He turned the computer to reveal the Sent items folder of the hacked Gmail account. Wallace could see the e-mail to Kate Baxter, but there were eleven other e-mails to seven different addresses. Each of the recipient's addresses was a seemingly random collection of letters and numbers. The preview pane showed that each e-mail contained a twelve-digit number.

"Look at the dates of these e-mails," Ash said. "Each one sent the day before a killing. Look at this one here. It was sent the day before you were attacked," she told Wallace, pointing to one of the e-mails.

"Can you solve the puzzle?" Pavel asked.

"Stop showing off," Ash advised him.

"The numbers are coordinates," Pavel revealed.

"Show me this one," Ash instructed, indicating the e-mail sent the day before Wallace was attacked.

Pavel input the coordinates 51°31'54", 00°10'57" into Google Maps, and Hamilton Terrace appeared on the screen.

"That's my place," Wallace declared.

"Try another one," Ash suggested.

Pavel selected the oldest e-mail in the folder and typed the coordinates 41°25'09", 73°53'38". Indian Brook Road, Garrison, flashed on screen.

"That's where Kye Walters lived," Wallace pointed out.

"This is a list of his victim's addresses," Ash said. "You think they're instructions?"

Pavel ignored her question. "And here's the most recent e-mail, sent yesterday."

He extracted the coordinates 40°45'35", 73°57'37" and put them into Google. The computer displayed a satellite image of the eastern edge of New York City and the red marker was centered on the Manhattan Regent Hotel.

"If this is a pattern, someone is going to be murdered there today," Ash said.

"We can catch this guy," Wallace said.

Ash nodded thoughtfully. "I'm going to need a favor, Kos," she said to Pavel.

"Don't Kos me," he responded, shaking his head and raising his hands fearfully. "Don't drag me into your mess."

"Hector won't listen to me," Ash countered. "But he'll listen to you. I don't care how you say you got the information, but you make sure he puts a team on this."

"Can I tell him you put a gun to my head?" Kos asked with a smile, which fell away when he noted Ash's steely expression. "Just kidding. I'll tell him we have an algorithm that looks for patterns based on locations. You guys will pretty much believe anything if we use the word algorithm."

"Can you monitor this address?" Ash inquired, ignoring the insult.

Kos nodded. "And I'll have one of my guys check out the IP logs and see if we can pinpoint the sender's IP address for each of these e-mails," he added. "We might get lucky and find his location."

"Come on, John," Ash said. "We need to go."

"Where?" Wallace asked.

"I want to be certain they get this guy," Ash said, turning for the door.

45

"This intelligence is less than an hour old," Hector told the agents assembled in the briefing room. There was Alexis Hale, who had command of seven field agents, and Jake Tanna and his five-man tactical unit. Parker stood near two plainclothes cops from the Fifth Precinct. "Pavel Kosinsky has provided us with information that suggests the Pendulum Killer will strike the Manhattan Regency Hotel sometime today. Special Agent Hale and her team will canvas the hotel. There are two hundred and thirty rooms, and we've got to check every single one. Agent Tanna and the tactical unit will set up surveillance on all entrances. We're going to do this quietly. This guy gets a sniff we're onto him and he'll vanish. Agent Parker, you get anything from the hotel?"

"The general manager knows to keep our presence confidential. The hotel is hosting a financial awards ceremony tonight. He offered to cancel it," Parker replied.

Hector shook his head. "We can't risk tipping off the killer by doing anything out of the ordinary. We all know what happened at the safe house. This guy is thorough. Any questions?"

Hector paused and glanced around the room at the diligent agents looking back at him. No one spoke.

"Okay, let's move out," he commanded.

Hale and Tanna led their teams from the room, while Hector collared Parker as he made for the exit.

"Agent Parker, Detectives Moses and Rollins," Hector said, as the two NYPD detectives approached.

"Hey," said Detective Moses, a trim, muscular African American in his late forties.

"Good to meet you." Detective Rollins smiled, the hard lights glinting off the top of his pasty bald head.

"Kosinsky fed me a crock about how he got the intel," Hector told Parker. "This wasn't some random algorithm; it came from Chris. Kate Baxter called earlier, said Chris had threatened her, and that she'd handed over her source's e-mail address. Same address Kosinsky gave us."

"You think she's going to be there?" Parker guessed.

Hector nodded. "She won't risk exposing Wallace to the killer, but I know Chris. She'll have eyes on us to make sure we get the guy. I've given Detectives Moses and Rollins photos of Chris and I want you guys to find her. And when you've found her, you'll find Wallace."

Wallace and Ash arrived at the Manhattan Regent Hotel just after five o'clock, as the sinking sun bathed the city in its last rays of light. The hotel was on East Fifty-Ninth Street, directly opposite the Queens-boro Bridge. The brown-brick building was fifteen stories high and abutted its neighbors. It was the sort of Midtown hotel that attracted midbudget middle executives. A sign in the entrance welcomed guests of the Annual Fund Management Systems Awards. Wallace followed Ash along the sidewalk, straight past the entrance.

"We need somewhere out of sight," Ash noted as she scanned their surroundings.

Wallace couldn't see an obvious vantage point. Fifty-Ninth Street was bumper to bumper with rush-hour traffic. On the other side of the street loomed the Queensboro Bridge, a vast latticework of cream-colored metal. Beneath it were deserted basketball courts encircled by a wire mesh fence. The river lay a couple of blocks east, and to the west was a series of stone-and-glass warehouses that had been constructed beneath the bridge. Between the first warehouse and the basketball court was an alley that was used as an unofficial parking lot.

"Come on," Ash instructed as she stepped off the sidewalk. Wallace followed, and the two of them picked their way through the crawling traffic until they reached the mouth of the alley. Wallace's ears throbbed with the loud rumble of slow-moving traffic reverberating from the bridge overhead. He and Ash hurried along the line of parked cars that snaked along the alley until they reached an old Pontiac. It was covered in dust and looked as though it hadn't been moved in months. Ash glanced around, found a strip of scrap metal among the junk that had collected beneath the bridge, and used it to force her way into the old car. The alarm sounded, but the noise was drowned out by the overhead traffic. Ash leaned into the car, popped the hood, and then bent over the engine until she found what she was looking for. With a decisive pull, she killed the screeching alarm. She climbed into the passenger seat and opened the driver's door for Wallace, who slid in beside her. The car was parked pointing south, and they had a relatively unobstructed view of the hotel, which lay to the southeast.

Behind them, to the north, lay Sixty-First, a narrow street that was clogged with traffic, and beyond its endless stream of vehicles, the other side of the road was lined with skyscrapers.

"We've got three ways out of here," Ash told Wallace. "North, south, or through the basketball court."

Wallace nodded and rubbed his arms in an attempt to keep warm. The car was cold, but the enclosed interior shielded them from the sharpest sting of the freezing air as they watched the hotel. After fifteen minutes, an unmarked white van parked to the east of the hotel entrance. Ash studied the driver, a gray-haired white man with a severe face wearing blue overalls.

"Okay," Ash observed. "They got Tanna. He runs one of the tactical units. Good guy," she told Wallace.

A few minutes later, Ash pointed at a man and woman heading for the hotel entrance. The African-American man wore a gray suit and was about six feet tall. His pale companion had long, dark hair and was only a couple of inches shorter than him. She wore a full-length coat and black boots.

"Alexis Hale and Lance Nelson," Ash remarked. "They're keeping it low-key. Getting the team into the hotel in twos and threes. That's how I would have done it."

Wallace could tell that Ash longed to be at the heart of the action and noticed her stiffen when she spied a dark-haired man walking toward the hotel.

"Hector Solomon," Ash noted. "My boss. Good. They're taking this seriously."

Parker trudged along Fifty-Ninth Street, checking the buildings west of the hotel. He pounded his feet, trying to keep warm, as he scoured the windows of the adjacent skyscrapers. Moses was checking the buildings east of the hotel and Rollins was canvassing the warehouses under the Queensboro Bridge. *If Ash is here*, Parker thought, *we'll find her.*

Hector Solomon sat in the contemporary lobby of the Manhattan Regent and listened to communications via a concealed earpiece. Hale had deployed her team in pairs, each working a different floor. The general manager had provided them with master keys to access any unoccupied rooms. It was going to take some time, but they would work through each floor to check the well-being and identity of every single guest.

The lobby was starting to fill up with people attending the fund management event. Tuxedo-clad men gathered under the sparkling chandeliers with women in expensive evening dresses as waiters circulated with trays of drinks and canapés. Hector had asked the general manager to instruct hotel security to search people entering the hotel and was pleased to see a line of guests waiting to have their bags checked by a team of three uniformed guards.

Ryan Silver stood on the corner of Fifty-Ninth Street and First Avenue and studied his friends' faces. Cassie, her face hard and unforgiving, looked ready to take on the world, as usual. Nate wasn't wearing enough clothes and his scrawny body was shivering as the ferocious wind whipped through the city. Lonnie was nervous but was too stubborn to admit it; as the biggest guy in the group, he had a reputation to protect. Only Wade, the wiry little weasel, was wearing his fear on his sleeve.

"I don't know, man," Wade whined. "We've never done anything like this before."

"Shut the fuck up, Wade," Lonnie admonished the little man, his long coat whipping in the wind. "Bail if you ain't got the balls for it."

"You're always bitchin', Wade," Cassie added sourly.

Ryan checked his watch. It was past seven and Ramon was late. Ryan fingered the contents of his coat pocket nervously, aware that they were supposed to hit the place at seven. He scanned the street in frustration.

"There's gonna be people," Wade complained. "Witnesses."

"The guy said he was a recruiter for the Foundation, Wade," Ryan barked. "They don't fuck around."

"This is war, man," Lonnie added. "We gonna do this or what?" he asked Ryan.

Ryan checked the street one last time. *Sorry, Ramon*, he thought as he started walking along Fifty-Ninth Street.

"Let's go, people," Lonnie told the group, and they all followed in Ryan's wake.

Ryan looked over his shoulder and saw his friends casting nervous looks at one another. They might be scared, but they believed in their cause, and that belief made them unstoppable.

Parker had been out on the street for an hour. He'd checked hundreds of windows for any sign of Ash but had found nothing. He'd seen Rollins popping in and out of the warehouses and envied the man the respite of their warm interiors. Parker had one more building to check; the skyscraper directly adjacent to the hotel. He looked across the street and saw Rollins heading into the last warehouse. It was then that Parker noticed the line of cars parked in the alley that ran beneath the Queensboro Bridge.

"Do you think he saw us?" Wallace asked, crouching beneath the dash.

Ash had dropped into the passenger footwell and responded with an anxious look.

"Hey, Rollins," Parker said into his concealed microphone.

"Copy," Rollins's voice filled Parker's ear.

"You want to check the cars in the alley?" Parker suggested. "I think I saw movement."

He saw Rollins shrug. "Sure," Rollins said, turning away from the warehouse and starting toward the mouth of the alley.

Parker tried to cross the sidewalk but almost collided with a group of kids who were covered in tattoos and piercings.

"Sorry," Parker offered, but he was met with cold, hostile looks. The guy at the front of the pack wore a one-percenter T-shirt beneath his denim jacket. Parker waited for the group of angry young anarchists to pass before continuing toward the street.

Fucking asshole, Ryan thought, as the guy in the suit passed behind them. He'd been eyeballing Ryan's T-shirt: *Fuck the one-percenters and their army of wage slaves.*

"Okay," Ryan told his friends. "It's time."

As he approached the hotel entrance, Ryan reached into his pocket and pulled out the mask.

NYPD would've shut the block down, Rollins thought to himself as he shone his flashlight through the windows of the first car in the alley. *Feds think they're all that, but the NYPD are the ones who always get the job done. Come in force, bring the pain, catch the bad guys, and go home again. Life can be that simple if you let it,* Rollins mused as he moved on to the second car, which was empty. *Fucking waste of time,* he thought as he continued along the alley.

"We've got to get out of here," Ash whispered. "I think he's a cop."

Wallace peered over the dash and saw the bright light of the flashlight held in the short bald man's hand. The guy was checking the cars up ahead of them and was no more than eight vehicles away.

Parker looked right to check for oncoming traffic and was about to cross the street when he caught a glimpse of a black mask that matched the description given by Wallace and Bruce Morton, the homeless man who'd witnessed Ken Pallo's murder. Parker didn't see it for longer than a split second, but he was sure the mask was on the face of the guy wearing the one-percenter T-shirt.

"Hey," Parker yelled, but his voice was lost beneath the sound of passing traffic.

The group of kids started running toward the hotel entrance.

"Command, I've got eyes on the suspect," Parker spoke into his radio as he broke into a sprint. "He's coming into the hotel hard and fast."

Rollins turned to face the hotel and saw a group of people stream up the steps toward the hotel doors.

"I see them. I count five heading for the main entrance," Rollins yelled into his radio as he started running.

Wallace felt his body sag with relief as he saw the fat man with the flashlight running away from them.

"We got lucky," he said to Ash, who shook her head in disbelief.

Wallace was startled a moment later when a hooded figure collided with the car as he ran past, sprinting down the alleyway at full pelt. The man must have been a full twenty yards away when he glanced back. Wallace froze when he saw the mask of his killer.

Ash was moving the moment she saw it. "Wait here," she instructed Wallace as she jumped out of the car. She drew her pistol and raced to catch the hooded figure.

Hector Solomon was on his feet, moving across the lobby, gun in hand.

"Get these people out of here!" he yelled at the security team. The lobby erupted in pandemonium as dozens of guests saw Hector's pistol and started to scatter, screaming.

Hot breath had misted the goggles that covered Ryan's eyes and he couldn't see properly. He hadn't fitted the mask correctly but had no time to fix it. They'd come here to do a job and their work had already begun. They weren't even through the glass doors, but Ryan could already see people fleeing in terror. The one-percenters and their slaves were weak, and soon they would be cowed by brave men and women who were determined to end injustice.

He put his hand to the brass doorplate and pushed.

With people scattering all around him, Hector struggled to get a clear line of sight. Panicked faces flashed past the end of his pistol. Beyond them, Hector saw the main door swing open.

"Freeze!" Parker yelled, his pistol leveled at the big guy at the back of the group. All around him pedestrians ran for cover, and the big guy in the long black coat turned to face Parker. He was wearing the black mask of the killer.

When Ryan stepped into the lobby, he realized he'd made a terrible mistake. The last of the guests had fled, leaving him to face a hard-eyed Latino guy who had a pistol leveled in his direction.

"Put your hands up," the guy yelled.

"I said put your hands up!" Hector repeated. The guy in the mask was frozen to the spot. Behind him Hector could see four or five other people all wearing replicas of the Pendulum Killer's mask.

"I've got you covered," Rollins told Parker as he reached the hotel steps. He had his pistol trained on the big guy in the long coat.

Parker nodded and produced a pair of cuffs as he approached the masked group. Rollins looked up the street and saw the Bureau's tactical unit racing toward them.

Fucking subway, Ramon thought as he sprinted along the alleyway. He reached the intersection with Fifty-Ninth Street and stopped dead. The sight of his friends robbed him of any desire to join them. They were surrounded by men in black body armor, the letters FBI emblazoned on their backs. The FBI agents were mustering Ryan and the others at gunpoint, and Ramon knew he needed to get away. As he reached up to remove the mask Ryan had given him, Ramon was knocked senseless.

Ash looked down at the fallen figure and wondered whether she'd hit him too hard. There was blood on the butt of her pistol, and when she knelt down and pulled his hood back, she could see more of it glistening in his hair. She glanced at the hotel and saw Tanna and his tactical team taking a group of people into custody. As she looked closer, she noticed that they were all wearing the same masks. With a growing sense of dismay, Ash pulled the mask off the man at her feet. A young Latino kid's face stared back at her, his dazed eyes full of fear.

"Please," he said weakly. "Please don't kill me."

"What are you doing here?" Ash demanded.

"It's a protest. We were just going to throw paint," the kid whimpered.

Ash trained her gun on him as he reached into his pocket and produced a handful of water balloons. One of them fell to the ground and burst in a splash of red.

"Shit!" Ash sensed movement but did not turn quickly enough, as a heavy, strong arm knocked the pistol from her hand.

She looked up to see the Pendulum Killer looming over her. She tried to stand but was smacked down by his heavy fist. She heard the dull thud of suppressed gunfire emanate from Pendulum's pistol, and saw the Latino kid's body shudder with the jarring impact of the shots. Ash scrabbled on the ground and looked desperately toward the hotel, where her colleagues were preoccupied with a group of masked kids. She turned and glanced along the alley, where she saw Wallace slumped over the Pontiac's steering wheel, a trickle of blood running down his temple. Ash tried to stand, but a heavy boot kicked her flat against the icy ground. She started to scream but was silenced by a rag, and as an acrid chemical flooded her nose and mouth, her body wilted. Reality grew distant, and her heavy head rolled toward unconsciousness. The last thing Ash remembered was the sensation of being dragged into darkness.

46

A wave of nausea washed over Ash as she came to. She vomited, and then, when her stomach had finished its somersaults, she forced herself to her knees. The first thing she noticed was the blistering wind. They were high up, and the immediate horizon was unbroken, which meant they were on the roof of the tallest building in the area. She could see the Empire State Building and the Chrysler Building to the southwest, and judging by the distance, they were still near Fifty-Ninth Street. She looked behind her and saw Pendulum standing several feet away, holding a pistol with a silencer pointed in her direction. He wore heavy black boots, black leather trousers, and black body armor over his torso. A black mask covered his face, and round, opaque black goggles capped his eyes. A full-length black leather coat fluttered in the wind, its purple satin lining catching the moonlight.

"Wake him up," Pendulum instructed, gesturing at a figure slumped a few feet away from her.

As she crawled across the concrete slabs lining the roof, Ash desperately tried to place the man's accent, but there was nothing distinctive about it. He sounded well-spoken but could have been equally at home in London or New York. She was relieved to see Wallace's face and immediately put her fingers to his neck to check for a pulse. Satisfied he was still alive, she gently patted his face. Wallace's eyes opened suddenly, and his first reaction to the world was exactly the same as Ash's; he rolled over and heaved.

"You knew we were coming," Ash said to the killer. "The e-mail account was bait. You knew how I'd react when you exposed my past."

Pendulum was ominously silent.

"Why are you doing this?" Wallace asked angrily.

The killer was impassive.

"Tell me why!" Wallace yelled. "Why did they have to die? Why did Connie have to die?"

"There is a cell phone on that vent," Pendulum said, indicating a metallic structure that protruded from the roof.

An enraged Wallace started to rise, but Pendulum gestured with his gun. "Stay down," he commanded, and Wallace reluctantly complied.

"I want you to make a call," Pendulum said to Ash. "Slowly," he added, as Ash got to her feet.

As she walked toward the vent, Ash looked over the edge of the roof and saw the unmistakable cream steelwork of the Queensboro Bridge. To her left was the East River, and beyond it, the spotlit red-and-white chimneys of the Ravenswood Power Station belched high clouds of dark steam into the clear night sky. They were on the north side of Sixty-First Street, directly opposite the Manhattan Regent Hotel. Ash didn't know the name of the building, but she surmised that they were on the roof of the new smoked-glass tower that overlooked Sycamores Park. A dangerous idea began to form in her mind.

"Who am I calling?" she asked.

"Hector Solomon."

"I won't do it," Ash protested.

"Then he dies now," Pendulum remarked, wheeling the pistol toward Wallace's head.

"Why?"

"Call it a test," Pendulum replied. "Don't think you're in a position to negotiate," he warned her. "There are many ways for me to achieve my objective. This is simply the easiest."

Ash picked up the phone. "I don't have his number."

"Just redial," Pendulum instructed. He held something to the side of his head, and Ash realized it was a Bluetooth earpiece; he was listening to the call.

Ash pressed Redial. She looked at the phone and, if the clock was to be trusted, saw that it was 01:06. After a few rings, she heard Hector's voice.

"Hello?" he said.

"Hector, it's me," Ash replied.

"Are you kidding? Do you have any idea what happened tonight? Someone shot a kid called Ramon Meza. You know anything about that?"

"What did the others say?" Ash asked quickly.

"So you were there," Hector observed. "They crumbled pretty damned quickly. Said some guy paid them. Told them he was a recruiter for the Foundation."

"Check he's in his office," Pendulum whispered, his voice tinged with irritation.

"Where are you?" Ash complied.

"Where am I? Where do you think I am? In the office going through a pile of paperwork," Hector replied. "I'm going to be here until Judgment Day."

"Tell him you know who killed Ramon Meza," Pendulum commanded.

"I know who killed Ramon Meza," Ash relayed.

Hector waited.

"John Wallace," Pendulum told Ash.

Ash shook her head, unwilling to pass on the lie. Pendulum drew closer to Wallace and prodded his head with the pistol.

"John Wallace," Ash relented.

"What?" Hector asked incredulously.

"Tell him Wallace was behind the Pendulum killings," the killer commanded. "He was working with a man named Leo Willard. Wallace was the brains, Leo was the muscle."

"Wallace is Pendulum," Ash complied, her voice wavering as she watched the dismay spread across Wallace's face. "He's been working with a man named Leo Willard. Leo was the muscle, Wallace was the brains."

"I don't have time for this, Chris." Hector sighed in disbelief.

"Tell him Wallace has sent him proof, and a confession," Pendulum said calmly.

"Wallace has sent you proof," Ash told Hector. She watched as the masked killer produced a small tablet PC from his coat pocket and swiped his fingers across the screen.

"It's here," Hector informed Ash, who heard the faint click of a mouse. "What the fuck!" Hector exclaimed suddenly. "What the fuck have you done?"

A split second later, the line went dead.

"What did I just do?" Ash asked the man in the mask.

"Did you get cut off?" Pendulum countered.

Ash nodded.

"Then the e-mail just uploaded a virus onto the New York Field Office servers," the masked man explained. "It's a particularly destructive one designed to take out every computer, server, and device on a network. It also attacks any backup nodes and ancillary systems such as power and telephones. You just sent the New York office back to the Stone Age."

"Why?"

"It will take months to repair the damage," Pendulum replied. "By then . . ." he trailed off, stopping himself from revealing any more. He reached behind an air duct and produced a black bag. As he riffled inside it, Ash saw the thick coil of a noosed rope. She looked at Wallace and saw that he'd also registered it. Pendulum continued gathering items for a few moments before tossing a bundle of stuff toward Wallace. "Help him get changed," he told Ash.

She looked at the bundle and realized that it wasn't just clothes, but body armor and a mask; an exact replica of Pendulum's outfit.

Wallace picked up the face mask and stared at it as he got to his feet, before tossing it back to the killer. "No," he said flatly.

"Then you can dress him after he's dead," Pendulum responded, raising his pistol.

"He'll do it," Ash interjected urgently. "You'll do it, won't you?" she asked Wallace, who was impassive as she approached. She moved slowly, fearful of triggering a violent reaction in their captor. "This isn't going to work," Ash observed. "John was in custody when you killed Ken Pallo and he was with me when Bonnie Mann was murdered."

"That's why you just told Solomon that he wasn't working alone," Pendulum replied.

"Who's Leo Willard?" Ash asked.

"Nobody important. A Vegas thug. He's dead now," the masked man continued. "But tomorrow the Bureau will be fed evidence implicating Leo and John in the murders. A sick scheme, twisted out of control."

"I guess after killing me, John is overcome by guilt and hangs himself?" Ash remarked.

"It isn't perfect," Pendulum noted. "But it doesn't need to be. It just needs to hold long enough to buy me more time. Sow enough confusion to get them to stop looking for a few days. Now, quit stalling, Agent Ash. Help him change."

Ash picked up the heavy leather coat and turned to Wallace. "When I say run, you've just got to trust me," she whispered.

Wallace replied with an imperceptible nod, fear writ large on his face. She glanced over the southwest corner of the roof and saw what she'd been waiting for. Her timing needed to be perfect.

"Go!" Ash exclaimed, pushing Wallace with all the force she could muster. She hurled the leather coat behind her and started running. Gunfire struck the ground behind her as she grabbed Wallace and bundled him toward the edge of the roof.

"We've gotta jump," she exclaimed. Ash looked behind her and saw Pendulum running to catch them, his pistol spitting fire with every step. "Trust me," she told Wallace, who looked at her as though she was insane.

She forced Wallace forward as bullets sliced the air around them. The resonant thump of suppressed gunfire assaulted her ears, pounding them with the urgent need to move. Ash felt every cell in her body recoil at what she was about to do, but she knew that if they stayed on that roof, they were both dead. Her head went light and her gut wrenched violently as she neared the balustrade and saw the street far below. She diverted her eyes toward the target, a red Roosevelt Island Aerial Tramway car, which was some eight yards south of the building, ten stories down. The drop would enable them to make the distance, Ash told herself as she pushed Wallace and then followed him over the edge.

Ash floated for a moment. The interior of the tram car was lit up with a brightness that drew her focus like the piercing beam of a lighthouse. The world around it shrank into insignificance as Ash went flying out from the building, soaring majestically before gravity kicked in and violently yanked her down. The world rushed past, but Ash kept her eyes focused on the illuminated cable car, which grew larger with every passing second. Her mind screamed the word *death*, but Ash forced the dark thought back. Ahead of her, Wallace struck one of the A-frame struts and bounced through the gap, across the tram car roof, slamming to a halt against the frame on the other side. The cable car shook violently and Ash hit a moment later, but her trajectory wasn't as kind and she struck the A-frame with her left shoulder and bounced away from it.

The impact had slowed her fall, but Ash realized with growing horror that she was sliding down the side of the cable car. She whipped her hands out, her fingers clawing at the cold glass that separated her from the horrified passengers who watched her slide toward her death. With a final, desperate effort, Ash grabbed at the thin metal foot rail that lined the base of the cable car. She felt her right shoulder scream in pain as her arm wrenched in its socket, but she directed the full force of her will toward her fingers, commanding them to hold. Her legs flailed wildly, but she was no longer falling, and she brought her left hand up to hook her remaining fingers around the foot rail.

Ash looked toward the sky and saw the terrible figure of the killer leaning over the edge of the roof. She could sense his hatred as he stared down at them, and she saw him load his pistol and take aim. She held her breath when he fired, but the distance was too great for a sidearm and the bullets flew wide and struck a Mercedes on the bridge below. Ash watched as the driver swerved and crashed into the central barrier. The dazed man emerged from his vehicle and stared up at the heavens. When he caught sight of Ash hanging precariously from the tram car, he hurriedly produced his phone. Ash returned her gaze to the roof and saw Pendulum lower his weapon and step away from the edge. They both knew it would not be long before the authorities arrived, and neither of them wanted to get caught. Ash could hear the tram car's shocked passengers trying to open the doors.

"Hold on!" one of the occupants yelled.

The doors wouldn't give, but, to her intense relief, Ash felt the tram car rock to a gentle halt. Moments later it started going backward, descending toward Manhattan and the station on Second Avenue.

47

Dazed and disorientated, Wallace heard his name being called over and over again. He lifted his fingers to his temple and felt a tender lump rising on the side of his head. The pain jolted him to his senses and he looked around urgently, realizing that he was lying on the roof of a cable car, suspended high above the city. Ash had saved him but she was nowhere to be seen, and Wallace was grief-stricken as he looked toward the night sky. He dared not look down; he did not want to see the remains of another savior lost to the murderous killer.

"John!"

Wallace tuned into the voice that had cut through his dazed stupor and realized that it belonged to Ash. He pulled himself to the edge of the roof and looked down to see the battered FBI agent hanging by her stubborn fingertips.

"I'm developing a real fear of heights," Wallace said faintly.

"We gotta get off this thing," Ash told him.

Wallace looked east and, beyond an off-ramp that cut beneath their path, he saw Roosevelt Station, a well-lit, four-story metal-and-concrete building that housed the red anchor girders and flywheels that kept the cable cars aloft. As he was watching, a blue-and-white police car pulled to a halt outside the building.

"Can you jump?" Ash yelled up at him.

Wallace nodded. "I think so."

"The ramp," she instructed.

Wallace looked at the approaching elevated section of road, which was connected to the bridge, and tried to guess the drop. The adjacent building suggested it was two, maybe three stories. Fifteen to twenty-five feet. Late-night traffic raced along the ramp at terrifying speeds. Wallace grabbed hold of the left A-frame strut and lowered his legs over the side of the cable car, looking along the bridge for an approaching gap in the oncoming traffic, which was starting to build up behind the crashed Mercedes.

"I'll go first," Ash shouted.

He followed Ash's gaze toward the station and saw two police officers peel away from the assembled crowd and start running toward them. He looked down and saw that the tram car had just crossed the concrete barrier that marked the edge of the off-ramp. Ash dropped but mistimed her fall and landed directly in front of an SUV that was gathering speed. The driver must have been startled but reacted quickly, and the brakes screeched as the tires trailed black rubber along the road before the SUV came to a jarring halt inches from Ash's face.

"Go!" she yelled.

Wallace surrendered himself to fate and released his grip. He struck the roof of the SUV, bent his knees, and rolled down the windshield onto the hood, where he came face to face with the shocked middle-aged woman who was driving. He felt a hand tug at his jacket.

"Come on," Ash said urgently. She pulled Wallace onto the road and led him along the dividing white lines that split the ramp into two wide lanes. As he stumbled on, Wallace noticed that Ash was hunched over, her right shoulder bent inward, forcing her into an awkward gait.

Horns blared and engines roared all around them, but more worrying than any of the immediate cacophony was the sound of approaching sirens. They struggled on for about a hundred and twenty yards before they reached the intersection with Sixty-Second Street. As the ramp leveled out and joined the island's surface, Wallace's heart plummeted as he saw the two uniformed policemen who'd been outside Roosevelt Station. A young African-American officer and an older Latino were running level

with Wallace and Ash on the other side of the northernmost concrete barrier.

"Stop!" yelled the African-American officer.

"Hold it!" the other cop cried. "Or we'll shoot."

Wallace looked at Ash and saw her eyes darting around for a solution as both cops vaulted the barrier and raced toward them.

"This way," Ash yelled, and she sprinted toward a white van with
black windows that was in the eastbound lane, two cars back from
the Sixty-Second Street intersection. Ash ran up to the driver's door
and yanked it open. "Federal agent!" she screamed at the top of her
voice. "Get out of the vehicle!"

The driver was a large tattooed white man with a shaven head.
After recovering from his momentary shock, he reached beside him
and drew a black pistol, which he swung toward Ash.

"Gun!" she exclaimed, as she ducked the shot.

Wallace saw the two police officers stop in their tracks and draw
their pistols.

"Shots fired! Shots fired!" the African-American cop called into
his radio.

Ash drove her left fist into the driver's nose, and as his head
lurched back, she punched his larynx. As he doubled over in pain, she
grabbed his pistol and slammed it into the top of his head, knocking
him cold. She leaned into the van, popped the safety belt, and rolled
the huge guy onto the asphalt.

"Get in!" she told Wallace.

He slid into the passenger seat while Ash jumped in and slammed
the door shut. She flipped the central door-lock switch just as the
African-American cop reached the passenger door and tried to pull it
open. Ash slipped the van into drive and gunned the accelerator, but as
the vehicle lurched forward, the African-American officer stepped back
and opened fire. His shots shattered the passenger window, whipped
past Wallace and Ash, and smashed the driver's window. The van
sped forward, colliding with the car in front. Ash stepped on the gas,
and the weight of the van forced the sedan into the intersection, where
it was sideswiped by a truck. The car spun clear and, as the police

officer leaned in and grabbed ineffectually at Wallace, Ash steered the van across the intersection. Wallace resisted the cop's attempts to grab him and punched the man in the face. He fell away, and when Wallace looked in the side mirror, he saw the cop roll to a halt at the top of the intersection. The dazed officer got to his feet and spoke into his radio as Ash sped away.

Wallace could hear sirens through the shattered window but couldn't see any flashing lights. Ash turned west on Sixty-Third Street and shot past other vehicles as she devoured the three blocks to Lexington Avenue. As they approached the intersection, Wallace saw an NYPD car speeding south.

"Buckle up," Ash instructed, and Wallace fumbled for his safety belt. The clasp clicked into place, and Wallace looked up to see the driver of the police car change lanes as he recognized their vehicle. Ash accelerated, aimed straight for the car, and drove the van into the police car, broadsiding it. Wallace was hurled forward by the force of the impact, but the air bags deployed and the safety belt caught, jerking him back onto his seat. He watched in horror as the cop car was driven across Lexington Avenue. Grinding steel shrieked, showering everything with furious sparks as the van pushed the car sideways over the slick street. The mass of metal came to a crashing halt when the police car hit an SUV parked on the far corner. The police officers inside the car were dazed and disorientated, their siren adding to their general confusion as it blared through the shattered windows.

"Come on," Ash urged Wallace.

He opened the passenger door and stepped into the road. Ash followed him and hurried toward the other side of Sixty-Third Street. She and Wallace stumbled toward the tiled stairs that led down to the subway station. As they descended the steps, sirens wailed, drawing ever closer. Wallace tried to rein in the pounding adrenaline, but his heart raced even faster when he saw a couple of transit cops round the corner at the bottom of the staircase. Drawn by the riotous commotion on the surface, the officers ran straight past Wallace and Ash. Wallace looked at the FBI agent, his eyes bright with relief.

"It's not over yet," she cautioned, continuing down the steps.

Wallace clung to the vain hope that Ash was wrong but found himself nodding slowly as he followed her into the station.

The F train spat them out at Second Avenue Station and they shuffled onto the street, where they moved slowly and silently along the icy sidewalk. Ash looked at Wallace and saw an exhausted, battered man. His skin and clothes were filthy, and Ash guessed that she didn't look much better. She certainly felt terrible and wondered about the nature of the injury that was causing her shoulder so much pain. She didn't think it was dislocated and guessed she might have some deep tissue bruising and torn ligaments. They staggered down the Bowery like a pair of degenerate drunks until they came to the Fresh City Hotel. Ash noticed the all-night pharmacy on the ground floor.

"You go up to the room," she told Wallace. "I'll get some supplies."

Wallace was too exhausted to argue and simply nodded as he stumbled into the hotel.

Ash entered the warm pharmacy and immediately felt her body sag with fatigue. The soporific heat of the well-stocked store made her eyes feel heavy and her bones leaden. She longed for the discomfort of the narrow bed in the tiny, dirty room above, but forced herself to load a large shopping basket with supplies: dressings, antiseptic, painkillers, and anything else that might help the walking wounded. She took her haul to the emo girl at the checkout. Working nights in the Bowery, the girl had probably dealt with more than her fair share of addicts and drunks and didn't even give Ash's disheveled appearance a second glance. Ash paid her and lifted the large, heavy bag of supplies with her good arm.

The night receptionist was an acne-ridden teenager who was busy watching something on a tablet and barely registered Ash when she entered the Fresh City Hotel. Ash hurried past as quickly as her aching legs could manage. The stairs were exhausting and she felt like she aged a year with each step. When she eventually emerged from the stairwell, she staggered along the corridor, leaning against the walls for support, before she finally made it to their room. She knocked on the door but found that it gave at her touch. Adrenaline suddenly pumping, Ash dropped the bag and drew the pistol she'd taken from the skinhead. She ignored the screaming pain coming from her shoulder and entered the room with her gun held in front of her. Despite her exhaustion, her senses were alert, and she could feel her heart pounding thunderously. What if the killer had followed them?

Ash took a couple of steps forward and peered around the corner to find Wallace lying facedown on one of the beds. "John?" she whispered.

Wallace responded with a gentle snore.

Ash smiled and shook her head as she lowered her pistol. She returned to the corridor and picked up the bag of supplies, which she dragged inside. She closed and locked the door and then pushed an old chair in front of it. She thought about cleaning herself up, maybe taking some painkillers, perhaps dressing her wounds, but for all her rational desires, a primal need overtook her; she had to sleep. She staggered over to the second bed, fell onto it, and was asleep a second after her head hit the pillow.

48

Wallace was falling through darkness. High above him someone screamed, and he turned to see Connie standing at the edge of a roof, looking down at her bloody torso in dismay. Wallace fell farther, until Connie's eyes were no more than pinpricks in the darkness. Bitterly cold air rushed past him and he heard the sound of his own scream moments before he hit the ground.

"Hey," Ash said gently. "Are you okay?"

Wallace opened his eyes and was surprised to find himself in the ghastly hotel room. He had no recollection of their return journey. He looked across the room to see Ash sitting in a chair by the door. She'd tied her wet hair in a loose ponytail and was wearing a clean pair of jeans and a garnet-colored pullover and was concentrating on Wallace's iPad.

"I've felt better," Wallace croaked. He cleared his throat. "Thanks," he continued. "Thanks for saving my life."

Ash smiled. "I bought some medical supplies. Painkillers. Bandages. They're in the bathroom when you're ready."

Wallace nodded his appreciation. "What time is it?"

"Three."

"In the afternoon?" Wallace asked incredulously.

"I've been up for an hour," Ash told him. "I figured I'd let you sleep."

"You okay?"

Ash shrugged ruefully. "Few cuts and bruises and some fatally wounded pride. I can't believe I let us get trapped."

"You followed the evidence," Wallace protested.

"I was careless. I let myself believe a lie," Ash countered. "Leaking my story, telling the world about my childhood had exactly the effect he wanted. It made me so angry I couldn't think straight. I thought I was being so smart tracking down that e-mail address, asking Pavel to hack into it. All the time, I was playing right into his hands. I should've known it would never be that easy. Pendulum isn't some psycho; he's smart, and he's got a plan."

Wallace hauled himself off the bed and shuffled over to the bathroom, where he found a large plastic bag loaded with medical supplies. He rooted around inside until he located a bottle of Advil and then scanned the room for a glass.

"You gotta take it straight from the faucet," Ash advised.

Wallace smiled and shook his head. His body protested as he leaned over the dirty sink and pushed his lips close to the cold water tap. He popped a couple of pills into his mouth and washed them down with a swig of worryingly warm water.

"I'm going to take a shower," he told Ash, but she was lost in her own world, distracted by whatever she'd found on the iPad.

The showerhead was clogged with years of green limescale that reduced the flow to a pathetic trickle, but Wallace couldn't have cared less as the gentle stream of warm water soothed his skin. It was a simple, pure sensation that reminded him how lucky he was to be alive, and he stood under the shower, his palms flat against the white tiles, his head bowed as though in prayer. A bloom of relief spread out from Wallace's core and rolled over his body as the Advil started to work. Freed from the relentless clutch of pain, Wallace's mind turned to his situation, which seemed dire. Pendulum had failed in his latest attempt, but no matter what he did, Wallace could not discern why this man wanted him dead. Ash was right; he did not seem deranged. Whatever his twisted logic, the man seemed extremely intelligent, and the fact that he kept coming back for Wallace suggested that his motivation was personal.

He stepped out of the shower and dried himself, frustrated that he was still no closer to understanding why he'd been targeted. He pulled on his last clean pair of black jeans and exited the bathroom to find Ash still using his iPad. She looked even more frustrated than him, and an air of defeat hung about her. Wallace had seen it before, at the hotel in Connecticut, when she'd been about to give up entirely and reveal their location to her boss.

"You okay?" he asked.

"I'm pissed," Ash replied. "At myself," she added by way of explanation. "The guy is smart enough to have stayed off the radar, and if it hadn't been for you we wouldn't have even known he existed. We can lay all these bodies at his door, but we have no idea what links them." She looked around the room awkwardly. "I wasn't sure how to tell you this, but he made good on his word," she said at last, turning the iPad toward him.

Wallace was dismayed to see his own face looking back, with Ash's photograph next to it, at the top of an article that revealed that the two of them were wanted in connection with the murder of Ramon Meza. They were also suspects in a cyber attack that had disabled the FBI's New York Field Office.

"According to a *Nightfile* report, you're now an official suspect in the Pendulum killings, and I'm wanted as a possible accessory," Ash explained.

Wallace slumped against the wall. He could empathize with Ash's defeatism. "Maybe we should turn ourselves in," he suggested morosely.

Ash shook her head. "We do that now, when we have nothing, and it's over. He will find you and he will kill you. And me, well, with this and the blowback from the *Nightfile* report, I'll probably be facing criminal charges. If you're an official suspect, that means the Bureau have swallowed whatever bullshit they've been fed and are a million miles from catching this guy. That means we've got to find a way to get to him."

She fell quiet as her eyes drifted into the distance and her jaw muscles clenched. Wallace could feel her frustration as she tussled with the problem, and the two of them were silent for several minutes.

"The trail led you to Erin Byrne. As far as we know, she was the first victim, before Kye, before Huvane, before you, before any of the others. The killer started with her," Ash said eventually. "We need to go back. See what we've missed, see what the family missed. There has to be something that links her to another victim, or directly to the killer. We need to find that link."

"You want to try Steven Byrne?" Wallace asked.

"No," Ash replied. "Not yet. The killer is resourceful and smart, and he knows more about computers than Pavel."

"So he's a suspect? You think Steven Byrne killed his own daughter?"

"I was going down that road. He's a computer genius and ex-military, so he fits the profile. But then I saw this." Ash swiped the iPad to reveal a gossip column article that detailed the comings and goings of a Republican Party fund-raiser the previous night. One of the featured guests was Steven Byrne, and his humorless face could be found in numerous photographs of the event. "I figure at least two hundred people would be able to give him an alibi for last night, and he was at public events during at least two of the other murders. No, it's not Byrne, but it might be someone from his world. An employee or maybe a rival."

"Why would someone with a grudge against Byrne start murdering people like me?" Wallace challenged.

"I don't know," Ash admitted. "None of this makes any sense. But I've worked serial killers before, and however twisted they might be, they always have a rationale. We just can't see it yet. One thing occurs to me: if Pendulum is from Byrne's world, the mother is more likely to give him up to us. From what I've read, there's no love lost between Mr. and Mrs. Byrne. I'm guessing she blamed him for Erin's death, and we can use that animosity to pump her for all the information she's got. Some piece of evidence she probably doesn't even know she has."

Wallace hesitated. As grim as it was, the hotel room was a safe haven, and the world beyond offered nothing but danger, pain, and death.

"We can't just sit here," Ash cautioned, as though reading his thoughts. "If the mother doesn't give us anything, we'll try Byrne senior. Something links their daughter, either to another victim or directly to the killer."

"Okay," Wallace said with a decisive nod. "I'm in."

49

It was shortly after four when they arrived at the tower that housed Canopy. Ash flashed her identification at the security guard to gain access to the elevators, and she and Wallace rode up to the thirty-second floor. The receptionist recognized them the moment they entered the Canopy lobby.

"Make that call, and I'll arrest you for obstruction," Ash called out to the receptionist, who had started to lift a phone to her ear.

The frightened woman replaced the receiver.

"Whatever you think you know, we're not here to hurt anyone," Ash reassured her. "We just want to talk."

Wallace led the way through the doorway to the inner corridor, and the workers in the large office didn't even notice as they passed. He pushed open the door to Marcie's office and he and Ash stepped inside. It was empty. They crossed the small space and opened the door to Philicia's office to discover her in conference with Marcie, seated on the couch on the other side of the room.

"Can I help you?" Marcie asked, standing, as Philicia reached for her phone.

"I told you what would happen if you ever came back here," Philicia told Wallace.

"Put it down," Ash commanded, hurrying across the room to take the phone. "I'm Special Agent—"

"I know who you are." Philicia cut her off. "I watch the news. They say he's the Pendulum Killer, that he had something to do with my daughter's death," she added, fixing Wallace with a cold stare. "What kind of game are you playing, you sick son of a bitch?"

"I didn't have anything to do with Erin's death, I swear," Wallace protested. "I hadn't even been to America before last month. Please, I came to you for help, Mrs. Byrne. Why would I do that? There has to be a link between your daughter and another victim. Either that or there's something that links Erin directly to the killer."

"A man like this doesn't select victims at random. There's got to be a connection," Ash put in. "Help us find it and you'll help catch your daughter's killer."

"Do you have any idea what it's like to lose someone you love to suicide?" Philicia said as she stood. "To know that life caused them unbearable pain? And to be totally unaware of their suffering?" She walked slowly toward the window, her head bowed. "And now you're asking me to accept that she might have been murdered?" She gazed out of the window, her back to the room. After a few moments, she turned to face them, her eyes glistening.

"Did Erin mention anything unusual in the days leading up to her death?" Ash asked. "Were there any strangers around your house, or unusual encounters? Phone calls? Anything?" she pressed.

Philicia shook her head. She moved to her desk and leaned against it, pressing both palms flat on the surface and curling her fingers round the edge of the desktop. "If there had been anything, I would've told the police."

The inner door flew open and Jacob burst into the room, pistol drawn, leveled directly at Wallace.

"Shit!" Ash exclaimed. "Panic button," she remarked, noting Philicia's position by the desk.

"Gun," Jacob commanded. "Slowly."

"Call the police," Philicia instructed Marcie, who hurried from the room.

Wallace felt a stab of panic as he watched Ash reach beneath her coat for her gun. Jacob kept his pointed in Wallace's direction the whole time, but despite the threat, Wallace still considered making a run for the door. A quick death would be preferable to any more time spent in Rikers, waiting for Smokie or someone similar to gut him with a shiv. Or, if he was lucky enough to prove his innocence, he could look forward to a few days in witness protection before Pendulum got to him. Wallace was about to move when Ash whipped her pistol around and pointed it at Philicia.

"Put your gun down!" Ash yelled at Jacob. "Do it now!" She didn't wait for Jacob to react. Instead, she rushed him and grabbed hold of his pistol, which he reluctantly yielded. "Sit down!" she commanded, and the humiliated bodyguard followed her direction, positioning himself on the couch and glaring at her insolently.

Wallace was in no doubt that the big man would strike the moment he had the opportunity, but Ash robbed him of the chance; she smacked Jacob across the face with the butt of her pistol, and he fell back unconscious.

"You've just turned this into a very intense situation," Ash told Philicia, training the gun on her as she cowered by her desk. "We need you to talk before the police arrive."

"I don't know anything," Philicia objected.

"You make out that you're some kind of saint," Ash gestured at their surroundings. "You con other people into funding your ego trip, so that you can work off your guilt by trying to save the lives of strangers. All the time you know you failed your daughter, and if that wasn't bad enough, you've left your son to rot in a nuthouse."

"Rot?" Philicia seemed genuinely puzzled. "Max isn't well, but he isn't rotting."

"Is that what you tell yourself? Drugged to the eyeballs with no visitors; if that isn't rotting—"

"Drugged? What are you talking about?" Philicia interrupted. "He isn't drugged, and he has visitors. Steven and I go to see him."

"What?" Ash asked. Wallace could see that Philicia's honest response had unsettled her. "What are you talking about?"

"It's difficult to see him so unwell, but I try to visit every month. It depends when his doctor thinks he's well enough to see me," Philicia replied indignantly. "This charity might make me feel like I'm doing some good with my life, but it hasn't replaced my children."

Ash walked over to the shelving unit that lined Philicia's office and examined the photograph of Max Byrne, then turned to Wallace. "Come on," she said, hurrying across the room. "We've got to go."

Wallace could hear the sound of distant sirens. He followed Ash into Marcie's office, and Philicia's assistant eyed them nervously as they rushed past.

"What's going on?" he asked Ash as they raced toward the elevators.

"We've got to get out of here before the cops arrive. I need to see Max Byrne." Ash pressed the call button.

The doors of the farthest elevator slid open and they started toward it before stopping in their tracks as two building security guards emerged. Ash gave the men no time to react, leveling her pistol in their direction.

"Get down!" she yelled. "On the floor!"

The guards hesitated.

"Down!" Ash repeated emphatically, and the two uniformed men complied, lying facedown on the marble tiles.

Ash joined Wallace in the elevator and kept her gun on the security guards until the doors finally closed. They rode the elevator in tense silence, and when the counter indicated they'd passed the tenth floor, Ash pressed the button marked "5."

"What are you doing?" Wallace asked.

"We need another way out," Ash replied. "There'll be guards waiting for us in the lobby. Police, too, probably."

The elevator doors opened onto the hospital-white reception of a design agency. Ignoring the nervous looks of the two assistants, who'd caught sight of the gun, Ash stepped out of the elevator and headed for the fire stairs, a few yards away. Wallace followed her into the stairwell and watched as she pulled the fire alarm. They hurried down the stairs as insistent Klaxons sounded all around them. Ash triggered another alarm on the floor below, and by the time they reached the third, the stairwell had started to fill with office workers, so they joined the swelling exodus and moved slowly down the stairs until they were eventually expelled into the street. A handful of police officers tried to vet the crowd, but they were severely outnumbered and Ash and Wallace drifted to the edge of the pack before slowly slipping down the street.

50

Something was troubling Ash. It played on her mind and Wallace could see her wrestling with it as they sat in the back of the cab and journeyed through the city. He tried to get her to talk, but she was resistant.

"It's better you don't know" was all she said, in a tone that made it clear she didn't want to discuss whatever was bothering her.

Wallace leaned his head against the window and watched the world pass. The embers of the day were rapidly fading to darkness, and the low light, the gentle rock of the taxi, and the somnolent warmth of its powerful heater soon conspired to send him to sleep. He didn't wake until the taxi pulled to a halt and the driver wound down his window, unleashing a blast of cold night air.

"Hello?" a man's voice crackled from the intercom beside the Cromwell Center's gate. The rush-hour drive from Manhattan had taken over four hours and it was a little after 8:30 p.m.

"Special Agent Alexis Hale, FBI," Ash replied, leaning out of her window. Wallace recognized the name of the agent who had been outside the Manhattan Regent Hotel. "We need to see one of your patients."

"The hospital is closed," the voice advised.

"This is an emergency," Ash countered. "Open the gates, or I'll come back with a warrant and arrest you for obstruction."

The voice didn't answer, but a moment later the gates swung open, and the cab rolled up the drive.

"Wait here," Ash said to the driver, as she and Wallace stepped into the cold night and climbed the steps to the heavy doors.

A squat security guard with a thick black mustache sat behind the reception desk. When Ash rapped the glass, he buzzed them through the inner security door.

"We're here for Max Byrne," Ash informed him.

"Ms. Kavanagh is on her way in," the man replied. "She's asked me to make sure you're comfortable until she arrives. Can I get you something to drink?"

Wallace saw Ash suppress her frustration. "I'm good," she said shortly.

"Nothing for me, thanks," Wallace added.

"Please take a seat," the guard instructed. "She won't be long."

They walked over to the seating area and sat in a couple of adjacent armchairs. As the minutes ticked on, Ash's frustration turned to brooding hostility.

"What are we doing here?" Wallace asked.

"You should wait in the cab," she advised, totally ignoring his question.

Wallace wasn't about to leave her side, and he turned his attention to the lobby's large watercolors, admiring the artist's composition and use of light. Every time he looked at Ash, her eyes seemed to have gotten narrower and her brow more furrowed. Finally, after almost half an hour, the heavy outer door swung open and Grace Kavanagh stepped into the security booth. The security guard buzzed her through.

"Thanks, Joe," Grace said. She turned her attention to the seating area and a stern look crossed her face as she approached. Wallace suspected her foul mood might rival Ash's. "You think Joe wouldn't recognize you? Your face has been all over the news. Give me one good reason why I should let you anywhere near my patient."

"I'm a federal agent," Ash replied halfheartedly.

"A federal agent using someone else's name," Grace observed with a sneer. "A federal agent who's on the run. There's no way you're getting inside, Agent Ash."

Ash stared at Grace, who returned the glaring hostility.

"Philicia Byrne told us that she and her ex-husband have been visiting their son," Wallace intervened. "The nurse we met said his family never came to see him."

"That's not possible," Grace replied. "Nurse Moore is Max's lead caretaker. He knows everything about Max's life here."

An exasperated Ash was about to speak, but Wallace cut her off. "Could you please check?"

Grace's expression softened. "We have a diary system," she said. "Visitors are required to check in and out," she added, turning toward the reception desk. "Joe, can you see if the system shows any visits from Philicia or Steven Byrne?"

Ash and Wallace followed Grace over while Joe typed at his computer. After a few moments, he shook his head.

"Nothing," he informed them.

"Could you check again?" Ash asked, as Wallace drifted toward the plinth that supported the large visitors' book.

Joe retyped his search into the computer while Wallace leafed through the pages of the thick book, which was full of handwritten remarks from friends and relatives commenting on the hospital.

"No," Joe said at last. "No visits. Not according to our records."

"Here," Wallace called out.

Ash hurried over to him, and Grace followed. The three of them looked down at a page that was divided into a grid of rows and columns. Each visitor was meant to use a single row. The first column was for the patient's name, the second for the visitor's, the third for the date, and the fourth for any remarks. There, in the center of the page, spread over two rows, was a comment from Philicia Byrne. Dated seven weeks ago, the remark, written in neat cursive, read; "Max and I spent time in the lovely garden today. We talked, but he's still the same, so quiet and withdrawn. I keep wondering when my little boy is going to come back to me."

"I don't understand," Grace said, her voice full of puzzlement. "If she's been here, she'd be in the system."

"Your computers may have been hacked," Wallace advised.

"Why would anyone do that?" Grace asked.

"Can we please see Max?" Ash asked, pressing home the advantage.

Grace glanced uncertainly at the main entrance and then nodded hesitantly. "Follow me."

She led Ash and Wallace through the security door on the far side of the lobby and along the corridor to the orderly's station, which was staffed by an elderly man with pale skin and white hair. Ash deposited her gun and Wallace handed over his belt. Somewhere in the middle distance, Wallace heard the deep rumble of a helicopter; probably a wealthy hedge fund manager commuting to his private estate.

"They'll be watching a movie," Grace told them as they stepped beyond the mesh gate.

Wallace and Ash followed her through the darkened exercise area into the dayroom, where the patients sat quietly and watched *Mary Poppins*. As Julie Andrews flew through the air clutching her umbrella, Wallace questioned the screening criteria for a group of damaged people whose grip on reality would be tenuous at best. Half a dozen nurses and a similar number of orderlies seemed to straighten ever so slightly when they caught sight of Grace, who picked her way through the room until she reached Max. He sat next to a large African-American nurse.

"Hey, Chuck, how is he?" Grace asked the nurse.

Chuck looked at Max and shrugged. "Same as always," he replied.

Grace crouched down and tried to meet Max's gaze, but his eyes were lost in another world.

"Max, it's Grace Kavanagh. I need to talk to you about your parents. They've been coming to visit you."

Max offered no response, not even a glimmer of recognition, as drool pooled in the corners of his mouth.

"What's going on, Ms. Kavanagh?" Chuck asked. "We don't have visitors on the secure unit."

"I know," Grace agreed. "But his mother's said she's seen him."

"I need to talk to him," Ash pushed.

"You can't. Not when he's like this," Grace replied.

"We could taper his meds," Chuck said. "There's a pretty good chance he'll become violent, but if it's important we can restrain him."

"How long would it take?" Grace asked.

"We'd need to check with Doctor Elise how fast we can bring him down, but last time it took two days," Chuck replied.

Wallace noted the grimace that flashed across Ash's face; they didn't have that long.

"There's got to be another way," she declared.

"You could give him a shot of adrenaline." Chuck's joke earned him a frown from Grace.

"Do it," Ash instructed.

"It was a joke," Chuck protested. "The shock would wreck his mind. In his condition it would almost guarantee a psychotic break."

"I have to talk to him," Ash said emphatically.

Wallace heard the turbulent thump of boots echo along the corridor outside the dayroom, and moments later he recognized Hector Solomon when he burst in at the head of a squad of four police officers.

"Shit!" Ash shot Grace an angry look. "You called them?"

"Of course I did," Grace said. "What did you expect? You're wanted for murder."

"Hector," Ash began, turning to her boss.

"You're done," Hector informed Ash, before speaking to a portly, droopy-eyed, middle-aged police officer who wore a badge that said "Chief." "Take them into custody."

The chief of Cromwell Police nodded to two of his officers, who approached Wallace and Ash.

"Hector, we need to talk to this man," Ash objected, signaling Max.

"Forget it, Chris. You're finished," Hector said.

Two more agents entered, and Wallace recognized them from outside the Manhattan Regent Hotel. He remembered Ash telling him their names: Hale and Nelson.

He could sense Ash's building anger and wasn't surprised when she wheeled around and punched Hale in the face. Ash's hands blurred for a split second and when they stopped moving they were holding a heavy pistol that Wallace assumed had come from Hale's holster. Ash fired a shot at the floor and all movement stopped.

"You!" Ash pointed the gun at Chuck. "Adrenaline! Now!"

Chuck looked at Grace, his eyes searching for guidance.

"Don't look at her," Ash commanded. "Look at me. Get me the adrenaline. Now!"

Grace nodded at Chuck, who hurried from the room.

"Put the gun down," the chief yelled, producing his own sidearm.

"Fuck you!" Ash turned her ire on the man. "I'll drill you, Chief! Put the gun down." She shot at his feet, and a couple of the more lucid patients started to become agitated.

"This is hard time," Hector observed sadly. "This isn't your career, Chris. This is jail."

"I need to get the patients out of here," Grace advised.

"Nobody moves!" Ash ordered. "Put your fucking gun down!" she commanded the chief, who looked at Hector.

Hector nodded slowly and the chief lowered his pistol to the floor.

Ash backed toward the wall, sweeping the room with the pistol to discourage the three Feds and the four police officers from doing anything stupidly heroic. Wallace could sense the tension of the two officers on either side of him, their bodies taut with violent potential. Moments later Chuck returned carrying a syringe and a vial and held the latter out for Ash to inspect.

"Do it," she instructed.

"This could kill him," Grace cautioned.

Ash looked at Chuck for confirmation, but he shook his head and said, "It won't kill him, but it will probably make him psychotic."

Ash considered the assessment. "Do it," she commanded with a wave of the gun.

Chuck stuck the needle through the rubber stopper and drew back the plunger. He pulled the collar of Max's smock and exposed the fleshy shoulder muscle before looking at Grace, who shook her head.

Ash stepped forward, grabbed the needle, and stuck it in Max's shoulder. She depressed the plunger and flooded his body with adrenaline. The reaction was instantaneous: Max rocketed out of his seat, knocking Ash backward. He grabbed her and drove her against the wall, wrestling for control of the gun in her hand. Chuck and two of the police officers grabbed Max and pulled him away. Ash rounded on him, bringing the pistol within inches of his head.

"What's your name?" she demanded.

"Back off, Agent Ash!" Hector yelled.

"Tell me your name!" Ash commanded, brandishing the gun.

Max looked around fearfully.

"I've got nothing to lose," Ash warned. "I'll put a bullet in you."

Max stared at Ash indignantly. She pulled the trigger, and the muzzle blazed fire a few inches from his head. The gunshot reverberated around the room, setting off a volley of fearful cries from the other patients.

"Agent Ash!" Hector roared, as Max clutched his ear in pain. The police officers and FBI agents all had their weapons trained on Ash.

"You're running out of time!" Ash told Max. "You've got three seconds. One . . ."

"Put down your weapon!" Hector instructed Ash. "Put it down or we'll be forced to open fire."

Wallace saw Max glance at the law enforcement officers, who were about to rain hellfire across the room. Realization dawned; he had as much chance of getting shot by one of the people trying to save him as he did by the unhinged woman with a gun to his head.

"Two," Ash continued, her resolve showing no signs of faltering as she pressed the hot muzzle against Max's head.

"Put it down, Chris!" Hector commanded.

"Thr—"

"Okay, okay." Max relented, interrupting Ash. "My name isn't Max Byrne."

51

Ash sat in one of the vacated chairs, her tightly bound hands stretched out behind her like an awkward rudder. The man they'd known as Max Byrne sat nearby, exhausted and deeply troubled. Grace Kavanagh had ordered patients and hospital staff out of the room, and the last of them were squeezing past the Cromwell police, who clustered in the doorway behind Wallace. He'd refused to leave Ash, and demanded to hear what the roused patient had to say. Hector, Nelson, and Hale stood around "Max." Occasionally Hale would glance in Ash's direction with unconcealed hostility. Ash was almost certain that Hale's shame at being robbed of her sidearm hurt much more than the punch.

"Who are you?" Hector demanded of the seated patient once the last nurse had left the room.

The patient looked at Ash and shook his head. She knew that he would be totally wired, his body flooded with adrenaline, his mind fighting the stupor of the sedatives and antipsychotics that still coursed through his veins. Hard interrogation wouldn't work on this guy; he needed the illusion of clarity.

"We can bring you in," she said quietly. "We can run your prints, dental records. It might take a couple of weeks, but we'll find out who you are." She looked up at Hector, hoping that he had the good sense to let her words sink in. "You'll be charged with obstruction," she added.

The troubled man was locked in conflict. His eyes met Ash's and she nodded gently, trying to encourage him to do the right thing.

Something inside changed and the man found some sort of peace in a decision.

"My name is Mike Rosen," he replied. "Max and I were in the army together. People always said we looked like brothers. After I got wounded in Iraq, I was discharged and things got pretty ugly, but Max came to me a couple of years ago and said we could help each other out. He offered me ten grand a week if I posed as him. He told me to do whatever it took to get into the secure unit. If they ever stopped sedating me, I was supposed to get violent until they put me back on the meds."

"You've been in here for two years?" Ash asked.

Mike nodded. "I was broke. Homeless. I would've done anything for that kind of money."

"Did you know why he wanted you to impersonate him?" Ash continued.

"No," Mike replied. "He said he needed to do some stuff without his folks finding out, but people don't spend ten grand a week to avoid getting grounded."

"Mr. Rosen is coming with us. I want to know everything," Hector said. He turned to Nelson. "Max Byrne's been running a false alibi for two years. Put out a nationwide alert for him; he just became our number one suspect in the Pendulum killings. Have units pick up Mr. and Mrs. Byrne and bring them in for questioning."

"What about us?" Ash asked.

"This puts everything in a new light. You and Mr. Wallace are no longer suspects, but Internal Investigations has already started building a disciplinary case," Hector replied. "Your earlier actions were reckless and dangerous, but what you've done here will play well for you. Unless Agent Hale objects, we won't add any other charges to your file as a result of tonight's conduct."

Hale shook her head slowly as she looked from Ash to Hector. "Whatever," she said.

"Cut her loose," Hector instructed Hale. "We still gotta bring you in to face renewed charges on the Washington shooting and for disobeying orders, dereliction of duty, and a whole long list of other infractions," he continued, as Hale produced a small pocket knife and sliced the ties that bound Ash's wrists. "I doubt you'll go to jail, but I don't see a future at the Bureau."

"What about him?" Ash asked, nodding at Wallace.

"Mr. Wallace is going back into WitPro," Hector replied.

"No. You can't protect me," Wallace objected.

"We can and we will. Thanks to Special Agent Ash's . . ." Hector searched for the correct choice of words, ". . . unconventional approach, we now have a real suspect." He turned to Nelson. "I want every piece of evidence reexamined when we get back to Police Plaza."

"Police Plaza?" Ash asked in puzzlement.

"We're bunking with NYPD until they can restore our power and systems. The virus you sent me wiped out everything," Hector informed her.

"We didn't send anything," she protested. "It was Pendulum. He had us at gunpoint. Forced me to make the call. He was trying to set us up before he killed us."

Hector looked at Wallace for confirmation.

"It's true," Wallace assured him.

"If so, it'll be one less charge on your sheet," Hector informed Ash. "Come on, let's go. We've got a chopper waiting outside."

Wallace followed the FBI agents out of the Cromwell Center, across the parking lot to a stretch of grass beside the hospital where a large helicopter waited. Its long rotors were turning, whipping icy wind into his face. He recognized the chopper as a UH-60 Black Hawk, an FBI version of the US Army workhorse he'd become familiar with in Afghanistan. Hale pulled open the rear sliding door, and Wallace, Mike Rosen, and the agents clambered into the large cabin, which was capable of carrying a fully equipped platoon of soldiers. Hale jumped in last and slid the door shut. The passengers split themselves evenly on the two benches that ran down either side of the aircraft, and Wallace slid between Nelson and Hale to sit opposite Ash. The pilot glanced at Hector, who wound his index finger to signal takeoff. The pilot spoke into his radio, and moments later Wallace felt the rotors run up to speed as the chopper climbed into the sky. He looked out the window to see the Cromwell Center drop away and glittering lights sweep into view as their rising altitude revealed more and more of the nocturnal landscape.

Ash looked across the helicopter and smiled. They were in custody and she was facing a disciplinary investigation, but they finally had a viable suspect and were no longer in the frame for murder. Wallace knew Ash would consider this a win, but he wasn't so sure. He felt safer with Ash than with anyone else, and he had a feeling that they wouldn't be together for very much longer.

Hector spent the first ten minutes of the flight on the phone to an agent called Alvarez, who, Wallace surmised, was in California leading the West Coast investigation. Hector told Alvarez about Max Byrne, taking care to highlight Ash's role in identifying him as a suspect. Wallace got the feeling that, despite their run-ins, Hector was a fan of Ash and that he was laying groundwork to help her fend off any charges.

"Hector," Ash yelled across the chopper, "I've been thinking. If we really want to find Max Byrne fast, there might be a better way than putting out a national alert."

"And what would that be?" Hector asked.

"Let's get people working for us," she replied. "You ever seen a missing person campaign go viral?"

Hector shook his head.

"Get hold of Kate Baxter. She runs *Nightfile*." Ash paused, noticing Hector's brow furrow at the mention of the name. "Yeah, I know. Let's just say she owes me a favor," she continued, "Ask her to run a story about how Max Byrne has escaped from a psychiatric hospital, how he poses a risk to himself. Find the cutest, most sympathetic photo of him, and use the truth. He's a troubled military veteran who poses a danger to himself. Play for people's hearts; make it sound like he's a tragic war hero who fell apart when he lost his sister. He's a wounded man who could commit suicide at any moment. Tell Kate to make some calls to her media contacts and get the story pushed hard. We get Twitter, Facebook—the world—looking for our man."

Hector stared at Ash impassively for a moment, before nodding at Nelson. "Get me Kate Baxter," he said.

Ash sat back and smiled at Wallace; she'd just scored another win. With creative thinking like that, it was easy to see why Hector wanted to help her stay on the team.

52

Dan Alosi turned his black AMG onto Cresta Via Lane and lowered his window to wave at Nate, the uniformed security guard, who raised the barrier. Alosi drove on, following the road as it snaked along the spine of the ridge overlooking Portola Valley. Alosi had chosen the area for its proximity to the Facebook campus so that on nights like this, when he'd been in the office past midnight, he could make it home inside half an hour. The custom-modified Mercedes hugged the road as it climbed the ridge. It was approaching one a.m. and there were no other vehicles to be seen, just the lush California vegetation caught in the brilliance of his headlights. Alosi had always prided himself on being a workaholic, but the load he faced in the coming weeks depressed him. It wasn't the quantity that weighed him down; it was the terrible event that had caused the increased workload. Zach Holz had been with Facebook for eight years, and Alosi considered him a close friend. Zach's wife, Ali, was utterly devastated, and Alosi could tell that the boys didn't fully understand what had happened. Nobody really did. According to news reports, Zach might have been a victim of a serial killer. The FBI had sent a team to interview Zach's colleagues, but the agent who'd questioned Alosi, a guy named Alvarez, had been very evasive when pressed on the subject.

It was a dangerous world, which was why Alosi believed in being careful. Security was another benefit of Cresta Via. The wealthy residents had clubbed together to build a gated security checkpoint at the start of the private road, and the guardhouse was staffed twenty-four hours a day. Alosi knew that the residents' money made them targets, and, never one to believe in taking risks, he'd deliberately selected the house for its inherent security advantages. It was located at the end of Cresta Via, which minimized passing traffic, so that anyone coming up to his house wasn't there by accident. The three-hundred-yard driveway meant the house was well hidden from the road, and the modern concrete construction had enabled Alosi to add a number of fortifications when he moved in. He'd installed a panic room and blast shutters across every window and door on the property. The building and any occupants could withstand a prolonged assault, but, with a three-minute alarm response time from the guardhouse and a full security team guaranteed to be on the premises within fifteen, Alosi never envisaged having to battle-test his fortifications.

He sped along his tree-lined driveway and pulled onto the gravel in front of his rectangular bunker of a house. He parked the AMG between his Tesla and his Ferrari 488 GTB and then checked his phone as he walked toward his home. The search for Max Byrne dominated his Facebook timeline, with dozens of people posting a link to a *Nightfile* special bulletin and a photo of the former soldier. Alosi had never met Max's father, Steven, but knew him by reputation. His standing within the tech industry and the tragic death of his daughter had given him a degree of notoriety.

The biometric scanner beside the entrance flared as a strip of light wiped over Alosi's palm, and the painted blue front door clicked open an instant later, triggering the alarm countdown.

"Deactivate," Alosi said as he stepped inside and shut the door. The countdown ended with a single tone, and he started across the lobby, the hard heels of his custom-fitted Foster & Sons shoes tapping the white marble. When he heard an unfamiliar noise coming from the front door, he stopped and turned; it sounded like air hissing out of a tire.

The explosion blew the door off its reinforced hinges and knocked Alosi onto his back. Dust and debris filled the vaulted lobby as he struggled to his knees, his eardrums aching with a numbness that silenced the world around him. He could not hear the sound of the masked man in the long coat as he walked over the wreckage and invaded his home, but he recognized the bleak figure from an artist's drawing that had featured in press coverage of the Pendulum killings. Sound started to return, first in the form of a high-pitched ringing that Alosi suspected was an aftereffect of the explosion. The sound inspired a thought, and Alosi looked at the alarm panel beside the door, his eyes locking on the red panic button. Realizing he had to reach that button, he pushed himself to his feet and started running, but the masked figure was faster. He leaped, lashed out, and caught Alosi with a Kevlar-plated forearm that clotheslined him and sent him tumbling onto his ass. A second, more precise blow delivered to the top of Alosi's head knocked him down completely. As the world bubbled and swirled, Alosi saw something he did not understand. Just before he passed out, he watched Pendulum walk over to the alarm panel and press the panic button.

53

If Pendulum had intended to incapacitate the New York Field Office's investigation, he'd failed. The Bureau had multiple contingency locations that it could deploy to in the event of a terrorist attack, but Ash had never expected a computer virus to force such a move. She surveyed the functioning chaos of the tenth floor of Police Plaza, the closest contingency site, and watched as sixty agents and administrators took calls from all over the country. *Nightfile*'s story and dozens of planted tweets and Facebook posts had been shared tens of thousands of times, which had led to the search being picked up by local and national news. A photo of Max Byrne, looking every inch the hero in full dress uniform, was clogging Facebook timelines and Twitter feeds, creating an army of thousands of unwitting bounty hunters. According to people phoning in, Max Byrne had been seen in each of the fifty states, and the current tally of sightings topped two thousand. The agents and administrators sorted the calls into obvious hoaxes, low probability, and high probability before coordinating with local law enforcement to check out every single one.

After she and Wallace had been debriefed, Ash had convinced Hector to let her answer a phone on the basis that they needed every available body, and now that they had a viable suspect, she had no reason to add to her burgeoning disciplinary file. Wallace had persuaded Hector to delay the handover to the WitPro team until morning, and Ash could tell that the Englishman felt safe only with her. He was currently curled up on a makeshift bed in a side office, and Ash could see him through the glass partition, sleeping soundly.

Hector was somewhere else in the building, interviewing Steven and Philicia Byrne. All of Ash's attempts at manipulation had failed to get her in the room, but she wasn't too disappointed. It was a relief to be back on the team in any capacity. Still, Ash thought, it wouldn't hurt to run a fresh pair of eyes over the case, so she pushed her swivel chair away from the chipped desk and picked her way through the rows of Bureau personnel until she reached Parker, who sat near Nelson and Hale. The three of them acted as extensions of Hector's will and supervised the search for Max Byrne. Ash noticed a stack of folders on Parker's desk.

"Hey," Ash smiled at Parker as he hung up his phone.

"What do you want?" he asked impatiently.

"To feel useful," Ash replied.

"Field calls," Parker suggested. "Getting the world searching for him was your idea."

"You mind if I take a look at the files?" Ash tried. "While I'm fielding calls."

"Solomon says your suspension won't come through until morning," Parker observed. "That means you're still an agent. An agent who will make my life a living hell until she inevitably gets her way. Right?"

"Probably," Ash responded honestly.

"Go ahead," Parker nodded at the files. "Let me know if you find anything."

He answered his ringing phone as Ash gathered up the stack of files and returned to her desk. She started flipping through the first file, which contained background information on Kye Walters. Her phone rang and she answered it, absentmindedly noting the details of an alleged sighting of Max Byrne as she studied everything the Bureau knew about the young victim from Garrison.

"I don't understand," Philicia Byrne said, her voice tinged with apprehension.

"Your son paid someone to impersonate him for two years, a former Ranger named Mike Rosen," Hector replied, studying the people opposite him. Max's parents seemed genuinely unsettled. Philicia was more demonstrative and her eyes welled with tears as she nervously played with the hem of her dress. Steven was silent, but he cast around the room with the disbelief of someone deeply troubled by the revelations. Steven's lawyer, Alan Cook, sat next to him. Hector knew the bald-headed, eagle-faced man as one of the most fearsome criminal attorneys in New York. Philicia's lawyer, Stephanie Ross, a somber woman with straw-blonde hair, whispered something to her client.

"That's impossible," Philicia objected. "I visited him in the hospital."

"Tell me about those visits," Hector urged.

"Max's doctor e-mails me with a visiting time," Philicia responded. "We always meet on the grounds. By his favorite bench."

"It's the same for me," Steven admitted.

"Our initial investigation suggests Max has been forging his doctor's e-mails and infiltrating the grounds in order to meet with you. Didn't you think it was strange you never saw him in a ward?"

"No. Of course not. They encourage patients to use the grounds," Philicia protested. "Why would he lie to me?"

"Having an imposter in the secure unit bought him an airtight alibi, but you'd have caused problems if you hadn't been able to visit your son or, worse, recognized the imposter. So we think your son manufactured your visits in order to maintain his alibi," Hector explained.

"I don't believe it," Steven Byrne spoke at last. "Max was angry, but he wouldn't do this."

The bare-walled interview room fell silent as Hector worked up to his next question. "Your attorneys will have informed you that your son is now the principal suspect in the so-called Pendulum killings," he said finally.

"No," Philicia objected, her eyes welling with tears. "Max wouldn't hurt anyone."

"Max served in the Seventy-Fifth Rangers," Hector continued. "He was dishonorably discharged—"

"That was a misunderstanding," Steven broke in. "Max didn't understand that politics has no place in the military."

"His file says he was accused of attempting to subvert his unit," Hector added. "He worked for you, Mr. Byrne, before your daughter's death. He's had combat training and is an expert with computers. If it hadn't been for his supposed incarceration, he would have been a suspect right out of the box. I've got to ask: did either of you know anything about what he was doing?"

Philicia responded with an indignant look and Steven shook his head sadly. Alan Cook leaned over to speak quietly to his client, and Hector was sure he heard the words "full disclosure."

"We'd like to show you what we've found," Steven said at last.

"I had my people make inquiries before we came in," Alan added, producing a document from his briefcase. "We discovered that someone has been accessing the fund my client established for his son."

Hector looked at the document Alan handed him: a bank statement that showed a series of offshore transfers.

"The fund was endowed with forty million dollars when Max was twenty-one," Alan continued. "As you can see, six million is missing, transferred overseas. We're working to find out where that money went."

"The Bureau would like to help," Hector replied.

Steven nodded and Alan echoed the gesture. They had no choice; the disclosure meant the fund now became part of the investigation and was most likely how Max Byrne had been financing his activities over the past two years.

"Thank you," Hector acknowledged. "I'm sorry, but I've got to ask this." He paused, certain that his next question would be painful for both parents. "Can you think of any reason why Max might have killed his sister?"

Philicia looked away, distraught, and Hector saw fury flush across Steven's face.

"Max did not kill Erin," Steven responded emphatically.

"I'm sorry to ask the question, Mr. Byrne, but how can you be so sure?" Hector pressed.

Steven stared at Hector with hard indignation. "My son did not kill his sister," he seethed. "He loved her. He would never do that. He was with me that night."

The ensuing silence was broken by the sound of a ringing phone.

"Are we done here?" Steven asked as he reached into his pocket and produced his cell. "I need to take this."

Hector nodded, and Steven and his lawyer left the room.

Philicia watched her ex-husband go, her eyes brimming with tears and bewilderment. "Max adored Erin. She was his little angel," she told Hector. "You've got this all wrong. There has to be another explanation."

Ash saw Hector rubbing his eyes as he entered the large office. He looked like a man who'd had a difficult couple of hours, but Ash needed to know what he'd learned from Max's parents, so she hurried across the room to intercept him. Hector grimaced slightly when she crossed his path.

"I can't tell you anything," he said instantly.

"That's okay," Ash lied. "I was looking through the files."

Hector glanced over at Parker and rolled his eyes.

"He didn't have a choice," Ash informed him. "I was looking through them and I noticed something weird. All the victims posted suicide notes apart from Zach Holz. He doesn't fit the pattern."

"Maybe by the time he got to Holz, he knew we were onto him and decided there was no point trying to cover it up?" Hector suggested.

"Maybe," Ash conceded. "But it doesn't fit the pattern, and I think it should be excluded. It might throw us onto the wrong track. Holz could have been killed for a different reason, or he might be the victim of a copycat."

"Why don't we just exclude everything that doesn't give us an easy answer?" Hector snapped. "I'm sorry," he added quickly. "It's been a long night."

"You've got links to organized crime with Bonnie Mann and Ken Pallo. Mann owed a lot of money in Vegas. The guy Pendulum tried to frame as Wallace's accomplice, Leo Willard—he and his colleague Eli Landsman were found murdered outside Vegas. His boss, a small-timer with a long record, Rusty Hausman, said Leo and Eli were last seen driving Bonnie Mann home. Ken Pallo had dubious investors, many of them indirectly connected to the underworld."

"You think these are mob hits?" Hector asked. "What about Wallace? Or the kid upstate? The British farmer?"

Ash shook her head in frustration. "I know. It's a stretch, but nothing fits them all. Without a common motive, we have no idea where he's going to strike next. He told Wallace and me that he needed more time. That means he's not finished."

Hector patted her on the shoulder. "I appreciate the effort, Chris, but let's focus on finding Max Byrne. We get him and I'm sure we'll fill in all the blanks."

The large digital clock hanging from the wall displayed a time of 04:47. Hector pushed past Ash and carried on toward Parker, who had just taken a phone call. Ash saw Parker's expression change and knew that he'd heard something important, so she jogged to catch up with her boss and drew alongside as Parker collared him.

"We've found Max Byrne," Parker announced. "He's in a house in Portola Valley, just outside San Francisco, and he's got a hostage."

Ash's head was shaking before she'd even consciously registered her disbelief. This guy didn't take hostages.

"Do we have confirmation it's him?" Hector asked.

"Local hostage negotiator is in contact," Parker replied. "He's identified himself as Maximillian Byrne and given details of each of the murders, including the attacks on John Wallace. Alvarez is twenty-five minutes from the scene, but he's reviewed surveillance footage from the community security system and says it's our man."

"Anything on the hostage?" Ash cut in.

"Dan Alosi. Chief technology officer at Facebook. The house belongs to him," Parker replied.

"Why would he start taking hostages?" Ash mused.

"He's working on a list of demands, but he's already said he wants you out there," Parker told Hector. "Wants the lead investigative agent. He asked for you by name, Assistant Special Agent in Charge Solomon. He also wants Christine Ash and John Wallace to go with you."

"So he can have another shot?" Ash protested. "You can't do this, Hector."

"If we've got a chance of bringing him in, I'm gonna play it out," Hector replied firmly.

Ash scowled and shook her head. "Not by this guy's rules," she advised.

"You and Wallace won't be coming with me," Hector assured her. "There's no need to put a witness in harm's way, and you no longer have any official role in this investigation. I'm expecting your suspension order to come through this morning, and you will be relieved of active duty." He turned to Hale. "We're going to need transportation. Make the arrangements," he said. "You and Nelson are coming with me. Parker, until we've got our own confirmation it's Max Byrne, I want you here following up every lead. Tell Alvarez to hold point till we get there."

Hector turned on his heels and marched purposefully through the office, with Hale and Nelson trailing him as they struck up urgent phone conversations.

Ash turned to Parker. "This sucks," she observed.

Parker shrugged. "Sometimes we catch a break," he replied before backing away. It was clear he didn't want anything to do with an agent whose career was almost certainly over.

Ash sighed with frustration. Max Byrne would only let himself get into a hostage situation if it furthered his twisted cause. Annoyed that she couldn't read the play, she sloped back to her desk.

Wallace opened his eyes and took a moment to remember where he was. His limbs semaphored their painful signals and his ribs echoed the message. He and Ash had concealed the full extent of their injuries to avoid being separated, but Wallace had resolved to inform the US marshals once he was in their custody. He felt utterly battered and wanted a doctor to ensure there wasn't anything that needed surgical attention. He sat up and looked out of the little office to see that the clock read 08:06. Dozens of smartly dressed men and women worked beneath the oversized timepiece, answering phones and sorting through reported sightings of Max Byrne. Wallace glanced toward Ash's desk and noticed that she was slumped over, asleep. He got to his feet and shuffled to the door, and when he opened it, the hubbub hit him: dozens of urgent conversations, commands, and instructions. As he picked his way past the busy agents and staggered slowly toward her, Wallace wondered how Ash could sleep through it all.

"Hey," he said quietly as he touched Ash on the shoulder. She stirred and then sat up suddenly.

"I think I was asleep." She rattled the words out so quickly that they ran into one another.

Wallace smiled; she was barely across the border that separated sleep from waking. "How are you feeling?" he asked.

"Like shit," Ash replied. "I could sleep for a week."

"What time am I being transferred?"

"I don't know," she said. "Hector took off. Quite literally. He's on a plane to San Francisco. Max Byrne has taken a hostage."

"Hostage?" Wallace echoed, puzzled. "He doesn't take hostages."

"Yeah, I know," Ash responded.

"Hey, Chris!" a voice called out. Wallace turned to see a tired junior agent with a phone cradled against his ear. "This one's for you. What's your number?"

"Three-two-three," Ash replied, picking up the phone as it started ringing. "Special Agent Ash."

Bailey watched an impossibly chubby Airbus A380 float across the crisp blue sky.

"Chris, it's Pat Bailey," he said, leaning back in his chair and placing his feet on his desk. His stomach muscles railed at the movement, signaling their complaint with a sharp stab of pain that made Bailey grimace.

"Bailey!" Ash exclaimed brightly. "How the hell are you?"

"Alive," he replied. "I'm on light duties for a couple of months."

"John Wallace is with me."

"Really?" Bailey asked in disbelief. "Can you put me on speaker?"

"We're kind of in the middle of something, so it's pretty loud here, but I'll try."

Bailey heard the acoustics change and the sound of a busy office filled his ear.

"John?" Bailey tried.

"DS Bailey?" Wallace's words rose above the din.

"It's good to hear your voice," Bailey said honestly.

"And yours. I thought you were . . ." Wallace trailed off.

"No danger," Bailey remarked. "I was really sorry to hear about Constance Jones," he added sympathetically.

"Thanks," Wallace acknowledged quietly.

"Chris, I tried to get hold of you before, but your mobile rings out and your office said you were unavailable," Bailey continued.

"Wallace and I had to go off the grid," Ash explained.

"I gathered. I've been following the news," Bailey replied. "Looks like this guy's been racking up bodies."

"Yeah. Too many," Ash agreed. "The prime suspect is holed up in San Francisco. Hostage situation."

"Doesn't fit his MO," Bailey commented. "Listen, I'd love to catch up and compare notes, but I've got something that needs to be checked out."

"Go ahead," Ash said.

"This information is coming through official channels," Bailey said, looking round the busy open-plan office on the fourth floor of the Paddington Green tower. "But since I'm chained to a desk, and you're the only federal agent I know, well, there's nothing I can do but meddle. When Pendulum broke into Riley Cotton's place he did something to the machines Cotton was running. This is way beyond my technical capabilities, but our cyber crime team analyzed the machines. Cotton was a hacker, and it seems Pendulum saw some value in his network. He used the back doors Cotton had created to embed a dormant application on dozens of enterprise servers around the world: banks, corporate communications, government networks, that sort of thing. Our cyber guys say Riley Cotton was one of the best they've seen, and they kept his network running; it's become a kind of training playground for them. They've figured out most of Cotton's stuff, but the application Pendulum implanted is next level.

They haven't been able to crack it, so they've been monitoring the network for activity. The dormant application was triggered a little over fifteen minutes ago. It's relaying data packets through a command chain that ends in the States."

"Where?" Ash asked.

"Our cyber guys say it's coming from a Facebook data facility in Twin Lakes."

"Any idea what it's doing?" Ash asked.

"Not a clue. At the moment it's just running data," Bailey replied. "But according to the geeks on this side of the pond, combining Facebook with this backdoor network means the application is connected to almost two billion machines. Like I said, this information is coming through our official liaisons, but I wanted to make sure it hits the ground fast."

"Got it," Ash assured him. "Thanks."

"DS Bailey," Wallace began.

"Call me Pat," Bailey interjected, sensing the awkwardness in Wallace's voice.

"Pat," Wallace continued. "I just wanted to say thank you. Without Salamander's help and Agent Ash's protection, I wouldn't have made it."

"When this is all over, you can buy me a beer," Bailey suggested.

"We'd better get going," Ash advised.

"I'm in the office if you need anything," Bailey offered.

"Keep us posted," Ash suggested. "Ask for Agent Parker, he'll know how to get ahold of me."

"Good luck," Bailey replied.

"Thanks. We'll talk soon," Ash said, hanging up. "Help me grab this stuff," she told Wallace, indicating the Pendulum files on her desk.

She and Wallace gathered the folders and set off toward Parker, who was on the phone. He gave Ash an incredulous look when she took his phone and cut him off.

"What the—" Parker began.

"We caught a break," Ash interrupted. "A British cop I know just called with information that Pendulum is running an illicit computer program from a data center in Wisconsin."

Parker looked blank. "So?" he asked.

"You remember what Pendulum said when we were on the roof?" Wallace asked Ash. "He said it was a test. I thought he meant a test of your courage or loyalty or something like that, but what if it was literally a test of the technology? What if he was testing a virus?"

Ash's eyes widened as she understood the significance of Wallace's words. "Call Hector," she instructed Parker. "Tell him I need a Bureau jet gassed and ready to fly. And I'm gonna need a police escort to the airport."

"You're not going anywhere," Parker told her.

Ash squared up to him and put her face within a hair's breadth of his. "Look down," she advised.

Parker slowly lowered his eyes to see a pistol in Ash's hand, the barrel pressed against his gut. Ash signaled him not to draw any attention to the situation.

"My gun," he said weakly. "How'd you—"

"My career is over," Ash interrupted. "So I can take any heat I need to. You might as well use that to your advantage," she counseled. "You've got one dead Facebook executive and another held hostage. We've got a backdoor network running from one of their data centers. And a killer who has developed a virus that destroys every machine in its path. Any of this starting to worry you?"

"No, that's impossible," Parker shook his head incredulously. "You're talking about billions of systems."

"All connected," Ash pointed out. "People have been trying to do this for years. You know what the Foundation did to First Atlantic and Square Pillar. You think someone like Max Byrne couldn't figure out a way to replicate it on a larger scale?"

"Maybe," Parker conceded.

"We're gonna need a police escort to La Guardia," Ash reiterated. "And I'll need a phone," she said as she took Parker's.

"Hey!" he objected.

"Thanks. You're a real sport." Ash smiled at Parker, before turning to Wallace. "You coming?"

Wallace nodded and followed her across the room. He had no intention of straying too far from this formidable woman.

"My gun?" Parker called after them.

"I'm gonna need that too," Ash shouted back.

Wallace glanced behind him and saw Parker borrow a phone from a nearby agent. "How do you know he isn't going to report you?" he asked.

"Parker might be a butt kisser, but he's smart," Ash replied. "He knows that if I'm right he can ride some of the glory, and if I'm wrong he can say I threatened him with a gun and feed me to the wolves."

"Did you really think you could requisition a Bureau jet? You're suspended." Hector's stern voice was clear above a steady hum of engine noise. He was en route to California, probably somewhere over the Midwest.

"This hostage situation is bullshit, Hector. There's a much bigger play," Ash countered, leaning against the steps of a Cessna CE-750 Citation X, which had been gassed and prepped at Parker's request. Despite the rush-hour traffic, the NYPD escort had gotten them from Police Plaza to La Guardia in a shade under thirty minutes.

"What do you think I'm gonna do here?" Hector asked.

"I think you're gonna cut me some slack," Ash replied. "Because you know my instincts are good. I gave you Max Byrne, Hector. You wouldn't even be on your way to California if it wasn't for me."

Hector fell silent.

"You can't afford to run the risk that I'm right," Ash added. "Because if I am . . ." she left the consequences hanging.

"Okay," Hector said finally. "But you keep me informed every step of the way, you hear?"

"I hear," Ash responded reassuringly.

"Give me a couple of minutes to make the call," Hector advised before he hung up.

Ash turned to Wallace, who shuffled on the runway and rubbed his hands together in an attempt to keep warm. "We're good," she told him.

"You're unbelievable," Wallace said honestly. "I've never known anyone so good at getting her own way."

Ash felt a pang of shame. She smiled uncomfortably at Wallace, who was oblivious to the fact that his words were double edged: just as much insult as compliment. Ash's father had left her many terrible legacies, including his ability to read and manipulate people. It was second nature to her, but whenever she paused to reflect on how easily she was able to exploit people, she felt the stigma that was attached to everything about her father.

"Hey, Agent Ash," a voice called out behind her, and she turned to see Buck Southwell, a Bureau pilot, lean out of the cabin. "You've been cleared."

"Thanks."

"Storm's closed Twin Lakes, so we're gonna have to go to Kenosha," Southwell added.

Ash nodded, but as she started up the steps, Parker's phone rang, so she paused to answer it. "Ash," she said.

"It's Parker. I've called the data center. On-site security says there's no unusual activity. The storm means they're running a skeleton crew, but nothing's going on out there."

"Okay, thanks," Ash acknowledged, somewhat deflated.

"You want me to send in local PD?" Parker asked.

"No. I don't want to tip Pendulum that we're wise to what he's doing," Ash said. "Tell them to set up a command station somewhere nearby, but have them do it quietly."

"Okay," Parker replied. "I'll keep you posted."

Ash hung up. "Let's go," she told Wallace, who followed her aboard the jet. Ash pulled up the airstair that was built into the door, sealed the cabin, and took her seat as the aircraft's twin engines started turning.

54

The Gulfstream V touched down at 8:37 a.m. Pacific Standard Time and taxied to a vacant stand in the northernmost reaches of San Francisco International Airport, near the huge flight support building. Hector, Nelson, and Hale disembarked and hurried toward a waiting convoy of vehicles: two gray Ford Expeditions, two San Francisco PD black-and-whites, and three California Highway Patrol Harley-Davidson Electra Glides. An earnest, athletic man in a black suit stepped forward and extended his hand.

"Agent Solomon," he said. "I'm Special Agent Casey Sommers. Assistant SAIC Dillon has asked me to get you to the scene. SSA Alvarez is already on-site."

"Good to meet you, Agent Sommers," Hector replied. "This is Agent Hale and Agent Nelson."

Sommers shook hands with Hale and Nelson before ushering them toward the waiting vehicles. "Your team can ride in the follow vehicle," he suggested to Hector.

Hale and Nelson climbed into the rear Expedition while Sommers and Hector boarded the lead SUV. Moments later, the convoy rolled out of the airfield along North Access Road, which skirted San Francisco Bay. Two of the CHP bikes sped ahead, sirens blaring, to clear a path through the rush-hour traffic.

"We had any more contact?" Hector asked Sommers, as the driver swung the speeding vehicle onto I-380.

"No, sir," Sommers replied with a shake of his head. "Negotiator has tried, but the suspect is refusing any further comms until you're at the scene."

"What kind of support do we have up there?"

"Full tactical unit," Sommers answered. "Plus SWAT. Agent Dillon wants to talk you through the options himself."

Hector nodded, and grabbed the handhold to steady himself as the Expedition swerved around a slow-moving semi.

"Sorry about that, folks," the driver said, glancing in the rearview.

"You only need to apologize if you hit something," Hector advised with a smile.

"Ain't gonna happen," the driver shot back confidently as he pushed the Ford along the highway.

The convoy cut onto I-280 and sped along the path cleared by the Highway Patrol outriders. Hector looked out over the Crystal Springs Reservoir, its surface glittering under the golden sun. He questioned the wisdom of giving Ash another chance but knew that if she did nothing the Bureau would almost certainly hang her out to dry. Hitting a home run was her only hope of redemption, and there was no way she could do that chained up in Police Plaza. The qualities that had led to her demotion and the current disciplinary investigation were the very traits that had enabled her to break this case. Without her determination and willingness to risk everything, there was no way they would have figured out that the man in the Cromwell Center wasn't really Max Byrne, and the perpetrator of the so-called Pendulum killings might never have been identified. The pressure she'd put on Max Byrne had forced him to change MO, and, instead of killing Dan Alosi, he was now trying to use him as leverage. Ash had at least one saved life to her name.

Fifteen minutes later, the convoy turned off the 280 and wound its way up Alpine Road. Thick banks of trees lined either side, some deciduous, their bare branches casting sharp shadows, others, like the interspersed redwoods, evergreen and heavy with spiny needles. Hector spied houses hidden behind the trees, and as they climbed the hill, the estates became more expansive and the homes increasingly secluded. The convoy turned onto Westridge Road for a short run before making a left onto Cresta Via, where a security guard waved them past a gatehouse. The Expedition slowed after about half a mile, and when they rounded the next bend, Hector saw why.

A fleet of local news trucks lined one side of the street, and a small crowd of residents mingled with reporters eager to relay speculative interviews back to their anchors. The CHP outriders peeled off and the Expedition carried on. The driver sounded his horn and the crowd parted to reveal a line of uniformed San Francisco police officers who stood behind temporary barriers and maintained the integrity of the scene. A couple of officers pulled one of the barriers aside to allow the two Fords through.

The road ended in a small turning circle half a mile farther on. A narrow driveway snaked into the trees, and the SFPD officer who stood guard signaled Hector's driver to continue. A couple hundred yards later, the driveway widened before terminating in an expansive graveled parking area that lay in front of a large white concrete house. Hector immediately noticed that heavy steel shutters covered every door and window. The driveway was crowded with a fleet of vehicles that had spilled into the surrounding yard: unmarked sedans and SUVs, San Francisco and Palo Alto black-and-whites, an ambulance, a fire department truck, an SFPD SWAT truck, and two gleaming white Santa Clara County sheriff's cars.

Hector jumped out of the Expedition as it pulled to a halt, and Hale and Nelson joined him as he followed Sommers across the driveway and down a small path running between the house and the abundant garden that encircled it. The shutters along this side of the house were all down, and as they rounded the corner, Hector saw that the rear windows and doors were similarly sealed. Sommers led them across a patio to a large section of lawn that was home to the mobile command unit, a battleship-gray ten-wheel truck that had been driven up a fire access road that lay to the rear of the property. Groups of law enforcement officers stood outside the large vehicle, some sheltering in the alcove created by the truck's expanded fore and aft compartments.

Sommers ushered Hector toward a group of men and women clustered around a Magliner. Hector recognized Alvarez.

"Art," he called out.

"Sir," Alvarez acknowledged, returning the greeting. He turned to the men and women standing with him. "Assistant SAIC Hector

Solomon, this is Assistant SAIC Dillon, San Francisco Field Office; Captain Reeves, SWAT commander; Undersheriff Michelle Hawkins, with Santa Clara County; Lieutenant Lianna Coleman, Palo Alto PD; Commander Dalton Freeman, San Francisco PD; and Assistant Deputy Chief Russell Mosley, San Francisco Fire Department. Lead negotiator is Special Agent Jeb Franks. He's in the command unit."

Hector turned his attention to a large field monitor on the Magliner, which displayed an infrared image of the interior of the house and showed two warm bodies somewhere near the heart of the building. The two men were seated on chairs in a small room that was packed with supplies. "What have we got here?" he asked.

"Deputy Chief Mosley provided a thermal imaging rescue camera to give us eyes inside," Agent Dillon replied. He was a tall, clean-cut man with dark hair and the intensely frank demeanor of a surgeon. "The place is more of a fortress than a home. Shutters are hardened steel: bullet and blast proof."

"We can get through them," Reeves, the grizzled SWAT commander, assured the group.

"But it'll make a lot of noise and give Byrne plenty of time to kill his hostage," Dillon added.

"Where are they?" Hector pointed at the screen.

"Panic room," Alvarez replied. "We pulled the architect's plans. It's a completely self-contained unit with its own air filtration system, three-foot reinforced concrete walls, and a Burton Defense armored door."

"Shit," Hector sighed. "Let's find out what he wants."

Dillon nodded and led Hector into the mobile command unit. Alvarez followed, while Hale and Nelson waited by the Magliner with the rest of the command team.

"This is Special Agent Franks," Dillon said, introducing Hector to one of the field agents who sat in front of the banks of communications and surveillance equipment that lined either side of the cabin. "Assistant Special Agent in Charge Hector Solomon."

"Good to meet you, sir," Franks said.

"Likewise," Hector replied. "You want to give him a call?"

Franks nodded and lifted the receiver of his field phone, which was preprogrammed to dial one number. There was a short delay while the line connected, and then Hector heard the ringing tone on the command unit speaker system.

"Yes?" came a man's voice.

"Agent Solomon is here," Franks said. "I need proof of life before I put him on."

There was a pause before they heard a nervous, hesitant voice. "This is Dan Alosi. I'm still alive."

Franks looked at one of his colleagues farther along the command unit and received a thumbs-up confirming the hostage's identity.

"Okay," Franks said into the field phone. "The next voice you hear will be Agent Solomon's."

Hector took the phone. "This is Agent Solomon. Who am I speaking to?"

"They call me Pendulum, Agent Solomon. I'm the one you want."

"And what do you want?" Hector asked.

"A simpler life. I'm willing to trade Dan Alosi for my freedom. I want a fully fueled Dreamliner ready to fly from San Francisco International."

"I'll need to take this up the chain of command," Hector explained.

"Take your time, Agent Solomon," Pendulum advised calmly. "Mr. Alosi and I are very comfortable. We have three weeks' supply of food and water, so we're not in any hurry."

The line clicked dead, and Hector rubbed his temples.

"This guy's good," Dillon observed.

"Byrne's ex–Special Forces," Alvarez noted. "We can't use a food delivery to cover an assault."

"And we can't blast our way in without giving him time to kill the hostage," Dillon added. "Gas won't work because the panic room has its own air system. We could wait it out, tell him we got the jet, and try and take him in transit?"

Hector shook his head. "I don't think so. It would be a death sentence for Mr. Alosi. Listen, the attorney general won't take the deal, but we've got to run it up the chain anyway. See what the AG says," he instructed Alvarez, before turning to Dillon. "In the meantime, we need to sit down with SWAT and figure out our minimal-loss scenario."

Hector stepped out of the command unit and returned to the Magliner. He looked at the fuzzy infrared image on the monitor and couldn't shake the feeling that Max Byrne was staring directly at him.

55

Wallace gazed out of the window as the Citation made its approach toward Kenosha Airport. He and Ash had spent the flight studying the Pendulum files and Wallace now had a growing feeling of unease. Bonnie Mann had triggered his discomfort. Before her gambling habit took over her life, she'd been a manager at You-Tube. Lost in the grip of her addiction, Mann had finally been fired when her boss discovered that she'd concealed her failure to respond to more than three thousand user complaints. The Bureau had concentrated on Bonnie's gambling, exploring links to organized crime, but it was her job that nagged at Wallace. An ugly idea began to form in his mind, and Wallace looked to discredit it with information from Ken Pallo's file, but he was only halfway through his search when the pilot announced they were beginning their approach.

The jet descended rapidly through the cornflower-blue sky, sweeping low over the icy waters of Lake Michigan. Wisconsin had been hit particularly hard by the snowstorm. Huge plates of ice shifted around the southwestern edge of the vast lake, and as they flew over the shoreline, Wallace saw drifts that had been swept as high as the cars abandoned along a deluged highway. The road ran parallel to a narrow beach and a couple of snowplows were navigating around the haphazardly parked cars, trying to clear a path. Neatly planned pockets of suburban housing gave way to white fields, and the jet flew over a clear road, low enough for Wallace to see the faces of drivers as they looked up. About a mile to his left, a collection of cars clustered beneath the ubiquitous golden arches, and the sight of a McDonald's made his stomach rumble; it had been over twelve hours since the curled sandwich he'd wolfed down at Police Plaza.

The Citation's wheels kissed the runway and smoothly slowed to taxi speed. The pilot brought the aircraft to a halt at a stand opposite Kenosha's tiny terminal, a single-story redbrick building with slatted windows. The pilot emerged from the cockpit and opened the hatch, sending freezing air into the cabin. Wallace and Ash pulled their coats tight.

"Kenosha," the pilot announced.

"Thanks," Ash replied, descending the short run of steps.

Wallace nodded his thanks at the pilot and followed her out. A man in a heavy blue parka waved at them from outside the terminal and hurried over, and as he neared, Wallace saw the letters "FBI" embroidered on his coat.

"Special Agent Ash?" the man asked, and when Ash nodded confirmation, he introduced himself. "Special Agent Lloyd Dorsey. Agent Parker gave Milwaukee a heads-up. I'm here to offer our support."

"And make sure we don't screw up on your patch?" Ash smiled as she shook Dorsey's gloved hand. "This is John Wallace; he's a witness under federal protection."

Wallace took Dorsey's hand. A thick crop of blond hair poked out from under the parka's hood. Dorsey had the easy good looks and beaming smile of a college quarterback at the top of his game.

"Nice to meet you," Wallace said.

"English," Dorsey observed. "I love the accent." Full of patronizing bonhomie and easy charm, Dorsey gave Wallace a hearty pat on the shoulder.

Wallace liked him instantly.

"My car's out front," Dorsey advised, turning for the terminal.

The clock inside the quiet building said 11:03, and as they walked through, Wallace saw Ash reset her watch.

"Central Time," she informed him. "These guys are a little behind us," she added with a wry smile.

"Gives us a chance to learn from your mistakes," Dorsey countered.

Dorsey's white GMC Terrain was parked next to a high drift of snow outside the building. Wallace and Ash followed him through a narrow gulley that had been cut through the drift and clambered into the car.

"If you guys are hungry, there's some food in back," Dorsey said.

Wallace found a large brown paper bag in the footwell, and opened it to discover a bounty of sandwiches, snacks, and drinks.

"I checked with Kenosha PD," Dorsey said as he pulled away from the terminal. "They got your request through Agent Parker, but they can't afford the manpower on a speculative investigation. All their people are working a missing person case. A local sheriff vanished this morning, so they've given us one officer. He's setting up at the Twin Lakes facility."

"Okay," Ash nodded. "We need to keep this low-key anyhow."

"You really think this Pendulum guy is doing something out here?" Dorsey asked skeptically as he scanned the snowbound rural landscape.

"I'd bet my life on it," Ash replied.

"Okay, I think we've got a viable way in," Reeves said, laying a large building plan on the Magliner. "Alosi's architect put us in touch with Decker Systems, who installed the house security and panic room. The whole place is networked and they've given us access to the operating system. We run an override code and everything opens up. Two teams, one through the front and the other through the garden door here." Reeves signaled an entrance on the plan.

As the rest of the group continued to listen to Reeves's plan, Hector looked around to see Alvarez signaling him from the command unit. Hector withdrew from Reeves's briefing and joined Alvarez in a quiet section of the garden a few yards away.

"AG won't go for the deal," Alvarez informed Hector.

Hector nodded. "Makes sense. It wasn't much of an offer."

"I got a call from Parker," Alvarez added. "Chris is at Kenosha, on her way to check out the Twin Lakes facility."

"Keep me posted," Hector replied.

Alvarez nodded and headed back to the command unit while Hector returned to the group beside the Magliner. Reeves and Dillon looked at him expectantly.

"Attorney general refused the deal," Hector revealed. "We go in and get him," he said firmly, looking at the infrared image of Max Byrne on the monitor.

The journey to Twin Lakes took three-quarters of an hour, most of which Wallace spent gratefully digging into Dorsey's supplies. The *Nightfile* report and the media coverage of the Pendulum killings had given Ash a certain notoriety, so Dorsey was keen to talk to her about the case and Wallace's role in bringing everything to light. He was impressed by Wallace's resourcefulness and endurance, but the memories troubled Wallace because they always led back to one place: the office on Victoria Street where Connie had died in his arms. The ugly idea that had been born on the flight from New York was growing into a horrific abscess that festered inside him. Wallace looked at Ash and Dorsey and wondered how he could possibly air his dark imaginings. *You're being paranoid*, he told himself.

He tried to suppress his thoughts and focus on his surroundings. Twin Lakes wasn't far from Kenosha, but the snow slowed everything down. Sixtieth Street was limited to one lane in places, and Dorsey had to give way to oncoming vehicles. As they made slow progress west, Wallace was struck by how flat the terrain was. When the tree line thinned, the distant horizon wasn't broken by anything taller than a house or an aerial mast. They climbed a couple of gentle hills as they neared Twin Lakes, but these only seemed like halfhearted attempts to break the languid Wisconsin landscape. Dorsey skirted the edge of town and drove south past a couple of farmhouses and something called the La Salette Shrine, a collection of low buildings obscured by tall evergreens.

A white "F" on a blue background was all that announced the Facebook facility. The single letter was embossed on the side of a gatehouse a hundred feet west of Wilmot Avenue. A high wall enclosed the property and stretched into the distance in both directions. Dorsey turned off the road onto a clear, impeccably laid drive that was smoother than anything the county could offer. He rolled down his window and produced his identification as a uniformed security guard stepped out to greet them.

"Special Agent Dorsey, FBI," Dorsey said. "I understand you have an Officer Finley on-site."

"Follow the road around. There's a fire access slip that branches off to the right. He's about a quarter of a mile down," the guard informed Dorsey.

"Thanks," he replied as the guard raised the gate, and the GMC rolled forward.

The two-lane road wound between copses of snow-laden evergreen trees. Dorsey stopped when they came to a fork. Directly ahead, no more than a mile away, they saw the sprawling Facebook data facility, a vast, low concrete building a quarter of a mile long and almost as wide. In front of the building was a parking lot for about a hundred cars, most of which was under snow. There were twenty or so vehicles parked in a small clear section directly opposite the main entrance, which was located in the northern third of the building. Tinted windows stretched north from the entrance to the upper end of the building. The larger southern section was entirely windowless.

Dorsey turned right and followed the narrow fire road that ran behind a line of trees. About a quarter of a mile up, Wallace saw a black-and-white cruiser parked in a turnout. Dorsey pulled in behind it, and a huge uniformed officer unfolded himself from the police car and sauntered over. Dorsey and Ash exited the GMC, and Wallace followed them out.

"Officer Finley?" Dorsey asked. "I'm Special Agent Dorsey. This is Special Agent Ash, and John Wallace. Special Agent Ash is calling the shots."

"Todd Finley," the bearlike officer introduced himself as they shook hands. "I checked in with Wayne Roach, who runs site security. He offered to set us up inside the building, but your colleague was very specific."

"We don't want to risk alerting anyone to our presence," Ash explained.

"Okay," Finley said, shrugging. "We've got a pretty clear line on the parking lot and entrance from here," he added, indicating a narrow gap in the tree line. "Site is running a skeleton staff because of the weather, but apart from Roach and the gate guard, nobody else knows we're here."

"That's good work, Officer Finley," Ash observed.

"What do we do now?" Dorsey asked.

"You and I are going to take a look inside," Ash replied, starting for Dorsey's SUV.

Wallace moved to follow, but Ash shook her head.

"You gotta stay here, John. I'm not putting you in harm's way. Officer Finley, you make sure you keep this man safe."

Finley nodded and drew alongside Wallace. After everything they'd been through together, Ash could tell that the Englishman was hurt by his exclusion. She might be reckless and hardheaded, but even she knew there was nothing to be gained by dragging Wallace into a potentially dangerous situation. She climbed into the SUV as Dorsey started the engine. He executed a sharp U-turn and moments later they were rolling along the access road toward the huge facility.

56

Ash had kept him alive and now she was gone. Wallace could not help but feel vulnerable as he watched the SUV disappear through the trees.

"All units, all units," a dispatcher said urgently, her voice crackling from Finley's radio. "Be on the lookout for a blue Chevrolet Express van, Illinois license number 'H' hotel, two, three, fiver, fiver, niner, two. The driver of the vehicle is wanted in connection with the abduction of Sheriff Douglas Simms."

Wallace looked down at the parking lot and noticed a blue van near the building. He squinted to read the license plate as Finley, who had also noticed the vehicle, leaned through the window of his black-and-white and grabbed his radio.

"Dispatch, this is Finley," the uniformed officer said into his radio.

"Copy that, Todd, you still up at Twin Lakes?" the dispatcher replied.

"Sure am, Janice," Finley responded. "You got any more intel on that van? What's the connection to Simms?"

"Gerry found Doug's car. They checked the dash cam and it shows Doug pulling the van over for a routine stop. When he approaches the vehicle, he's pulled into it," Janice explained. "The van sped off with Doug inside."

"I've got eyes on the van, Janice," Finley informed her. "It's right here in the parking lot."

"Copy that," Janice replied. "All units, all units, proceed to Walton Avenue, Twin Lakes. Suspect vehicle on-site."

★ ★ ★

Hector hurried to join Hale in his assigned place at the rear of the group that would enter through the front of the building. There were six SWAT officers in black body armor, each carrying a Heckler & Koch MP5. They were to be followed by Dillon, Hale, and Hector. Reeves was leading the second team, which would assault the rear entrance, and he had Alvarez and Nelson with him.

"Move into position." Reeves's voice came over the tiny radio that was pressed into Hector's ear. He looked across the garden to see the SWAT commander and his team stalk toward the back door, which was still covered by a steel shutter. Hector followed his SWAT squad around the side of the building to the front door, which was also sealed.

"We're in position," whispered McDaniel, the officer leading Hector's team.

"Copy that," came Reeves's voice. "Run the override program."

Somewhere in the command unit one of Dillon's techs was using the information they'd been given on the house's security operating system to override the settings. Moments later, the shutter over the front door shot up.

"Go! Go! Go!" McDaniel commanded.

Two SWAT officers were prepared to use a battering ram, but they dropped the heavy implement when they saw that the front door had been blasted off its hinges. The squad surged into the building, moving in pairs, running a cursory cover-and-clear formation, with the FBI agents sweeping up behind them. They hurried toward the heart of the house; infrared had already told them where the target was located.

Hector watched the armor-clad men move swiftly through the expansive living room into a whitewashed corridor that led to the bedrooms. Halfway along the corridor was a branch that ran down to the panic room. McDaniel and his squad arrived there moments before Reeves, whose team had blocked any possible escape through the rear of the building. Reeves waved McDaniel and his team down the branching corridor, which ended in a single solid-steel door. McDaniel moved ahead and pushed the heavy door, which gave at his touch. The override program had worked, but Hector saw McDaniel look back in surprise; he had obviously expected some resistance.

McDaniel raised his MP5 and flung the door wide open. Hector craned to peer over the heads of the SWAT officers in front of him, and saw two seated men. The first was an elderly Latino man in a checked shirt. A gag covered his mouth, and his arms and legs were bound to his chair. The second man was wearing Pendulum's mask and body armor, but instead of standing to fight, he remained seated, struggling against bonds that tied him to his chair. *Why would Byrne restrain himself?* Hector asked inwardly as he suddenly realized that something was very wrong, and that the old man's muffled cries, which could hardly be heard through his gag, were warnings. Hector followed the old man's gaze as his eyes darted frantically around the panic room, desperately searching for hope among the half-dozen shoebox-sized bombs placed around him. Hector's blood curdled and his heart skipped a long, hard beat when he saw receiver rigs wired to each of the powerful devices.

"Bomb!" McDaniel yelled, but even as he saw the man turn and start running, Hector knew that it was too late. He looked at Alvarez's dismayed face as he too realized that death was upon them.

Inside the panic room, the rigs received simultaneous signals that activated the detonators and ignited the thermobaric explosive packed within the six devices. A huge blast tore through the room, shredding the walls, and a searing firestorm shot along the natural chimney created by the corridor. The last thing Hector saw was the approaching vortex of flame engulfing the bodies of the brave men and women ahead of him. Like them, a split second later Hector was consumed by fire.

57

It took Dorsey less than a minute to drive to the Facebook building. As they exited the GMC, Ash's phone rang; it was Parker.

"Hey?" Ash said.

"I've got Wallace for you," Parker told her, before patching through his call.

"John?" Ash peered up at the tree line where Wallace and Finley were concealed.

"You see the blue van?" Wallace asked.

"Yeah," Ash replied.

"It was used in the abduction of that sheriff. Officer Finley says it looks like a routine traffic stop that went wrong," Wallace told her. "Be careful."

"Thanks," Ash said, suddenly on edge. She hung up, pocketed the phone, and slowly drew her gun. "Van," she advised a puzzled Dorsey.

He drew his sidearm and the two FBI agents crept toward the vehicle. There was movement inside as a masked figure pulled back the inner curtain and slid into the driver's seat. Ash was aghast to see Pendulum, and her mind struggled to comprehend how he could be here. Dorsey started shooting as the engine roared and the van lurched forward.

Wallace peered through the trees and watched the van speed toward Dorsey, who was no more than twenty feet away. He couldn't see the driver, but he did see Dorsey fire a volley of shots, which hit the oncoming vehicle. Dorsey tried to run out of the way but slipped on a patch of black ice and went down, flinging his hands up in a pathetic attempt to prevent the van driving over him. Wallace watched in horror as Dorsey's body bucked and twisted like an enraged bronco when the wheels rolled over it, before it fell utterly still.

"We've got to get down there!" Wallace yelled at Finley, who nodded. Both men turned and sprinted toward the police cruiser.

Ash fired at the van, which gathered speed as it drove toward her. Pendulum ducked as bullets pierced the windshield, and Ash turned and ran toward the building, sprinting across the parking lot as the engine roared behind her. She made it to the glass doors, which slid open to allow her into the large lobby, and raced toward a horrified security guard who sat behind a desk against the far wall. As she ran, she turned to see the reason for his horror; the van mounted the sidewalk outside the building and smashed through the plate-glass doors, careening across the lobby toward her. Ash attempted to leap out of the way, but she was hit by the Chevrolet, and the impact sent her into a flying roll that came to an abrupt halt when her head smashed against the lobby wall, knocking her cold.

Finley pulled up beside Dorsey's body. As Wallace hurried from the car, he heard a loud Klaxon inside the building and looked toward the wrecked entrance. The glass frontage had been shattered and the lobby was obscured by a thick cloud of smoke, but even through the dust, Wallace could see the warm orange light of a fire glowing within the darkness. He turned to Finley, who crouched beside Dorsey's mangled body, his fingers pressed against the FBI agent's neck.

"He's dead," Finley said, before speaking into his radio. "Dispatch, this is two-one. We have a federal agent down at the scene. Suspect has fled into the building. I am in pursuit."

"Two-one, this is dispatch," Janice's voice came over the radio. "Todd, the chief wants you to wait for backup."

Wallace shook his head. "We can't wait," he said. "Ash is in there."

Finley nodded and set off across the parking lot, walking between the tracks laid by the Chevrolet. Wallace watched for a moment, then picked up Dorsey's pistol, which had been thrown into the snow a few feet from his body, and concealed the gun in his coat pocket as he hurried to catch up with the police officer.

Finley did not try to dissuade Wallace. He simply nodded slowly and drew his sidearm as they stepped over broken glass and entered the dark lobby. Dust and smoke filled the air and debris was scattered everywhere. Wallace could see the red brake lights of the van at the far end of the room, and he followed Finley toward them. The rear door of the Chevrolet was ajar, and Finley aimed his pistol at the gap as he stepped through the hazy smoke toward the vehicle. Wallace peered up the side of the vehicle and saw a man, a security guard, crushed between the hood of the van and the concrete wall. The man stared at Wallace with lifeless eyes as a small fire burned in the engine beneath him. Wallace looked away in disgust and joined Finley by the Chevrolet's rear doors. The police officer kept his gun poised as he pulled one of the doors open.

Wallace peered inside to see the interior of the van was lined with communications and surveillance equipment. Some of it was scattered over a body that lay on the flatbed, but most of the video screens were in place. They broadcast an image of the same location from different vantage points. It looked like a battle scene from a war movie, but Wallace realized it was actually a house that had been partially demolished and was on fire. Strewn about the sun-drenched garden that surrounded the white concrete building were the bodies of fallen police officers and FBI agents. Wallace stood, mesmerized by the horror, while Finley checked on the debris-covered body in the van. It was a man wearing a sheriff's uniform, and Wallace guessed it was the missing Doug Simms. Finley turned the sheriff's head to reveal a single gunshot wound drilled through his right temple.

Wallace heard movement outside the van. He jumped off the flatbed, ran over to a pile of debris, and pulled at ragged pieces of wood to reveal an injured man stirring underneath.

"Get out, get away," the dazed, bloody man slurred quietly, forcing Wallace to concentrate on his voice. "Bomb."

The word shocked Wallace and he followed the dazed man's eyes as they focused on the van. Finley was by the doors, trying to pull the sheriff's body from the vehicle.

"Hey!" Wallace yelled toward the van. "There's a bomb!"

The startled police officer fixated on something inside the vehicle, and, as Wallace followed his gaze, he saw what had caught Finley's attention. Pressed up against the partition separating the back of the van from the cab was a gray brick wired to a timer that flashed 00:07.

"Move!" Finley yelled, as he started running.

Wallace pulled the injured man to his feet, and Finley grabbed hold of both of them and bundled them through the lobby. As they ran haphazardly, stumbling over debris, Wallace willed time to slow, but he could do nothing to prevent the inevitable. They were six feet from the entrance when the countdown cycled to zero, triggering the device. The powerful bomb exploded and the blast tore through the van, twisting and shredding the chassis. The initial shockwave was immediately followed by a furious firestorm that incinerated the vehicle and surged through the lobby, scorching everything in its path. Wallace, Finley, and the dazed stranger were lifted off their feet and hurled through the entrance into the parking lot, where they landed heavily on the icy ground.

Wallace recovered first and turned to peer toward the entrance. The violent firestorm engulfing the lobby died away almost as quickly as it had begun, and the sprinkler system activated, unleashing a heavy shower of water onto the pockets of flame that glowed in the smoke-filled gloom. Wallace turned to Finley, who exhaled deeply as he got to his feet. Neither man said anything about how close they'd come to death; their stunned expressions conveyed more than words ever could.

"He's going to kill me," the injured stranger cried out in despair.

Wallace and Finley hoisted the unsteady, punch-drunk man to his feet. His shirt was crusted with old blood, his face swollen with the marks of a multitude of injuries, and he was shaking.

"I have to get out of here," the man said when he finally came to his senses. "He's going to kill me."

"Who are you?" Wallace asked.

"Dan Alosi," the trembling man replied. "He kidnapped me. Made it look like a home invasion. But he'd already been in the house. Set everything up. He brought me here on a private jet. He hacked into my security camera system. He's been watching every move the feds made. He set up a relay from my home line to a satellite phone, so they'd think we were inside. I wanted to warn them, but he would've killed me. He kidnapped a couple of innocent men . . . I think they were gardeners. He dressed one of them in his suit. He wanted the feds to think we were in my panic room. They're all dead! He detonated those bombs without even blinking. He killed them all." Alosi broke down at the memory of his experience.

"Why's he here?" Wallace asked, willing the man to compose himself.

"I don't know, but he wanted access to the main server room," Alosi replied eventually. "He got the security architecture from Zach. He beat me until I gave him the systems structure. He's planning something, but I don't know what. He's just been sitting in the parking lot, watching my house and playing the feds. He went nuts when he saw the woman."

"Ash?" Wallace asked.

"I don't know," Alosi replied. "I think she was a fed. I saw him dragging her further into the building after he'd knocked her over with the van. I couldn't do anything. I have to get away. He kept me alive in case there was a problem with the network, but he doesn't need me anymore. That bomb was supposed to kill me," he added fearfully.

"We've got to go after Ash," Wallace told Finley.

The huge police officer nodded. "Sir, can you walk?"

Alosi looked at them uncertainly. "I think so."

"I'm gonna need you to wait in my car," Finley told him. "Backup is on its way."

Wallace watched Alosi limp toward the police cruiser before turning to Finley.

"You should wait with him," the huge police officer suggested.

Wallace shook his head and gave Finley a grim stare. He'd already lost too much to this maniac. He owed Ash his life and had no intention of letting Pendulum take her.

"Let's go," he said as he headed toward the smoke-filled building.

58

Dorsey. The man's name was the first thing to hit Ash's mind when she came to. She was moving, being dragged into a cold blue hell where the Devil was screaming an ugly tune. Ash's eyes focused and she saw her own feet, her heels trailing limply against a smooth polished floor. She was in a narrow alley, flanked on either side by row after row of server racks, the machines fitted with low-intensity blue lights that made the chill air seem even colder. Her hearing kicked in and she realized that the Devil's scream was a fire alarm, relentless in its urgent call for people to evacuate the building.

Ash tried to gauge the length of the alley but there was no obvious end; the icy lights simply stretched toward the horizon. She looked up to see Pendulum, the man who had murdered Dorsey. He was hunched over her, hands clasped around her chest, half-lifting, half-pulling her backward to some unseen destination. When he glanced down and saw Ash watching him, he dropped her to the floor, drew up his right fist, and punched her square in the face. The fiercely powerful blow sent her reeling, and the blue server lights swirled in a kaleidoscope as the edges of reality frayed and folded in on themselves.

"Fight and you die," came the harsh voice from behind the mask. "Run and you die."

Strong hands forced their way under Ash's arms and clasped together over her breasts, and she lay limp as she was dragged on. Ash's mind was cast adrift in a dazed sea of confusion and she lost track of time and distance.

Her senses found their way back when she was roughly deposited on the floor in the heart of the server farm. There was a clear thirty-foot-square patch that was only broken by four computer terminals that protruded from the gleaming floor like monoliths. As she lay on her back, Ash looked around to see a silhouetted figure at one of the terminals. She tried to focus, but her eyes drifted as though she was in a dream.

"The cops are on their way," she heard Pendulum announce.

"It's nearly done," the silhouetted figure remarked.

"You have to leave. You can't afford to be here when they arrive," Pendulum cautioned. "I can finish it."

"California?" the shadow asked.

"They're gone," Pendulum replied. "The van's destroyed."

"We've done what we had to." The shadow's voice was tinged with regret.

"If I have any trouble getting out, I'll use her for leverage," Pendulum added, gesturing toward Ash.

"She's awake," the dark figure noted.

"Don't worry, she won't be able to talk," Pendulum said, approaching Ash. He swung a mighty punch, driving his fist with such force that when he hit Ash's head, it rebounded against the floor and sent her into dark oblivion.

Finley moved at a deliberate pace, his gun held out ahead of him, and Wallace followed a few steps behind. They were in a long, windowless corridor that stretched out from the lobby. Finley was a few paces from an intersection when a man and a woman ran around the corner and almost barged into him. The startled woman cried out.

"Take it easy," Finley said calmly. "We're not gonna hurt you."

"We need to find the server room," Wallace added.

"Down there," the flustered woman yelled above the Klaxon. She pointed to a corridor that ran off to the right. "The security door at the end."

"Thanks," Finley replied, before starting toward it.

"Here," the woman called out to Wallace as she produced a key card from her pocket and handed it to him. "You'll need this."

The two Facebook employees hurried toward the nearest fire exit as Finley and Wallace stalked on, taking the corridor that led off at a right angle. A heavy, glass-paneled security door lay at the other end, and Wallace could see the low blue lights of dozens of computer servers beyond it. Finley's pace quickened and Wallace hurried after him.

Ash felt the cold floor beneath her and slowly opened her eyes. Lights danced in front of her as she struggled to make sense of the world. She raised a hand to her head and touched a tender bruise. The motion attracted the attention of Pendulum, who stood beside a nearby computer terminal.

"Remember what I told you," he warned.

Ash focused on him, and her quadruple vision diminished to double before it returned to normal.

"You didn't have to kill him," she said.

"Who? The man that was with you?" Pendulum asked.

"He was a good man.".

"They were all good men. Assistant SAIC Hector Solomon, Supervisory Special Agent Arturo Alvarez, Hale, Nelson, all of them," Pendulum replied.

Outwardly, Ash remained impassive, but she felt her innards ripped away by the revelation, and grief swelled in the void they left behind.

"They're all dead," Pendulum said flatly, before rounding on Ash, filled with sudden animosity. "Because you wouldn't back off. Turn every weakness into a strength, that's what the army taught us," he continued more calmly. "The manhunt you instituted was problematic, until I realized I could use it as a lure to get the feds focused on entirely the wrong thing."

"You didn't have to kill them!" Ash protested.

Pendulum crouched beside her and raised his fist. Ash thought he was going to strike her again, but instead he reached out and stroked her cheek with the tips of his gloved fingers. They trailed down her face and came to a halt on her bottom lip, where they lingered for a moment, before they were suddenly withdrawn. Pendulum grabbed at his mask with both hands and pulled it off, revealing his true identity: Max Byrne.

"Sometimes it gets to be too much. Sometimes I just can't breathe in this thing," he observed, drawing close to Ash. "I did have to kill them, Agent Ash. It was the only way to ensure my own survival. Everyone's going to think I died in an explosion at Dan Alosi's house. Nobody will be looking for me anymore. A new identity will leave me free to continue my work."

"Your work? All those people . . ." Ash lamented quietly.

"All those people," Max mocked as he drew within inches of her. "What do you think this is?" He gestured to the vast array of servers surrounding them. "We're at war. We're at war with a machine. A machine that no one asked for. A machine that has marched over the face of the Earth. Billions of narcissists crying out for attention, gratifying their most disgusting urges, destroying all that is beautiful." As Max spoke he grew increasingly agitated. "Do you even know what this is about?" he asked angrily.

"No," Ash replied quietly. "Why don't you tell me?"

The gentle hiss of escaping air sounded like a hurricane when Finley pulled open the pressurized security door. Wallace followed the police officer into the server room, where row after row of computers stretched into the distance, their blue lights glowing like cold eyes, watching as he and Finley crept deeper into the dark cavern. As they moved farther away from the door, Wallace heard the resonant tones of a man's voice.

"Two years ago last September, my sister posted a video on You-Tube," the man said, confirming Wallace's worst fears. "She looked for validation from total strangers and asked them to rate whether she was hot or not."

Wallace recalled the mess he'd been in the night he'd broken up with Connie. He recalled his drunkenness, his rage at hearing that he'd been discredited by the Masterson Inquiry, the self-loathing he'd felt at having pushed Connie from his life.

"They tore her apart," the man continued. The words that followed confirmed his identity. "Six of them, they ganged up on Erin, trolling her with hateful comments, and when she tried to argue with them, they attacked her, humiliated her, hounded her until they'd convinced her that she'd be better off dead."

Max's words stirred Wallace's memory. He had a dim recollection of trawling through YouTube that night, looking for trouble, seeking to spread his misery. He couldn't recall exactly what he'd done, but he remembered becoming so disgusted and enraged that before the night was through, he'd smashed his computer to pieces.

"You know about John Wallace, Kye Walters, and Stewart Huvane," Max said. "There was also Shane Boyce, a financial adviser from Perth; Danielle LeRoy, a stripper from Cape Town; and Joshua Logan, a college student from Gainesville. John Wallace is the only one still alive."

"They couldn't have known what would happen, how fragile Erin was." Wallace recognized Ash's voice, but she sounded weak and fearful.

"We're all just one heartbeat away from death. We're all fragile," Max countered. "They didn't care. They thought they could hide behind their anonymity, but I found them."

"You can't be sure they were responsible," Ash protested.

"Erin's suicide note quoted words they'd used about her. I hacked into her YouTube account and deleted the video, which removed the comments and concealed the role those people played in her death. I didn't want them to be found out. I didn't want them to be shamed, or made to feel guilty. I wanted them to die the way she had. In her note she said she was worthless, that she had nothing to offer the world. Those were the things they'd said about her. They put her in her grave."

"What about the others? Bonnie Mann? Ken Pallo? Zach Holz?" Ash asked.

"Zach Holz was a casualty of war. He had nothing to do with Erin's death. I just needed information from him. But the other two were involved. Bonnie Mann failed to respond to Erin's abuse complaints. Not just from Erin, but from other users who saw what was happening and tried to stop it. Ken Pallo secretly ran a suicide advocacy website, Next Life. Porn wasn't enough for him. He used to get his kicks telling people how to die. My sister went looking for a way to kill herself, and when she found his sick site, Pallo spent hours convincing her that hanging was the answer."

"I'm sorry." Wallace heard the sadness in Ash's voice.

Her response triggered a tremendous sense of remorse, and Wallace's surroundings spiraled into insignificance as he realized his role in the dark events that had destroyed his life. He should have recognized Erin Byrne, but he didn't. He'd devastated an entire family with casual, rage-fueled venom that he'd been too drunk to remember. All of it, everything that had happened, could be laid at his door. *Connie.* Wallace felt his body heave as he suddenly realized the part he had played in Connie's death. His cruelty had set everything in motion. He leaned against a server rack for support as his legs gave way beneath him.

"You okay?" Finley whispered, glancing over his shoulder.

Wallace nodded and pushed himself upright before following the tall policeman farther into the darkness.

59

"I don't need your pity," Max growled as he returned to the computer terminal. "You think this is just about Erin, but you're not thinking big enough. She was the impetus. The final falling snowflake that set the avalanche in motion. Her death got me thinking clearly for the first time. It made me realize I had to bring it all crashing down. I'm going to free people from the grasp of the beast. Free them from the chains that bind them to a life they never wanted."

"This isn't about freedom," Ash countered. "This is murder."

"There is no murder in war!" Max yelled. "I've seen the consequences of our enemies congregating in the shadows of the digital world. I've seen attacks in Paris, New York, London, Boston, all organized from those shadows. Islamic State, Hamas, al-Qaeda. We have given our enemies a strategic weapon to use against us. What I'm doing here will cripple them."

"You'll set the world back thirty years," Ash retorted.

"This world is sick!" Max spat. "Pornography in every bedroom. Gambling in every home. Children watching people being decapitated. Watching other kids being abused and killed. Murdering friends to please a Slender Man. Secret markets for drugs, weapons, body parts. Corporations making hundreds of millions of dollars destroying families, encouraging husbands and wives to cheat on each other. This," Max gestured at the computers that surrounded them, "has brought nothing but evil into the world. And governments sit by and let it happen because they think it makes money, but people are poorer now than they've ever been. The riches of the world are concentrated in the hands of the few."

"People like you," Ash pointed out. "People like your father."

"Don't you talk about my father!" Max snapped.

"You can't reverse progress," Ash said.

"Just because it's new, doesn't mean it's progress." Max calmed himself as he continued to type at the terminal. "Sometimes civilization can take a wrong turn, and when that happens, we need to return to the fork in the road and take a different path."

"None of this will bring Erin back," Ash tried.

"But it will stop the same thing happening to another innocent, Special Agent Ash. Alice—"

"Don't ever call me that," Ash interjected. "How did you find out about me? Those records were sealed."

"Sealed!" Max hissed contemptuously. "Privacy is dead, Agent Ash. Binary lays bare all our secrets. Did Marcel Washington remind you of your father? Is that why he had to die?"

"You can stop this," Ash said quietly, trying to change the subject. "I understand why you're in pain."

"This isn't about my pain. It's about correcting a mistake. Human existence has changed beyond all recognition. The Internet exposes every single one of us to the entire world. All the good. All the evil. None of us were prepared for it. Nobody asked whether we wanted it. It just happened. And we're not ready. We can't cope. A young teenage girl alone in her bedroom, vulnerable, searching for a place in the world, looking for love, for hope, for something to believe in. She's bombarded by a Twitter feed full of vacuous nonsense, by narcissistic Facebook friends timelining the illusion of their perfect lives, by advertisers promising things that they can't possibly deliver. Darkness that previously existed in the concealed corners of the world is all out there in the open, ready to be found by anyone, by that sensitive girl. You think it's not going to change people? All that noise. All that violence. All that evil. There's a mental health epidemic devouring people, making them vulnerable. And when, bewildered by it all and desperate to fit in, that young girl exposes herself to the world, looking for approval, she's hit by a barrage of hateful abuse from people who tell her to kill herself. Strangers who think the world would be better off without her. I'm giving my sister justice."

"This isn't justice," Ash countered.

"I've spent years developing this virus. The dissemination program is compiling. Once it's finished, it will spread through my network and every Facebook account on the planet. All the noise. All the hate. All the evil. Everything will simply stop. Then, in the quiet that follows, we can decide what kind of world we really want. This is justice, Agent Ash."

"The one you uploaded to the Bureau took out communications, power, and security systems," Ash said, looking at the status bar marking the progress of the compiler. It was 5 percent complete. "You'll shut down power stations, hospitals."

"And why are power stations and hospitals online? People need to realize the dangers of a connected world," Max replied. "Sometimes it takes a sharp shock to wake people up, and if some die in the process, well, that will only serve to make the experience more memorable. I'd like to stay, Agent Ash, but this is only the beginning. I must help shape the new world that rises from the ashes." He produced a Beretta M9 from within the folds of his coat.

Ash crawled onto her knees. "Who are you working with?" she asked, gratified to see that the question unsettled her captor.

Max glowered at her and swung the pistol toward her head, his thumb popping the spring-loaded safety switch. Ash didn't wait for his arm to reach the end of its arc. She pushed up and back with all her strength and collided with Max's torso, throwing him off balance. A gunshot rang out and a bullet tore through a nearby rack.

Ash started to run, but her feet were knocked from under her as Max executed a sweeping low kick that brought her tumbling to the floor. She rolled onto her back to look her killer in the face as he drew alongside and raised the Beretta.

Ash flinched when she heard the gunshot, but when she opened her eyes a split second later she saw that Max had been hit in the back. A rapid volley of blasts followed, sending Max flying forward. As he barreled over her, Max turned and unleashed a hail of bullets at his assailant.

Ash sat up and saw Finley, the big police officer, go down with multiple gunshot wounds. She got to her feet and kicked the fallen Max in the head. A second kick sent his pistol flying, and a single thought filled Ash's mind: *reach the gun*. She chased after it as it spun toward the computer terminals. Behind her, Max got to his feet and drew a second Beretta from a holster concealed beneath his coat. He raised it, took aim, and opened fire. Ash felt the scorching agony of a slug slicing through her abdomen, and the force of the shot sent her sprawling, just shy of the fallen pistol. She touched her wound and felt warm liquid on her cold fingertips. She drew them up to her face and saw they were covered in dark-red blood.

Ash realized that her breathing was shallow and fast and wondered whether it was panic or the approach of death. She watched as Max drew near, willing her legs to push her along the floor, to bring her within reach of the pistol, but her feet just slid around ineffectually. *My wiring's fucked*, she thought darkly.

She cast around, desperately searching for a way to stay alive, and caught sight of something between the servers to her left: a pair of eyes at her level. Ash recognized Wallace, his face outlined by blue server light. Max had not seen him, so she had to be careful. When she glanced in Wallace's direction and locked eyes with him, she recognized the fear that filled his eyes. It was the same look she'd seen in the eyes of countless frozen rookies, and she knew that Wallace stood little chance against a seasoned killer like Max. She had to find a way to help Wallace save her.

Max raised his gun.

"Wait!" Ash exclaimed, as an idea sparked to life. "Tell me one thing. What was John Wallace's suicide note going to say?"

Wallace heard the question echo around the vast room. He longed to move, to take Dorsey's gun and kill the man out there, but he couldn't. Instead, he shook with fear, his mind replaying every death he'd witnessed. He'd experienced the terrible moment of feeling his life slip away and knew that he didn't have the strength to face it again. He tried to focus on Connie, to use her memory as leverage to induce his frozen body to move, but the thought of her death only terrified him more. He looked between the racks and saw Ash lying wounded. Shame overwhelmed him at the thought that he was going to let her die at the hands of the man who had already taken Connie.

"John Wallace is a coward," Max Byrne said in reply to Ash's question, his words cutting through Wallace's paralyzing fear.

"John Wallace watched Afghan men, women, and children get murdered," Max continued. "Worse than that, he had photographs that could have brought the killers to justice, but he allowed them to destroy the evidence and ruin his credibility. John Wallace's suicide note would have told the truth. That he was a weak man who couldn't live with the guilt of his cowardice."

The words scorched Wallace's soul, sparking an uncontrollable fury.

As Max brought the Beretta up toward her head, Ash saw a bullet tear through his shoulder a split second before she registered the sound of the report. Another bullet cut into a gap in the body armor that covered his back and shredded the muscle beside his neck. A third shot hit Max's throat, ripping it wide open. Ash saw Max's face contort in bewildered agony as he pawed at the horrific wound. He dropped to his knees and looked at Ash with hatred blazing in his eyes. He tried to raise his pistol, but as it came level with Ash's head, a final gunshot echoed through the room and a searing hot bullet tore through his skull.

Ash watched Max's lifeless body crumple and staggered to her feet to see Wallace holding a smoking pistol. The look on his face turned from one of shock to horror when he took in the severity of her wound. Ash collapsed as Wallace sprinted over.

"Hey," she smiled weakly. "You did good."

"We need to get you to a hospital," Wallace said urgently.

Ash shook her head. "No. We need to stop that."

Wallace followed the line of her index finger, which pointed toward one of the computer terminals standing at the heart of the huge room.

"Alosi's outside," he told Ash.

"Get him," she commanded.

Wallace hesitated.

"Go!" Ash exclaimed with sufficient passion to get Wallace's feet moving.

Ash watched Wallace cast her concerned looks as he hurried from the room. She dragged herself over to the computer terminal, where the status bar showed that the program was 53 percent compiled. Ash leaned against the monolithic machine and looked at the blood oozing out of her right side, offering a quiet prayer that she would stay alive long enough to put things right.

The persistent wail of the fire alarm merged with the sound of approaching sirens as Wallace crossed the building threshold. He ran through the scorched, shattered entrance, stumbling over fallen masonry and broken glass, and saw the police car parked near Dorsey's body, but it was empty. Wallace cast around the parking lot and saw a small group of about two dozen men and women clustered some distance from the vehicle. Occasionally someone would steal a look in the direction of Dorsey's body. Six or seven of the group were on their cell phones.

Wallace ran forward. "Alosi! Dan Alosi!" he yelled.

Alosi pushed through the group and looked at Wallace uncertainly.

"I need you inside," Wallace said urgently. "We have to stop it!"

As Alosi took a step back and shook his head, Wallace remembered he was holding a gun and brought his arm up, aiming the weapon at the man's head.

"Move!" Wallace yelled. "Or I swear I'll shoot!"

Alosi looked at the people around him, who all took a step back as Wallace grabbed his collar and pulled him forward.

"Move!" Wallace shouted.

"Okay, okay," Alosi responded submissively.

Wallace turned to the man he and Finley had encountered on their way to the server room. "My friend's been shot," he said. "When the police get here, tell them we need help. We're in the main server room."

The man nodded.

"The main server room," Wallace reiterated as he pulled Alosi toward the building.

Ash sat alone in the room surrounded by the low hum of hundreds of servers. Her head was light and the world had taken on an unreal haze. She wondered whether she was experiencing the effects of blood loss, or the comedown as the adrenaline that had flooded her system dissipated. She pressed her hands against the bullet wound. *Pressure*. Pressure might save her. Pressure might kill her. The pressure cooker, that's what they'd called it. The discipline cell. Her father stalking the hall outside, determined to make her a good girl. Pressure will kill you. Pressure will keep you alive. The delirious absurdity of her inconsistent, rambling thoughts scared her. Ash focused and tried to keep her mind rooted in reality. She heard a noise beside her and turned to see figures approaching through the shadows.

Ash looked terrible. Her bloodless white face was tinged by the blue light of the surrounding servers, which gave her an unnatural, ghostly appearance.

"I've got him," Wallace called out as he pushed Alosi toward her.

"It's uploading a virus that will shut everything down," Ash told Alosi, her voice shallow and breathless. "You've got to stop it." She pointed toward the screen above her head, which showed the compiler was 82 percent complete.

Wallace crouched beside Ash as Alosi stepped up to the terminal.

"There was someone else." Her voice was almost inaudible.

"What?" Wallace asked.

"Someone else," Ash repeated weakly.

"Just rest," Wallace advised her. "Help is on its way. Keep the pressure on."

Ash grimaced as he pressed her hands against her bloody abdomen.

Wallace longed to scream. He wanted to turn on Max's fallen body and rip the flesh from its bones. He fought to prevent himself from trembling with the angry impotence that consumed him as he watched Ash's life slipping away. He knelt beside her and felt a sudden stab of grief as he remembered Connie. *This is how she died*, Wallace thought bleakly.

"You're going to be okay," he heard himself lie, but the look on Ash's face suggested she didn't believe him.

"I can't fix this," Alosi declared, his urgent words cutting through Wallace's dark thoughts. "He's changed the software architecture and security protocols. I'm gonna have to shut it down. You," he pointed at Wallace. "Come with me!"

Wallace hesitated; he did not want to leave Ash alone.

"Go," she told him.

The status bar was at 92 percent.

"Come on!" Alosi yelled. "We don't have long!"

Wallace got to his feet and followed Alosi, who started running toward the far end of the room.

Ash watched Wallace and Alosi until they were lost to the forest of servers. She fought the urge to close her eyes as her breathing became ever more rapid and shallow. Her heart pounded erratically and she was sure that she could feel it skipping beats as blood leached out of her body.

She looked up at the status bar and saw that it was at 94 percent.

"Hurry," she cried, the feebleness of her voice surprising her.

She refused to simply fade and made a conscious, painful effort to take a deep breath.

"Hurry!" she yelled, as the status bar hit 95 percent.

* * *

"Hurry!"

Wallace heard Ash's voice echo around the vast room, and he and Alosi redoubled their efforts and sprinted on.

"There are six circuit breakers. If we pull them the power will overload, shorting the entire facility," Alosi told Wallace as they reached the far wall, which was covered with heavy cable ducts and an intricate latticework of pipes.

Alosi hurried along the wall until he found six huge junction boxes. He opened the first box to reveal a large circuit breaker held in place by claw-like clasps. Alosi released a paddle lever and the clasps retracted. He grabbed the handle and yanked the circuit breaker out.

"We gotta do them all," he instructed Wallace, who immediately went to the junction box at the end of the row, and hurriedly replicated Alosi's actions.

Ash looked up at the terminal to see that the compiler was 97 percent complete. She thought she was hallucinating when she heard a sound behind her, but turned to see someone moving through the server farm. Not one, but two people. She looked around for something she could use as a weapon, but saw nothing. *There was someone else*, Ash thought darkly, as the figures drew closer.

Wallace's hands shook as he fumbled with the fourth breaker. *You're out of time*, he told himself. *You're out of time and Ash is dying alone.* He ignored his fears, took a deep breath to steady himself, and extracted the fourth breaker with a decisive pull.

A few feet away, Alosi pulled the penultimate breaker and watched as Wallace flipped the paddle lever of the final box and yanked the last device from its housing.

Ash saw the compiler hit 99 percent when the power surged. The lights flared brightly for a split second before every piece of electrical equipment in the building failed and the cavernous room was plunged into total darkness. She could hear the indistinct voices of two men talking to each other, and a moment later she saw the beam of a flashlight, the bright light terrifying her as it moved in her direction.

"It's over here," Alosi said, fumbling in the darkness.

Wallace heard him release a catch, and something fell on the floor. A moment later there came a blinding beam of light as Alosi turned on a powerful flashlight. He reached into the emergency supply box next to him and tossed Wallace a second flashlight. Wallace switched it on and hurried back toward the heart of the sever room, with Alosi following a few steps behind.

Light danced ahead of him, the bright beam cutting through the gaps in the server racks. Long shadows were born, but quickly shortened and died away as he ran on. As they reached the middle of the room, Wallace froze in his tracks when he saw the shadowy shapes of two men crouched over Ash. They were backlit by a flashlight that rested on a server rack and cast them into solid silhouette. The gun felt heavy as Wallace raised his arm and took aim.

"What the fuck are you doing?" Alosi asked, shining his flashlight directly on the two men to reveal their brightly colored paramedic uniforms.

"I thought . . ." Wallace started, but the sentence died as relief took over. He slipped the gun into his pocket and ran to Ash as the paramedics lifted her onto a gurney.

"Is she okay?" Wallace asked.

Ash was unresponsive beneath the oxygen mask that was fastened to her face.

"Please stand back, sir," one of the paramedics requested.

The paramedics double-timed the gurney through the server room, and Wallace ran with them, his tired legs struggling to keep up. Alosi followed as they pushed on through the building into the wrecked lobby, where a squad of firefighters worked to extinguish the flaming van, and out through the shattered entrance.

The parking lot was jammed with vehicles. Police black-and-whites lined up with sheriffs' cars, a fire truck, and three ambulances. Law enforcement officers spoke on their radios or took statements from the employees huddling outside.

"If anyone asks," Wallace said, turning to Alosi, "tell them I'm going with her."

Alosi nodded before peeling off and approaching a pair of police officers.

Wallace hurried to catch the paramedics, who moved quickly but carefully over the packed snow until they reached the farthest ambulance, which was parked on a clear stretch of asphalt. They loaded Ash into the back, and the driver ran around to the front. Wallace climbed in and sat beside Ash while the attending paramedic crouched over her and shook her gently.

"Stay with me, honey," he instructed. "You can sleep later, when we get to the hospital. For now I need you awake. You work with her?" the paramedic asked, turning to Wallace.

Wallace looked down at Ash, whose skin had turned parchment white. "She's a friend," he replied. "Her name's Christine."

"Stay with me, Christine!" the paramedic commanded. "You stay awake!"

Fighting whatever foul darkness snatched at her conscious mind, Ash opened her bloodshot eyes, looked up at Wallace, and gave him a thin smile.

"That's good," the paramedic said. "You keep smiling."

Wallace kept his eyes on Ash. For the first time in months, he felt free of fear: the man who had tried to kill him was gone. The sense of freedom came with tremendous shame, as thoughts of Connie filled his mind. He knew he would carry the guilt of her death for the rest of his life and, resigned to his everlasting burden, made a solemn vow to himself that he would try to live a good one. He could never bring Connie back, but he could honor her memory by striving to do something worthwhile with whatever time he had left. It was poor consolation for the loss of the woman he loved, but it was the only thing he could think of that would give him any sense of purpose as he tried to rebuild his life.

Wallace gave Ash a sad smile and leaned forward to take her hand, then squeezed it gently as the ambulance sped out of the parking lot.

EPILOGUE

A sh watched the members of the Disciplinary Review Board file back into the room. It had been three months since Twin Lakes, but she could still feel the dull throb of the bullet wound. She shifted in her seat and winced as her stomach muscles spasmed. Assistant Director Randall glanced in her direction as he took his seat, and the other five board members also acknowledged her as they sat. Ash looked at Isla Vaughn, her attorney, who smiled.

"Promising," Isla whispered.

Ash nodded and turned to see SAIC David Harrell sitting in the otherwise empty row of seats at the back of the room. He slouched forward, his head buried in his hands, but when he realized proceedings were about to recommence, he sat up, catching Ash's gaze. His gray face was topped by a neatly cut crop of straight salt-and-pepper hair, but Ash thought he looked gaunt and washed out. Two years away from retirement, Harrell had been devastated by the loss of Hector, Alvarez, and so many of his team. Ash nodded at Harrell, who offered a sad smile in return. She turned to see Ed Omar watching her, but there was none of the animosity of the previous hearing. Ash got the distinct impression that the Bureau's attorney had been going through the motions because, like many others, he believed she'd suffered enough.

"Special Agent Ash," Randall began, "the Disciplinary Review Board has been asked to reconsider your appeal in relation to the Marcel Washington shooting. We've been asked to reassess it in light of information that has emerged about your background. We've also been asked to review your conduct during the Pendulum investigation. Your attorney, Ms. Vaughn, has argued that your childhood records were sealed and were only made public as the result of a criminal invasion of your privacy. We've reviewed the records and believe that your past has already caused you enough pain. We see no reason to believe that it had any bearing on the Washington shooting, and our decision in respect of that appeal stands."

Ash glanced at Isla, who returned a relieved smile.

"With regard to the Pendulum investigation," Randall continued, "you disobeyed orders, destroyed private property, assaulted fellow officers and members of the public, and generally behaved erratically and irresponsibly. However, it is also abundantly clear that had it not been for your dedication, John Wallace would almost certainly have been killed, and we would never have discovered that Max Byrne was responsible for the murders, nor would we have been able to prevent the devastating cyber attack he had planned. For that reason, the board recommends that you receive a citation for your work and that you are promoted at the first opportunity."

Ash nodded and smiled at Randall. "I'd like to thank the board for reviewing my case so thoroughly," she said gratefully. "Good work," she told Isla, patting her on the shoulder.

She turned to see Harrell leaving the room. "Excuse me," she announced, wincing as she stood to follow him.

Harrell was halfway along the corridor when Ash finally caught up with him. They stopped by a large picture window and Ash felt the warmth of the late afternoon sun soaking into the fabric of her dark jacket.

"I wanted to speak with you, sir," she began.

"That was a good result," Harrell replied, his voice devoid of enthusiasm. Backing away, he added, "I don't really have time to talk. I'm late for a meeting."

"When are you going to do something about the second man?" Ash challenged loudly.

Harrell stopped in his tracks and bowed his head for a moment, before looking up and glancing at the faces of the agents passing by.

Ash could tell that he did not want to be embarrassed. "I saw someone else at Twin Lakes," she persisted.

Harrell drew close to Ash, his face inches away from hers. "You think you saw someone, but the investigation has shown that Max Byrne was acting alone. Isn't it possible that you made a mistake? That you experienced a hallucination brought on by a blow to the head?"

"The cameras were disabled," Ash protested. "We can't be sure he was alone."

"The cameras were always disabled," Harrell argued. "London, the safe house, the Manhattan Regent. Max Byrne shut down all those cameras too. That was his MO."

Ash wavered, unsure of herself. Harrell was getting it from every direction. The Pendulum killings had dominated the media, with the Bureau coming under fire for many perceived failings, the most damning of which was the accusation that it should have made the connection between the victims sooner. Ash sympathized with Harrell. Max Byrne had deleted Erin's YouTube video, and Ken Pallo's involvement with Next Life had been a shameful secret he'd worked hard to conceal. Agents from the Los Angeles Field Office discovered the Next Life servers in an apartment Pallo rented via a dummy corporation. Pallo had a death fetish, with a particular fascination for strangulation, and used Next Life for his own perverted sexual fantasies. Bonnie Mann's involvement with the Vegas underworld had sent the investigating agents down the wrong path. Erin's harassment complaint was one of thousands that Bonnie had concealed from her bosses as her gambling addiction had spun out of control.

The Bureau had learned a great deal from the Pendulum case. It had proved that the digital world connected victims and criminals in ways that had never previously been possible. If it hadn't been for Wallace, they might never have made the link, and Max's crimes could have gone entirely undetected.

In addition to those who criticized the Bureau for not acting fast enough, there were some who attacked it for having prevented Pendulum's final crime. Max's attempt to reverse decades of technological progress had divided opinion. There were many who agreed with his objectives, and a small anonymous minority online who approved of his methods. Censorship was cited by those who sought to argue against any form of control, as though free speech should trump child protection, social cohesion, and even human life. Ash empathized with the suffering caused by Erin's death—she knew what it was to lose a loved one and understood how the desire for revenge could twist the mind—but she could not condone Max's desire to punish the world for the perceived failings of a few.

Ash looked at her beleaguered boss, his eyes pleading with her to be reasonable. With the controversy and public outcry that surrounded the case, she could understand why Harrell was keen to hold the official line.

"We've spent two months on this, Special Agent Ash," he said calmly. "We lost thirty-two people at Alosi's house. Four of our own. Hector was a friend. If there was any evidence of a second man, we'd be scouring the Earth for him."

Ash studied the experienced old agent for a moment before nodding slowly.

"You did good," Harrell told her. "But it's time to move on," he added before turning away and heading down the corridor.

Ash stood in the sunshine and watched her boss walk wearily away. She wanted Harrell to be right; she wanted to accept the simple explanation, to take the easy option, to fit in, but she couldn't shake her deep-rooted belief that someone else had been working with Max Byrne. Ash looked at the agents passing her and wondered how many of them would suppress their beliefs, ignore their instincts, and follow orders. She envied the ease with which they assimilated, their willingness to be functioning parts of a whole, a communal approach to life that stood in stark contrast to her own difficult solitary existence. For all the horrors he'd inflicted, Ash's time with her father had marked her with a deeply ingrained distrust of authority and an inherent belief in her own instincts. She couldn't be part of the pack. She couldn't ignore what she believed. Whatever the Bureau saw in her, she was only of value to it if she had the courage to be an outsider and stand alone. As she watched Harrell recede into the distance, vague ideas of investigation began to crystallize as lines of inquiry, and Ash knew that her work on the Pendulum case was far from over.

The bright-green sycamore leaves danced in the gentle breeze and sheltered Wallace from the late afternoon sun. The chill he felt had nothing to do with the shade of the towering trees that lined the road. Like the pounding beat of his racing heart, his cold, numb limbs were a symptom of his anxiety. He'd been afraid for so long that he'd almost forgotten what it was like to be at ease. Every passing car, every sudden movement, every loud noise provoked the primal fight-or-flight response.

Given the choice, there was no way that Wallace would have opted to return to London. He tried to tell himself that there was nothing to be afraid of, that Max Byrne was dead, but Ash's words ate away at him. She had been so sure of herself, so certain that there had been someone else working with Max, and the more Wallace replayed the day's events, the more he wondered what Max had been doing in the parking lot. Why hadn't he been inside? Who had programmed the computers and triggered the machines that alerted Bailey to what was happening? The official explanation was that Max had started the process remotely from inside his van before moving into the building to finish it, but Wallace wasn't so sure. Ash had earned his everlasting trust, and if she said there was someone else . . . *then I'll never be safe. I'll never be free to live a normal life.*

Wallace wondered what constituted a normal life for him. Perhaps the fear might gradually fade, but he was certain his memories wouldn't. He longed to turn back time and unsay the evil words that had helped drive Erin Byrne to suicide, the tragic event that had set Pendulum in motion. Every time he saw Connie lying in her own blood, dying in his arms, Wallace could not help but blame himself for her violent, traumatic murder. Being in London made it worse. Terrible memories lurked all over the city, each one the father of a new nightmare. This street was particularly potent, and he was haunted by the recollection of the last time he'd walked beneath these trees. Sweepers had been brushing dead leaves off the pavement and he'd had the misguided sense that they were symbolically clearing a path for him and Connie. If he'd listened to her, if the two of them had disappeared together, perhaps she would still be alive. But instead—

He shook his head in a pathetic attempt to dislodge the dark thoughts that plagued him. Thoughts that were made all the more powerful by the prospect of what lay ahead. He tried not to think about where he was going, or who he was going to see, but apprehension clouded his mind.

He'd recognized the same fear in Bailey when they'd met at the Monkey Puzzle. The detective who'd saved his life had looked well and claimed to be fully recovered, but Wallace could see the familiar sadness is his eyes, a dark uncertainty born out of trauma. Salamander and his crew had been there, congratulating them both on their survival and role in bringing Pendulum down, but Bailey and Wallace had shared the same muted response. Wallace knew there was no joy to be found in the moment of celebration; it wasn't the end of anything, but the beginning of what was certain to be a difficult process of recovery. And no matter how the echoes of events dwindled, or how dull and faded his memories became, Wallace was certain that one would stay with him forever: Connie's death. Whatever the future held, he faced it alone, and that gap, that everpresent space beside him, the cold sheet, the empty passenger seat, the table for one, was a constant reminder of their shared moment of horror.

Even being in the Monkey Puzzle had been hard. To Salamander, Bailey, and the others, it was just a pub. To Wallace it was one of the last places he'd been with Connie, and if he'd listened to her, perhaps . . . He'd forced himself to stay for one drink, handed over the money he owed to Salamander, and promised to keep in touch with Bailey before making his polite excuses and leaving for an appointment he'd long dreaded. He'd drifted east on public transportation, ambling, shuffling, moving unenthusiastically toward his destination. He couldn't have stayed where he was, troubled by the history of the Monkey Puzzle and the company of people who'd known Connie, but he had no desire to reach his journey's end. Wallace wanted to keep moving, hoping that eventually he'd be forgotten by the world and could vanish entirely. But he owed Connie at least one last mark of respect.

No matter how slowly Wallace moved, his sense of obligation made his arrival inevitable, and he eventually found himself outside Connie's building. He looked up at her flat and his heart leaped when he saw her familiar silhouette standing in the window. He hurried forward, his mind spinning as though he was in a dream. The buzzer sounded as he reached the door and he flung it open, barely able to contain his excitement at the impossible joy of the situation. How had she survived? How had the news reports got it so wrong? Had there been a cover-up? A ruse to protect her? He raced up the stairs, breathless with elation, but as he turned the corner and peered toward Connie's doorway the beautiful dream died. Wallace stopped in his tracks, the wind knocked from him with remorseless brutality. Standing in the entrance of Connie's flat was her mother, Sandra. Apart from the lines on her face and the flecks of gray in her hair, she was Connie's double.

"Sorry if I startled you," Sandra said with a sad smile.

"It's okay," Wallace replied, struggling to swallow his disappointment.

Connie's father, Peter, appeared at Sandra's shoulder. "Why don't you come in, John?" he suggested.

Wallace trembled as he crossed the threshold and made his way into Connie's flat. Peter and Sandra led him into the living room, which was piled with boxes. Most of the furniture was gone. Only the small dining table remained, and Wallace had to look away as he recalled the last conversation he and Connie had there, when she'd tried so hard to persuade him not to leave with Bailey.

"Oh, John," Sandra said quietly, looking at his shaking hands. Tears welled in her eyes as she drew close to Wallace and embraced him. "It's okay," she murmured. "It's okay."

Wallace bowed his head and pressed his face against Sandra's shoulder. He felt Peter pat him gently on the back. This was not the reaction Wallace had anticipated.

"I'm sorry," he sighed as he stepped back. "For everything. I'm sorry."

"It's not your fault," Sandra assured him. "Constance. Connie . . ." Her voice faltered, and she took a moment to compose herself. "Connie was so happy you were back. We spoke almost every day, and she was lifted. Those first few months after you split were hard on her; she never quite recovered. But when the two of you got back together, even though it was only for a short time, she, well, she was back to her old self. She was happy. You were the love of her life."

"I didn't mean for her to . . ." Wallace trailed off. His words sounded pathetically inadequate.

"We know what happened, John," Peter said. "It wasn't your fault."

Wallace couldn't meet their gaze. He turned to look at the tops of the sycamore trees, the branches swaying beyond Connie's window. It didn't matter what these people said; he'd taken their daughter to her death.

"Connie didn't make any arrangements," Peter explained. "So we're sorting through everything as best we can."

"Is there anything you want?" Sandra offered. "Something to remember her by?"

"The postcards," Wallace replied instinctively. "The ones in her bedroom. I'd like to remember her through all the people that loved her."

Sandra was moved by Wallace's request and could only nod as she choked back her tears. The three of them stood in peaceful silence for a moment.

"What are you going to do now?" Peter asked.

Wallace shook his head. "I don't know."

They stood in silence again, until Wallace asked, "You?"

"The flat's been sold," Peter replied. "We're just going to finish up here and then go home."

Wallace nodded sympathetically, and silence descended on the room once more. Wallace felt ashamed to be in Connie's flat, sharing her space with her gracious, forgiving parents. He was the one that should be lying in a cold grave in Stoke Newington Cemetery.

"Well, I should get going," he said finally.

Peter nodded, but Sandra shook her head. "Won't you stay for some tea? We can unpack some cups."

Wallace could see the misery in Sandra's eyes. She was desperate to cling to every possible trace of her daughter, but he couldn't face the prospect of tea from Connie's mismatched cups; the experience would be too painful for all of them.

"I have to go," he said softly.

Sandra nodded, then quickly turned on her heels. "Wait," she instructed.

Peter and Wallace stood in the still room and glanced awkwardly at each other until Sandra returned moments later.

"The postcards," she explained, thrusting a thick brown envelope into Wallace's hands.

"Thank you," he replied and wrapped his arms around her.

Sandra returned his embrace and seemed to sag slightly as he held her. Peter lent his wife a supporting hand as Wallace withdrew, but she brushed it away gently.

"I'm okay," she told him, the lie too big and bold to be contradicted.

Peter extended his hand toward Wallace. "Thanks for coming," he said as Wallace shook it. "We both needed to see you."

"If you're ever in Australia . . ." Sandra's offer trailed away to nothing.

"Thanks," Wallace replied. "If there's anything I can do—"

"We're fine," Peter cut him off. "There's not much left now."

"Good-bye," Wallace said as he backed toward the door.

"You won't forget her, will you?" Sandra called out, but her tone wasn't one of admonishment; it was almost as though she was talking to herself.

"I could never forget Connie," Wallace assured them, his voice cracking as he said her name.

Peter nodded and Sandra turned toward the window as Wallace left the room. Clutching Connie's postcards, he hurried down the stairs and out of the building. He glanced up at the flat as he walked down the path and saw Sandra weeping. When she caught his gaze, she retreated from the window and was swallowed up by Connie's flat.

Wallace had honored Connie's memory and knew that was the last time he'd ever see Peter and Sandra. With no ties left to bind him to the world, Wallace was free to lose himself. He quickened his pace and almost broke into a run when he turned onto Cazenove Road, desperate to escape his own grief, determined to keep moving until he drifted into oblivion.

Acknowledgments

For my wonderful wife, Amy, without whom this adventure would never have been possible. Our three gorgeous children, Maya, Elliot, and Thomas, earn gold stars for always making me smile.

Thanks to Hannah Sheppard, my very capable literary agent, whose hard work and insight will always be appreciated.

Thanks also to Vicki Mellor, my inspiring UK editor, who has been instrumental in nurturing *Pendulum*.

I'd like to express my appreciation to the team at Quercus US for all their hard work and enthusiasm, in particular Jason Bartholomew, Elyse Gregov, Amelia Iuvino, and Nathaniel Marunas, who are a pleasure to work with.

Thanks to Shane Eli, an extraordinary artist, for helping me see the potential of *Pendulum*. Thanks also to my manager, Pat Nelson, for all the ardent encouragement along the way.

My thanks also goes out to everyone who takes the time to read *Pendulum*. I hope it was time well spent.

About the Author

Adam Hamdy is an author and screenwriter who works on both sides of the Atlantic.

Pendulum is Adam's third novel. Prior to becoming a writer, Adam was a strategy consultant and advised global businesses operating in a wide range of industries. He lives in Shropshire, England, with his wife and three children.

Follow Adam on Twitter @adamhamdy.